Sins
of
Deception

The Cletus Efferding Novels

Sins of Intent
Sins of Omission
Sins of Deception

Sins
of
Deception

Randy Roeder

Dusty Typewriter Press · Cedar Rapids

Cover design by Jenn Roeder

Dusty Typewriter Press
5001 1st Ave SE
Ste 105 #243
Cedar Rapids, IA 52402
http://dusty.typewriter.press

ISBN 978-1-940509-35-8

First Edition June 2023

Version 1.0.2

In memory of the late Don Kraft, a man of the land.

Chapter 1

"Last one," my personal banker said as he pushed a sheet of paper across the desk.

I placed the page in front of me, angled it, and wrote Cletus A. Efferding on the line at the bottom—Palmer style. The capital E was a work of art. Mrs. Meyer, my third-grade teacher, would have been proud of me. My signature complete, I moved to the next line and added the date: March 18, 1983.

"I guess that's it then," I said, unhappy to be taking on a loan for an unnecessary business expansion. "It's time to be on my way. I'm meeting someone for lunch."

Hal, a soft-spoken gent, rose halfway from his padded leather chair, extended his hand, and said, "It's been a pleasure doing business with you, Cletus. If there's anything I can do for you—anything at all—don't hesitate to give me a call."

I rose. "I prefer Clete."

As I got up, my banker, an executive vice president, did so too. "Sure thing ... Clete. Do you play golf?" He rounded the desk. "One of our foursome has developed some health issues and is going to have to drop out."

"Thanks, but I don't play."

Hal clapped me on the back. "Too bad, you'd fit right in."

Yeah, right.

He walked me through the outer office, past a potted *ficus* that towered over an elderly secretary tapping away on an IBM typewriter. Hal breezed by his peon as if she didn't exist and led me into a plush, carpeted hallway where he took my hand again and gave it a vigorous shake. "Remember—"

"—anything at all." I finished his sentence for him.

I strode down the hallway into the grand lobby of Merchants National Bank. The square-pillared, high-ceilinged room spoke of reliability, security, and no-nonsense financial dealing, appealing qualities now that I had something to lose. After a quarter century of pinching pennies, borrowing to make the rent, and covering emergencies with an overloaded credit card, my luck had changed.

Flogging men's clothing for Killian's Department Store hadn't been lucrative, and the demise of the place last fall left me in dire straits. The small dance studio I ran on the side barely paid for itself. Oh, there'd been some good times—a couple of modest inheritances and a nicely profitable dance business when the disco fad hit, but I'd socked the windfalls away in trust funds for my kids.

They weren't impressed. I hadn't seen my daughter Tammy in eighteen years, and my son Mike in seven. Seven, if I counted the time he didn't recognize me. Still, I'll never forget the day. If not for that chance encounter, he'd be at the eighteen-year point too. Neither of the kids wanted any contact with me. I'd made a parental mistake or two. Actually, I screwed up big time. Reconciliation was off the table.

A blustery wind greeted me as I exited the revolving door. After Hal's soul-killing financial prattle, the fresh air felt good. The only thing that got me through an hour of the man's oily good cheer was the lunch date ahead of me. Flipping up my collar, I turned north and made for the Top of the Seasons, a downtown eatery where my fiancée, Dusty waited for me.

The Top of the Seasons sat atop a concrete box that city officials considered dynamic architecture. The restaurant's windows offered a panoramic view of the town—a grand sight if rooftops are your thing. Though the new chef was at the top of his game, I had no illusions.

Cedar Rapids enjoyed a reputation for driving out its better restaurants. Both crowds and chef would be gone by next year, and the once-glorious venue would install a salad bar and feature Sunday buffets on Mother's Day. Pending its certain descent into a coupons-for-granny hell, I intended to dine at the Top whenever possible.

I stepped out of the elevator and shed my coat. Dusty had given my name to the hostess, a comely young woman who directed me to our table. Its location surprised me. We'd scored one of the coveted window tables, but on the side of the building looking out at the Quaker Oats factory.

I bussed Dusty on the cheek and smiled broadly as I took my seat. "All that Sutherland family influence, and we get the industrial side?"

"It's a popular place, Cleatzy. Even a Sutherland can't manufacture extra floor space."

I don't remember when she started calling me Cleatzy, but word got around, and the name stuck. Her family and friends used nothing else. I can't say I liked the handle, but Dusty's circle was gung-ho for nicknames. It had something to do with going out east for college. Her dad came back as Steele and her brother as Tanner. Dusty got the treatment too; her given name was Jane.

Her mother, an Italian *baronessa*, escaped the curse. Too bad, with a name like Consuela, she could have used some help. Then again, why trifle with a nickname, when what the woman needed was a whole new personality.

Dusty placed her menu on the table. "Uncle Gib and Aunt Dora invited us to the club for dinner and drinks next week Saturday. Mom and Dad are coming too. Can you make it?"

As if I had a choice. Steele and Gib Sutherland were funding my new menswear business. I'd be bored out of my skull but can't say I minded that much. The Cedar Rapids Country Club served prime-grade rib eyes, and Gib would order enough single-malt scotch to keep the conversation moving.

"Sounds great," I lied. "Gib is always a good time, and your Aunt Dora is a peach." Actually, more of a prune, but I didn't want to rain on Dusty's parade. She idolized her aunt and uncle. The fact they were childless didn't hurt any. They doted on their niece, and Dusty could expect to inherit a few million, their palatial home, and a summer house on Lake Superior.

We spent a few minutes exchanging gossip and got down to the business at hand—ordering. I decided on a Caesar salad, *coq au vin*, and a *crème brûlée* for dessert. The mission-critical part of the lunch over, I looked up from my menu.

"How did it go with Hal?" Dusty asked while unfolding her napkin.

"I thought the guy was going to ask me to marry him. Fell all over himself making sure I was happy about taking on more debt."

"That's Hal. You should see him kiss up to Dad."

Poor Hal had no choice; he had to like me. Steele Sutherland was president of Merchant's National Bank and largest shareholder. His vice presidents enjoyed the life expectancy of mosquitos. Sucking up to Steele's future son-in-law meant survival.

Our salads arrived, and I dug in. The great thing about a Caesar is that it's about the dressing, not the greenery.

Dusty looked up from her plate of walnuts and spinach. My fiancée was a vegetarian, something she'd picked up during an extended stay in India. "Did you think when you opened Cleatzy's it would be such a hit you'd need to double your floor space in just three months?"

She still didn't get it. I never doubted the business would take off. When it comes to selling menswear, I'm a natural. My family was in the business for three generations. I'd have kept Cleatzy's small but didn't have much choice in the matter. My backers, Steele and his brother Gib, insisted on expansion. I'd run the numbers inside and out, but they wouldn't take no for an answer—even after I explained the added overhead canceled out the extra revenue. They never said it aloud, but I knew the backstory. Running an intimate little clothing store didn't meet their definition of an acceptable occupation for a new member of the family. Size mattered.

"I'll miss the old place," I sighed.

Dusty's face fell.

"But who can argue with prime retail space on the ground floor of the Roosevelt Hotel?"

My quick response saved the day. On a roll, I went for the extra points. "I don't know how your uncle latched on to it. He's a genius."

"You didn't know Gib owns the building?"

"He never mentioned it."

"Gib's twice as smart as Dad. I suppose it's time to 'fess up. I didn't come up with the slogan *Where the man about town shops*. Gib did."

The tagline stank, but Dusty insisted on it. Now I knew why. The woman worshipped her uncle.

"Originality has never been Gib's strong suit," I noted.

I'd have continued, but my chicken plate arrived. The genius who came up with the idea of pairing a hen with brandy, red wine, and bacon deserves a shrine at the Place du Panthéon in Paris. The stuff tasted so good I forgot to make conversation.

Dusty laughed. "Earth to Cleatzy. I'm talking to you."

I came up with a hundred-watt smile for the best-looking woman I'd ever dated. She giggled a bit more than I liked, but I respected the brain behind the packaging. She'd make a good wife. "Sorry, I zoned out for a bit."

"I know you're not thrilled with Gib's slogan, but you don't have to keep it forever. You have to admit I hit the jackpot when I came up with the idea of using your nickname for the store. Cleatzy's has class."

I did a double take. "Cleatzy's has class. Now there's a slogan for you. When the time is right, the man-about-town tagline goes."

Dusty took a dainty bite of her salad. She'd have no entrée or dessert. "You might not think much of Gib's slogan, but it beats the hell out of *Efferding's Menswear—the Home of Mr. Neat*."

I blotted a stray bit of sauce from the corner of my lip. "You need to look at it from another angle. The Mr. Neat thing is so corny, it's good. It worked for my father. Mr. Neat and Efferding's Menswear are a family tradition."

"Your family business went broke, Cleatzy."

I hadn't mentioned the real reason Efferding's Menswear went broke. I glossed over it along with other parts of my past Dusty wouldn't like. I was waiting for the right time to fill her in, but somehow, it never came. Now, in three weeks, we'd be married. I wasn't thrilled with the deception, but Dusty never pushed for more. Why mess up a good thing?

I almost spaced out again but caught myself and kept the conversation going. "You're all about new ideas and living in the moment, and I'm a traditionalist who will keep you down to earth. That's why we're a good match."

Dusty's reply flowed over me like warm syrup on a hot pancake. "You don't know yourself, Cleatzy. You're sentimental, not traditional, and as good-looking as a man can be. I always wanted to marry a handsome dog, and Sweet Cheeks, you qualify."

God, she was beautiful—dark brown hair that barely touched her shoulders, eyes so deep they were nearly black, pouty lips, a great body, and brains to match. Fifteen years my junior and good in bed, she had money to burn. She'd take care of me when I got old. My fiancée had more than enough of everything a man could want.

There was just one problem—I wasn't in love.

Chapter 2

"You are making a mistake, Clete."

We were sitting in my best friend Lumir's workshop, a wood-frame building once used as a livery stable. Furniture patterns and hand tools hung on the walls. Pieces of a rosewood jewelry cabinet lay on the glue-up table. Lumir sat in his captain's chair, his back to his desk. A fire crackled in the woodstove.

Lumir had recently resumed work on the cabinet after a case of pneumonia that laid him up for close to a month. Since his recovery, he'd been using the shop more for sitting than doing anything productive. I loved the man. Over the years, he'd become my father, counselor, and brother.

"I don't think it's a mistake," I said. "Dusty and I aren't starry-eyed kids. We enjoy spending time together, and that's enough. I'm fifty years old for pity's sake. Dusty's been married before. We're way beyond all that 'I love you' crap."

Lumir leaned back in his captain's chair and folded his hands over his belt. "Who said anything about love? The Sutherlands are not like you and me, and you are making a mistake to think you can ever be one of them. Why do you think Dusty waited until you were engaged to tell them about you? Mark my words. You will always be an outsider."

My friend was level-headed and generous with his time and modest financial resources. When it came to the ways of the world, he was as perceptive as anyone I knew. But for all his good sense, Lumir had one blind spot. He simply could not believe the wealthy were ordinary people with the same wants and needs as the rest of us.

I leaned forward in my pressed-back chair and put my hands on my knees. "You're not still sore I asked her brother to be best man, are you?"

Lumir snorted. "I am far too sensible to care whether I am best man in your wedding. I am worried you are putting yourself in a situation that will turn out badly."

Yup, Lumir was still sore. The wedding was to be an intimate family affair at a stylish Episcopal church. Lumir, a retired packing plant worker, wouldn't have been comfortable making small talk with the swells. After the nuptials, he and the rest of my friends were invited to attend the swankiest reception the city had seen in a quarter century. Dusty eloped the first time around, depriving her mother of the chance to play the grand hostess. Consuela intended to do this one up right. Outstanding food, top-shelf liquor, the classiest venue in town, and an eighteen-piece dance orchestra from Los Angeles. My friends would have a great time.

I retrieved my coffee from the stand alongside the chair. Still hot. "You've met Dusty, and the two of you hit it off. She likes you and is thrilled you're feeling well enough to get back to work on her wedding present. She comes to visit you when I'm not around. Not only that, she likes your coffee."

"She is a wonderful woman, and I enjoy speaking with her. And why wouldn't she like my coffee?"

Lumir made his coffee in a stovetop pot. His method was simple: throw in a couple fistfuls of grounds, pour water over the top, and boil the heck out of it for twenty minutes. I'd grown to tolerate Lumir's swill, but a full mug of it can clean out a first timer. I never told him that Dusty valued his concoction for its purgative qualities. She claimed it beat the heck out of the herbal brews she'd tried in India.

"If you like Dusty so much, why don't you want to see her happily married?"

My friend rose from his chair, picked a piece of firewood from the nearby pile, opened the stove door, and pitched it in. "White oak, it burns twice as hot as pine."

"You're stalling, Lumir. What's wrong with Dusty and me sharing a little happiness now that we're not kids anymore?"

Though born in the United States, Lumir's English gets convoluted and his Czech accent is more pronounced when I put him on the spot. Today his agitation manifested itself as a problem with word order.

"I am stalling because you will not want to understand that which I am preparing to say to you. You are not the man who is able to make such a woman happy. Knowing how to wear the right clothes and small-talk-making her rich friends does not turn you into one of them. When the romance wears away, she will become embarrassed by you."

I shook my head. Lumir would never understand. "There is no romance to wear away. Dusty and I are a mature, level-headed couple who enjoy each other's company. We know what we want."

Lumir stroked his snow-white mustache—one of his better features. "I have seen the way the woman looks at you. No matter what she tells you, she is in love."

"Of course, she is," I kidded. "Who wouldn't be in love with the best-looking guy in town?"

Best-looking guy in town might have been stretching it a bit, but I bear a strong resemblance to the film star Warren Beatty. The years have not been kind to the man. I'm four years older but don't have the wrinkles.

"You can joke all you want, but Dusty is going along with your good-friends foolishness because she does not want to scare you off. When she understands you are still not over the death of your wife, she will be heartbroken. How did she take it when you told her about Myra?"

Lumir has a way of taking me down a peg. I once believed in total honesty but found out the hard way it's for fools. I tried it with my kids.

When the youngest turned eighteen, I asked a lawyer to send registered letters explaining that the man and woman who raised them were not their mother and father, but their grandparents. I had him follow up with another informing them I'd set up trusts to fund their higher education and disclosing their birth mother's death by suicide. They rewarded my efforts with a letter from their attorney asking that I not contact them and threatening a restraining order.

Lumir looked at me over the top of his eyeglasses. "You told her, didn't you?"

I was about to answer when Mrs. Hemsky, Lumir's neighbor, breezed through the workshop door bringing the crisp night air in with her. She handed him a brown paper bag from the Hy-Vee grocery. "You forgot these," she said.

Lumir took the bag, a puzzled look on his face.

"Your slippers," she said.

"I have been looking for them," he replied.

Mrs. Hemsky smiled. "I would have brought them sooner, but they were under the bed where I couldn't see them." She looked up. "Hello, Cletus. Ready for the big wedding? Nice to see you, but I must get home. The New Glarus polka program starts in ten minutes."

A whirlwind of activity, ninety-year-old Mrs. Hemsky seldom waited for the answers to her frequent questions. She had her hand on the doorknob before I was able to collect myself. I couldn't believe Lumir was dating again. A widower, he made the rounds after his wife's death but swore off the opposite sex when he hit eighty. I could understand his wanting companionship, but Mrs. Hemsky? The woman was eight years his senior. Most of Lumir's love interests had been ten to twenty years younger than he was.

Mrs. Hemsky breezed out, and Lumir put the bag on the floor. "Dusty—did you tell her?"

"You're dating Mrs. Hemsky?"

Red-faced, Lumir didn't respond.

I couldn't resist. "Are you sure you can keep up with her?"

"It is nothing. She is a good neighbor who brought me soup when I was laid up. We are talking about you and Dusty."

Lumir didn't want to talk about Mrs. Hemsky, and I didn't want to talk about Dusty because I'd been less than candid about my past. She knew my wife Myra had taken her life and that my kids—toddlers—were raised by grandparents, but I skipped the part about gram and gramps deceiving the kids into thinking they were Mom and Dad. Though Dusty understood the children and I were estranged, she didn't know my severely depressed wife drowned herself after the police arrested me in a raid on a house of ill repute. The story of the bust, complete with a photo of the police escorting me from the scene in handcuffs, made the front page of the local newspaper. I didn't mention I'd abandoned the family business by turning it over to an incompetent cousin and moving to Cedar Rapids. It seemed a wise decision given that Myra's father threatened to kill me.

There was more. Dusty hadn't heard about my arrest for manslaughter. The charge was dropped. Or that I killed another man in self-defense—a bloody, violent incident involving a fishing spear. Those omissions didn't seem to bother Lumir. He'd been in World War I and considered them the sort of thing best kept from the fair sex. I doubted Dusty would agree.

Lumir shook his finger. "You do not want to talk about Dusty because you have been holding out on her. I can tell by the look on your face. Are you crazy? What if Mr. Steele Sutherland hires a detective to check on you? How will you explain it then?"

"There's still time," I protested. "The right moment hasn't come up yet."

"What right moment? The right moment was a year ago. You are getting married in three weeks."

Lumir's disapproval cut like a knife. I'd intended to tell Dusty but the thought of a life free of financial worry made it easy to keep putting it off.

"Clete, you are marrying a woman you do not love. I do not fault you for that. You have discussed the matter with her, and however she might feel, she understands the situation. You owe it to her to come clean about your past. You must tell her what happened the day before Myra took her life and that you are not over her death. You will either lose her or keep her, but she deserves the truth. I am happy you did not ask me to be your best man. I would not want to be part of this deception."

I slumped in my seat. My friend was right. I might be able to hide the truth from Dusty, but the deceit would eat at me and poison our relationship.

Lumir thumped the arm of his chair with his fist. "If you do not tell the woman about your past, I will not attend your wedding reception."

His words smacked me like a punch to the gut. I knew the man. Failure to level with Dusty could cost me his friendship. "You're right," I conceded. "I've never had very much, and Dusty's money will give me something I always wanted—security. I don't want to lose it, and I don't want to lose what might be my last chance to have a family."

"Never had very much? What is wrong with you? Instead of appreciating what you have, you focus on what you think is missing. You have a dance studio, are the best haberdasher in the city, and people like you. In France, I buried dozens of soldiers, young men killed before they'd had the chance to marry, have children, or own a business. You are fifty years old. It is time for you to act like a man."

I stared at the floor. Lumir's experiences on a wartime graves detail gave him perspective I lacked. "You're right. We're going on a picnic this afternoon. I'll tell her then."

My friend wasn't finished with me yet. "What about Eddie? Did you ask if he could tend bar?"

Eddie, a neighbor fifty years Lumir's junior and the apple of his eye, played in a rock band and worked at a nearby factory that manufactured cornstarch. Though he wanted to be part of my wedding, the thought of an evening at the Cedar Rapids Country Club terrified him. Nervous about mixing with the crowd, he asked if he could tend bar at the reception. I'd yet to give him an answer.

I looked up expecting to see disapproval on Lumir's face but found something worse, disappointment.

"Lumir, in Dusty's world, wedding guests aren't asked to tend bar. The Country Club has a professional mixologist with trained assistants. Eddie would be as uncomfortable behind the bar as he'd be out in the crowd."

"And the Steele Sutherland family, they do not have the influence to see that Eddie gets a place behind the bar at this country club? If Eddie feels useful, he will get over his shyness and enjoy himself. The problem is not Dusty's world. It is you, embarrassed by a young man who has been your friend for a dozen years."

I didn't reply but looked around the woodshop, the remnant of a simpler time. I treasured the hours that Lumir, Eddie, and I had spent there. Our young friend grew from boy to man helping Lumir with his many projects. Tools and woodworking weren't my thing, but the friendship shared in that sawdust-filled room helped me through some of my hardest hours. Tonight, Lumir's woodshop felt less like a refuge and more like the proverbial woodshed where a father straightens out a son grown too big for his britches. Embarrassed by my friends, deceiving the woman I was about to marry—what had gotten into me?

Chapter 3

I turned off First Avenue and into the short drive leading to Blair House. I'd popped Stevie Wonder's *Songs in the Key of Life* into the cassette deck of my Chrysler Cordoba and was humming along to "Isn't She Lovely" as I looked for a parking place. Dusty and I were moving into one of the classy top-floor condos in a few weeks, and she wanted to give me a preview.

Dusty's DeLorean pulled up next to me before Wonder had finished his song. With its stainless-steel body, gull-wing doors, and sumptuous leather upholstery, the car was stunning. Despite its allure, I had cautioned her not to buy it. A DeLorean on Rodeo Drive might not attract attention, but in Cedar Rapids, Iowa? No matter where she parked it, Dusty returned to find her pride-and-joy surrounded by gawkers wanting to know how its doors worked and how much it cost. Now reserved for special occasions, the car spent most of its time in the garage.

I slid out of the Cordoba and leaned on the roof. "The DeLorean? What's the occasion?"

"You," Dusty laughed as she made her way to the vehicle's front storage compartment. "It's not every day a woman gets to show her intended she knows how to turn an apartment into a home." She retrieved a picnic basket and turned to face me. "The appliances aren't in yet, and since it's a little cold to be outside, I thought we'd picnic in-doors."

I hadn't seen the condo. A wedding present from her Uncle Gib, the place needed some work. Though Dusty hoped to have the remodel completed before showing it to me, she'd grown tired of waiting. I'd have preferred a cozy cottage outside town, but it's hard to turn down an unbelievably generous gift from a major investor in your business.

I relieved Dusty of the picnic basket, took her arm, and escorted her up the walk to the main entrance. The doors opened onto some-thing Dusty called the Commons.

She waved her arm as we walked through, "We can reserve these rooms for gatherings that are too large for our apartment." After un-locking an inner set of doors, we entered a small atrium providing ac-cess to the elevators. A gent in an unfigured charcoal suit waited in front of them. His jacket fit like a glove. He turned as we entered.

"Why, Dusty Sutherland," he said, extending a hand and taking a step toward us. "Look at you, all grown up. It's been a long time."

Dusty took his hand and shook it. "Grown up? I was a sophomore in college when I worked on your campaign. It's good to see you, Bob."

I'd been struggling to place the man, but Dusty's remark gave me the context I needed. The guy was Robert Ray, and he'd just stepped down after three terms as Governor of Iowa. The elevator arrived, and we got in. Dusty and Bob talked non-stop. I learned he had just been appointed CEO of the biggest insurance company in town and taken a condo on the floor below ours. When we got to his stop, I pushed the button to hold the doors while he and Dusty continued their conversa-tion.

After inquiries into Steele and Consuela's health, Ray gave Dusty a hug and stepped into the hallway.

"Oh Bob," she called after him. "I almost forgot. This is my fiancé, Cletus Efferding."

I voted for the man and would have liked to shake his hand, but it was too late. The door had already closed.

A gas fireplace flickered in the condo's great room. Gib had purchased two adjoining units and hired a contractor to knock out a wall and combine them into one. The place wasn't quite finished— the trim and cabinetry were incomplete. Dusty had stopped by earlier in the day with an air mattress and massive throw pillows. We lounged on them, sipping wine, and nibbling tropical fruit.

Dusty extracted herself from my arm and reached for the wine bottle. "I wanted to surprise you so didn't say much about the project. Guess I succeeded. I can see you like the result by the look on your face."

Though I'd been underwhelmed, Dusty was beaming. Off the hook for an insincere expression of delight, I smiled and let out an inaudible "Thank you, Jesus."

"Mom didn't think you were the type to appreciate mauve carpeting and teal-green accents, but I told her she underestimated you. Wait until you see the royal blue furniture and salmon-colored drapes I've picked out."

Truth be told, Consuela hit the nail on the head. When I painted my apartment, I gave the walls and ceiling two coats of an off-white called Sears Ivory Linen. My broken-in couch and recliner would have helped me feel at home in our new place, but Dusty had talked me out of bringing them with me. She said they'd look shabby in the new environment. She was right, of course.

Though I promised Lumir I'd fill Dusty in on the gaps in my personal history, the time didn't seem right. My fiancée, filled with excitement and delighted to be picnicking on the floor, babbled happily as we snacked and sipped. Destroying her carefree mood would have felt like shooting Bambi. When I took a break from the food, she put her hand on my chest and pushed me back into the throw pillows.

"Time to get cozy," she murmured.

I settled back as she nestled into my shoulder. The food, the fire, the wine—contentment washed over me. I wasn't in love but try as I might, I could think of no better substitute. I'd almost nodded off when Dusty brought me back to the present.

"Cleatzy?"

"H-m-m."

"We need to talk. You've been so trusting and open with me, but here we are three weeks from our wedding, and I've been holding out on you. There are things about me you should know."

I made a comforting noise. I'd been worried about how to tell Dusty about my role in Myra's suicide and run-ins with the police, and now the opportunity to make a clean breast of it came marching boldly over the horizon. Best of all, she was going first. I readied myself to hear about a lover she'd neglected to mention. At my age, there wasn't much that could shock me.

She kissed my cheek. "When I lived in India, I felt so happy I didn't ever want to leave. I believed I would never find a better group of friends. Sattguru Dev had mastered the essence of all religions. If we stayed on the path and followed him, we'd build a society filled with love, one where everyone could find fulfillment and prosper. He promised we would become saints, the People of Light. I believed Dev was a living god."

She paused, waiting for me to comment. She hadn't told me anything I didn't already know, so I made the appropriate noises. "There's nothing wrong with being part of a religious community, even if you chose to leave it. Go on, tell me what's really bothering you."

"I didn't leave the group willingly. Dad and Gib hired someone to bring me back home. One night when I went out to solicit donations, two men came out of nowhere and pulled a cloth bag over my head. They threw me into the back of a van and drove me to a walled compound where they locked me in a room without windows. The next day, a deprogrammer showed up. I had to stay in that room and listen to the guy tell me over and over I was living in a fantasy. After a few days, I realized he was right. The People of Light weren't a caring, loving community. The group was a cult."

Dusty began to sob, and I held her closer. "It's okay," I whispered. "Everyone makes mistakes. The important thing is that you got out and are safe."

She broke into full-bore crying. Though I only got fragments of what she said, I understood enough to know she felt guilty and stupid. I waited for her to get control of herself. When she did, I assured her I still cared for her and asked if there was anything else. She nodded.

Her voice quavered, but she soldiered on. "Dad and Gib raised holy hell with Senator Jepsen, and he complained to the State Department. Nothing happened until the Indian government realized the *ashram* was cheating on its taxes. That got their attention, and they forced Sattguru Dev to close it. He fled the country, and now he's moved to New Mexico where he and his followers have set up again. With our First Amendment, nobody can do anything about him."

I touched her hair and stroked her cheek. "You can't help that they're still in business. There's a limit to what you and your family could do. Now aren't you glad you've got it off your chest? I don't care about it. It's in the past."

She pulled herself away, sat up, and turned her back. "You need to hear all of it. When I'm done, you might not want to marry me."

"I can't imagine that would happen."

"There's more, Cleatzy. When I realized what happened to me, I didn't trust anyone. My family paid to have me abducted, and my friends at the *ashram* wouldn't talk to me. I was angry with all of them, so I moved to Switzerland and married the first guy who came along. I never told you, but the reason Baron divorced me is I quit sleeping with him. Because of everything that happened, there wasn't enough of me left to share with anybody. I had a nervous breakdown and spent a year recovering at a rest home in Vermont."

Though I wasn't thrilled about the breakdown and freezing out her husband, her reaction made sense. "It's no surprise you had a breakdown. After what you'd been through, it was bound to happen. You shouldn't have felt like you needed to keep all this to yourself." I moved a hand up to her shoulder and gave a gentle tug, a sign that she should settle back onto the pillows with me. She did.

I kissed her on the lips, pulled back a bit, and met her gaze. Her eyes reflected the light flickering in the fireplace. My best friend hurt, and I wanted to soothe her. "Now that wasn't so bad, was it?" I whispered.

She shook her head. "You don't understand life at the *ashram*. The path to enlightenment involved harnessing our tantric energy. At tantric therapy, we'd strip to rid ourselves of our inhibitions and give each other massages. The encounters were intense. Sometimes we got carried away and had sex right there in front of everybody. Cleatzy, I did that more than once. I was even in some three and foursomes. Sattguru Dev encouraged us to take part in the groups to strengthen the community. I kept count. I had sex in tantric therapy with forty-seven people over three years."

If I'd been in love, I would have been devastated. But a friend can catch breaks a lover cannot. Still, sixteen a year? And that was just in the tantric groups. I'm not a prude, but after all, we were getting married. The number forty-seven bounced around my brain like a Ping-Pong ball at a table tennis convention.

"We were on the front lines of the sexual revolution, Cleatzy. Before AIDS, before we knew the revolution was more about guys getting laid than love and commitment. I got lucky and didn't catch anything that couldn't be cured. That was then, and this is now, but you need to go into our marriage with your eyes open."

My eyes were open, and my guts were quivering. A failed marriage, a sanitarium, and enough lovers for several lifetimes. Though I felt like I knew Dusty, there were dimensions to her personality I could only guess at. I had trouble forming thoughts, let alone words.

Get a grip Efferding. Do you want to blow your best chance at marriage, kids, and financial security? Fake it.

I managed a few sentences. "You didn't need to tell me this, Dusty. What matters is the person you are today because that's the person I want to marry. You wouldn't be that person you are if you hadn't lived the life you lived."

Hadn't lived the life you lived? My brain was spewing nonsense even I didn't understand.

Dusty rolled on top of me and kissed me like I'd never been kissed before. When she pulled away, she sat up and hugged herself. "You understand, Cleatzy! I wouldn't have worried so much except you're so perfect. You told me all about yourself and didn't hold back. You want to marry me despite my mistakes and holding out on you. I'm not like you. You're good, honest, and kind. I wouldn't be able to take it if I discovered you were keeping secrets from me. My world would shatter."

Her world would shatter.

I promised Lumir I'd fill Dusty in on the details of Myra's suicide, the flight from my hometown, and the loss of my parental rights. She had the right to know I'd killed another human being, but her revelations made it hard to think straight. The truth could upend our relationship.

To heck with it, I pulled her down on me and tried to kiss her like she'd never been kissed before. With well over forty-seven notches in her belt, the task would have broken a lesser man. I gave it my best shot, and by the end of the smooch, I knew I'd outdone them all.

Chapter 4

He slouched in the doorway of my office, his hands in the pockets of ill-fitting jeans and his expression a sneer. Engrossed in scheduling instructors for April dance lessons, I hadn't noticed him. I didn't know how long he'd been standing there watching me. Though the years had passed, I recognized him at once. I'd imagined the moment thousands of times, but nothing prepared me for the reality. The young man at the door was my son.

Radiating hostility, he didn't speak. The gulf between us, a veritable Grand Canyon of loss and missed opportunities, stretched before me like a life sentence without parole. Everything about him, his posture, his timing, his attitude, seemed awkward and wrong. A meeting between a long-separated father and son should have felt like a warm embrace. Ours was anything but.

Tears blurred my vision. I stood to move toward him, if not to hug, to shake his hand. My tongue finally moved, and an unsteady "Hello, Mike" came out.

He glared. "So, this is it. Efferding's dance fantasy, the kind of place where you tricked my mother into believing you were marriage material."

I put my hands on the desk and sat back down.

He gestured toward the dance floor outside. "Guess that's where you spend your nights. Kind of a desperate way to get laid, don't you think? Not much, but I suppose it's better than hiring prostitutes."

Guilt, shame, anger, and grief struggled for dominance. He'd managed to push all my buttons at once. Not bad for the first few sentences out of his mouth. I blinked hard.

"Do your lady students get free lessons if they beat you up, or do you have to give them a little extra on the side?"

"You're making it difficult for me to like you, Mike."

"You made it pretty hard to feel warm and fuzzy about you."

He had me. Though she'd been severely depressed, his mom killed herself on the heels of my arrest at an apartment the newspapers dubbed a sadomasochistic dungeon. It wasn't, but I doubted Mike would care the whips-and-chains thing was nothing more than a reporter's fevered imagination. His mom took her life, and he blamed me. So much to explain, but really, would it make any difference?

I had to try. "Mike, your mother suffered from severe depression. The doctors wanted to try shock treatments, but I couldn't let them do that to her. Maybe the treatments would have helped, maybe not. It's been eighteen years, and I still second-guess my decision every day. I loved your mom. She's the only woman I've ever loved."

Slight of build, he had his mother's oval-shaped face, her mouse-colored hair, her brown eyes. The physical likeness magnified his contempt for me, as if Myra stood in the door, passing judgment.

But it wasn't Myra. It was Mike, and he hadn't finished yet. "If my real mom was the only woman you ever loved, why are you getting married again? Yeah, I know all about your kind of love and feel sorry for her. You laid out good money to get a whore to beat you while your sick wife sat at home with two little kids. Worse yet, you were stupid enough to get caught."

I ran my hands through my hair. Though my son was twenty-one, I needed to be the adult in the room. "I made a mistake, Mike. I'll live with the consequences the rest of my life. I'm sorry beyond words for what I did. If there was a way to take it back—"

"Take it back? You live with the consequences? What happened isn't just about poor Cletus Efferding. What about me? What about Tammy? We live with the consequences every day. We grew up calling our grandparents Mom and Dad. Our whole life was a lie. Where were you?"

Whatever I said would sound like self-justification. My son imagined I had some control over the situation. Devastated by Myra's death, I'd gone on a year-long bender. By the time I straightened out, a judge had terminated my parental rights. No need for Mike to know the details of my descent into hell, so I sidetracked, laying it all on his grandpa Brutus.

"Where was I? Rebuilding my life. Brute threatened to kill me if I didn't leave town and promised to take me out if I ever came back. The guy was county sheriff. He'd killed two men in the line of duty—one with his bare hands. When somebody like that wants to take you out, it's time to go. Your grandfather cost me everything—my family, my home, my business. I tried to contact you, but the letters came back marked 'Return to Sender.' Your Christmas and birthday gifts came back unopened. He and Velma monitored the phone. One day Brute called to tell me he'd come to Cedar Rapids and beat me with a tire iron if I sent more packages or phoned again."

My son extracted his hands from his pockets, shifted to the other side of the door frame, and leaned on it. He crossed his arms. "As if you cared about our birthdays. You probably don't even know how old I am."

"Twenty-one years, six months, and three days. Tammy is nineteen. You want the months and days for her too?"

The clock ticked. No response. Finally, I'd gotten through to him.

"Big deal. So, you're some kind of math whiz. Do you know what it's like to live with a man who's proud of beating someone to death? A guy who thinks the way to raise a kid is to toughen him up by taking a leather belt to him? My life was hell."

"Mike, I didn't know."

"Didn't know? If you were any kind of father, you'd have checked in on us. The day the old man died was the best day of my life. You could have come then. There was nobody to stop you, but I didn't see you at the front door."

I sighed. There's nothing like the collapse of your every claim to human decency to take the edge off the day. The evidence of my abject failure as a father stood in the doorway. I leaned back in my chair and taking a cue from my son, folded my arms—on the defensive, but unable to walk away. Whether he hated me or not, he deserved answers.

"I'm sorry, Mike. Brute and Velma shouldn't have raised you as their own kids. I didn't know about it until he died, and I read the obituary saying they were your parents. I talked to a professional psychologist. He said to butt out until the two of you were adults. That's why I didn't contact you until Tammy turned eighteen. After I sent those registered letters, I was going to wait a couple of weeks to let it sink in and then call. But the next thing I knew, your lawyer phoned and threatened me with a restraining order if I tried to communicate with either of you."

Mike shook his head. "As if a couple of letters could make up for eighteen years. You washed your hands of us when our real mom died. Abandoned your kids and waltzed off without a care in the world—a shining example for your children."

Worried adrenaline might get the better of me, I held up my hands, counted to ten, took some deep breaths, and counted again. It didn't work. Images of me punching him in the face came out of nowhere. I grabbed the arms of my chair and squeezed with everything I had.

"It wasn't like that, Mike. I've never had much, but whenever I caught a break, the money went into trust funds for you and Tammy. There should be enough there for four years of college for each of you."

Mike rolled his eyes. "Never had much? I stopped by Cleatzy's Menswear last night. Not too bad I'd say."

Comfort unimaginable would be mine in three weeks, but it would be Dusty's money. "Cleatzy's belongs to the investors. I'm a figurehead, drawing a salary just like the years I worked in a department store." I felt the anger welling up again. "But I have a question for you, Mike. Why are you here? Stop by just to use the old man for a punching bag? I might disgust you, but there's nothing I can do about that. What do you want from me?"

"The money from my trust fund."

Game, set, match. The chances of a father-and-son relationship died with his reply. My body unknotted as jingly shakiness replaced anger. No need to be defensive, the stranger at the door meant nothing to me.

I leaned back, put my elbows on the arms of the chair, and steepled my hands. "I can't make a distribution from your trust; only the trustee can do it. It's the way the thing works. When I set up the trust, I gave directions for its dissolution. The money pays for tuition. If you don't use it for an education, the balance stays in trust until your twenty-eighth birthday. You're twenty-one years old. You must know the terms by now."

"I need the money. A group of us are investing in ourselves so we can reach our maximum potential and promote world harmony."

I didn't understand a word of his gobbledygook and couldn't care less. "It's out of my hands. You'll have to take it up with the Trust Department at Merchant's National Bank."

"I know you're marrying the head banker's daughter. It was in the newspaper. Pull some strings for me."

I might have been able to pull strings. Maybe, but that would imply letting the kid waste the money while he stared at his navel searching for his maximum potential. "I don't have that kind of influence."

"Could I borrow ten thousand dollars, then?"

My jaw dropped. "No."

He sniffed. "Your son wants to invest in himself and make the world a better place, but all you can say is one word."

"There's nothing to lend. I'm already in hock forty grand for my part in getting Cleatzy's off the ground."

With that, he turned on his heel and marched on out across the dance floor. "You're cold, man," he shot back. "Really cold."

I nodded to myself. *Yep, that's me, Cletus Efferding, unfeeling parent and heartless skinflint—an emotional icebox.*

Chapter 5

The Cedar Rapids County Club. My greeter directed me to Steele Sutherland's table. I can't say I was looking forward to our lunch. Though Dusty and I had been dating for a year and a half, I'd yet to spend more than a quarter-hour alone with her father. On those occasions, he intimidated me with what Dusty called his favorite trick—leaving long pauses in the conversation to keep his companion off balance. I was five minutes late and let out a sigh of relief when the table proved to be empty. I didn't know much about the world of CEOs but suspected a minute of his time would buy a pair of Bostonian wingtips.

It took fifteen minutes for him to arrive. By then I was on to his game. Making someone wait ensures they're aware of your importance. I made a mental note to be twenty minutes late if we had another lunch together. Tardy he might have been, but when the man entered the place, he looked impressive. Six-foot-five, athletic, with silver hair and a confident stride, his commanding bearing set him apart from the other diners.

Steele strode up to the table and stuck out his hand. "Sorry, Cleatzy, my board meeting ran late."

The man had such presence I almost rose to take his hand, a mistake that would have forever condemned me in his eyes. Protocol demanded that I lean forward and lift my butt two inches off the chair to give his extended mitt a firm shake. In return, Steele nearly broke the bones in my hand.

"It's good to see you," I replied as I returned my rump to the chair. "I took the liberty of ordering a glass of wine while I was waiting. Hope you don't mind."

"Not at all, not at all," he said as our waitress set a partially unfolded napkin in his lap.

It didn't take a psychic to see he did mind. If I hadn't said anything, my future father-in-law wouldn't have noticed. I made a second mental note: never say anything that in any way, shape, or form could be construed as an apology. Though I'd known him almost a year, I hadn't scratched the surface of the multitude of *faux pas* constituting breaches of decorum in his clubby, hyper-masculine world.

Steele ordered a Scotch, neat. He must have known the lunch menu by heart since he coupled his directive with an order for food. I frantically searched my menu so as not to hold up the process and ended up with a cold veal dish and an endive salad.

After our waitress left, Steele sat silently with one hand on the table and the other rubbing his chin. Not wanting to play his game by making idle chatter, I didn't speak but tried to look thoughtful by leaning forward and furrowing my brow. When the silence got to me, I decided to take the direct approach.

"Steele, I've been dating Dusty for a year and a half, yet you and I have never really spoken. You have something on your mind. What is it?"

His piercing blue eyes met mine. I flinched. He shifted in his seat, a movement so subtle I almost missed it. The seconds of silence stretched into minutes, then days as the meaning of the word *gravitas* became clear to me.

He finally spoke. "Cleatzy, you'll be marrying my only daughter in three weeks. I hired a detective to investigate you and have had the report in my safe since November."

I waited. Nothing more.

I finally gave in. "Then you know all about me. It's three weeks before the wedding, and you've waited six months to have this conversation?"

Silence, wait, response.

"I wanted to make sure the nuptials would take place. Dusty has been engaged twice and called off the weddings—the last time, four weeks before the ceremony. Since we're at a little less than three weeks, it behooves me to assume your union will come to pass."

"So, what do you want to talk about?"

"You."

What, no controlling pause? Maybe we'd have a regular conversation. I replied with a question: "And?"

"Well, you're not exactly what we've been looking for. Losing an established family business, I don't understand how a man can allow something like that to happen."

The family business? No mention of bondage, Myra's suicide, and the prostitution charge. Nothing about abandoning my kids, the manslaughter arrest, or killing someone. Steele's detective must have done a half-baked job, and I was the luckiest man in Cedar Rapids.

I lied a little.

"My objective was to keep the business in the family." In truth, I unloaded the business on the first person to come around—my cousin. Nothing like the County Sheriff promising to kill you to inspire a hasty departure to another jurisdiction. "I didn't foresee my cousin would have a nervous breakdown and let the business fail."

Steele drummed his fingers on the table. "You'd have been able to keep an eye on things if you hadn't spent your time staring at the bottom of a table in a dive on Sixteenth Avenue."

My heart sank. Dusty's father knew more than I imagined. "My wife's suicide, I … it threw me."

The waitress arrived with our orders. Steele's Caprese salad looked magnificent. My veal had the appearance of wet cardboard. After asking if there were anything more we wanted, she left, and Steele started in again.

"You've signed the prenuptial agreement, so you understand that while Dusty has considerable financial freedom, ultimate control of her assets resides with the family trust. Your poor business sense precludes our bringing you into the arrangement. Neither you nor the children you abandoned are in line to receive income from, or assets belonging to, the trust. That includes the transfer of assets or income by inheritance."

The detective may have done a better job than I gave him credit for, but Steele needed to know I didn't abandon the kids.

"The situation with the children was complicated. They weren't abandoned but went to live with their grandparents. I did what I thought best."

Silence again. I'd come across as apologetic.

He let me stew a full minute before speaking. "As I was about to say, the children of a previous marriage are of no concern to Dusty or the family trust."

He didn't get it. I tried again. "My in-laws sued for custody of the children. Myra's father was the County Sheriff and—"

"Give me some credit," he interrupted. "I know all about the death threats and your highly publicized arrest for prostitution. You blabbed to half the population of Bohemie Town when you were drinking." He glanced at his watch. "Let's talk about your upcoming marriage while I still have time."

I looked at him with disbelief. "I believe you said I'm not what you're looking for."

"That may be true, but Dusty wants to marry you, and frankly, Consuela and I are relieved. Dusty says the two of you would like to start a family, and we want grandchildren. My daughter isn't getting any younger, and her brother Tanner is unlikely to produce offspring."

Dusty had mentioned Tanner was "light in the loafers," but until Steele referred to him as an unlikely to have kids, I didn't understand her meaning. Dusty's father hadn't scheduled our luncheon to give me the brush-off. He wanted to make sure I didn't have any illusions about my bottom-tier place in the scheme of things. I sat quietly, waiting for my almost father-in-law to continue.

Eventually, he broke the silence. "Consuela and I had just about given up on the possibility that Dusty would re-marry. She's so gullible she joined a cult. We had to buy off her first husband when she banned him from her bed. After that, she underwent a complete nervous breakdown and subsequently backed out of two engagements to scions of good families. Word gets out, and successful men don't marry women as unstable as Dusty, so for better or worse, you're the future of our family."

That future didn't seem as rosy as it did two days ago. I was about to ask him for background on Dusty's mental collapse but didn't get the chance. Steele had become positively loquacious.

"In a way, you're a godsend. Your children prove you're fertile. Because of your experience with your first wife, you understand mental illness and how to deal with it. It doesn't hurt that you've killed a man. I know it was in self-defense. It's unlikely to happen, but if a break-in occurred, you'd likely sacrifice yourself to protect her."

Now I really felt guilty. I knew everything possible about Dusty, but her father knew more about me than she did. It wasn't right. I didn't have much time to tell her, but she deserved better. I'd set things straight.

"I have a confession to make, Steele. Dusty doesn't know I've killed a man. She doesn't know Myra killed herself after I disgraced her publicly or that some people call what I did abandoning my kids. I promise you I'll tell her everything."

Steele's momentary weakness disappeared. "No, you won't. You'd unload and have a clean conscience for five minutes, but my daughter would be devastated. She might cancel the wedding. The shock could even send her back to the mental hospital. Gib and I set you up in business so you wouldn't be an embarrassment to her. Dusty needs peace and stability to raise our grandchildren, and for better or worse, that stability is you."

"Steele, Dusty deserves to know."

He shook his head. "You can go now and process what we've talked about. It'll certainly be easier than digesting that miserable excuse for veal on your plate. I need to finish my salad and get back to the office."

I stood. "It's not right."

Steele looked up at me, annoyed. "Don't go moral on me, Cleatzy. You haven't told her, and if we hadn't talked today, you'd have been content to keep your little secrets from her."

"But—"

"Let's get one thing perfectly clear. If you sabotage your engagement or hurt my daughter in any way—emotionally or physically—I will find someone to castrate you and break every one of the two hundred and six bones in your body. Understand?"

I understood.

Chapter 6

I surveyed my apartment and took in the well-worn furniture, the newspapers stacked next to the TV, the walls covered with mementos of my fascination with the city's minor league team. The place wasn't much, but I liked it, and it should have been enough for me.

Funny how things work out. As a young man, I wanted nothing so much as to live in my hometown, manage the family clothing shop, marry, and raise kids. My folks wanted me to go to college instead. My sole consolation after their death in a car accident was the chance to leave school and take over the store. Within a few years, I'd managed the whole package: loving wife, two kids, weekend bowling, a Jaycees membership, the works—until an afternoon's indiscretion snatched it away. Now, eighteen years later, I had a chance at a do-over, but I'd have traded the whole shebang for a sunny afternoon walk with Myra. Carrying a torch for a long-dead woman made no sense, but that's the way it was. I doubted anything would change it.

I'd planned a few quiet beers in front of the television so retrieved the latest issue of *TV Guide* from the magazine rack. The Friday night lineup didn't amount to much, but I got home early enough to catch the start of *The Dukes of Hazzard*. A trip to redneck country it would be.

I pulled a Budweiser from the fridge and settled in for an hour of car crashes and Daisy Duke's legs. The show's plot wouldn't have challenged a first grader, but the short shorts exposing a good part of Catherine Bach's backside almost made up for it. The storyline went from bad to worse when a character named Cletus Hogg made an appearance. I sat transfixed, unable to look away as my namesake blundered his way through scene after scene, spewing unending stupidities. Horrified the show's writers had paired my given name with the common term for swine, I turned off the TV.

The end of my first beer inspired me to fetch a second and a bag of cheese puffs. I returned to the couch. My upcoming marriage had begun to feel like a trap, one of those golden-handcuff contracts corporations use to chain employees to miserable jobs. For my part, I'd sire grandchildren and take care of Dusty. In return, the Sutherland machine would see I enjoyed a comfortable existence. Maybe it wasn't worth it.

I looked at Dusty as a free spirit who embraced the opportunities that came her way and picked herself up when she fell on her face. Her father saw an unstable woman with mental problems. The guy didn't run the most successful bank in town by being a bad judge of character. If Dusty went into a depression like Myra, my new life could become a nightmare. She'd quit sleeping with her first husband. What if she did the same to me?

I loved Myra unconditionally, and her depression-induced refusal to be intimate hurt worse than anything I'd ever experienced. My inability to deal with it led to the ill-fated bawdyhouse visit that ruined my life. I would never love like that again and didn't want to. If Dusty shut me off, I'd be miserable. I reached for a handful of cheese puffs and froze. What if she lost it and went the other way?

Licking my cheesy fingers, I thought about marriage to a cheating nymphomaniac. After all, my fiancée had at least forty-seven lovers in just three years. Since I wasn't in love, I'd probably get over the infidelity, but flagrant cheating can't be hidden. I'd become a public cuckold. Snickers, elbowed asides, pity for my inability to hold a wife, the shame.

I reached for my beer and downed it without thinking. Trapped with a frigid nymphomaniac in a loveless marriage, dependent on the Sutherlands for every penny, I pictured a future anything but rosy.

My imagination, on a wild ride, got the best of me. One minute, I imagined a disastrous marriage because Dusty was frigid and the next because she was a slut. I struggled to get a grip on myself. If things went to hell, I could always leave. Heck, if I wanted to, I could call off the engagement. Dusty had done it twice. There'd be financial ruin, but I'd been through it before and survived. After a few deep breaths, I settled down, my imaginary problems in perspective—until Steele's words came back to me.

If you sabotage your engagement or hurt my daughter in any way ... I will hire someone to castrate you and break every one of the two hundred and six bones in your body.

I threw my empty beer bottle against the wall, got up, and ran out the front door.

"Looks like I caught you orange-handed."

I looked over to the guy on the next bar stool and contemplated getting up to leave.

"Your fingers," he said, "you've been eating cheese curls."

I turned my head back to center and stared down at my second gin and tonic. I'd switched to gin after downing a pair of Seven and Sevens. The number of drinks I consumed was the bar's fault, not mine. I'd come to Pete's Pub in search of a Wisconsin Old-Fashioned, but the barkeep looked at me like I was daft.

"We don't make any of those frou-frou drinks here. It's whiskey, gin, vodka, and rum with a mixer, or else beer," he said.

Though the Sutherland men drank scotch, I generally avoid spirits. Hard liquor short-circuits the part of my brain that tells me I've had enough. After the first of the gins, I saw the handwriting on the wall. Come hell or high water, Cletus Efferding would drink himself blotto for the first time in fifteen years.

"Friendly sucker, aren't you?" the guy who commented on my fingers said. "I make a living by noticing things about people. I'm a cop, and your fingers stuck out like a sore thumb."

Fingers, sore thumb, the guy had a strange sense of humor. I glared. "If you didn't notice, I don't feel like talking. You must not be very good at your job."

He shrugged his shoulders. "Suit yourself. You wanna sit there and get hammered all alone, knock yourself out. Most people go to bars to be around other human beings. I guess you don't qualify."

He had a point.

"Sorry, didn't mean to be a Class-A jerk. I've got a lot on my mind. Actually, they weren't cheese curls but el-cheapo cheese puffs."

"Crappy cheese puffs—you must be on a downer. I wouldn't have said anything about your fingers, but they reminded me of a bust I made last summer."

I smiled at him. He looked like a good enough egg. I put him at fifty-five, with half of the hair that once graced the top of his head. Had bachelor written all over him. No woman would have put up with the guy's purple shirt and checked polyester pants.

"The bust—the guy rob a grocery store?"

"No, broke into one of those fancy houses up on Grande Avenue. He didn't steal anything, but he was high as a kite on Colombian pot. Got the munchies, made for the kitchen, and loaded up on junk food. The dude split by the time we got there, so my partner and I fanned out through the neighborhood. I saw a guy leaning against a light pole and went up to question him. He gets huffy and starts waving his arms around complaining about police harassment. That's when I see his orange fingers. When I point out he's got cheese dust all over himself and the burglar was eating cheese curls, he raises his hands in the air and says, 'You got me, man.' The dude's a regular, always getting hauled in for something, but my bust made him famous. Now everybody at the station calls him Cheeto, you know—after the Cheetos Bandito."

I didn't bother to tell him it was the Frito Bandito. The story didn't do much for me, but it broke the ice. I introduced myself and learned his name was Burl. "So, you notice things. Ever think about applying for detective?" I asked.

"No and wouldn't want to. Most boring job in the world. I'd sooner be out on the street where the action is. Besides, who wants to take a test and then kiss up to the brass? Me? I can rip into the captain when he needs it and nobody cares. What's he gonna do? Put me on night shift? I'm already there."

"You could get sacked."

"Nah, the union would raise holy hell. Anyway, all I ever do is tell it like it really is."

I nodded, happy the man didn't work for me. Before long, Burl was filling me in on his divorce. One morning after he rotated to the graveyard shift, he came home to find his wife and a neighbor passed out in bed, an empty fifth of peppermint schnapps on the nightstand.

"Passed out cold and naked," he continued. "She's the dirty cheat, but her lawyer takes me to the cleaners. Now I live in a dump. I tell ya, never again. Marriage is the worst deal a guy can get himself into."

His comment inspired me to order another G & T, and after a moment's hesitation, I gave him the gory details of my upcoming engagement. When I finished, he looked at me as if I'd just stepped off a spaceship from Pluto.

"Let me get this straight," he said. "You're marrying a rich babe who's good in bed, and you like her enough to start a family. Her relatives set you up in a business and a penthouse apartment. All that, and you get cold feet? Cletey Boy, I can't see the downside. The worst that can happen is you bail out and end up where you started."

Yeah, but in a body cast and minus the family jewels.

I tried to explain about the golden handcuffs, about her parents wanting me to take care of their unstable daughter and demanding we produce grandchildren. "I'll be trapped in a situation with in-laws who don't respect me," I complained.

Burl was having none of it. "You need to get a grip on yourself," he laughed. "So, they expect you to be nice to their emotional daughter and want you to make grandkids. I never seen a man who gets handed everything complain so much."

I tried again. "She used to sleep around and belonged to a cult."

Burl raised his brows and rubbed the stubble on his chin. "That changes things; those cults are a bad business. We had a couple of teenagers here in Cedar Rapids run away with the Children of God. They use their young women to lure in new members by having sex with them, hookers for Jesus. They target horny teenagers who end up running away from their families so they can get laid."

"And think about the People's Temple cult down in Jonestown," I added. "One visit from a congressman and Jim Jones convinces 900 people to drink poison Kool-Aid."

"A bad situation," Burl agreed. "What group was she in?"

"They call themselves the People of Light, and they follow somebody called Sattguru Dev."

"Think she'll ever go back?"

"She's put it all behind her. Even if she wanted to, they wouldn't take her because they got into trouble with the government of India and blame her for it."

Burl shrugged. "So, whatcha worried about? If they don't want her, she'll never go back to 'em. Hell, life's a risk. Marry the lady. You'd be nuts not to go for it."

"She had forty-seven lovers in three years!"

"Nobody's perfect. If you had that many, you'd wear your tonsils out crowing about how great you are with women. Think about the life coming your way, and you'll get over the forty-seven."

Maybe Burl was right. I would be nuts to back out on Dusty. I thought it over as we chatted over a steady stream of drinks, and my alcohol-besotted brain could come up with no good reason for my reluctance. No good reason except I still loved Myra.

The next morning, I woke up on Burl's couch, my shirt covered with vomit.

Chapter 7

Dusty came over to my apartment after our dinner with her parents, her Uncle Gib, and Aunt Dora. The place looked good considering I'd returned that morning to discover I left the door wide open during my flight the night before. Miraculously, no one took advantage of the situation. Though I found myself cleaning up a hairball left by the neighbor's cat, my stupidity had gone unpunished.

Well, almost unpunished. My self-indulgent night at Pete's put me so far behind at Cleatzy's I would need to pull an all-nighter. A late-season flu bug had turned staff scheduling into a hopeless mess, orders for the upcoming fall season were beyond late, and worse yet, my quarterly tax reports were so far behind I needed to ask for an extension.

At least our evening at the club had gone well. Steele sipped his scotch and acted as if our come-to-Jesus lunch never happened. After a few martinis, Gib started telling lame jokes and slapping me on the back. Consuela dominated the conversation; Dora didn't crack a smile.

My fiancée and I made for the couch, turned on the TV, and settled in. Still nursing an all-day headache from last night's epic binge, my body let me know it would kill me if we attempted anything serious. I put my arm around her, pulled her close, and kissed her lightly.

Dusty must have read my mind. "Not much passion in that one. Still hungover from your spree at Pete's? You should have taken Dad up on that peated scotch tonight," she teased. "It would have made for a good male bonding experience."

"After last night's bender, the last thing I needed was more booze."

"When you went to the restroom, Dad said your tee-totaling didn't impress him. What did the two of you talk about at lunch?"

Probably not a good idea to bring up castration and broken bones. I decided to shade the truth. "We talked about sponsoring me for the Country Club." And we had, but earlier in the week at Cleatzy's.

Her face lit up like a Christmas tree. "The club? I'm happy he likes you so much. I think Mom's coming around too."

"That reminds me, what's the dustup with the club's caterer? Sounds like Consuela really got into it with him."

"Oh, that's my fault. I wanted potato chips on the snack tables for the reception. When Mom told them she wanted the broken chips removed before they put them into the serving bowls, the guy went ballistic."

Too bad the dragon lady was about to become my mother-in-law. "I hope she's in a good mood when you ask her about Eddie tending bar."

"I'm not crazy enough to ask. Besides, it's already taken care of." Dusty began playing with my earlobe. "I went to high school with the head bartender's son, so it was easy to arrange. What Mom doesn't know won't hurt her."

I wished I could have said the same thing about Dusty. What she didn't know could hurt her big time. She believed me an honest, decent man, and I was—sort of. Sort of, but not honest and decent enough to share secrets she needed to know. Sort of, but willing to lie to a friend so he'd come to my wedding.

Dusty shifted, pulling away from me so she could see my face. "Cleatzy, what's wrong? You haven't been yourself today, and going out and getting drunk last night, that's not like you. Are you having second thoughts about our marriage?"

Time to lie again. I'd gone beyond second thoughts, was all the way to nineteenth or twentieth. I fudged the truth.

"No, no second thoughts. I haven't told you, but my son came to see me at the studio Thursday night. I'm upset because it didn't go so well. He told me how much he hated me, then had the gall to ask for ten thousand dollars."

Dusty took my face in her hands and kissed me. "Sit on the floor," she commanded.

Knowing I was in for one of her fantastic neck rubs, I readily complied. Dusty excelled because she had lots of practice. The folks at the *ashram* took the art of massage seriously. She began kneading my shoulders, then worked her way up along my neck bones. Moans of pleasure passed my lips.

"Poor Cleatzy," she said as she kneaded, "All these years you've wanted to reconnect with your kids, and this is what happens."

"Yeah, he came on like a real jerk and then asked for the money. Said he and his friends wanted to invest in themselves so they could reach their maximum potential and promote world harmony."

Dusty stopped rubbing. "Reaching their maximum potential and promoting world harmony? Are you sure, Cleatzy?"

Sensing my massage had come to a premature end, I got off the floor and returned to the couch. "That's what he said."

"Those are the words Manoneetas use to describe their quest."

I shook my head. "Manoneetas? Quest? I don't know what you're talking about."

"Manoneetas are followers of Sattguru Dev. The quest is a Manoneeta's search for spiritual fulfillment."

Dusty's experience at the *ashram* still haunted her. She sometimes saw the cult's hand at work in activities that had nothing to do with the group. "I don't know, Dusty. Investing in yourself and promoting world harmony are common ideas."

"When Mike asked you for money, he mentioned investing in his friends as well as himself. Add in the 'maximum potential' bit, and it's the standard fundraising pitch. He wanted funds for the People of Light."

"Dusty, Mike lives in Iowa City, a half-hour drive. The cult is in New Mexico, eleven hundred miles away. He just wants to sponge off me."

"Your son is involved with them whether you want to believe it or not."

I didn't think so, but what difference did it make? My son hated me.

"Maybe, maybe not, but he did everything but spit in my face. If he wants to rot his life away with a bunch of kooks in some godforsaken hellhole, it's his choice."

Dusty looked disappointed with me. She leaned back into the couch and crossed her arms.

"I'm glad my family didn't think that way."

The next morning. Margaret, my assistant manager at the dance studio, called the apartment to report she had fallen in love and would no longer be working for me. Though I failed to understand the connection between finding love and employment, the link between her departure and the effort required to train a replacement was easy enough to see.

The Sutherlands insisted Cleatzy's welcome the buying public ten hours a day, 360 days a year. Though I hired experienced staff who'd lost their jobs when Killian's Department Store went out of business, the new shop ate up fifty to sixty hours a week. Managing Steppin' Out took another fifteen; it should have been twenty-five. Fatigued beyond belief, I didn't have the energy to handle both operations and decided to close the dance studio. My future in-laws would be thrilled. Consuela wanted me to shutter the operation because she considered it "lower class" and Steele and Gib because they feared it would detract from my effort at Cleatzy's.

When Margaret's call came in, I'd been in the kitchen, cradling a cup of coffee and mulling over Dusty's reaction to what she called my "callous attitude" toward my son. Dusty was still in bed. The phone must have awakened her, for she soon appeared in the doorway, wearing nothing but a pair of panties and one of my barrel-cuffed Arrow shirts. Her hair in disarray and stifling a yawn, she made for a vision so lovely I nearly fell from my chair.

"What was that?" she asked, raising her hands over her head to stretch.

The results of the stretch beat the heck out of the yawn.

"Margaret called to tell me she's in love. She's resigning."

"M-m-m," Dusty replied as she made for the Mr. Coffee. "Sucks."

"Tell me about it," I said. "I'm closing the studio."

She pulled a mug from the cupboard and poured. "Makes sense. Between your schedule and our honeymoon, there's not much you can do about it until you get a replacement."

I waited until she joined me at the table. "No, I'm closing it for good. I just can't do it anymore. I'm fifty years old and don't have the oomph to run two businesses. If Steppin' Out can't be a first-class operation, it's history."

Dusty stood, rounded the table, and sat on my lap. The kiss that followed came close to taking the top of my head off. Apparently unhappy with the results of her effort, she kissed me again, leaving me nearly comatose.

"I know how much you love teaching dance," she said when she'd finished with me. "And I know you could run both businesses with your hands tied behind your back."

"Huh?"

"You're doing it for me. When my family wanted you to give up the studio, you said 'no' and meant it. I haven't said anything about wanting to spend more time with you, but you picked up on it and are closing Steppin' Out, a business you love, just for me."

"I wanted to surprise you," I lied. "It's been a hard decision, and I didn't know how to tell Margaret. She's taken on a lot since Cleatzy's opened. Closing the studio felt like rewarding her loyalty by letting her go. Now I don't have to. Her resignation made me so happy I forgot the shutdown was a surprise and let the cat out of the bag."

I should have felt guilty about the whopper but hoped appreciation for my apparent sacrifice would replace Dusty's disappointment with my attitude toward my son. The lies and deceptions were piling up, but I had a lot on the line—a rosy financial future, the success of

Cleatzy's, and my last chance to have a family. The wedding had to go through.

Chapter 8

I checked the mirror and gave my bowtie a last-minute adjustment. My hair, once nearly black, showed the first signs of salt and pepper. The idea of going gray didn't bother me. With my nice thick head of hair, I might look different, but the change wouldn't do anything to alter my innate good looks.

My Rolex, a gift from Dusty, lay on the top of the dresser. I'd put it on and taken it off three times. Convention has it that a man in a tuxedo does not wear a watch, but I had deadlines ahead of me—the photographer, the church service, the grand entrance at the reception. I opted for the cautious approach and put it on a fourth time. The break with tradition wouldn't have been necessary had my steadfast friend Lumir been my best man, but Dusty's disorganized brother couldn't be trusted. I picked up the box containing the rings and put them in my jacket pocket. Tanner wouldn't get them until he got to the church.

My tuxedo, a product of three trips to a Chicago tailor, looked fantastic. Though I've measured customers for made-to-order suits with good results, tailored garments are in a class of their own. Sol, the owner of Dorn's Haberdashery, measured me in places I didn't know I had. When he discovered I danced, he brought out the tape again. A master tailor, Sol wanted to add gussets to the jacket sleeves to give me greater freedom of movement, creating a jacket that kept its shape when I held my arm in standard dance position.

Though the tux looked grand, I was less than happy about being seen in it. Modern weddings have played hell with traditional fashion rules. A tuxedo is considered evening wear; a gentleman never dons one before six p.m. Though a morning coat with a vest and striped trousers were called for, Dusty's mom insisted on a tux. When I pointed out that President Reagan wore a morning coat for the visit of Emperor Hirohito, Consuela insisted they'd gone out of style during the Kennedy inauguration. I tried to compromise, offering to wear a dark business suit for the ceremony and the tuxedo for the evening reception, but the Iron Lady would not be moved.

Determined not to let the obdurate maven spoil my day, I looked in the mirror, struck my best man-about-town pose, and strode off to meet my future. On the way to my freshly washed Cordoba, I found myself whistling "Get Me to the Church on Time." Life's benevolence smiled from horizon to horizon. Money, a pretty wife, and the good life were soon to be mine.

I pulled into the Sutherlands' driveway ten minutes late for the pre-wedding photography session. Lakeside, the family manse, was an impressive heap of rock. Built during the Great Depression, the limestone house featured slate roofs, a Norman tower, and an exterior walkway supported by hand-hewn wooden columns. Dusty claimed her grandfather modeled the house after one of Marie Antoinette's summer homes. Whether true or not, Consuela certainly believed it. Every stick of furniture in the place was French provincial.

Black Cadillacs and Lincolns lined the drive. When I reached the house, a valet appeared out of nowhere to take charge of my car. It took a second to place him. Burl, my drinking companion from Pete's Pub, would be parking the Cordoba.

I opened the door, got out, and reached for his outstretched hand. "Burl, never expected to see you here."

"Never expected to be here," he said giving my hand a firm shake. "I'm working security."

Burl had mentioned he sometimes moonlighted for a private security company.

"Nice cover," I replied. "Nobody would suspect a valet to be an off-duty cop."

"Ex-cop," he said. "I got into it with the captain one time too many, so the chief called me in last week and said I could resign and keep my pension or get fired and lose it. It'll be jobs like this until the paperwork for my private shield goes through."

"Jeez, Burl, sorry to hear you got sacked."

Burl put a hand on the Cordoba's open door. "Don't feel bad about me leaving the department. I've been fed up with management for a long time. Not going into that nuthouse every day—it's like getting out of prison."

"Well, good luck, but I've got to get going. I was scheduled to be in front of the photographer ten minutes ago."

"I'll see you later," Burl replied. "I'm on duty for the church ceremony and the reception."

Hiring security for a wedding seemed a little over the top, but the Sutherlands took comfort in the fact that interlopers would be bounced before they made it to the door.

My tardy arrival went unnoticed. After Dusty's solo poses, the photographer set up a series of shots with me, her parents, and a herd of relatives. Time crawled. I shuddered at the thought that we'd be repeating the process at the church. After the equivalent of fourteen hours in a dog's life, the session ended with shots of Dusty and her maid of honor, Bunny Hamilton.

Dusty introduced me to Bunny last winter. She couldn't hold a candle to Dusty in the looks department, and though Bunny's family had money, the Sutherlands' pile put them to shame. In the world of the rich, the little things like the school you attended are a big deal, so when Dusty's family sent her to Dartmouth, the Hamiltons shipped their less-than-gifted daughter there as well.

Poor Bunny never caught on to the origins of her Ivy League handle. Considered "a dumb bunny" by her brainy classmates, it didn't take long for the characterization to become a nickname. Still, I couldn't help but like the woman. She accompanied Dusty to those wives-with-abusive-husband flicks, freeing me from a good chunk of the movie industry's three-tissue weepers.

"Since you don't have a family, we'll have you stand at the side of the chancel and have you join the wedding party when Steele escorts Dusty up the aisle."

No family. The words spoken by the Reverend Williams at last night's rehearsal still haunted me as I stood in my assigned place awaiting my bride. I hadn't expected the big day to bring back memories more appropriate to a funeral than a wedding. The unexpected death of my parents, Myra's suicide, the murder of my sole surviving cousin, the estrangement of my children—the losses that made my world smaller tormented me. Marriage to Dusty held the promise of something better. I pushed the troubling visions to the back of my mind.

Lumir had warned that the Sutherland family would never accept me. The photo session at Lakeside drove his words home with the force of a hammer. The Sutherlands barely talked to me, a snub that left me feeling like a stand-in proxy for the real groom. Small wonder, Dusty's Carolina Herrera wedding gown cost more than I earned in a year and a half at Killian's Department Store.

I should have realized how dramatically our worlds would collide when my attempt to buy an engagement ring went down in flames. A diamond ring and matching wedding band that once belonged to Dusty's grandmother magically appeared the day we were to go jewelry shopping. Though Dusty was thrilled, I understood the motive behind Consuela's gift. She wanted to avoid the shame of her daughter wearing the sort of rings I could afford.

The organ sounded, pulling me back to the present, as the bridesmaids and attendants began their walk down the aisle of Grace Episcopal Church. No man should have to go through a church wedding twice. I felt as nervous as the first time but had to deal with something new this time around—the feeling I'd dishonored Myra by re-marrying.

Worried my emotions might get the best of me, I shoved my nerves and guilt into a box, shut the lid, and hoped they'd stay there. When Bunny and my best man Tanner reached the halfway point, I moved from the side of the chancel to the center and waited for Steele to escort his daughter to me.

I hope it's okay, Myra. I'm sorry I messed up. I've been so lonely and won't forget you.

Steele and Dusty started down the aisle.

I forgave you long ago, Cletus. Be happy.

My knees nearly buckled. I'd heard Myra's voice as clearly as if she stood next to me. It had been eighteen years, and now at the big moment, my mind was playing tricks on me. I looked down the aisle and tried to relax. My imagined Myra had given me her blessing and my bride looked as happy as I'd ever seen her.

I couldn't say the same for Steele. As grim as a pallbearer at a funeral, his distaste for his bottom-of-the-barrel son-in-law came through loud and clear. I looked over at Consuela. No motherly wedding tears, the woman looked as if she'd just stifled the urge to pass gas.

I put it all behind me as I took Dusty's hand and for the first time realized I loved her. We breezed through the Declaration of Intent, and after Steele presented Dusty, the congregation was slated to sing "Abide with Me." Either Episcopalians aren't much for hymns, or the wedding guests were unfamiliar with one of the greatest pieces of church music ever written. The miserable squeak emanating from the pews was nothing short of embarrassing.

And then, out of nowhere, a pure, sweet tenor floated above the discordant mess. We hadn't arranged for a vocalist. I looked over at Dusty. She raised her eyebrows and shrugged. A strong singer inspires others to lose their inhibitions, and the congregants responded to the newcomer with the skill and enthusiasm of a professional choir. I turned to Dusty again. She nodded, and of one mind, we broke protocol and turned to find the owner of the golden pipes.

Halfway back in the small nave stood the source of the sweet sound—my son, hymnbook in hand. I don't know how Mike managed to slip by security. Guests were required to show their invitations before entering. He'd gotten a haircut and spiffed himself up. He hadn't donned a suit but wore a navy-blue blazer with gray slacks, a classic look if a bit informal. My son wore his clothes well. I couldn't fault him for not understanding the fine points of wedding attire. Several of Dusty's snobby cousins had done worse.

Stunned my son wanted to attend my wedding, I gave him what I hoped was a warm smile. He didn't smile back. I couldn't blame him. He'd been forced to sneak into his father's marriage ceremony. Dusty and I didn't invite either of my kids because of their lawyer's threat of a restraining order. I wondered if my daughter had snuck in, but no one stood next to Mike.

Mike, present at my marriage to the woman I loved. His harsh words had hurt, but I forgave him. He came to see me on the big day. No matter how high the barriers, I'd see we reconciled. Blinking back tears, I hoped my children would understand my love for their mother would never die. A second marriage wouldn't change that. Nothing could.

I turned back to the altar realizing I'd misjudged my son. The sloppily dressed, angry young man who confronted me at the studio had the gift of music. He wanted answers from me and didn't get them. A better man than I, he just met me more than halfway.

Reverend Williams moved through the ceremony at a good clip. When we got to the part about speaking now or forever holding your peace, it occurred to me that Mike might have come to the church to disrupt our wedding. When nobody objected, I took a deep breath and relaxed.

We'd joined hands, and the Reverend Williams had just begun the 'Do you Jane?' bit when it happened.

"This farce has got to stop! Now!"

I didn't need to turn around to see who'd interrupted. I recognized the voice. Mike didn't come to the church to share in the ceremony; he came to ruin my day.

The look in Dusty's eyes went from shock to disbelief. We turned simultaneously and saw my son standing in the aisle.

Mike pointed to me. "A church wedding and beautiful hymns can't hide your hypocrisy. My mother, the woman you married, killed herself because you couldn't stay away from whorehouses. You called yourself my father, but you cheated one time too many and got caught. It made the newspapers. After that, you abandoned your children and stabbed a man to death." He held up a packet of papers. "It's all here."

Burl, at the back of the church, made for the aisle.

I stood rooted to the spot as my son continued his abuse. "What kind of man does that? I'll tell you. A cheating sleazebag!"

Burl closed the gap, grabbed an arm, and twisted it up behind Mike's back.

"He hired women to beat him up. His cheating killed my mom!" shouted Mike.

Burl forced him to the floor and cuffed him. Mike screamed "Bastard!" Burl must have used a chokehold on him then because Mike went limp. I turned to Dusty to get a read on her reaction. I couldn't. She stared at the commotion. I looked back again and saw Burl dragging a motionless Mike by the jacket collar. An usher helped him get my son through the door.

Guests began to murmur as all eyes turned to the front of the church, their focus on me. Sweating like a prisoner on his way to the electric chair, I felt my lips forming a weak smile. Mike had it wrong; it hadn't been like that.

"We can start the vows again as soon as he's out the door," the reverend whispered. "If you're feeling a little shaky, you can take some time out for a break. I can lead the congregation in a hymn or two while you compose yourselves."

Unsure of what to do next, I looked to Dusty. The hurt in her eyes ripped me from top to bottom. If I'd come clean about my past, she wouldn't have been blindsided and would have recognized Mike's acting out for what it was—the ill-timed outburst of a disturbed young man. Instead, I took the easy way out and deceived the woman who loved me.

"Dusty, I can expl—"

A blow from nowhere nearly detached the head from my body. I struggled to remain upright. It took a few staggering steps to recover my balance. Dusty had slapped me. Slapped me so hard my ears rang. The room spun. I forced my eyes to focus and searched her face for tears but saw none.

"You killed a man and didn't tell me?"

"The guy—"

"You lied to me, Cletus," she hissed. "You lied about your wife and your kids. I deserved to know. I trusted you."

"I didn't lie, Dusty. I kept things to myself. Everybody deserves a little privacy. The man I killed, it was self-defense. The police arrested me at an apartment, not at a torture chamber. The police led me away me before the girl and I did anything. I didn't abandon my kids. I drank so much after Myra's death that I wasn't organized enough to make it to the custody hearing."

Dusty folded her arms. "Don't try to hide behind your excuses. You pretended to be someone you're not. That makes you a liar. I can't believe I was crazy enough to marry you."

The reverend stepped between us and whispered. "You're loud enough for the first pews to hear. I take it that the wedding is off. Should I make an announcement?"

I stepped around him and dropped to my knees. "I was wrong Dusty. Forgive me. I'll do everything in my power to be the best husband anyone could ever have."

She walked away.

Consuela and Bunny met her before she reached the first pew and put their arms around her. Dusty began sobbing.

The reverend announced the wedding was off and asked the congregation to remember us in their prayers. That's when Steele exited the front pew and approached me. Devastated, I'd yet to stand. He spoke quietly. "For God's sake, stand up, man. Your groveling is making the situation worse."

He was right. Our wedding guests, still in their seats, were getting the show of their lives. I stood and adjusted the sleeves of my tux, trying to salvage some sense of dignity. I turned to see Reverend

Williams at the side door of the chancel. He cleared his throat and motioned that I should leave by that exit.

Steele patted me on the shoulder and looked me directly in the eye. "I'm sorry things didn't work out, Cleatzy. I truly am. One last thing. It won't make sense now, but you'll look back and thank me."

Puzzled, I searched Steele's face, trying to find a reason for his apparent concern. As far as I knew, he didn't like me. There was no longer a need for pretense. Wondering if I'd misread the situation, I waited for his parting words.

His intentions became clear when I noticed his fist just inches from my eye.

Randy Roeder

Chapter 9

Eddie appeared in the doorway of Lumir's workshop cradling a large paper bag. "Holy crap, Clete. What happened to you?"

Leave it to a young guy like Eddie to come right out with something you don't want to talk about. Lumir had just been reading me the riot act because I lied to him about misleading Dusty.

"Steele Sutherland and I had a frank discussion about my future," I replied.

Eddie put the bag on Lumir's glue-up table, alongside Dusty's still-wrapped wedding gift. He rolled up the sleeves of his flannel shirt, grabbed a pressed-back chair, and turned it so the back faced me. Straddling the seat, he rested his elbows on the back and stared. "Can you see out of that eye? Looks like it's swelled shut."

"I don't want to talk about it," I snapped.

Lumir cut in. "Clete is a little touchy right now. I warned him not to keep secrets from Dusty. When it all came out at the church, Dusty decided to hit him instead of marrying him. He is embarrassed, and that is why he hasn't been answering his phone."

Eddie's eyes grew large. "She did all that?"

"I said I don't want to talk about it," I muttered as a headache, my constant companion since Steele bopped me, went back on the warpath. I shifted in my chair and reached into my pants pocket for the container of aspirin.

Lumir cut in. "I think Clete does not want to repeat his story, so I will tell you for him."

Eddie shook his head. "If he doesn't want to talk to anybody, he should have stayed home in bed."

"I think he is here because he is stir-crazy."

I hate it when people talk about me as if I'm not present. I'd come over to apologize to Lumir for luring him to my aborted wedding reception. To say he wasn't happy about my deception was putting it mildly. He'd yet to accept my regrets. Four aspirin made the trip from the bottle into my hand. After bolting them, I followed up with a swig of Lumir's coffee.

Lumir left his captain's chair, pulled up a pressed-back, and assumed a pose like Eddie's. "Mr. Steele Sutherland cleaned Clete's clock after Dusty hit him. Clete is lucky the man stopped after one punch."

"Wow, twice in one day," said Eddie. "He's a real punching bag."

"He got socked just once," Lumir explained. "His fiancée slapped him before she called him a liar."

"Not the best way to start married life," said Eddie. "Good thing the wedding didn't happen, he'd be a battered husband. You think he would phone his friends to explain why the big event got canceled."

I'd spent the last two days holed up at the apartment with the phone unplugged and an ice bag for company. Steele's punch had resulted in a double fracture of my orbital bone. The doctor at the emergency room told me I was lucky. A fist to the eye often results in triple or quadruple breaks, a real problem since there's no way to set an orbital bone. Though he expected my vision to clear up, he wanted me back in a week because complications are frequent and can result in permanent damage. I told the doc I didn't feel lucky.

Dusty had slapped me harder than I believed possible. Her smack to the side of my face left marks. She'd gone for a pre-wedding manicure and come back wearing those artificial fingernails that are all the rage. Either she raked my cheek as she pulled her hand away or made a second pass while I recovered from the first. I can't be sure. When

Steele landed his haymaker, he rattled my brain, so the memory of the details in the minutes leading up to it was a little fuzzy. Now scabbed over, the cuts made by Dusty's nails only added to the monstrous mess that once passed for my face. Yup, I was lucky alright. Any more luck and I'd come down with a case of bubonic plague.

Lumir stroked his mustache. "I wish I would have been there to see it. Clete got what he deserved. At any rate, the man did him a favor. His bride smacked him in the middle of the church service, in front of everybody. Clete would have looked foolish watching his bride walk away after she hit him. Steele Sutherland's punch made it man-to-man."

My friend was right. People would remember Steele's blow rather than me on my knees, pleading with his daughter for a second chance. All said and done, I'd have preferred humiliation. The only positive thing to come out of getting clobbered was the hope Steele had satisfied his need for vengeance. A broken eye socket beat the hell out of castration.

"I was getting an orientation to the bar setup when this dude walked in and announced the wedding was canceled," said Eddie. "You could have knocked me over with a feather. The lie musta been a real whopper for her to smack him right there in church. The woman doesn't mess around."

"Dusty should have used her fist on Clete," Lumir huffed. "Her daddy might not have hit him if he was already down."

Feigning sympathy, Eddie shook his head.

Lumir glared at me. "Clete's been telling a lot of lies lately."

I shouldn't have visited Lumir. My head hurt, my vision was cloudy, and I was unprepared for the depth of his anger. Eddie's arrival interrupted an intense conversation—one that might well have determined the future of our friendship. As stubborn as only an eighty-two-year-old Czech can be, Lumir had a strong sense of right and wrong. I came up on the wrong side of the line.

Eddie must have noticed the edge in Lumir's voice. He changed the subject. "I didn't know what to do with your wedding present, so I brought it over thinking you could pick it up sometime. It's a toaster oven. I've already got one, and now that you'll be a bachelor again, it'll come in handy."

Dusty wouldn't have been caught dead using a toaster oven.

Lumir turned to Eddie. "How a man, a man I call friend, could pull as many fast ones as Clete has, is beyond me. It makes me wonder if I am a bad judge of people."

I'd known Lumir for fifteen years and had seldom seen him angrier. I worried about what might follow, the calm that sets in when someone decides nothing short of an earthquake will alter. I'd seen Lumir in that state. He'd been preparing to lynch the man who'd murdered his granddaughter. I was the earthquake that intervened, but miracles don't happen twice. If he lowered the boom on me, I'd be dead to him. My gut told me to leave before it happened.

I rubbed my forehead and sighed. "Sorry guys, my head is killing me. I'm seeing double and need to get home."

Seeing double—another lie. Dishonesty had become a habit. I needed to get my head straight, but the time for self-examination could come later. I rose and slipped into my windbreaker.

"You shouldn't be driving," said Eddie. "I'll give you a lift home."

Trapped again. I didn't want to ride with Eddie but couldn't very well drive home if I was seeing double. "Thanks," I replied. "I'll take you up on that."

Eddie returned his chair to its original position and clapped Lumir on the back. "I'll stop by to pick you up for the tool collectors' meet. There's going to be a demonstration on timber framing."

"Maybe I can teach them a thing or two," said Lumir. "I helped frame Uncle Janek's barn."

Eddie laughed. "I bet you can. See you then." He turned for the door.

I followed. "Bye, Lumir."

He didn't answer.

––––––––––––––––––

When I returned to Cleatzy's, a half-mug of cold coffee greeted me from a coaster on my desk. My number one employee, Reg, was using the space in my absence. Once my boss, he retired from the Killian's menswear department a year before the place shut down. Retirement wasn't as much fun as he thought. When Reg heard I opened my own shop, he asked if I had a position for him. I jumped at the chance to bring him aboard. His experience and work ethic were a godsend. I'd scheduled him to manage the shop while Dusty and I enjoyed a Hawaiian honeymoon.

The cup left on the desk surprised me. Reg was a neat freak. I'd come in at 5:30 a.m. and planned to be gone before the place opened. It wouldn't do to have the shop's namesake show up looking as if he'd come out on the losing end of a bar fight. My bruises had gone from horrific black and purple to appalling red, yellow, and blue. Unhappy that I still looked like hell, I took some comfort in the fact that my vision had cleared.

I pulled out my chair, sat, and retrieved a stack of paper from the inbox. Wanting to work oldest to newest, I turned the pile upside down and retrieved the first item, an envelope bearing the address of the city's foremost law firm. I can't say the contents surprised me.

Dunn, Whipple & Dows
Attorneys at Law
4042 1st Ave. NE
Cedar Rapids, IA 52402
April 11, 1983

Mr. Efferding,

J. H. Sutherland has asked us to inform you that he is severing business ties with you. He intends to liquidate his share in G&S enterprises. Your loans have been assumed by a third party. The line of credit extended to you by Merchants National Bank …

I'd expected Steele to bail on Cleatzy's and close my line of credit. It would cost me but wouldn't destroy the business. Steele wasn't the sort to shoot himself in the foot. He'd lose most of his investment if he forced the business into closure. The man wanted me out of his hair, not on the street. With Cleatzy's prospering, he would have no problem finding a buyer for his piece of the operation. As for the line of credit, I'd find his competitors willing to work with me. Without the Sutherlands' backing, my interest rates would be higher, but the financials still worked. As for the loans themselves, no problem. The paperwork I signed required fraud or substantial misconduct on my part before the holder could call a loan.

When Steele referred to my "bad business sense," during our lunch at the country club, he got it wrong. I might not be the one to start an enterprise, but I knew the menswear business inside and out, and if I couldn't make a profit on it, I deserved to be out on the street. Dusty's father operated by a strange personal code I'd never understand. He'd have no problem hiring someone to assault me but would find harming a thriving enterprise unthinkable.

I worried more about my landlord, Gib. If he wanted to get rid of me, I'd have a hard time stopping him. My lease allowed for an annual renegotiation of the rental rate prior to renewal. Any increase had to be in line with market rates, but we'd made so many improvements to the property Gib could easily justify a hefty increase. My gut told me not to sign the document, but Dusty insisted I was paranoid. Now that relations with her family had gone to hell, the lease could come back to haunt me.

I dropped the letter from Steele's attorneys into a file and dug into the stack of invoices and time sheets. About halfway through, I found a scented blue envelope without a return address. I recognized the handwriting immediately—Dusty. I couldn't imagine why she'd written. Instead of tearing the end of the envelope, I retrieved my Fred Astaire letter opener from the top right drawer. After taking a deep breath and exhaling slowly, I slit the envelope and discovered a single sheet awaiting me. I unfolded it with shaking fingers and began to read.

Cletus,

I apologize for striking you in church. It's no excuse, but my emotions got the best of me. I wish I could say I don't understand why you kept so much from me, but the reason you did so is clear. You feared if I knew more about you, I'd end a relationship that benefitted you financially.

I could have accepted your past, but I can't forgive you for misleading me. You should have known I'd get over your visit to a hooker almost twenty years ago. Many men have done as much. What I can't forgive is the extent to which you concealed things from me—your role in your wife's suicide, your flight from your hometown, the time you spent seeking consolation in a bottle, taking the life of another human being. How you could hide the defining moments of your life from the person you planned to marry is beyond my understanding.

It doesn't matter that Mike's accusations against you were exaggerated or that you killed someone in self-defense. You owed me the truth. There's something wrong with you, Cletus. I should have seen the warning signs when you were willing to let a disturbed young man, your own son, "rot his life away" in a cult.

Of course, there's no way we'll get back together. Please don't attempt to contact me. Dad is talking about getting a restraining order. I wish he wouldn't because I don't think it's necessary. On the other hand, I don't care enough to stop him.

I should have listened when Mom called you a gold digger. As much as I hate to say it, she was right. It's the only logical explanation for your actions.

Dusty

Cletus instead of Cleatzy. Funny how something little can hurt. I reread the letter. Steele seeking a restraining order? The idea that I'd try to contact Dusty or her parents had never entered my mind. He had no legal grounds to justify an order, but given his power and influence, it would be a snap. My kids and their grandmother threatened to get one if I tried to contact them. I honored their wishes. The idea that Steele thought a court order necessary didn't sit well with me.

I put Dusty's letter back in the envelope and walked back to the breakroom where I ripped the packet into a half dozen pieces. After stuffing them down through the rubber fingers of the garbage disposal, I turned on the water, flipped the switch, and ground my one-time fiancée's kiss-off to pieces. Losing Dusty felt as bad as losing Myra. The rupture between us, as final as death, left a void just as bleak. It would have been easier if I hadn't realized I loved her. For the first time since my aborted wedding, I cried.

A few sodden tissues later, I returned to my desk and tore into the stack of accumulated paperwork. It soon dwindled to the second last item, an envelope from a law firm a tad less prestigious than the first.

I tore the end of the envelope and extracted the contents. Steele worked fast. His portion of the business now belonged to an entity referred to as Everest Property Management. I had more than a nodding acquaintance with Everest Property Management. Gib Sutherland served as president, his wife Dora as treasurer.

My landlord now owned my business.

Chapter 10

Late Friday afternoon, six days after Steele pasted me in the eye. I still looked like hell but came to the shop nervous about an event I originally planned to skip—the annual YWCA fashion show. The organization's primary fund-raising event, donations from attendees enabled the organization to provide housing for homeless women. They'd asked Cleatzy's to dress the men. Since the event paled in comparison to a honeymoon in Waikiki, I'd chosen the outfits and asked Reg to cover it.

Tonight was the big night. Though Reg had an endearing persona, when it came to showmanship, he was no Cletus Efferding. A less-than-stellar production could dent Cleatzy's reputation, but an outstanding performance would cement its status as the city's foremost men's shop. My battered face precluded participation in the all-important schmoozing and glad-handing, so the only contribution I'd be able to make would be backstage.

Reg had just left the office after some unnecessary coaching when Gib Sutherland appeared in the doorway. He looked good in the lightweight gabardine trench coat I sold him last month. I'd gotten a heck of deal on them last February because the supplier wanted to unload and focus on his summer line. Though comfortable for a late April cold spell, the coat screamed 'out of season.' Gib should have toughed it out in his suit jacket.

Now that his niece and I had split up, a visit from her rich uncle, a man capable of putting me out of business, didn't make for a relaxing situation. Unsure of how to handle the situation, I didn't stand and offer a handshake, but looked up and greeted him.

"Hello, Gib. What can I do for you? By the way, it's too late in the year to get away with a trench coat."

"Think so?"

"Definitely. Have a chair."

"No, thanks. I'm on a tight schedule. There are some things we need to talk about."

My heart sank. The ax, razor-sharp, was about to fall. Gib and Dora saw Dusty as the child they never had, and he'd come to seek his revenge. I cursed myself for believing I'd somehow made it through the disaster at Grace Church with my business intact.

"I expect you're here to lower the boom on Cleatzy's," I said. "The paperwork gives me legal protection, but if you're intent on putting me out of business, there's nothing I can do. Just know I never intended to hurt Dusty and am sorrier than you can ever imagine for the way things worked out."

"Sorry for the way things turned out? I'm not. Dusty has escaped marriage to a man entirely unsuited for her, and Steele sold me his interest in Cleatzy's. I now own ninety-five percent of a successful retail operation located in a space I had trouble leasing. My brother may be a good businessman, but he's emotional and lets his feelings get in the way of sound judgment."

"Emotional? The guy threatened to hire somebody to break my bones and castrate me if the wedding didn't come off."

Gib shrugged. "Sounds like Steele."

"Do I—"

"Cletus Efferding?" A burly guy with a bad haircut and worse sports coat appeared in the doorway, his eyes hidden by cheap sunglasses.

"Can't you see I'm busy right now?"

"But you are Cletus Efferding," he said as he barged into the office.

I stood to give him a piece of my mind.

He held out an envelope. When I didn't reach for it, he let it drop on the desk. "Cletus Efferding, you've just been served," he announced and walked out before I could think of a reply.

"I hoped to get here before Steele's restraining order," Gib said. "That's one of the reasons I stopped by. The order covers Dusty, Steele, Consuela, Dora, me, and our places of business. Steele went off half-cocked and asked his lawyers for the moon. Since he and the judge are golfing buddies, he got everything he wanted. I don't know what he was thinking. The way the order is written, you're enjoined from setting foot in Cleatzy's."

My temper flared. "Then how the hell am I supposed to run the goddamned store? I'm the one who needs a restraining order. Your brother is the one who assaulted me!"

Gib motioned for me to calm down. "I've already spoken to my attorney and asked to have the order amended. It'll be straightened out early next week. In the meantime, you can safely ignore the part about staying away from the shop and me. You're barred from Merchant's Bank. You should be able to telephone instructions about your accounts, but I recommend waiting until the situation is clarified. Now, I realize you're angry but understand the sheriff's office took care to have you served by someone in plain clothes."

I sat back down. "I can't believe it. Your brother threatens me with bodily harm and follows up by assaulting me. My vision might be permanently damaged, and somehow, I'm the bad guy."

Gib cleared his throat. "As I said, Steele is excitable. I doubt he'll hit you again."

"Yeah, but what about having someone do it for him?"

Gib looked unconcerned. "He could, but if he arranges something like that, you'll never prove it. The incident brings with it two concerns: that you might seek damages for your injuries and that it behooves me to take out a life insurance policy on you."

"A life insurance policy on me? Have you lost your mind?"

"Hear me out, and you'll thank me for stopping by. Let's talk about the wisdom of suing Steele for damages first. If you do, I will liquidate Cleatzy's. Without the income the shop generates, you'll find yourself unable to make payment on your substantial debts. Given your personal history and our family's financial resources, there is not a lawyer in town who will waste time on you. If you do find one, Steele and I will see your lawsuit tied up for years. My brother has authorized me to offer you twenty-five thousand dollars to ensure you don't take him to court."

"Twenty-five thousand dollars?"

"The offer is dependent on your signing the release from liability that I have with me today. The offer expires at five o'clock, an hour and a half from now."

"I need time to think," I replied.

Gib didn't comment but went on with his spiel. "Let's get back to the life insurance. Acquiring Steele's interest in Cleatzy's substantially increases the risk inherent in my investment. I'd be a fool not to recognize the business is a one-man show. Your importance to the enterprise gives me what's known as an insurable interest in your continued well-being. Taking out a life insurance policy on you is simply good business. I've brought with me a second document for you to sign, a form giving your consent to such a policy."

"So, you can clean up if your brother has some goon take me out? No way."

"The result of your failure to sign this second document will be identical to that of your failure to sign the first. I will liquidate Cleatzy's."

"You're bluffing. Liquidate and you lose most of your substantial investment as well. I wasn't born yesterday."

"Substantial in your eyes, smaller in mine. I invested in Cleatzy's because Dusty begged me to. I assumed I'd never see my money again. Somehow you managed to leverage your meager abilities and make a go of it. You're too weak to walk out on the operation. I have you over a barrel and intend to press my advantage."

I ignored the insult, tried to appeal to reason. "Gib, think about how this looks from my point of view. Having you as the beneficiary of a life insurance policy is like declaring open season on me. If Steele hits me again, I could lose vision in that eye. If he hits me hard enough, I could even die. From where I stand, if he has to worry about his brother losing money he'll think twice."

"You're sitting, not standing, and for goodness' sake, taking out a policy on a key employee is commonplace. As for Steele, he got carried away in the heat of the moment and made a mistake. The man is the driving force behind Merchant's National Bank. The last thing he needs is a run-in with the law or bad publicity."

"That may be true, but Steele said he'd hire someone to put me in the hospital."

"He is very unhappy with you, but I doubt my brother would go to such extremes. At any rate, the policy includes a rider that protects me if you are blinded or otherwise disabled and unable to fulfill your duties."

"You doubt Steele will go to extremes, but you're covering your ass anyway?"

"Really, Cleatzy, your options are simple. Sign both documents and receive a cashier's check for twenty-five thousand dollars, or refuse to sign, and Cleatzy's is liquidated. Given your outstanding loans, the liquidation of Cleatzy's is certain to force you into bankruptcy. It will be years before anyone lends to you again."

I signed both documents.

Chapter 11

Saturday morning, my kitchen table. The *Cedar Rapids Gazette* lay next to my elbow. I'd yet to look at it. The paper had scheduled the feature article on the YWCA style show for tomorrow's edition, so I had no incentive to rush. Last night's extravaganza had gone like clockwork. To tell the truth, it went better than clockwork. Cleatzy's participation was an unqualified success. Reg exceeded my expectations, even filling in as substitute emcee when the scheduled radio personality came down with strep throat. A gaggle of well-wishers came backstage afterward to shake my hand. Though no one seemed to notice my face, I ducked the KCRG crew with the big video camera and spent time with a print reporter instead.

A howling success and I didn't care. Gib's afternoon visit managed to drain the last bit of self-respect in the tank. Learning that Dusty begged the Sutherlands for the funding to start my business only added to the shame of kneeling before her, pleading for her to marry me. Steele's punch to the eye didn't do much for my ego but leave it to Gib to kick what was left. There'd been no real reason for him to insist on the life insurance policy. He'd done it to demonstrate my vulnerability by grinding my face in the dirt. The fact I signed only added to his triumph. I may have sold my soul for twenty-five grand, but I had one up on him—I'd have done it for less.

I glanced back at the kitchen counter. A gift-wrapped box next to the coffeemaker beckoned. The shape of the box made the contents obvious, but I got up to unwrap it anyway. Reg gave it to me after the show, telling me he knew from the get-go we were sitting on a success. And then he said, "Take tomorrow off." Old habits are hard to break. Sometimes Reg forgets he works for me now.

It shouldn't have, but his unintentional slight bothered me. Then too, we'd worked together for years. How could Reg forget I'd sworn off hard liquor? I rose from my chair, shredded the festive paper, and discovered a bottle of Jameson Irish Whisky. The connection between Irish whiskey and my morning coffee proved too much to ignore. I retrieved my Snoopy mug, dumped the contents, and glanced at the coffee pot. It seemed a shame to dilute a product that generations struggled to perfect, so three fingers of unadulterated nectar from the Old Sod made their way into Old Snoopy. After guzzling half, my mug and I returned to the table.

I unfolded the newspaper. "Double homicide at I-380 rest stop!" screamed the headline. I rewarded the editor's efforts by doing what was expected of me—shifting my gaze to the accompanying photograph. It looked like the cops kept a tight lid on the crime scene. The cameraman managed little more than a shot of a half dozen vehicles parked alongside the highway.

The *Gazette* goes to bed early so information was sparse. The unidentified victims were found in a luxury sports car riddled by shotgun blasts. A witness to the act was taken to an area hospital for observation. I looked at the photo again. The accompanying credit revealed the cameraman had been a woman. I made a mental note to start using the term photographer.

Local pessimists had been saying for some time the new Interstate would bring more crime to Cedar Rapids. It looked like they were right. The highway had been completed just a bit past the downtown, and already the new rest stop was the scene of a horrific murder.

Other than the double murder, the big news involved the signing of a peace treaty between Lebanon and Israel. Apparently, they'd been in a state of war since 1948. The treaty made sense to me; thirty-five years of fighting would wear on anybody. I shook my head in disbelief. Peace in the Middle East—I never thought it would happen in my lifetime. A small celebration seemed in order, so I downed the rest of the cup. My now-empty mug looked forlorn, a situation I remedied by pouring another three fingers of Jameson into it. One sip led to another, and before long, I headed to the couch for a well-deserved nap.

Something was wrong. Somehow Steele Sutherland had gotten inside my skull and was hammering on it with both fists because he wanted out. "God damn it, Steele. Knock it off!" I yelled. He didn't, and I realized he couldn't hear me because nothing came out when I opened my mouth. I tried shouting again and again but to no effect. My vocal cords couldn't operate because there was no air in my lungs. I struggled valiantly to breathe. I tried kicking, but my legs wouldn't move. Life-giving oxygen denied, I was dying.

The hammering grew louder, and I woke with a start, gasping for breath. Some inconsiderate slob was beating on the door. Asking myself why someone would pound on my entryway when I had a perfectly good bell, I got up to put an end to the yammer. The room spun, and the blood coursing through my cranial arteries throbbed. The hell with the door. I lurched to the kitchen sink and emptied my guts.

The knocking continued, interspersed with bouts of the doorbell. I grabbed a dish towel and wiped my face. I didn't want to answer, but anything to quell the racket. Leaning on the wall with one arm, I opened the door with the other. It took a bit for my eyes to focus, but when they did, I recognized the jerk who'd served me Steele's court order. He'd changed his shirt but wore the same sports coat and pants.

"What's it this time?" I asked, extending my hand to receive yet another court-ordered atrocity.

Misreading my gesture, he took my hand and gave it a robust shake. "Orrin Dietz, Linn County Sheriff's Department. May I come in?"

"We've already met," I growled.

"Sorry about that," he replied. "Nothing personal, but a job's a job —even when you don't like doing it."

"Don't like doing it? You should have seen the smirk on your face."

"Probably nerves. I hate serving papers. All the deputies do. When you hand someone an order, they tend to take it personally."

"Maybe you'll be on the receiving end someday and realize it is personal."

"I'm not here to serve a court order, it's just that the Sutherland situation has gotten complicated."

He took a step forward. I'd either have to tell him to get lost or allow him to come in. Too hungover to assert myself, I let him in and headed for the kitchen table. My dinette-sized table seated two. I picked the chair farthest from the counter, leaving him the one nearest the vomit in the sink. He made a face as he sat. Though I had allowed him in, there seemed no reason to be pleasant.

"Well?" I asked.

"The department is looking into the recent activities of Jane Sutherland. I understand you are acquainted."

"We are," I replied, unwilling to give him more.

"Do you have any reason to believe she has been involved in a bad business deal or done something illegal?"

Dusty caught up in a police investigation? If I'd been feeling better, I would have laughed in his face. "No," I replied.

"When was the last time you saw her?"

My alcohol-addled brain struggled to come up with an answer. Had it only been a week? A pause. "Seven days ago, last Saturday."

He shifted in his chair. "The day she refused to marry you, and her father gave you a black eye?"

"That's right."

Another knock on the door. "Excuse me," I said and got up to answer it. A wave of dizziness hit, and I staggered a bit. My second visitor proved to be another Linn County Sheriff's deputy, this one in full uniform.

"I'd like to speak with Orrin Dietz," he announced.

They were ganging up on me. I wasn't about to invite the guy in so called over my shoulder, "Orrin, it's for you."

I stood aside when Orrin came to the door, hoping the new visitor might cause his departure. Though Orrin stepped outside, he held the door open with his butt.

The second deputy glared at me. "Do you mind? We'd like a little privacy."

I backed into the room and watched as the second deputy leaned toward Orrin and began whispering. When he finished, Orrin looked back at me and then turned to whisper something to the new guy. I didn't like it.

Without so much as a by-your-leave, the second deputy followed Orrin back into the apartment. "I didn't invite you in," I said to him. He didn't reply but glared. I shrugged and went back to the kitchen.

They followed me. Orrin didn't sit but stood facing the new arrival. He motioned toward me with his thumb. "Guy's drunk and threw up in the sink."

His partner smirked. "Why do you get all the good ones?"

Their attitude wasn't doing much to inspire cooperation. "You guys are no prize either," I snapped. When they didn't react, I upped the ante. "Go to hell."

I knew their game and wasn't going to volunteer anything. The question about Dusty and illegal activity was a red herring, an opener they'd use before getting down to their business—harassing me. It didn't take a genius to see Steele's hand in the background. The man had influence. Judges, the sheriff's department, it didn't matter. If one of the city's foremost power brokers wanted law enforcement to make my life miserable, his wishes were not to be denied.

Orrin and the new guy glared at me. I glared back. After silently hating each other for something like three lifetimes, Orrin finally spoke. "Efferding, you might think the highlight of my day is interviewing hostile drunks who reek of vomit, but let me clue you in. It isn't. You, your apartment, and your miserable life stink."

"Now you've pissed me off," I said. "Dusty hasn't done anything illegal, and I haven't seen a warrant. There's no crime in progress, and no one is in danger. I didn't give your buddy permission to enter my home. If the two of you don't leave, I'll have my lawyer file a complaint."

I was bluffing.

Orrin scowled. "We're leaving, but you haven't seen the last of me. When I see you again, you better have answers. Any more of this I'm-not-gonna-cooperate bull, and I'll see you held as a material witness."

Now Orrin was bluffing.

"Swell," I replied. "I'll worry about it when you find a judge willing to sign off on the papers."

Orrin's buddy took a step forward. "Your failure to cooperate makes you look like an accomplice."

"Accomplice to what? Dusty get a parking ticket?"

No answer.

"Leave, or I'll call my lawyer. Don't let the door hit your backside on your way out."

"Hasn't happened yet," Orrin muttered. "You're gonna regret this."

I knew then they'd leave. Without another word, my visitors made for the door. When they didn't bother closing it, I got up and did it myself.

I returned to the kitchen and scooped the undigested food from the sink and into a trash bag. Following a pair of aspirin and a glass of lukewarm water, I headed back to the couch.

The deputies' mention of Dusty had been a not-so-subtle message that Steele intended to grind me into dust. Nothing the woman might have done could have been of interest to law enforcement. She didn't take drugs, didn't drive drunk, and wouldn't think of cheating anybody in business. Heck, she didn't even have a regular job.

I fluffed up the pillow and settled in. Dusty might have missed the boat when she didn't marry me, but she was nonetheless a fine person, one more likely to be victim than villain. I'd begun to drift off when the word *victim* popped back into my head.

I opened my eyes. Dusty came from money. Maybe she'd been the target of a criminal scheme, something along the lines of blackmail.

Fortunes aren't made by being nice to people. Steele Sutherland was a ruthless businessman who must have made dozens of enemies. Someone could have tried to get back at him by making life difficult for Dusty. But the Sutherlands were no longer my business. I was under a court order prohibiting contact with them. I got horizontal again and had almost drifted off when I went from prone to upright in something like a tenth of a second.

The luxury sports car at the I-380 rest stop—it was Dusty's DeLorean.

Sitting at the kitchen table, I reread the article in the *Gazette*. There were two occupants in the sports car, a fact that only served to increase my apprehension. Dusty and Bunny often drove to Iowa City for yoga classes or to take in a concert. I got up and fetched a week's worth of back issues from the pile of newspapers next to the TV. I selected the earliest and started scanning the ads. Halfway through the third paper, I spotted a notice for a Friday night screening of *Singing in the Rain* at Hancher Auditorium. The show was to be followed by a lecture and question-and-answer session featuring the movie's star, Gene Kelly.

My heart sank. Dusty and I talked about the affair when the season's ticket brochure came out. Dusty didn't dance but found Gene Kelly's singing irresistible. I didn't think much of man's pipes but liked his dancing. We'd wanted to go, but the date of the event conflicted with our honeymoon.

The KCRG evening news confirmed my worst fears. The reporter read from his script in front of blowup portraits of the victims. The residents of a nearby farm had called the Linn County Sheriff's Office at 11:00 Friday night to report a series of gunshots sounding as if they'd come from the direction of the Interstate. Another call at roughly the same time complained about the detonation of illegal fireworks. When officials arrived at the scene, they discovered a vehicle perforated by multiple shotgun blasts with two bodies inside. I learned that Linn County had asked for the assistance of the Iowa Division of Criminal Investigation. The segment concluded with a snippet of the County

Sheriff promising to do everything in his power to take down the culprits. I turned off the TV.

Dusty—gone. It didn't matter that we were on the outs. And Bunny, poor Bunny, never asking much of the world except that people not be mean to her. While I had been at the style show reveling in back slaps and congratulations, their lives were taken. The contradiction ate at me. I stared at the wall until my brain shut down. It stayed that way until the realization I was a murder suspect hit me like a hammer to the face.

The deputies who'd rattled my cage this morning must have known I had an alibi, or I wouldn't have gotten rid of them so easily. Still, it didn't take a detective to realize the murders were a hit, and if they were, that I might be involved. It wasn't hard to imagine a jilted lover one step away from Easy Street hiring a thug to take out the ex-fiancée who'd brought his dreams to an end.

Orrin and his buddy had stopped by to shake the tree, hoping a low-hanging apple would fall. If they got any useful information—fine. If not, they'd applied enough pressure to see which way I'd turn. No doubt about it, I needed a lawyer. God knows enough of them shopped at Cleatzy's, but I wanted the kind of guy who could get Lee Harvey Oswald off for shooting John Kennedy.

Only one of my customers filled the bill, Harold Hardesty, a mild-mannered man with a penchant for conservative suits who underwent a personality transplant the second he entered a courtroom. Feared by prosecutors and hated by judges, if anybody could give me good legal advice, Harold was the guy.

It's not easy to find a lawyer on a Saturday evening, but I'd been advising Harold on his wardrobe for years and had a seldom-distributed card with his personal number. His wife answered and asked me to wait while she asked him to pick up the extension. Once on the line, he told me I'd done the right thing in stiffing the deputies but bungled the job by antagonizing them. We arranged for an early Monday morning conference.

Harold wouldn't come cheap. Though I signed away my right to sue Steele for the damage caused by his assault, his check for twenty-five thousand had yet to show up, and I didn't know if I could count on it now that Dusty had been murdered. For now, the best I could do would be to hock the diamond-studded jewelry and Rolex she gave me. If worse came to worst, I'd try to sell my share in Cleatzy's. I borrowed tens of thousands against it but with luck might realize a small profit.

I returned Harold's card to my wallet, microwaved a cup of the morning's leftover coffee, and returned to the kitchen table where I made a mental inventory of the people who might want Dusty dead. No need for a pencil and paper, my list was too short: Dusty's ex-husband, a nut from the cult, and my son.

She'd banished ex-husband Baron from the marital bed, but he seemed like a long shot. He and Dusty exchanged Christmas cards. A guy who includes photos of his wife and kid with a holiday card seemed an unlikely suspect. Baron lived in England. I doubted he would travel all the way to the Midwestern States to seek revenge.

Dusty bailed on the cult five years ago. She'd been blamed for the group's problems with the Indian government. Since then, not a peep out of them. It didn't seem likely anyone connected to the group would care enough to hold a grudge that long.

My son Mike hated me and went out of his way to ruin my wedding. His actions at the church pointed to an unstable personality. He ruined my big day, but was he capable of killing the woman I loved just to get back at me? Try as I might, I couldn't believe he was that twisted.

The Sutherlands had enemies. What better revenge than killing the daughter of a man who'd bested you in business? Then too, a frustrated attention seeker, someone whose attentions she once rejected, may have been stalking Dusty. Some guys hold a grudge for years, and one day, for no apparent reason, act on it. I had more questions than answers, but try as I might, the one I preferred not to think about came back time and again.

Did my son hate me enough to gun down the woman I loved?

Chapter 12

My Rolex said 8:30. Three hours had passed since KCRG confirmed my suspicion that someone murdered the woman I almost married, and I didn't feel a thing. I'd been upset when she left me at the altar. I cried when I thought she might have been murdered, but now that my suspicions were proven true—nothing. I'd already lost her when she discovered I kept much of my past to myself, so what difference did it make? One way or another, I wouldn't be seeing her.

The lack of emotion puzzled me, but I learned from the loss of Myra there's nothing rewarding about grief. It sucks you in, and when it spits you back out, you're a fourth of the person you'd once been. At some point, you manage to add back on to that fourth, but you're never whole again. I didn't need it. Nobody does.

I wasn't grieving, but I'm not a stone. The news of Dusty's death left me restless. A visit to Lumir was out of the question, so I checked the *Gazette* and discovered Ken Paulsen was playing a dance at Hofer's Ballroom. I could think of no better alternative, so showered, put on a clean suit, and fired up the Cordoba for the twenty-minute drive to the venue.

I hadn't gone far when I realized going to a dance the day after Dusty's murder was a bad idea. Hofer's would be filled with folks who didn't travel in the same circles as the Sutherlands. As far as they knew,

I'd recently married. Seeing me out dancing the day after my new wife's brutal murder wouldn't do much for my popularity.

On my way back to the apartment, I passed Pete's Pub. The idea of a quiet beer in the little green building appealed to me, so I pointed the car in its direction. Maybe Burl would be there. We'd never be good friends, but the guy was easy enough to talk to.

I took the last parking place in Pete's lot and entered to discover a dozen people inside—enough to thwart my hope for a quiet drink. Apparently, the other customers didn't share my opinion that Burl was easy to talk to; the sole vacancy at the bar was the stool to his left. I took the empty seat, a location that put me directly opposite the bartender who stood silently, drying a glass.

"What'll it be?" he asked.

"Budweiser."

He turned around, reached into the cooler for my order, then plunked down a bottle and the glass he'd been drying in front of me.

"Dollar twenty-five," he said.

I laid two dollars on the bar. "Keep it."

Burl turned to me. "You sure you should be here tonight?"

"How's that?" I asked.

"What with your girlfriend getting killed and your drinking problem and all."

"Girlfriend, fiancée, whatever, it's in the past. She threw me over. I should have listened to my gut and saved myself the embarrassment. I can see now we didn't have much going for us, so live and learn. By the way, I don't have a drinking problem."

"Last time I saw you here, you got shit-faced, and I had to take you home. Remember? You puked all over my couch. Now, I hear you were hungover before noon today."

I poured the Bud into my glass. "Fired by the police department but still plugged into law enforcement gossip—should be a big help in your new career. My business got a major boost last night, and I was still celebrating."

"Really, Clete, you don't have the stomach for it. Orrin said your sink was full of vomit. Guys like you who get sick so easy don't last long when they start puttin' the booze away. Their bodies can't take it."

I took a hefty swallow and returned my glass to the bar. "Damn that loudmouth Orrin Dietz, it figures he'd blab my business all over town."

"Hey, a guy's got a right to complain about his job to his brother. You really acted nasty."

"Orrin's your brother?"

"Yup, third-generation law enforcement. Grandpa was a Pinkerton, and Dad was highway patrol. Orrin and I didn't want to listen to gossip about each other, so when he signed on with the county, I joined Cedar Rapids' finest. Junior wanted to go into the military police, but it didn't work out."

"I was at a fashion show last night and didn't have anything to do with what happened to Dusty."

"Hell, I know that. No way a guy who has a hard time deciding to marry a rich lady is gonna be decisive enough to kill her. When you see Orrin again, you ought to apologize. He's got a job to do, and he can't do it if he thinks you didn't kill her."

"That doesn't make sense."

"Orrin is an investigator. To be good at it, he's gotta assume everybody is guilty. You might not like it, but that's the way it is. I woulda put in a good word for you, but he would just ignore me anyway."

I downed the rest of my bottle and thumped it on the counter, a signal I wanted another.

Burl raised his eyebrows. "Better slow down. I ain't about to take you back home so you can throw up on the furniture again. You made a real mess."

"I don't have a drinking problem, but I have to do something about the stress. Think about it. Somebody killed the woman I almost married. On top of that, her father breaks the bones around my eye socket, an investigator thinks I killed her, my son hates me, and the guy who owns most of my business is busting my chops. A man under pressure has to let off a little steam."

Burl fiddled with his glass. "There's lettin' off steam, and there's makin' things worse."

"I'll be okay as long I stick with beer and stay away from the hooch."

Burl shrugged. "Maybe that will work for you. It don't for most."

Pete stopped by with my refill. Another two dollars made its way from my wallet to the counter. I wanted to know more about what transpired at the rest stop but wasn't sure if Burl knew anything, or if he did, if he'd spill.

"News report didn't give much detail," I offered, "but it looked like a hit to me."

Burl nodded and checked out the room. "Had to be," he said quietly. "And from the entry angles on the DeLorean, two shooters."

"Two? Whoever did it meant business. They were out for Dusty. Bunny Hamilton was such a driz, nobody would care enough to shoot her."

"A driz?"

"A wet noodle, a limp dishrag, spineless."

Burl looked around again. "Maybe, maybe not. At any rate, the guys who did it used some real firepower. The DCI guys estimate over twenty rounds went into the car. With as fast as it happened, the theory is they used South African Strikers."

I reached for my glass. It was already empty. "Paid assassins from South Africa?"

"No, Striker shotguns, semi-auto riot guns. They come with twelve-round canister magazines. Makes 'em look like Tommy guns. With one in the chamber, you can get thirteen shots off in twenty seconds. By the time they got done, the front of the DeLorean was gone. So much lead hit the driver's door that it disintegrated. DCI found enough single-ought buckshot in the car to sink a battleship. They say a Striker puts out projectiles faster than some machine guns."

I must have looked pale because Burl asked if I wanted to hear any more. I felt shaky, but the urge to know everything possible about the murders had taken control.

"I heard there was a witness," I said, hoping Burl would continue.

He did.

"Two, a mother and her daughter. They stopped so the little girl could use the bathroom. They was on the way out, almost to the door, when the fireworks started. They ducked back inside and hid in one of the stalls. When the mother heard a car tear out, she figured it was all over. She told the girl to stay in the bathroom while she went to use the pay phone. It was out of order."

"They were lucky the guys didn't see them."

"Yeah, but now they got a lot to deal with. The mother is a nurse so she checked out the car to see if there's anything she could do. Of course, there wasn't, but the little girl got tired of playing hide-and-seek and went out to be with her mom. The woman didn't notice until it was too late. The poor kid saw everything. Right now, the mom's in the hospital under sedation. And the kid . . . who knows if she'll ever be right again."

The warm, tiny bar grew warmer and tinier as images of what the crime scene must have looked like sank in. Sweat started running down the sides of my face. The room swayed. I don't know what happened next, but somehow Burl had a hand on my shoulder and another on a door's exit bar. I felt a rush of cool air as he herded me outside where he leaned me up against the side of the building.

"You oughta cut the alcohol, Buddy."

"I only drank two beers."

"You guzzled 'em, and you been drinking all day."

I shook my head to clear it. "I needed to know what happened to Dusty. Didn't think it would get to me like that."

"I shouldn'ta told you so much. The stuff isn't for general knowledge. You need to let on like you don't know what happened. By the way, I gotta tell my brother everything you said tonight.

"Sounds like I should have been more careful about talking to you, but there's nothing I said that will make any difference."

Burl smiled. "Guess you're not as dumb as you look."

"Sorry about getting woozy. The idea that somebody could do that to Dusty and Bunny ... I started picturing how they must have looked."

"Guys like me, who spent years in law enforcement, see a lot. We never get over it, but we get used to talkin' about it. It's easy to forget that civilians aren't the same."

A cab pulled into the lot. Burl started pushing me toward it.

"I asked Pete to call you a cab. You shouldn't be driving tonight."

For reasons I can't explain, I began crying.

Burl shook his head. "You're a tough guy, alright. Losing the woman you're crazy about and not letting it get to you. Now go home and get some rest."

I'd never convince Burl I hadn't been drinking all day but took the cab because he meant well. As I settled into the seat, the horrific images of the interior of Dusty's car came back. I took a deep breath to compose myself. The murders were the product of an organized hit squad. My son was off the hook. Nasty as Mike was, he'd be incapable of the cunning needed to organize that kind of firepower and of finding a partner to pull it off. The realization should have been comforting, but it wasn't. The murders were too close to home.

What if I'd been in the car with Dusty?

Chapter 13

I tossed my fedora on the office desk and plopped into what I like to think of as my executive chair. I'd just returned from Siegel's Pawn Shop where I surrendered my Rolex, gold tie bar, and cufflinks. The paltry sum I got in return would barely make a dent in my legal bills. Still, Harold Hardesty did a good job for me. I went to our meeting ready to turn my financial records over to the investigators to prove I hadn't hired someone to kill Dusty. He'd cautioned against it, pointing out that they'd want originals, and I'd be unlikely to get them back. Besides, he argued, they'd do nothing to prove my innocence.

Now that a week had passed, I saw the wisdom of Harold's advice. My status as a jilted fiancé didn't constitute grounds for an arrest, especially when I had a bulletproof alibi. He prepped me for our meeting at the sheriff's office like one of those top-gun defense lawyers on TV. The interview went like clockwork; we were out in less than an hour.

If only the rest of my life were going as smoothly. My blasé attitude toward Dusty's murder lasted about three days, long enough to lull me into the delusion that I'd get through the experience without falling apart. Instead, sleep went out the window, food tasted like cardboard, and my gut hurt twenty-four hours a day. Sometimes my chest got so tight I had trouble breathing. I don't know what I'd have done if Lumir hadn't taken charge of my hours away from Cleatzy's.

Lumir showed up at my apartment the day after the news of Dusty's death with a tuna casserole in hand. He didn't say anything when I opened the door but walked into the kitchen and put the dish in the oven. After a short lecture on the wonders of oven cleaner, he pulled a thick deck of cards from the pocket of his Cardigan sweater and set up a game of double solitaire. Unsure of what to say, I stood at the entrance to the room, my hands in my pockets and my tongue glued to the roof of my mouth.

"Well, are you playing or not?" he asked.

I sat down and took up my cards. We didn't talk much, and after munching down on the casserole, he set up another game. We played until eleven o'clock, and Lumir beat me every time. He left as abruptly as he arrived, without a word about our spat.

Since then, I'd seen him almost every day. He'd show up for lunch, have me over for chili, or drag me along to play dominos with his friends. Yesterday he'd taken me to a family dinner at his son's house. The one day he missed, Eddie stopped by to take me to the Cedar Rapids Boat Show at the Five Seasons Center. I got the feeling Lumir arranged that as well.

My friends' ministrations helped me settle down enough to return to work. Today was my first day back. Now that my eye had healed a bit, I could face the public without scaring them off. Paperwork had piled up, so I settled into the tedium of orders, invoices, and schedules. When I did, I realized how much Reg had taken care of in my absence. No doubt about it, the guy's next paycheck would include a bonus.

By midday, I'd gotten through the worst of it and decided to go to the Little King sandwich shop for lunch. I debated whether to take my fedora. The hat had become sort of a good luck piece ever since I wore it to a playoff baseball game. The home team pulled off a win after being down a half dozen runs. Certain the only explanation for their comeback was my fedora, I'd taken to wearing it when my spirits needed a boost. I reached for the hat and left the office.

On my way out through the sales area, I noticed a scruffy young woman toting a large shopping bag, going through a table of Izod shirts. It didn't take a genius to see she had no intention of buying anything. Her furtive glances about the store and massive bag screamed shoplifter.

I walked up and greeted her politely. "May I help you, miss?"

She turned with a start. "Uh, I …"

About to pilfer a first-class sports shirt, my presence rendered her speechless. I was ready to show her the door when I realized the look on her face was one of recognition rather than guilt.

"Are you Cletus Efferding?" she asked.

"That's me," I replied, wondering how she knew me.

She stuck out her hand. "Name's Tamara. And you're taking me to lunch."

My brain did a somersault. "Tammy Hinkley?" I asked.

"None other, but I use my full name, Tamara."

She didn't look like me, and she didn't look like Myra. I don't know if it was the spiked hair, the purple eye makeup, or the safety pin in her nose, but I couldn't wrap my mind around the idea that I was looking at my daughter.

"You're Tamara Hinkley, and you want to go to lunch with me?"

"Never figured you'd be a little slow on the uptake. You're taking me to lunch and paying for it. I like Mexican, and that's a hard find in Maquoketa. I want to go someplace authentic."

I know nothing about Mexican cuisine, but the guys in the shop talked about going to Papa Juan's up on Center Point Road. "Okay, but the only Mexican place I know is a few miles away. We'll have to take the car."

"Let's go," she said.

We left the shop and headed for the parking ramp. She talked about the weather and her drive over to Cedar Rapids. I learned she was spending a few days with a cousin who attended the local junior college. When I finally thought of something to say, it was a doozy.

"Shouldn't you be in school today?"

"Senior skip day. I decided to take tomorrow off too. I don't have to be back home until my shift starts tomorrow night. I waitress at the Green Mill Restaurant."

"You're cutting classes tomorrow?"

Tammy stopped walking, so I did too. I turned to see her put her hands on her hips and look me firmly in the eye. My daughter and I were the same height, so it was hard to miss the determination marking her face.

"Okay, this is where you realize you blew the parental role, and if we're going to get along, you're going to have to treat me like an adult. I'm nineteen years old and have been taking care of mom since I was fifteen."

I held up my hands, the universal sign of surrender. "Sorry, I'm nervous. A guy doesn't meet a long-lost daughter every day."

She started walking again. "Not lost. I've been in Maquoketa ever since you dropped me off at Mom and Dad's place."

Trying to explain would only get me in deeper. I struggled for another conversation starter. "So how is school?"

She burst out laughing. "You're so out of touch it's charming."

And then she began talking about her life at Maquoketa High—all the way to the restaurant.

Though I'd never been to a sit-down Mexican restaurant, the decor was about what I expected: walls covered with bullfight posters and the chintzy tourist sombreros you'd find in Mexican tourist shops. *Ranchera* music drifted from hidden speakers. A waitress with a south-of-the-border accent set down our menus and left. Tamara ordered soft tacos. I tried something called a bean burrito. The thing was massive, but it didn't intimidate. When it comes to food, Cletus Efferding hangs in there with the best of 'em.

"Man, you can pack it in," my tablemate observed.

I put down my fork. There were so many questions, so much I wanted to know. "Tam ... uh, Tamara ..." The name was going to give me trouble. "Look, I know you're Tamara, but I hope you cut me some slack. I'm going to mess up. I've thought of you as Tammy all these years. It'll take a while."

"You've got until we get back to the car."

My face must have fallen. She laughed.

"You'll be okay as long as there's a sincere effort. You think you have a problem? What am I going to call you? Forget Cletus, it ain't gonna happen, and Cleatzy is too cutie pie. You're smart enough to know Dad won't work. He might be dead, but I already have a dad."

That hurt, but I hadn't earned the title. "As long as you don't call me grandpa, I'll be okay."

"Wouldn't work anyway. Already taken. Remember? I had a grandpa, and he was my dad."

Had Mike mentioned Brute's threats to kill me? Since I didn't mention it in the registered letters I sent, my daughter might not know. "I need to explain about that," I said.

"Don't. Whatever you have to say, I won't like it."

I looked down at my plate. The remains of the burrito stared back. No matter how hard I tried, I never understand how a lifetime of logical decisions could leave me without a family. I wondered if I was depressed.

Tammy's voice brought me back to reality. "I think I'll call you Gramps. Pop or Pops doesn't sound right. Besides you're old-fashioned. It fits."

My fork clattered to the tabletop. "Gramps? Old-fashioned?"

"Yeah, think of it as a reminder of what you did to us. Hey, by the way, how was your honeymoon?"

She didn't know.

"We didn't get married."

"So that's why you look so sad. What happened?"

You will not break down Efferding. Not now.

I slid partway out of the booth and bent down to re-tie my shoe. The distraction helped. I straightened back up, under control.

Tammy continued. "I know about your wedding because Mike sent me a newspaper clipping of the announcement. That's how I recognized you, from the picture. Nice looking lady. You guys must have had a really big fight. I hope you didn't cheat on her."

Tammy thought I cheated on Dusty because I cheated on her mother. She was fishing for an answer. And really, she deserved one.

"She died," I said.

After she threw you over. Your daughter deserves a straight answer.

"We broke up because I didn't tell her things about myself that she deserved to know," I continued.

Tammy raised her eyebrows. "About Mom?"

"That's part of it, yeah. She was murdered."

Tammy sat quietly, looking at me as if I was the Devil incarnate. "Mom?" she asked.

"No, you weren't misled. Your mother took her own life. Someone killed Dusty, the woman I was going to marry, two Saturdays ago."

Myra, Dusty, my son, my daughter—the dam holding back an emotional flood was about to break. "Excuse me," I said, "call of nature," and made a beeline for the restroom.

Once inside, I locked myself inside the stall while I worked to compose myself. It took twenty minutes before I looked presentable enough to be seen in public. Tammy didn't deserve to be involved in the melodrama that was my life. She'd be gone when I returned to the booth.

Except she wasn't.

Tamara Hinkley sat where I'd left her, a spoonful of ice cream halfway to her lips, a large bowl of the stuff sitting in front of her. Her father's daughter, the girl knew how to eat.

I took my seat. "I thought you'd be gone by now."

"No car."

She'd chosen to ignore what I'd been doing in the restroom. "Oh," I said, flagged the waitress, and ordered a dish for myself.

"Tamara, you have no idea of how sorry I am that I ruined our lunch today. Somebody like your mother comes along once in a lifetime. Dusty understood that and accepted it. Even though we broke up, she was a big part of my life. I'm having a hard time coming to terms with the idea that someone would kill her."

"That's what your friend said when he called. Well, not exactly. He said you were having a really bad time, and if I ever wanted to meet you, I should come now. He wouldn't tell me any more than that. Said it was up to you to answer my questions. I didn't want to lose both the people who brought me into this world to suicide, so I came over."

"Called you on the phone?"

"Yeah, some guy called Boomer. He was really hard to understand."

"I can't believe he did that. His name is Lumir. He grew up speaking Czech. He has an accent."

The waitress brought my ice cream. We both dug in, emptying our bowls in record time. The task complete, I put down my spoon and looked Tamara straight in the eye. "I'm not about to kill myself. Lumir shouldn't have called you. Everything is ok."

Tamara nodded, then uncomfortable with the intensity of my gaze, looked away. "If you say so. I never thought a guy locking himself in the men's room so he could have a mini-breakdown made for a picture of someone happy and relaxed."

"You've got me there, but let me clue you in, if I ever did the deed, I'd be sure to load up on ice cream first. Want a second bowl?"

"Sure," she said.

Our server must have had second sight, for she appeared out of nowhere wanting to know if I wanted more coffee. I nodded and said, "And bring two more bowls of ice cream. While you're at it, triple the chocolate syrup."

She looked dubious. "Whatever you want. Nobody's ever asked for that much chocolate."

I winked at her. "That's because I've never eaten here before."

Tamara laughed. "Not only old fashioned, but corny too. You're definitely a Gramps."

"Sure you can't come up with a different name? Gramps sounds like somebody old."

"Nope, you're no spring chicken, and that wink at the waitress sealed the deal."

"You saw it, huh? Say, you mentioned something earlier about taking care of Velma since you were fifteen. What happened?"

Tamara tapped her bowl nervously. "Mom had a stroke in the fall of my freshman year. She has brain damage and sometimes forgets where she is. If nobody is watching her, she does things like leave the house in her nightgown when it's cold outside. Aunt Maidie and Aunt

Mary helped a lot, but she's been getting worse. Sometimes she chokes on her food. We put her in the nursing home last month."

"I'm sorry. I didn't know. It must have been rough."

"I wouldn't have made it if Maidie and Mary hadn't pitched in. They saw to it that I had a social life and could play volleyball. Mike doesn't have the caretaker personality. He helped some, but that ended when he went away to college. The restraining order was Maidie's idea. She flipped out when your registered letters telling us Mom and Dad weren't our parents arrived. So did Mike, even though he hated Dad."

"What happened between Mike and Brute?"

She sighed. "Everything was fine until Dad came home one day and found Mike wearing lipstick and one of my dresses. He was just ten, but Dad went crazy and hit him. After that, they never got along. I shouldn't be telling you, but Mike said he argued with you when he visited your dance studio. I don't know why but he blames you for what Dad did to him, but he does."

"Mike is gay?"

"None of your business, Gramps. It's none of mine either unless he decides to talk about it. You're not one of those guys who doesn't like gay people, are you?"

"I'm not, but Mike's my son."

Tamara cocked her head. "And?"

"Well, if he is, maybe I could get him some help. I hear there are places with programs to cure it."

"Hello. It's 1983, Gramps. They don't do that anymore."

"No, they do. I read about it in *Time Magazine*."

Tamara looked disappointed. "I like you better when you're not playing parent. Let's say you put things in their proper perspective and quit worrying about it."

I came up with a smile that must have had embarrassment written all over it. "Let's say I will, and we get back to our ice cream."

My daughter looked relieved and smiled back. "Let's."

We finished the ice cream and walked back to the Cordoba. "What are you driving?" I asked as we settled in for the trip back downtown.

"Volkswagen Bug," she answered. "She's not much, but I'll miss her when she goes to that junkyard in the sky."

I put the car in drive and turned back onto Center Point Road. "Do you think your bug will ever find its way back to Cedar Rapids?"

"It would have to leave first. Boomer and a guy named Eddie are meeting us tonight at a place called the Flamingo for dinner. The Bug and I will pick you up at Cleatzy's when you get off at eight."

"It's pronounced 'Loomer' and spelled L-u-m-i-r," I replied. "How'd you know when I get off work?"

"I'm not stupid. I asked Bloomer."

"Not to mention that you should quit pulling my leg."

"That'll be the day, Gramps," she said and tuned the radio to a heavy metal rock station and turned up the volume.

I realized then my lucky fedora had come through for me. I liked my daughter, safety-pin nose jewelry, raccoon makeup, and all.

Chapter 14

The Flamingo Restaurant's parking lot was surprisingly full for a Monday night. If Tamara's Volkswagen hadn't been small enough to squeeze into a space alongside a dumpster, we'd have had to park a half block away. I managed to open the passenger side door far enough to squeeze out, and as we rounded the corner of the building, the venue's unelectrified pink flamingo sign caught her attention.

"Cool," she said, "they just don't make 'em like that anymore."

How a nineteen-year-old could have any idea of how they used to make 'em was beyond me. I looked at the sign, one familiar enough since I'd eaten there dozens of times. I can't say Tamara's remark caused me to see it with new eyes. The thing had needed a coat of paint for ten years, maybe longer. Still, a response seemed called for.

"Yeah, they've used the same sign for years. I guess you could say it's become iconic."

"What's iconic mean?" she asked.

"That it's been there a long time."

"You already said that. Why'd you have to come up with another word for it?"

I didn't want to get into a discussion of the distinction between symbolic and old. "Let's go inside," I said.

We did. I knew without looking we were the last to arrive. I'd seen Eddie's motorcycle and Lumir's pickup, but Mrs. Hemsky's presence at the table came as a surprise. Eddie saw us and waved. I knew by his smile that Lumir was giving him a lecture on the finer points of good living.

Tamara grabbed me by the sleeve. I was beginning to think she couldn't walk and talk at the same time. "The young guy who just waved is Eddie?" she asked.

"And the guy with his back to us is Lumir. The lady next to Lumir is his neighbor, Mrs. Hemsky."

"You should have told me Eddie isn't old."

"What?"

"Never mind. I'll be with you in a minute."

Tamara did a sudden turn and made for the ladies' room. I joined the group at the table, where I discovered Mrs. Hemsky made an unscheduled visit to Lumir's shop and he invited her to join us. We were about five minutes into our chat when Mrs. Hemsky dropped a bombshell.

"Lumir's been wanting to get married."

My friend's face turned thirty-six shades of red.

"I told him 'no'. We've been living alone for so long we'd get on each other's nerves. I'd lose my Social Security widow's benefit. Besides, marriage can ruin a good thing. Look what happened to you, Cletus. A girl's got to take care of herself."

Lumir let out a quiet groan. He'd blabbed the details of the disaster at Grace Episcopal Church after I asked him to be discrete. Mrs. Hemsky must not have heard him for she barreled right on.

"I don't need the heartbreak of losing another spouse. I might be older than Lumir, but at his age men drop like flies." She stopped and put her hand to her mouth. "Oh Lord, I talk too much. You just lost someone, and here I am going on about people dying. I'm sorry, Cletus."

Lumir's obvious embarrassment made the show priceless. Besides, who could be angry at a ninety-year-old dynamo like Mrs. Hemsky. I reached across the table and touched her arm.

"It's okay, but you'll have to do some penance." I flashed my baby blues. "Since you know so much about me, the Mrs. Hemsky thing won't do. From now on, you're Millie." My declaration met with flushed cheeks and a demure smile. Women are putty in my hands when I turn on the Efferding charm.

"Hi."

I looked up and saw my daughter. The reason for her trip to the powder room became clear. Tamara had taken the opportunity to freshen her makeup. I didn't think it was humanly possible to add more gunk to the skin around her eyes, but somehow, she managed. She'd smudged enough pink powder on her cheekbones to put Millie Hemsky's blush to shame and enough coral lipstick to repaint the restaurant's flamingo sign. She headed for the vacant chair next to Eddie.

"This is my daughter, Tamara," I said. *My daughter—*the words felt good.

Lumir, ever the gentleman, stood and extended his hand. "Lumir Sedlak. Pleased to meet you. Your dinner is on me."

I gestured toward Eddie and introduced him. He managed a nod and a "hi." I introduced Millie as Mrs. Hemsky. She responded with a finger wave.

When our waitress arrived, Lumir, Millie, Eddie, and I ordered the broasted chicken. When Tamara's turn came, she asked, "What's broasted chicken?"

Time to educate my daughter. "The ambrosia of the gods, sent down from the heights of Olympus so mere mortals might enjoy a taste of paradise."

Our waitress looked up from her order pad and rolled her eyes. "Chicken, deep-fat fried in a pressure cooker, Honey."

Tamara ordered the chicken.

The Flamingo was busy. It took all of forty minutes for our dinners to arrive but when they did, we made short work of them. As we waited for our desserts, Lumir spotted an old friend. He and Millie excused themselves and went over to chat with him. They'd no sooner left than Tamara and Eddie began talking about rock bands. I didn't have much to contribute other than observe that the groups were so loud you couldn't speak to the person next to you.

"So, what about Duran Duran?" Eddie asked.

Tamara, clearly excited, began hopping up and down in her seat. "They're, like, totally bitchin.' John Taylor lays down a mean bass line."

"He's the best," Eddie replied, "The guy's bad to the bone. I spent hours trying to figure out his licks."

"You play bass?" Tamara asked.

"Yeah, some friends and I have a band. We're playing at The Freeway Express in a couple of weeks. It's a neighborhood bar. You should come out and hear us."

"I just might do that. I noticed the bike on your tattoo. You really have one?"

Lumir and I had been giving Eddie grief over what he referred to as 'body art' since the day he turned up at the woodshop with the design on the inside of his forearm. Why anyone would permanently mark his skin with the word "knucklehead" was beyond our comprehension. Worse yet, he had it spelled out in oversized bold letters above the image of a flame-belching motorcycle. He put up with us good-naturedly at first, but as time passed, his tolerance for our teasing evaporated. We no longer mentioned it.

Eddie perked up at Tamara's question. "You know about knucks?"

Tamara looked genuinely surprised. "Don't tell me that's your knuck in the parking lot."

"Yup. You know what they say. If it ain't a knuck, it ain't—"

"Eddie!" I cut him off and completed the sentence for him. "—ain't any good."

Tamara looked annoyed. "It's okay, Gramps. I've heard it all before."

I frowned at Eddie. "Everyone has heard the word before, but at least have the decency not to use it when I'm with my daughter."

"Sorry, Clete. Sometimes I forget you're still living in the last century."

"I'm not old-fashioned. Do it again, and I'll tell Lumir."

Eddie's eyebrows jumped. "Okay, okay, I won't. Just don't tell Lumir."

When Lumir straightens someone out, they stay straightened out.

Tamara turned her chair to face Eddie, leaving me with a view of the back of her shoulder. "My old boyfriend had a shovelhead."

Eddie ran his fingers through his locks. "I traded a panhead to get the knucklehead and never regretted it. Wanna go for a ride?"

"Sure," said Tamara.

I didn't know how I felt about the idea. Motorcycles are dangerous. "Don't you think—"

Eddie didn't let me finish. "See ya in a bit," he said and got up.

Tamara followed, leaving me alone. The desserts came. I'd just finished mine when Lumir and Mille returned.

"Tamara and Eddie have gone for a ride on his motorcycle," I explained.

"He seems to have taken a shine to your daughter," Lumir observed.

"He's twenty-nine and divorced," I countered. "He's too old for her. Not only that, he invited her to see his band at a bar. I know nineteen is the legal drinking age, but that doesn't mean Tamara should be spending time in the lowlife dives Eddie frequents."

Lumir shook his head. "You should hear yourself, Clete. Tamara is a fine young woman with a good head on her shoulders. She has been taking care of her mother since she was fifteen. What is wrong with her having a little fun? You should be ashamed. Eddie is your friend and a good man. If you are lucky enough, one day someone like Eddie might become your son-in-law."

"He's right," Millie harrumphed. "It's not Eddie's fault his wife left him for someone with a fancy car."

Chastened, I dropped the subject. No matter what my companions thought, Eddie was too old and too wild for Tamara. A father watches out for his daughter, even if she doesn't like it. I'd met her a few hours ago and already felt as if she were slipping out of my hands. One blunder eighteen years ago and still paying for it. Would the fallout from an ill-timed visit to a prostitute ever end?

Chapter 15

A warm smile came to my face as I stuck my Fred Astaire letter opener under the envelope's flap and slit it open. It had been two weeks since Tamara visited, and now she'd chosen to write me. Though the envelope bore no return address, the line directing the missive to Gramps Efferding, care of Cleatzy's Menswear, served as a dead giveaway.

Though Tamara was miffed when she went for her ride on Eddie's motorcycle, she drove me back to my car bearing no ill will. "Eddie said you were a little weird, and I should take you with a grain of salt," she explained. Not exactly words I wanted to hear but being in the same car as my daughter made her honesty easy to take. Though certain I was in the doghouse for eating her dessert while she was with Eddie, it must have been a minor infraction—she only mentioned it twice.

Tamara wrote her letter on what must have been her favorite stationery. The outer edges of the single-page sheet sported a black border festooned with skulls, daggers, and apes. I read slowly, savoring every word.

May 4th, 1983

Dear Gramps,

I'll be in Cedar Rapids on Saturday. I want to hear Eddie's band at the Freeway Express.

I'll stop by your store around noon, so you can take me to Papa Juan's again. Something really, really important has come up, and I need to talk to you.

By the way, I quit my job at the Green Mill Restaurant. I'm going to blow this pop stand and relocate to someplace massively cool. I realized I needed to get out of Dodge when I talked about somebody going "hog wild." I don't want to stay here anymore and turn into a hillbilly.

Tamara

A short letter, it gave me enough to chew on. Tamara planned to leave her home base for parts unknown, she liked Eddie enough to drive over to see his band, she trusted me enough to ask for advice, and last of all, she would be at the shop in an hour or so.

I leaned back, put my hands behind my head, and stretched, wishing she'd mailed the letter earlier. I had no conflicts for lunch, but knowing she planned to visit would have made for a bright spot in an otherwise lousy week. Deputies had shown up at Cleatzy's on Monday with a warrant allowing them to seize my business records and search the premises for firearms. I knew it might happen, but there's nothing like having law enforcement hauling a guy's stuff away to remind him of how small he is in the eyes of the system. I'd taken Harold Hardesty's advice and been prepared, storing copies of all my records in Lumir's woodshop.

He also advised me to take photos if law enforcement served a search warrant. The idea was to intimidate them into not making a mess. A great concept in the abstract, but it didn't turn out well. The deputies frisked me, saying they needed to ensure I wasn't carrying a weapon, and removed the three rolls of unexposed film in my pocket. Before they left, they demanded the camera as well, justifying its seizure by stating it might contain images of my financial records. The process didn't do much to raise my regard for the Office of the Linn

County Sheriff. When I called Harold Hardesty to tell him about the search, he didn't seem concerned.

"Remember, the search means they don't have enough to arrest you. I suspect they've convinced a judge that you have motive and that your arrest for manslaughter and the self-defense killing back in Jackson County prove you're capable of violence."

"They took my camera and film. I couldn't record the search."

Harold chuckled. "I wondered if they would. Don't worry about it. The camera thing was just to keep them on their toes."

"That was a two-hundred-dollar camera," I grumbled.

"Compared to me, it's cheap," he laughed. "If they haven't tossed your apartment already, it'll be next."

As if I needed a reminder. I'd already cleared the apartment of everything from my birth certificate to the water bills. Harold may have worn the most conservative suits of any lawyer I'd met, but he knew what he was doing. Nobody arrested me, my records were safe, and the investigative hoopla would soon be on the downswing.

Good thing I opened Tamara's letter in the morning, rather than the afternoon. She showed up just forty-five minutes after I learned of her intention to visit. We made the drive to Papa Juan's with the windows open, enjoying the beautiful May weather. Tamara seemed puzzled by Lumir and Millie's relationship.

"Are Lumir and Millie dating?" she asked.

"They've known each other for years," I replied. "Millie lives across the alley from him."

"Eddie says Lumir wants to get married. Do you think they still do it?"

"None of your business, Tamara. It's none of mine either unless he decides to talk about it."

"Maybe I'll ask Mrs. Hemsky if I see her again."

"I don't recommend it," I replied. "But if you find out, be sure to let me know."

She laughed.

We parked in a nearly full lot, entered the restaurant, and escorted ourselves to a booth. A swivel-hipped waitress sashayed over, presented our menus with a flourish, and wiggled away. When she was out of earshot, Tamara went straight to the reason she wanted to talk with me. "Mike needs help, and by the way, you look a lot better than the last time I saw you."

When I read her letter, I expected "something important" to be more along the lines of a romantic problem or a few bucks to spend in Cedar Rapids. I no longer wanted anything to do with my son. He'd insulted me and ruined my wedding. I studied the menu, stalling for time to formulate a response. "That burrito thingy I had last time was tasty. Yup, I'm getting that and a diet cola. What about you?"

When I looked up, I found Tamara leaning forward, arms on the table, frowning. "You don't want to help, so you're sidetracking me. But since you asked, I'm having the chicken enchiladas and a margarita."

"A margarita for lunch? Aren't you a little young, and isn't it a little early in the day?"

"Remember? I like you a lot better when you don't pretend to act like a parent. I'm legal age and having a rare Saturday treat. By the way, you're paying for it, Gramps, just like the rest of my lunch."

I gave in and ordered a Corona and lime to go with my burrito. Tamara sat quietly, waiting to see what I had to say about Mike. Borderline lies and deceptions had gotten me into so much trouble, I decided to go with the truth but to ease into it. "Mike told you we fought when he came to the studio. Did he tell you why?"

"He said he wanted to borrow money."

"That's right, he wanted me to lend him ten thousand dollars. When I told him I didn't have it, he asked me to take it out of his trust fund. I can't do that. The tax code requires that it be used for the purposes described in the documents."

Tamara's eyes grew wide. "Ten thousand dollars? I thought he hit you up for a few twenties."

"He and his friends want to invest in something they call reaching their maximum potential and promoting world harmony. Dusty said his spiel sounded a lot like the language of the People of Light, a cult she got tangled up with. I doubt that was the case. Dusty never got over the time she spent with them in India."

"Gramps, the People of Light is the group he wants to go live with. They have a settlement in New Mexico. I'm worried. He's not answering his phone, and I think he's moved out of his apartment. A lot of people go into those cults and never come out. Sometimes they even commit suicide like that group down in Jonestown. Some of them didn't drink poison because they wanted to. They were forced to do it at gunpoint—they were murdered."

Our orders arrived. Appreciative of the distraction, I once again tried to redirect the conversation. "You know, I could get the hang of eating Mexican food. It's tasty."

"Don't change the topic. You're the only one who can help Mike, and you won't because you don't like him."

I didn't know how to answer and toyed with the hot sauce bottle. Finally, I came up with something profound. "I didn't say that."

"Maybe, but it's true!" she countered.

"Mike hates me and scotched my wedding. He showed up in church yelling his lungs out about me being addicted to prostitutes and wanting women to beat me up. Then he called me a killer. I wouldn't lift a finger to help him."

Tamara looked as if she'd just made sense of a difficult puzzle. "So that's how your fiancée found out you were hiding things from her. If you'd been honest, you'd be a married man." She pointed her fork at me. "My brother might be a snot, and he might be messed up, but he doesn't deserve to be brainwashed—no matter what you think." She brought her fork closer to my face, waving it just inches away from the tip of my nose. "He's your son. Find him and bring him back to Iowa. You abandoned him once. Act like a father and don't do it to him again."

I sat back, away from the fork. "I didn't abandon your brother, and I didn't abandon you. I knew where you were—living with your grandparents. I'm sorry Mike didn't get along with Brute, but that doesn't change the fact he despises me and ruined my last chance to marry and have a family."

Tamara put down her fork, her lower lip quivering.

"No family? What about Mike and me?"

I didn't have time to answer. My daughter stood and fled the table. By the time I fished a couple of ten-spots from my wallet and threw them on the table, she was already out of the building. I rushed to follow but encountered an elderly couple struggling with the heavy door. I helped, waiting impatiently as they tottered inside, but the delay proved my undoing. When I stepped outside, Tamara was nowhere to be seen. I waited in the parking lot for a half-hour, thinking she needed a ride back downtown, but to no avail.

My daughter had run from me.

Chapter 16

I pulled into the Coe College parking lot, switched off the ignition, and sank back into the seat with a sigh. When I mess up, I don't monkey around. I jump into the cesspool of stupidity and wallow in it like a pig on moonshine. My attempts to mend fences with Tamara had been in vain. She was done with me. Three returned letters and two weeks of unanswered phone calls left no doubt. I tried in vain to get Eddie to intercede.

"Not me. Not gonna happen," he said, shaking his head. "You were a major-league jackass, and she's really pissed off. Don't ask me again."

What I got from Lumir was an unsympathetic sermon followed by his standard 'How a man can be so stupid is beyond me.'

Tamara wanted me to act like a father, but I'd acted like a parent. I had never given much thought to the difference between the two. Parenting ends when a child turns eighteen. Fatherhood is a lifetime gig.

I fully believed Mike had gone to the cult's ranch. The longer he stayed, the harder it would be to get him to leave. But I wasn't up to the job. Still sleepless from Dusty's murder and breaking into tears at the drop of a hat, I struggled to keep Cleatzy's afloat amid Gib Sutherland's hectoring about margins and profits. I didn't know where I stood with

Steele. He'd indemnified me twenty-five grand not to sue him, so it seemed unlikely he would have me beaten and castrated.

I tried to get Burl involved in his new capacity as a private detective. "I got my hands full gettin' this business up and runnin'," he complained. "I got no time to traipse down to New Mexico. Besides, you're the guy with the best chance of talkin' him out of there. Lie if you have to. Just drag him out and take him to one of those deprogrammers."

Springing Mike by myself and getting him to a deprogrammer would be next to impossible, but I wanted my daughter back in my life. Fulfilling her vision of what a father should be seemed the only option.

"I don't think I have it in me, Burl. I don't like the kid and like the idea of messing with a cult even less."

"Like it or not, you oughta do it yourself. But before you give up, get some more information. There's this professor at Coe College named Flanagan. He came down to the station to give us a class on cults in case we needed to deal with one that targets minors. He's been down to their ranch. Talk to him, then decide."

So here I was, ready to talk to Professor Flanagan. I found his office in the music building, a strange location for an anthropologist, and the cause of my being twenty minutes late for our appointment. Expecting anything but a warm welcome, I was pleasantly surprised when a bearded, bespectacled, gray-haired man beckoned me inside. Though his Donegal tweed sports coat had seen better days, a smile lighting up a face as Irish as a pint of stout put me at immediate ease.

"Have a seat," he said as he made for a side table where he filled two mugs with coffee. "The departmental secretary said you wanted to see me because you have a relative who's joined the People of Light and plan to visit Shiva City."

So that was the name of the place. "My son. My daughter is worried and wants me to bring him back."

Flanagan handed me a steaming mug, "I can add a touch of Jameson's if you'd like."

I shook my head. "Thanks, but spirits and I don't get along."

Rather than taking the chair behind his desk, the professor pulled up a pants leg and plunked his rear on an uncluttered corner of its top. The action put him a head and a half above me. I'd have read it as a dominance move but knew it was anything but. Though sunlit and cheerful, his office was small, and the only alternative to his perch would have put the desk between us. After studying me a moment, Flanagan leaned forward, raised his bushy brows, and asked, "So you go there, and then what? If he knows you're searching for him, you won't see him, and if his new friends—and I use the term loosely—discover you're looking for him, they'll do everything possible to see you don't find him."

My face flushed. "I doubt my son will recognize me. We've been estranged for eighteen years. His grandparents took custody of him when he was a toddler, and I can count on three fingers the number of times we've seen each other since. It won't take much to keep my identity from him. I plan to grow a beard, get an ear pierced, and shave my head. And weight is easy enough to change. With enough banana splits and milkshakes, gaining an extra twenty pounds will be a cakewalk. I've been working on that piece of it and am already halfway there. As for the other loonies at the ranch, I might as well go back to kindergarten if I can't outthink a few blissed-out crazies."

Flanagan took a sip from his mug. "Splurging on dairy products will be the easy part. Don't underestimate the people in Dev's cult. Some are highly intelligent. When I visited Shiva City for my fieldwork, I met doctors, lawyers, entrepreneurs, and a boatload of psychologists. True believers they may be when it comes to the Sattguru, but their mental faculties are fully intact."

I realized then that I'd already decided to go. "Doesn't make any difference if they're all PhDs.," I replied. "I messed up the fatherhood gig royally. Now, for the first time since she's been a baby, I can do something for my daughter. She's worried about her brother and wants him back home. My son may be a bad apple, but if I don't look for him, she might do it on her own. I don't know as much as I should about the People of Light but letting a nineteen-year-old get anywhere near them sounds like an outstandingly bad idea."

Professor Flanagan set his cup on a pile of papers and unparked his backside from the desktop. "Let's take a drive," he said.

"Where?" I asked.

"To the Kool Moo, to work on the easiest part of your task. You're trying to gain weight, and I'm an expert on their milkshakes. Their pineapple is the best in town. I'll drive. You can fill me in on what you know about the cult."

After he handed me a book of the Sattguru's writings, we left the office and rode to the Moo in Flanagan's Volvo. I gave him the lowdown on Mike and my abortive wedding on the way. When I finished, he didn't comment but let out a low whistle. I've been around the block enough to realize a vocalization that doesn't require an answer is used to keep an interviewee talking. The professor needn't have bothered, I was on a roll and spilled everything Dusty told me about the Manoneetas. None of it was new to him.

After the girl behind the Moo's order window handed us our milkshakes, we made for a concrete table where the professor took a healthy slurp. "Okay, suppose you go to Shiva City. Over three thousand Manoneetas live there and—"

"Three thousand? That's the size of a small town!"

Flanagan nodded. "People still think of it as a ranch, and three years ago, it was. Let's assume you're lucky enough to find your son. Then what? Are you going to hire someone to snatch him and deliver him to a deprogrammer? Your fiancée's parents had it easy. The *ashram* was in India. A rescue in New Mexico is a different kettle of fish. Mike is an adult and free to associate with whomever he wants. From a legal standpoint, what you think of as a rescue and deprogramming can be viewed as kidnapping and psychological abuse. If someone complains and you are charged, you could be looking at twenty years in a federal penitentiary."

I spooned a piece of pineapple from my double extra-large shake. "I don't like my son, so snatching him never occurred to me. I want to locate him, tell him his sister wants to see him, and talk him into coming back. The cult is bad news, but if Mike is at the ranch, I can't keep my promise to my daughter without going there."

Flanagan stroked his whiskers. "I never thought of the People of Light as particularly dangerous until I visited Shiva City. I can't tell you why, but I came to believe something dark lies behind the façade of a group of smiling Manoneetas seeking enlightenment. Naming the ranch after Shiva, the god of destruction should have been a clue. I didn't read much into it at first because Hindus view destruction as a natural part of the cycle of life. But now I wonder. Some of the security people carry sidearms, and I heard gossip about a place in South Dakota where those who fail the Sattguru are sent for re-education. Rumor has it some never come back. Probably just a case of a Manoneetas disgusted with the reassignment who returned home. Still, true believers can go to extreme measures when their core beliefs are threatened. The literature is filled with examples."

"Not to mention the Jim Jones Kool-Aid thing," I interjected. "At any rate, I'm making the trip. Do you have any suggestions for me?"

"Not many," he replied. "The best part of anthropology may be fieldwork, but I left the ranch after three weeks. I'm not a quitter, but the game got too weird for me."

"How so?"

"There are three levels of involvement with the group: client, seeker, and *sadhu*. To get anywhere in my research, I would have had to make it to the *sadhu* level—full membership. To make the cut, you're expected to put your entire life into the hands of the guru. I could have faked that, but there's also the expectation you've gotten rid of your negative energy by sharing the joyous, sexual side of yourself with your peers. I doubt my wife would have approved. You're single, so that might not be a problem, but there's another hitch. I got to know one of the medical people. He let it slip that gonorrhea is rampant and something like eighty percent of the group has herpes. His attempts to get the word out about condoms met with only mixed success."

I returned my half-consumed shake to the table. "So, it's a sex cult. I'm not into that sort of thing but earning my daughter's trust is important to me. If necessary, I'll grab a rubber and give it the old college try. My son is a new member, so I doubt I'll need to become a *sadhu*. He's probably still at the client level."

Flanagan shook his head. "I doubt it. Clients aren't members, but visitors who enroll in the self-discovery programs at the Devesha Harmonic Convergence Center. Most of them think of the People of Light as saints who gave up everything to follow the Sattguru. Clients are more interested in feeling better about themselves than in abandoning their upper-middle-class lifestyle. They lay out outrageous sums to hear motivational speakers, join encounter groups, and get meditation coaching. The braver ones sign up for induced-stress therapy and the sensory-deprivation tanks. Ordinary Manoneetas are cautioned to avoid associating with clients outside the center. Unless your son Mike has done an exceptional favor for Dev or bought his way in, he's likely living in one of the seeker compounds."

"You can buy enlightenment? Dusty said it took years."

"Maybe in India, but here in the U.S., the People of Light never miss a business opportunity. Once they're satisfied that they've squeezed as much out of you as they can, you're good for early promotion. Did you know the Self-Discovery Program rakes in tens of millions and the worldwide publishing operation millions more? They irrigate something like three hundred acres of desert and distribute produce throughout New Mexico. Seekers and *sadhus* are expected to earn their keep by working at the ranch or bringing in money from the outside. Most work eight hours a day, seven days a week, and it all flows to the top. Dev has twenty-five Bentleys and a fleet of top-end Mercedes Benzes."

I shook my head. Dusty's youthful infatuation with the *ashram* and nirvana I could understand. The poor girl's domineering father, ice-cube mother, and sheltered upbringing left her susceptible to the hollow promise of a meaningful life in the arms of a loving community. But how Myra and I managed to produce a son gullible enough to fall for the Sattguru's hogwash was beyond my ken.

Maybe he belonged to the milkman.

Chapter 17

A crescent moon shone on a vacant landscape, and more stars than I knew existed pierced the dome of the night sky. The gray-haired woman next to me, her head resting on my shoulder, snorted softly when the bus hit an unexpected bump. Now sleeping soundly, she'd boarded at Oklahoma City, picked her seat, and got straight down to business, fingering the beads of a rosary she picked from her dress pocket. Mexican or Indian, I don't know which, but given the shy smile she sent my way before she sat, I doubt she had more than a word or two of English.

I checked my watch—three a.m. I'd scored a window seat on the redeye Greyhound to Albuquerque. The scene at the Oklahoma City station confirmed I'd soon put the Great Plains behind me. The farm folk and oilfield workers heading for home disappeared, leaving behind sleep-deprived passengers bound for the Old Southwest. A family, its belongings in twine-tied boxes, a ranch hand lugging a saddle, an adolescent boy struggling with a TV set, the appearance of my fellow travelers spoke of bad luck, hard lives, and dim futures.

The new cowboy hat resting on the overhead rack above me would protect my recently shaven head from the summer sun, and the patterned boots on my feet would shield them from the desert scrub. A silver buckle the size of a dinner plate cinched the hand-tooled belt circling my waist. An unexpected present from Eddie, I suspected the impetus behind his gift lay in his appreciation for my daughter.

Wanting to support me in my quest for my son, he'd offered to accompany me to the Saddle and Leather Shop, the Barta family's store on Bohemie Town's Sixteenth Avenue. Lumir came along as well, using the trip as an excuse to spend a few minutes gossiping with the elder Barta sister. On the way out of the shop, he chastised me for referring to the neighborhood as Bohemie Town.

"You must keep up with the times," he cautioned. "The name Bohemie Town is outdated. We are now the Czech Village. Call the wrong person a Bohemie nowadays and you could get punched in the nose."

The bus's luggage compartment held my suitcase, a beat-up piece of Samsonite donated by Lumir. A pastel pink number from the 1950s, it held the rest of my new wardrobe: three cowboy shirts with contrasting yokes and mother-of-pearl buttons, spare pairs of bootcut jeans, a flannel-lined denim jacket, and the obligatory red bandanas. There were the necessities of course, and my one splurge—a bolo tie with a bear-claw slide I'd need if invited to a formal event. The shirts had been an object of considerable discussion. Eddie encouraged me to choose from the ones with fringed yokes. Lumir argued against the idea, telling me I'd look like a refugee from a Gene Autry movie. Operating on the theory you can never be overdressed, I went for the fringe.

I settled back in my seat, closed my eyes, and slept until the driver pulled up beside a small-town post office and called out "Santa Rosa." My signal that it was time to get moving, I stretched, bid my aged seatmate farewell, and grabbed my hat. When the driver retrieved my suitcase from the luggage compartment, he handed it to me saying, "Never stopped here until the People of Light moved in. Now it seems like there's one of you every trip. Hope you find what you're looking for. I'm into Jesus myself."

"Thanks," I replied. "Hope you find him."

I pulled the Foster Grants from my shirt pocket, perched them on my nose, and walked to the corner to see what might be stirring. A small sign identified the thoroughfare as U. S. Route 66. A row of single-story buildings interspersed with vacant lots and abandoned businesses flanked the street. Bypassed by Interstate 40, the town's once-thriving hub had taken a hit. The only sign of prosperity looked to be a half-mile away—a gleaming three-story building I took to be a hospital.

The New Mexico climate doesn't mess around. The temperature must have been in the high nineties, and the midday sun burned through my Foster Grants like they were dime-store toys. Midwestern folks talk about the southwestern heat as if there was nothing to it. "It's dry heat," they say. "Why, you hardly sweat at all." They don't mention a few minutes of it drains every shred of ambition from your body.

Already tired and in need of directions, I made for a nearby sign identifying a sunbaked building as the Club Café, home to world-famous sourdough biscuits and Tex-Mex cooking. Bells tinkled as I opened the front door. The layout looked familiar enough—cash register and trinkets upfront, a lunch counter on one side, booths on the other, and tables in back. I put my Stetson on the counter, removed my sunglasses, and took a seat. A sloe-eyed waitress took my order for coffee. I studied the menu, and when she returned, asked for an egg dish called huevos rancheros.

"Red, green, or Christmas?" she asked.

I had no idea what she was talking about. My confusion must have been obvious.

"Your chilis. Red, green, or mixed?"

"Christmas," I replied decisively.

A woman in pastel blue hospital scrubs took the stool next to mine. She wasn't shy. A tap on my arm and "Hi there" made her presence hard to ignore. I turned to take in a bead-wearing, freckled carrot top whose frizzy shoulder-wide mane dwarfed her face. If not for a pair of green-framed eyeglasses, the unruly mass might have obscured her features entirely. "My name's Ma Prema," she said extending a hand. "Welcome to Santa Rosa. I drive one of the shuttles to Shiva City."

I took her hand, gave it a shake. "I'd never have guessed. You look like you work at the hospital up the street."

"It's not a hospital. It's the Devesha Harmonic Convergence Center. Clients from all over the world come here for counseling and enlightenment coaching. And I'm not in health care. I'm a mechanic and drive a shuttle three days a week. The scrubs are an easy way to meet the Seeker Dress Code. I'm leaving for Shiva City at two. Be on time."

Wondering how she knew I wanted to go to the ranch and not wanting to seem too eager, I played it low-key. "Just passing through, ma'am. Hadn't thought about staying."

Ma's smile seemed to come from far, far away. "You can drop the phony ma'am business. If you were from around here, you'd put your hat on the counter upside down. When you put it right side up, all the luck runs out of it. And with a voice like that, you can only be from the Midwest. The dude getup, the silly belt buckle—give me a break—of course you're here to visit the ranch. If you were a Convergence Center client, you'd be wearing pricey clothes. And that chubby little tummy, I'd like to give it a rub sometime."

"Now Ma—,"

Her eyes twinkled. "I'm not your Ma. It's Ma Prema. When a seeker is on the way to becoming a *sadhu*, the seeker is given a set of rosewood beads, a title, and a new name. *Ma* is a mark of respect, just like Mrs., and Prema means love—something I excel at. You can call me Prema. Sattguru Dev told me I've been gifted with second sight because I sense things about people. I can see you're on a quest, something you're not sure of, and that's causing you to be afraid."

The woman made me uncomfortable. She wasn't bad-looking or anything, but really, I didn't want her rubbing my tummy, and the last thing I needed was her reading my mind.

I held up my hands. "Okay, you've got me. I'm here to see the ranch, but I'm not on a quest and can't imagine there is anything to be afraid of."

She patted me on the shoulder. "Don't worry," she whispered. "The search for enlightenment is not easy. Everyone has fears and doubts." She rose from her stool. "I need to check the Center and the Sahara Diner to see if anyone else needs a ride. You should be finished with lunch when I get back here at two o'clock. Don't make me wait. And by the way, what's your name?"

I was ready for the question. "Cliff, Cliff Krabbenhoft."

Prema giggled. "Well, that's an easy one to remember. It's colorful, like your boots, and you're the type to get crabby now and then."

I raised my eyebrows. "I never get crabby."

She poked me in the shoulder. "Uh-huh, I have second sight, remember?" And with that, she left.

I've never understood why some people skip lunch, but happy she'd departed and with my transport to the ranch in place, I relaxed. The woman might believe she had second sight, but her vaguely worded attempt to read me failed to pick up anything significant. When my huevos thingy arrived, I attacked it with relish.

A post-lunch peek in the restroom mirror revealed bits of egg clinging to the hairs around my mouth. Keeping food out of a four-week-old beard was proving harder than expected. After blotting my lips, I made for the cash register to settle up and retrieve my suitcase. On my way out the door, I checked my watch. Three minutes to two. Prema proved as good as her word. A dusty eight-passenger van, its side decorated with a flaming eye, waited outside.

Prema got out, opened the rear storage compartment, and tossed my pink suitcase inside. "Steal that from a life-size Barbie?" she asked. "Take the front passenger seat. The people sitting in back dressed in purple are *sadhus*, but they also teach at the Center. They may be enlightened, but after putting up with clients all morning, the last thing they want is to chat with a grunt."

Thoroughly put in my place at the bottom of the totem pole, I made for my designated seat. Professor Flanagan hadn't mentioned anything about grunts, but he did tell me it would take a few weeks to become a seeker. Until then, it was best to shut up and do what you're told.

Heeding the professor's advice, I sat quietly as we traveled south on a narrow road through country anything but breathtaking. We drove through barren scrub dotted with scrawny cactuses and scraggly evergreens I took to be junipers. Our path took us parallel to a line of silver-leaved trees punctuated here and there by the skeleton of an abandoned windmill.

"The Pecos River is on the other side of those trees," Prema announced as she caught up her unruly locks in one hand and twisted them into something resembling a ponytail. Taking her other hand off the wheel, she pulled a rubber band over the works to hold it in place. A vision of myself as the sole survivor of an overturned van, crawling through the desert beneath a vulture-filled sky, prompted me to grab for the wheel. A sharp slap on the back of the hand rewarded my effort.

"You trying to kill us?" Prema scolded. "I can't remember the last time I ran into somebody so nervous. A few weeks at the ranch, and you'll be a new man."

To tell the truth, I was happy with the old me.

"Sattguru Dev," she continued, "chose the location of Shiva City himself. He wanted it away from the distractions of Santa Rosa but close enough to the Interstate to make it easy for clients to come for counseling and classes. That's why the Harmonic Convergence Center is located in town."

I should have sat quietly, but my curiosity got the best of me. "What's this Harmonic Convergence business all about?"

"The most important event in the history of mankind, and the ranch has everything to do with it. Some of Dev's enemies spread the word that the People were expelled from India because of a disagreement with the government. The truth is that Dev chose to relocate because of our mission. Shiva City is just a few miles south of the old Catholic church at Puerta de Luna, the most important of the earth's power centers."

"Power centers?" I asked.

"Places where spiritual energy is especially strong. Four years from now, on August 16th and 17th, one hundred forty-four thousand enlightened saints will converge at power centers all over the world to meditate for peace. The event will bring on a new era of spiritual harmony. Those meditating in the lesser power centers like Mount Fuji or Mount Shasta won't know the unsurpassed bliss enjoyed by Manoneetas."

The view from the windshield seemed particularly devoid of mountains. "So, how far is it to Mount Puerta de Luna?" I asked.

"Puerto de Luna isn't a mountain. It's a town up ahead."

We drove a little farther, passing a handful of sun-bleached buildings and crossing the Pecos River—a stream that would have barely qualified as a creek back home. We were driving by a junkyard when I asked, "How far to Puerto?"

"We're in it."

"The most important spiritual power center on earth? There's nothing here."

"You must not know Spanish because you're missing the obvious. The shamans who named the place knew exactly what they were doing. Puerto de Luna means Gateway of the Moon."

The most important spiritual power center on earth a god-forsaken junkyard in New Mexico? So much for Professor Flanagan's belief in the intelligence of the Manoneetas.

Just outside the main gate to the ranch, a pink sign with navy blue letters announced, "Shiva City—Invited Guests Only—No Trespassing." The message seemed unnecessary. A ten-foot-tall chain-link fence separated the ranch from the rest of the world, extending as far as the eye could see. A crossing arm stretched over the road discouraged unauthorized access, but not as much as the assault rifles slung over the shoulders of the gate's pink-clad attendants. Though Professor Flanagan had mentioned security people with handguns, I was unprepared for long-range, semi-automatic weapons.

Prema picked up on my discomfort. "We get death threats all the time," she explained. "The Blanton family had their eye on this property for forty years, and we bought it out from under them. Before the fence, we'd have pickups full of drunken ranch hands driving through, throwing firecrackers, and shooting guns in the air."

On the surface, the explanation made sense, and for all its threatening appearance, security looked lax. The smiling attendants raised the crossing bar as we approached and waved us through with good-natured bonhomie.

Just inside the gate, a blacktop road divided by a landscaped boulevard replaced the dirt track we'd driven in on. Rows of tidy two-story adobe buildings lined the street on both sides. Behind them, an expanse of lush cropland interspersed with greenhouses spoke to the Manoneetas' agricultural expertise.

"Compared to what's outside, Shiva City is the Garden of Eden," I remarked. "Who'd have thought you'd find enough water in the desert for all this."

Prema rolled down her window and waved at a scrubs-clad pedestrian. "I know it looks dry to you, but technically this isn't the desert. It's the dry side of the New Mexico High Plains."

The woman could get as technical as she wanted, but no ifs, ands, or buts, we were in the desert.

"We're some of the lucky few who get to take water from the Pecos," she continued. "We have access to an irrigation channel that was grandfathered in back when the water laws changed. That's why the Blantons wanted the property so much."

We passed a blue-clad crew surrounded by wheelbarrows adding hefty stones, plants, and gravel to the landscaped boulevard. They looked hot, dirty, and tired.

"Every Manoneeta earns their keep by contributing to the greater good," Prema continued. "The same goes for newcomers. Once you're settled in, you'll be given a work assignment. Of course, the plum jobs go to those with seniority or special skills. If you decide to stay, you'll start at the bottom—most likely doing fieldwork. I was lucky because I'm a mechanic and got assigned to the motor pool. They wanted me to stay, so I earned my beads and Advanced Seeker status in just four weeks. For most folks, it's grunt work until their promotion, usually for something like twelve to eighteen months."

I thought about the tired, miserable-looking grounds crew working eight hours a day, seven days a week, and shuddered.

Chapter 18

Prema pulled my suitcase from the back of the van and set it on the pavement. "This is Harmony House, the administration building. When you get inside, take the hallway to the left. Registration will be one of the first offices."

"Wish me luck," I replied.

"You won't need it. By the way, don't be offended if someone calls you a grunt. It's the unofficial name for a newcomer." And with that she gave me a hug, squeezed a butt cheek, and kissed me hard on the mouth, scaring the living bejesus out of me.

"*Shaanti*," she said, turning to go. "It means peace."

I *shaantied* her in return, picked up my suitcase, and headed up the walk. Except for the lack of bicycles and playground equipment, the adobe building could have been an elementary school. I passed through a small, unattended lobby, took the hallway on the left, and came to a door identified as *Registration & Orientation*. I opened it and stepped inside.

A bald, bearded man stood at a counter beneath a three-by-four-foot portrait of a bearded guru—one of those jobbies where the eyes seem to follow you wherever you go. A full-length, life-size photo of the same guy hung on the wall to my left. On the opposite wall, a corner-to-corner, floor-to-ceiling mural showed the man standing on a flower-strewn platform, waving to an adoring crowd. I'd seen photos of the Sattguru in *Newsweek* and the book Professor Flanagan gave me, but the man on the walls looked to be twenty years older. He must have been the guy who handed Dev the wisdom of the ages.

I cleared my throat to get Baldy's attention. "Is that the Sattguru's guru?"

The man behind the desk looked up, horrified. "That's Sattguru Devesha. You've never seen a picture of him, never read one of his books? Why are you here?"

So, the guru used older publicity pictures to show the world outside a more youthful face. I decided to play dumb and gave Baldy the Cletus A. Efferding look of total innocence.

"Don't know anything about the guy, but it's weird," I answered. "I was on the bus to Albuquerque and saw a sign that read: Santa Rosa 10 miles. An irresistible urge to see the town came over me, so I asked the driver to let me off. As soon as my feet hit the ground, I experienced an overwhelming sense of relaxation—the kind you get when you finally make it home after a long trip. The Club Café looked like a good place to eat, so I went in and took a seat at the lunch counter. I was looking through the menu when a woman with a face like an angel sat down next to me and told me about Shiva City. After she left, I heard a man's voice in my head—deep, low, almost a murmur. 'Come to Shiva City,' it said. 'You will find a life of serenity and meaning.' Then a feeling of happiness like I've never known washed over me. A guy would have to be nuts to ignore something like that."

The skeptical look on Baldy's face disappeared, replaced by an extended hand and a distant smile. "Sattguru Devesha must have something special in mind for you. A personal call is rare—very rare. Still, everyone must take the prescribed path." He handed me a three-page form and gestured toward a table and chairs. "Fill this out and bring it back when you're finished."

I took a seat and went to work on the registration form. I used my phony Cliff Krabbenhoft name and made up a history that included selling men's clothes in Texarkana and Muskogee. If anyone asked about my work, I'd have a lot of detail on the rag trade. There were questions about family to which I replied, "no living relatives" and re-quests for information on income and financial resources. Not wanting to be hounded for a contribution, I painted a picture of an out-of-luck haberdasher headed west in search of opportunity. Baldy took my form when I finished and looked through it.

"Looks like you've had some bad luck. Can I see your ID?"

Time to lie. "Don't I wish. It fell out of my wallet when I bought my bus ticket in Oklahoma City. I was double-checking to see if the clerk got it right and absentmindedly put it in my shirt pocket. It must have fallen out."

Baldy shook his head. "ID loss is more common than you think—especially when people travel. Since you've been called, I can overlook that minor technicality. I'll issue you an identification card you can use anywhere in Shiva City. Wait here."

He took my registration papers with him and came back holding a card embossed with a flaming eye and bearing my name and birth-date.

"Your room and board are free tonight but building Shiva City isn't cheap. Since you have no assets to speak of, you'll be given a work assignment after your orientation tomorrow. The assignment allows those of modest means to contribute to the community while earning their keep. We don't have many positions open right now, but I'll see what I can do to give you a choice."

"I want to be part of the world you're building." I almost gagged on the whopper. "I'll be here tomorrow, ready to work."

Baldy handed me the ID and reached under the counter to re-trieve a key. "We assign most newcomers a bunk in one of the big tents, but I'm putting you in room 232 at the guest house. Here's a map. The guest house is circled in blue. The area circled in red is *sadhu* housing. It is off limits to newcomers."

"Be here tomorrow at nine sharp. I don't usually do orientations, but you've been called, so it's important I get you off on the right foot. By the way, I'm Babba Bahru. *Shaanti.*"

I thanked him and left, happy I had inadvertently BSed myself into some sort of special status. The old Efferding luck was holding.

The guest room was spartan but clean. I tossed my Barbie suitcase on the bed and opened the curtains. The bed, a nightstand, a three-drawer dresser, and a small desk made for the entirety of the furnishings. A tug on a sliding door revealed a bathroom the size of a phone booth. Next to it, a board fitted with four pegs served as a closet.

I stowed my belongings and made for the bed where I tossed a pillow aside and leaned back against the headboard. Surveying the opposite wall, I found myself staring into the riveting gaze of the Sattguru courtesy of a portrait I hadn't noticed when I came in. As far as eyes go, Dev's were humdingers. They gazed at me as if he knew my darkest secrets, the ones I did my best to hide but weren't important in the greater scheme of things. I stared at the eyes for a long time, trying to fathom the enigma of their attraction. No answer came, but by the time I quit looking, it occurred to me that maybe I wasn't such a bad guy after all. Everyone makes mistakes.

I must have fallen asleep pondering the mystery of my disordered existence. I awoke a couple of hours later from a recurrent dream in which some dirtbag murdered Dusty and kidnapped our children. Uncomfortably close to reality, the blasted nightmare had been repeating itself every three or four days, and I was damned tired of it. When it came to family, fate dealt me a bad hand. I'd lost Myra to suicide, Dusty to assassination, and my son Mike to his unrelenting resentment. To be fair, Mike wasn't much of a loss, but at the very least, fate could have gifted me a mentally sound son.

What bothered me most about the errand I'd undertaken was its almost certain failure. If Mike were at the ranch, the odds of finding him were slim, and the odds of convincing him to leave astronomical. Tamara expected results. Returning home without her brother would make for an indelible black mark in the book of fatherhood, one that might add her name to my personal losses column.

As for the home front, I didn't worry about Cleatzy's. I put Reg in charge and had no doubt he'd do a fine job. I'd instructed him to tell Gib Sutherland I was taking an extended vacation to recover from the shock of Dusty's murder. Gib would be livid, but tough rocks, he'd have to get over it. The money-grubbing weasel had the smarts to know Cleatzy's success was a one-man show and angry as he might be, adding a few shekels to his swollen coffers would take priority.

Napping in bed wouldn't help me find my son, so I got off my butt and went to the desk to study the map Baldy gave me. The map identified the street Prema and I came in on as Shiva Boulevard. It looked to be the ranch's only divided street and the only one opening onto the outside world. Shiva City's four other main streets ran north and south and carried Hindu-type names like Rama Road and Vishnu Avenue. The People of Light had divided the town into square blocks and given the cross streets English names. I'd taken Enlightenment Street to get to the guesthouse and despite its promising name, arrived in my room as benighted as ever.

A large, crosshatched area on the east edge of town identified Kali Court, the location of temporary housing. Next door lay something called the Serenity Center and the Sattguru Devesha Residential School. Gray blobs indicated a children's play area, the motor pool, and a brickyard.

The west side was home to the Krishna Amphitheater, the *sadhus'* Blissful Haven, and Harmony House–a.k.a. the administration building. The Mercantile Center, the Shiva City Clinic, and the municipal utilities were located nearby. A green-shaded area surrounding the town on three sides and labeled "P. O. L. Fields of Abundance" spoke to the group's agricultural prowess.

The part of the map that really got my attention was a scrawled notation above a circle in the middle of Kali Court, the temporary housing area. Though the handwriting wasn't much, it didn't take a lot of effort to make out the words "guest dining." I checked my watch—7:30 p.m. I'd forgotten dinner.

Shaking my head in disbelief, I pocketed the map and headed out the door.

Chapter 19

"Too bad. We quit serving a half hour ago," the guy wiping down the tables said. We stood in the middle of a large tent. I don't know what I expected, but a meal under an oversize army surplus canvas wasn't on the list. With its canvas sides rolled up to let in the evening air, the dining pavilion felt comfortable enough, but the number of picnic tables jammed onto its huge wooden floor meant aisle space was in short supply. I figured a seating capacity of three hundred in an area designed for two-thirds of that.

"So where can I get something to eat?" I asked.

He shrugged. "This was it. Guests and folks in temporary quarters eat here. Everyone else eats in their compound. We feed three hundred people three meals a day here, so the schedule is important."

I must have looked pathetic. He dropped his rag into a bucket and wiped his hands on his apron. "Let's see if Ma Ananda's crew left anything in cold storage. Come on. Follow me. By the way, my name is Al."

"My name's Cle— uh, Cliff. I appreciate your helping me out."

"No problem."

Al looked to be in his late twenties and wore his blue scrubs with a surgeon's cap. The headgear wasn't stylish, but it beat the hell out of a hairnet. Al didn't wear beads and used his given name. I assumed that put him in the unadvanced seeker category. He led me past a trio of now-empty buffet counters to an unimposing frame structure just outside the tent where he opened the door to reveal a kitchen populated by a half dozen workers in surgeon's caps washing pans and dishes. No one looked up as he grabbed a still-damp tray from a stack and handed it to me. He picked up a plate and utensils as we made our way to a walk-in cooler.

"You're in luck," he said after opening the door. "We still have leftovers." Al spooned a blob of rice onto the plate. The rice taken care of, he removed the lid from a large kettle and added another blob—green stuff this time.

"What is it?" I asked.

"Brown rice and bok choy. I can't heat it up for you because once we turn the stoves off, we're not allowed to turn 'em back on again until we make the next meal. Looks like the soup is all gone, but you're in luck, we have some carrot juice."

He poured the orange fluid from an oversized thermos into my mug. I tried to look appreciative. "Thanks, Al," I said with as much enthusiasm as I could muster.

"It's the least I could do," he replied. "Take your tray to one of the tables on the far side of the tent—they aren't washed yet."

A diner who'd lingered over the evening meal was scraping the remnants on her plate into a garbage can when I returned to the dining area. I put my tray down on an unwashed table and sat. Both Dusty and Professor Flanagan said the Manoneetas were vegetarians, but I'd somehow overlooked that their preferences would become my diet too.

I managed the cold glop on my plate without triggering my gag reflex. A shadow fell across my plate as I finished off the carrot juice. I looked up to see Al. Like Prema, the guy wasn't shy. He took a spot alongside me. I'd have preferred him across the table. Though the air had cooled, he'd spent most of the day working food service in ninety-degree heat and needed a shower.

"Decide to stay yet?" he asked.

"For now," I replied. "I get a work assignment tomorrow. I'm staying at the guest house, but I expect they'll set me up in temporary housing before long."

Al smiled. "Temp housing's not so bad, I've been here in Kali Court for two years and don't mind it at all."

"Two years in temporary housing?"

Al flushed. "I sort of messed up. But no matter how you slice it, life's been better since I joined up with the People of Light. On the outside, I bussed dishes and had so much trouble making the rent I slept on friends' couches. Here, I bus dishes, have a place to live, and the girls are easy. Manoneetas believe all work is honorable, so nobody looks down on me."

The guy seemed happy enough, but it was hard to imagine he would ever make it very far—even in Shiva City. "How'd you mess up?" I asked.

"My friend Elvin and I got assigned to kitchen duty at the Convergence Center in Santa Rosa. When our shift was over, I shoplifted a twelve-pack from the Quick Mart down the block, and we drank half of it while waiting for the shuttle. The driver caught us when we tried to smuggle the rest of the bottles on board. The Inner Circle wasn't happy we broke the 'No Alcohol or Drugs' rule, so they put us at the bottom of the housing list."

Now certain that Al wouldn't make it far in Shiva City, I asked, "Doesn't it get cold here in winter? How'd you ever stand it in a tent?"

"There were over ninety of us in temporary housing when the weather got bad, so the Inner Circle rented trailers. When the weather got better, the trailers went away, and it was back to the tents. Elvin and I were still at bottom of the list last fall, so it was the trailers again."

I shook my head. "Sounds harsh for a minor infraction."

Al smiled as if he hadn't a care in the world. "Sattguru Dev isn't happy about the trailers and wants everybody in permanent housing before the weather gets cold. Whatever Dev wants—he gets."

Al looked up. I followed his gaze and saw an older guy in a blue cowboy hat walking our way. Tall and rangy, maybe sixty-five years old, even his belt and boots were blue. The only non-blue on the guy's person: a gray-brown hat band.

"Well, what do you know," said Al. "Here comes Elvin now." He motioned for his friend to sit. "I was just telling Cliff here how we ended up at the bottom of the permanent housing list."

Elvin nodded a greeting and took a seat across from us. "I got big news, Al. Babba Pappa put me in charge of the Brickyard today. He's unhappy about production falling behind schedule, so he gave Babba Kam the boot."

Al shook his head. "Never heard of a seeker replacing a *sadhu*. Why, you don't even have your beads yet. You'll have a target on your back."

Elvin put his cowboy hat on the table—bottom side up. "Not worried. Nobody important likes Babba Kam. The I. C. is sending him up to Fargo to start a pod there. If there's a worse place to send a *sadhu*, I don't know of it."

I felt like they were speaking a foreign language. "How about giving a poor grunt a break, what's with all this Babba and I. C. business?"

Elvin looked at me as if I were a particularly slow student. "Most people know this stuff before they get here. *Sadhu* means holy person. Sattguru Dev chooses especially deserving Manoneetas for this honor. They're the ones you see in purple."

"I know about all that, but what's with all the Babbas, the pods, and the I. C?"

Elvin frowned. "You're an impatient little cuss. I'm getting around to it."

I tried to look chastised.

"*Sadhu* men are given the title *Babba* and the women *Sri*. The I. C. is short for Inner Circle, the top twelve *sadhus* in the People of Light. Babba Pappa is Devesha's second in command. He's been with Dev for twenty years and oversees housing and security."

A pause signaled my lesson was at an end. Since Elvin already considered me hopeless, I opted to forgo asking about pods and congratulated him on his promotion. Smart move. The guy beamed.

"Babba Pappa called me into his office himself and asked why we're so behind in making adobe bricks. I knew then the boss was in trouble. *Sadhus* never ask a seeker's opinion on anything—especially when the seeker doesn't have his beads yet. I told him the truth. We'll never fix the housing shortage as long as Babba Kam treats his workers like they're doing him a favor whenever they turn out a brick. Then I let him know that most of the crew do whatever they want to—like playing cards or disappearing for naps. I said that some days they move so slow they'd lose a foot race to a snail on crutches. And just like that, he made me head of the Brickyard."

"Well, he needed to know," I offered. "Otherwise, newcomers like me would be stuck in temporary housing forever."

Elvin nodded. "And here's the best part. If we have enough housing for winter, Babba Pappa promised me I'll get my beads. Just imagine, me a swami. I'm gonna work those loafers like dogs. No matter how hot it is or how tired they are, that crew is gonna sweat. I don't care if they're crying and puking their guts out, they're gonna make adobe. Babba Pappa says any of 'em give me crap, they'll get sent to South Dakota for re-education."

Al cut in. "Sure, Elvin. And when Dev picks out your new name, you'll become Swami Hardass."

I could see Elvin wasn't enlightened yet. His face grew an angry red. It didn't take much enlightenment on my part to recognize a deteriorating situation. I'd been getting good information and didn't want a squabble to interrupt the flow. Time to sideline the shouting match. "Say, Elvin, I can't help but notice your blue boots. I've sold some footwear in my day but never imagined you could buy anything like that. How do you keep them looking so good when you spend your day in the Brickyard?"

Elvin seemed as happy to ignore Al as I was to tone things down. "These are my dress boots," he explained. "I don't wear 'em to the yard. Didn't buy 'em blue, I found the right color Krylon and spray painted 'em."

The toxic atmosphere seemed to subside. Another wardrobe question or two and peace would be restored. "Your hat doesn't look sprayed. Where'd you get it?"

Elvin picked up his hat, studied it, and plopped it on his head. "You can buy 'em at the Shiva City Mercantile Center. It used to be a special order, but the company that makes 'em ended up selling so many that now there's a standard color: Shiva City blue. My hatband is custom made though, and I ain't about to paint it."

"You know," I said, "I've sold a lot of hats over the years and looked through hundreds of catalogs but never saw anything with a band like yours. It's not alligator, or python, or any of the custom leathers I'm familiar with. What is it?"

Elvin removed his hat. Holding it in front of him, he rotated it and inspected the band. "I've worn cowboy hats on and off for over fifty years, and I can tell you there's not another band like it anywhere on the face of the earth. I had it made from a piece of my colon."

All I could manage was a "what?"

"About ten years ago, I had surgery. I worked in hospital house-keeping, so I knew it would get tested and tossed. I didn't want that to happen to a part of me so to make a long story short, one of the lab guys was stealing drugs from the crash carts. I let him know I'd rat him out if he didn't get my colon for me. He did, and a friend who does taxidermy tanned it. He did a nice job. It's been ten years, and it looks as good as new."

I blanched, felt the congealed blob in my stomach rumble.

Al looked disgusted, then angry. His face flashed red, and he rose halfway from his seat. "That's the sickest thing I ever heard of. And they put you in charge of a crew? The kind of guy who'd go to a morgue and think lunch?"

So much for my attempts to defuse the situation. I stood to go. "Excuse me," I said. "I have a big orientation tomorrow and should get back to the guesthouse to meditate."

By the time I reached the edge of the tent, they were trading accusations about who had the most offensive body odor—Al or a week-old corpse. Though I didn't know much about Manoneetas, my gut told me that neither Al nor Elvin would make it very far along the path to nirvana.

Chapter 20

The chirps and tweets of birds outside the window brought me back to consciousness. Who'd have thought New Mexico would be home to so many. I didn't mind the interruption—their gentle chatter left me feeling all was well with the world. After drifting off again, I woke to realize someone with a flute joined the chorus. My eyelids parted when a delicately played violin joined the ensemble. As my mind cleared, I identified the source of the sound as the portrait of the Sattguru on the opposite wall.

The pastoral sounds faded, replaced by a deep, low mechanical drone coming from Dev's portrait, which slowly illuminated as the tone grew louder. I recognized the hum as a male voice pronouncing a drawn-out letter O. The guy dragged it out for half a lifetime before closing his lips to make an M sound. It took a bit to realize what was going on, but I'd read enough about hippies and mystics to recognize the great Om, a sound supposed to bring inner peace. The Om slowly began repeating itself. I tried to relax into it and was almost there when the birds returned and the light over Dev went out. After a bit more twittering, a new, unhurried voice came from the portrait's hidden speakers.

Welcome guest. Welcome to the wonder that is Shiva City, the home of the new consciousness and the hope of the world. It is our wish that the joy and contentment you find here today will bring you closer to your true divinity. Each of our residents has dedicated their lives to building a world of light, a new world where each soul is worthy of respect, where hatred is unknown, and where Sattguru Devesha's teachings guide us gently along the path to self-actualization.

Not bad as far as alarm clocks go—if you could make your way through the gobbledygook. After another minute of flute, chirps, and twitters, yet another voice came on, this with the most important information of the day.

Breakfast will be served in the Kali Court dining area between seven and eight-thirty a.m. Shaanti.

Mike hadn't been in Shiva City long, so there was a good chance he'd be staying in Kali Court's temporary housing and taking his meals in the big tent. My plan: locate Mike before he recognized me and went into hiding. At least then I'd know he was at the ranch. Later, when I better understood the inner workings of Shiva City, I would formulate a plan for making my approach.

After a quick shower, I checked the mirror to see if my beard needed trimming. It did, but worried tidy facial hair would make me more recognizable, I abstained. My ear had yet to take to the ring I put into it. In fact, it had gone beyond minor redness and become swollen. I took it out. It didn't do much to disguise me anyway. A bigger concern was the vegetarian diet. The pounds I gained were an important part of my deception. I couldn't afford to lose them. The thought of the amount of brown rice and boiled green stuff I would need to ingest weighed on me. With that pleasant thought in mind, I squared my shoulders, put on my cowboy clothes and sunglasses, and went out to meet the world.

At the bottom of the stairway, I encountered a blond seeker with a wispy beard, flexing his muscles and doing deep-breathing exercises.

Seeing me, he abandoned his routine and asked if I was going to breakfast. I allowed that I was, and he stepped in beside me.

"What do you think of Shiva City so far?" he asked.

"I don't know," I answered. "Just got in yesterday afternoon."

"Last night, for me," he replied. "I've been a seeker for over a year. My pod's *sadhu* said I was ready for the next level and sent me down here to get my beads. Me, face to face with the Sattguru himself—unbelievable."

"Where you from?" I asked.

"You really are new," he replied. "It's bad form to ask other Manoneetas about hometowns or families. Many find it necessary to put aside the ties binding them to their old lives so they might focus on their quest. If someone brings up their past, then it's okay to talk about it."

"Sorry, I didn't know." The information threw a spanner into my plan to find Mike. I'd hoped passing references to Iowa might elicit mention of a Mike who'd lived there. "Any other *faux pas* I should know about?"

"Not really, there aren't many serious mistakes a grunt can make. In general, avoid asking people about their pre-Manoneeta lives. Never ask a beaded seeker or *sadhu* their birth name."

"Doesn't sound so hard," I said as the search for my son grew more complicated. If Mike managed to get his beads, a good chunk of Shiva City would know him only by his swami name.

"Say," I said. "You're the second person I've heard mention pods. What are they?"

My companion beamed. Except for Elvin, everyone I encountered seemed to be all smiles. I was beginning to think of the ever-present grins as "the look"—upturned lips designed to keep you at a distance rather than welcome you in.

"The pods are People of Light Development Centers. There are some 250 of them scattered throughout the world, and each is run by a *sadhu*. People visit them to get counseling and discover the fundamental truth of Sattguru Dev's teaching. Most Manoneetas never visit the ranch, and of those that do, most come only to get their beads. I'm so happy to be here I could fly like an eagle."

I didn't share his enthusiasm. "Now that you've come all this way, why don't you stay?"

"I'd like to, but I can't. I'm an investment banker and can do more for the People by contributing my *hissa* than here in Shiva City."

"A *hissa*? What's that?"

My companion's smile was full of pride. "Sixty percent of my income. Those of us who are fortunate enough, contribute financially. Those who can't, contribute in other ways. In a way, I envy you. Staying at the ranch—it's a dream for most Manoneetas."

"I don't get it," I replied, "you make financial donations but can't live here. I hop off the bus, and as far as I know, can stay if I want."

My rich guy walking companion responded with a spacey smile. "You are here because this is your destiny. Mine is to live in Boston and earn the money we need to create the new world."

I still didn't get it, but by then we were approaching the chow tent, and he turned the conversation to the weather. I got into the food line dreading the swill in store for me but was pleasantly surprised by a large bowl of oatmeal and raisins covered with brown sugar. I grabbed three bananas and made for a table.

"You can't do that," a voice behind me called out. I turned around, resigned to the loss of extra bananas.

I approached the server nearest the fruit piles. "Sorry," I mumbled, "didn't know there was a limit on bananas."

Again, the spacey smile, this time from a young woman who might have been twenty. "You can eat as much as you want, but you need to sit at the grunts' table." A pointed finger directed my attention to a long table occupied by a dozen newcomers in civilian clothes.

I joined the group. Most of the diners around us looked to be under thirty, and most wore cowboy hats. They must have been outdoor workers. Too bad their mothers didn't teach them to remove their headgear when eating. I estimated the size of the breakfast gathering at 200, about two-thirds of the population of Kali Court. Between the blue duds and hats, it was hard to pick out possible Mikes. Engrossed in my observation of the crowd, I neglected the social niceties.

An elbow jostled me. "I said, are you going to dye your hat?"

I turned to the baby-faced young man at my side. "Hadn't thought of it," I replied absently.

"The hats at the Mercantile Center cost an arm and a leg. Maybe you can spray it."

I shuddered at the thought of painting a top-of-the-line Stetson. After muttering something about a straw hat being better for the desert anyway, I bent over my tray hoping he'd lose interest in a conversation. Things went downhill from there.

The oatmeal was made with water instead of milk.

We stood in front of the Mercantile Center, our first stop on my personal tour of Shiva City.

"You may have noticed we have no telephones, network or cable TV, no radios, or newspapers," Babba Bahru announced.

Getting Bahru's name right was going to be a chore. I'd never think of him as anyone but Baldy. "I haven't been here long enough to pick up on it," I replied.

My companion raised his index finger. "In Shiva City, we seek to avoid the distractions of modern life. The path of the seeker is difficult enough without them."

I faked a nod of agreement. "Makes sense to me." Actually, nothing about the place made sense, but hey, why deflate the guy?

Bahru nodded and pointed to a long, single-story adobe building with multiple entrances. "The Mercantile Center is where you can buy seeker clothing, personal necessities like toothpaste, books on Sattguru Devesha's philosophy, videotapes, and the like. The selection of videotapes is extensive. The People may not watch network television, but we're not hermits. The center stocks the latest in music, plus classic Hollywood videos, and quality literature up through 1960."

No books, TV, or movies from the last quarter-century? So much for keeping up with the times.

"Is this where I can mail letters, get stationery and postage stamps?" I asked. "My daughter will want to know where I am."

Baldy gave me the sappy smile. "Shiva City has no Post Office. The nearest one is in Santa Rosa."

"Then how do people get their mail?" I asked.

"Most of them don't bother. Shiva City is a special place. Those who live here have given up everything to follow the Sattguru—careers, money, family, friends—all of them stumbling stones on the path to enlightenment. Four of ten will become *sadhus*. On the outside, only one in twenty earn their purple. If you want to mail a letter, you can get a pass to take the shuttle to town."

"A pass?"

"It's free and for your own good. Last fall, two of the People tried to hitchhike to Santa Rosa. The locals beat them so badly they were hospitalized. One ended up in a wheelchair. It's important to know who is at the ranch and who isn't."

Good news, bad news. No need to hitchhike into town to sneak a hamburger or send a letter, but when I got there, the locals would hate me. Of course, slaving for the People of Light fifty-six hours a week wouldn't allow much time for outings.

We continued our tour with Baldy pointing out such highlights as the Serenity Center, Blissful Haven—the gated neighborhood where Dev and the *sadhus* lived, the outdoor meditation grounds, and the Sattguru Devesha Residential School. The children of Manoneetas lived at the school, rather than with their parents, a perk freeing future saints from the distraction of childcare. My guide seemed especially proud of the Shiva City Municipal Utilities building.

"We generate our own electricity and maintain our own water services. Our sewage treatment plant is first-rate. Water is precious here. That's why we use single-ply toilet paper, and the Kali Court residents use privies. Four days a week a tanker arrives with a supplemental water supply. We built a delivery pad and hookup outside the fence so the trucks can unload there. Our streets are too narrow for the big rigs."

Baldy checked his watch, leading me to believe keeping track of the time did not count as a distraction. "We'd better go for lunch," he said. "We'll be eating at one of the communal centers."

Adobe walls surrounded each of the Shiva City residential blocks. The outer walls of the two-story residences formed part of the fence that enclosed each compound. Baldy opened a wooden gate located halfway between a pair of corner residences and beckoned me to follow. After closing the gate, he gestured at a single-story building occupying the center of the square created by its neighbors.

"The communal building in the center of each compound houses a kitchen, dining area, showers, and laundry facilities," explained Baldy. "The residents of the *haciendas* surrounding it plan the compound's meals and are responsible for keeping the buildings and grounds tidy. Since each compound accommodates something like eighty people, there are enough hands to keep the workload manageable. Once you get out of temporary housing, you'll live in a place like this."

When we entered directly into the communal building's dining room, a beaded seeker, female, in scrubs and a surgeon's cap approached us. "Babba Bahru, welcome!" she exclaimed, giving him a hug and lengthy kiss on the mouth.

When the kiss reached its conclusion, Baldy spoke. "Ma Laxmi, *shaanti*. I brought a newcomer for lunch. Can you accommodate us?"

Hand on her hip, she gave her pelvis a forward thrust and flashed a grin. "I can accommodate you anytime you want, Bahru."

Baldy, oblivious to Laxmi's come-on, asked, "What's for lunch?"

A sigh escaped Laxmi's pouted lips. "Potato burritos, rice, and for tea, Red Zinger." She pointed to a short cafeteria counter. "Help yourself."

Finally, food I could get into. Piles of red and green peppers sat beside a chafing dish of already-rolled burritos. The rice dish looked passable but was flecked with unidentifiable, black-colored bits that might have been anything from dead flies to dried fruit. I pointed to one with my fork and looked at Baldy with a cocked eyebrow.

"Dried ancho pepper flakes," he said. "Not very hot, but a great taste."

I piled a heap on a second plate, added a tea bag and hot water to the tray, and waited for Baldy. He caught up and led the way to an unoccupied table where he began a long-winded discourse on the finer points of Dev's teaching. I tried hard to pay attention, but after packing my lunch away, dozed off. When my head bobbed, I roused myself. Baldy, in love with the sound of his voice, hadn't noticed my lack of enthusiasm.

When we left the communal center, Baldy continued his babble, a lecture that continued until our return to Harmony House. When we arrived at the Orientation Office, he told me to take a seat and disappeared into the bowels of the office behind the reception counter.

He must have taken his time before returning. I awoke from a well-earned snooze when a coughing sound from behind the counter beckoned me to return to the ranks of the suffering. I rose and rejoined Baldy. The man let out a low whistle and looked up at me over the top of his reading glasses.

"Most unusual. I've done orientations for over two years and have yet to see a newcomer invited to permanent housing on his first full day. Do you know someone here in Shiva City?"

"Not a soul," I replied.

"Then without a doubt, you have been called to Shiva City, and without a doubt, you are fortunate indeed. I shouldn't mention this, but most newcomers find temporary housing to be a trying experience. Tent life's lack of privacy, the extremes of hot and cold, the privies, and the unending dust go far in testing the commitment of our new arrivals. Your adobe home will be cool in the daytime and warm at night. You'll have a private room, indoor toilets, and the guidance of established Manoneetas. The *haciendas* might be home to the occasional scorpion or biting centipede, but they are comfortable accommodations indeed."

I felt my flesh crawl. "Scorpions?"

"Not much to worry about. The scorpions in this part of the state are small and though their stings may cause minor discomfort, they are not toxic. The centipedes are the bigger problem. Like the scorpions, they are sometimes attracted to our cool, dark adobe structures. Centipede bites can be very painful."

Scorpions? Flesh-eating centipedes in the choice accommodations? I cursed my son for his choice of cults. If he joined the Hare Krishnas, I'd be looking for him in almost-heaven West Virginia.

Baldy plowed on. "Your *hacienda* is located at the corner of Tranquility Street and Durga Drive. Go there with your belongings between five and six o'clock. That way, you'll arrive after most residents have come home from work but before the evening meal."

"You've been assigned to the nine-p.m. spiritual development group. It meets Mondays, Wednesdays, and Saturdays in the Serenity Center. These folks will form the basis of your socialization, meditation coaching, and Tantric training. Though we try to balance the number of men and women in the spiritual development groups, they reflect the composition of our new arrivals. Your group will skew female which might be a problem for the Tantric sessions but make for more peaceful group encounters. Your first session is tonight. Any questions?"

My mind still back at the scorpions, I accepted the piece of paper he handed me and shook my head.

"And now for your work assignment," Baldy continued. "Most newcomers are assigned fieldwork, but once again you're proving the exception to the rule. We're trying to speed up the construction of permanent housing, so the Inner Circle has assigned you to the Brickyard. You'll be making the adobe blocks we use for construction. Be there tomorrow at nine."

Visions of Elvin driving his puking brickyard workers like dogs assaulted me. The powers that be gave him the okay to send slackers to South Dakota for re-education. I didn't know much about South Dakota, but if there was any place in the Lower Forty-Eight as isolated as New Mexico, the home state of the Mitchell Corn Palace would be a contender. And then there was Flanagan's mention of some folks never coming back. Based on what I had seen so far, I doubted the Manoneetas were killing anyone. The bigger problem: no way I'd find Mike if I got sent away and couldn't return to the ranch.

"Are you sure there hasn't been a mistake?" I asked Baldy. "Making bricks doesn't sound like a proper assignment for someone who's been called. And really, if it came right down to it, I wouldn't mind working in the fields. You could give my assignment to somebody who isn't cut out for farm work or has allergies to pollen."

Baldy looked sympathetic but handed me my work papers. "Cliff, all work is honorable, and Manoneetas serve when and where they're called. If the Inner Circle began making work assignments based on preference, there'd be chaos. Remember all your effort will be for the good of the community. *Shaanti*."

The tour over, I went to the Mercantile Center and laid out an outrageous sum for a pair of blue work gloves and a tube of sunblock. At the end of my first week, I'd be paid in scrip for my brickyard work. Since the Manoneeta means of exchange was valid only in Shiva City, once I ran out of funds, I'd have nothing to spend in the outside world. The only way to get real cash would be to have it wired to me.

A dollarless Manoneeta would find it difficult indeed to leave the ranch.

Chapter 21

I took in the compound at the corner of Durga Drive and Serenity Street. Save for the blue paint covering every wall, the interior courtyard proved identical to the one Baldy and I visited earlier in the day. I made for what looked to be the entrance to a building I guessed to be my new home. I knocked and waited. A young woman barely out of her teens, her shoulder-length hair held in place by an Indian headband, answered the door. A half dozen turquoise bracelets adorned her wrists. Though located hundreds of miles from the reservation, the Manoneetas seemed to be in love with everything Navajo.

"You must be the old guy Prema talked about," she said. "You're gonna be in the minority here in Shiva City, but don't worry, nobody will hold your age against you. Once you get rid of the cowboy shirt and pink suitcase, you'll blend right in." We entered a stubby hallway where she stopped to point out a bulletin board.

"This is where you'll find your service assignments."

"Service assignments?" I asked.

She gave me a gap-toothed smile. "Each of us is responsible for the well-being of the other residents of the compound. Our *hacienda* prepares meals for one week a month. The next week we're in charge of our communal center. We clean the showers and toilets, keep the laundry room spic and span, and make sure the public rooms are picked up. The week after that we take care of the compound's grounds—the plantings and stuff like that. The fourth week, we rest. Then it starts all over again. By the way, I'm Ma Astra."

"Nice to meet you, but how does everyone have the energy to work, much less to stay organized, when they have seven-day-a-week jobs?"

Astra laughed. "Ma Shivani, the mayor of our compound makes it easy. She sees we have everything we need for our service assignments and takes care of the scheduling. We have the best food and nicest compound in Shiva City. Still, you'll want to watch out for her. She's a real maneater,"

"Hates men, huh?"

"Just the opposite, she can't get enough of them. The problem is she chews on her partner when she gets going. We may believe in freely sharing our sexual selves, but once is enough for most guys. I can see why. The bruises and bite marks look nasty."

I made a mental note to avoid Ma Shivani. "Thanks for the heads up, but I don't plan on getting intimate with anybody for a while."

It took a moment for Astra to come back from outer space. "I shouldn't gossip. You're new, and still believe you have control over your life. If you're fated to spend time with someone, it will happen. It's just that Shivani likes to hit on new arrivals."

I smiled. "I'll avoid enclosed spaces if she's nearby."

The vacant smile again. "Some of us think privacy is overrated."

"Is Ma Shivani one of those?"

"Don't worry about something that might never happen. Prema was right when she said you were a bundle of nerves. A few months with us, you'll be the man you were created to be."

"Ma Prema lives here?"

"How do you think you scored *hacienda* status your second day? She talked us into inviting you because she believes our *hacienda* will be more of a real community with an old guy living here. The rest of us thought you'd be a pain, but Prema said there's more to you than meets the eye and that was enough to convince us. She has second sight you know."

"She told me."

Astra nodded. The spacey gap-toothed look again. "Our *hacienda* is blessed. There are two of us with special gifts."

I wondered what could top telling the future. "When do I meet the other one?" I asked.

"You have. It's me. I have out-of-body experiences. My spirit and my body can be two different places at once. It's called astral projection. That's why Dev named me Astra."

We passed into a large room, its wooden floor covered with throw pillows and Navajo rugs. Opposite a vacant futon, a television and stereo set held center stage. The standard portrait of Dev overlooked the works. It was hard to miss the most prominent feature of the space: two big guys draped over floor cushions, snoring like lawnmowers at full throttle.

Astra raised her voice enough to be heard over the din. "The one in front of the window is Swami Raj and the other is Swami Madhuk. They had a hard day picking beans and didn't make it to their rooms upstairs. Actually, most days are hard for them. They generally collapse as soon as they get in. Prema likes to say they've perfected the yoga of sleeping. They'll be out like lights for another hour."

I had visions of myself sprawled among the sleeping giants, comatose after slaving for Elvin in the heat of the Brickyard. "Where's everybody else?"

"This is our week to rest, or we'd be busy with community assignments. Some of us might be out running errands or visiting friends. Most are in their rooms napping or meditating. Ma Nakti, Amanda, and Ma Star are in Albuquerque dancing at the Silver Spur. Nakti doesn't have a work assignment because she earns enough in four weeks to make *hissa*. She dances for a month and then comes back to the ranch for a month. Amanda and Star just got their beads and are hoping to do the same. I tried to talk them out of it. They have to pay *hissa* every day they're away, so it's a tough row to hoe. Besides, who wants to be away from Dev and Shiva City?"

I wondered if Mike might be away from the ranch, working to earn money for the cult. "How much is this *hissa*?" I asked. "And how does it work?"

Astra gap-toothed me again. "*Hissa* is different for everybody and must be approved by the Inner Circle. Ordinary people usually don't earn enough to make *hissa*. The only way Nakti has the dough is by being super friendly to the Silver Spur's clients. Get my drift?"

I got it. As far as I knew Mike possessed no marketable skills, and I doubted the local Albuquerque cowboys would be motivated to stuff money down his G-string. Unless my son had an off-ranch work assignment, he'd be in Shiva City.

My new housemate pointed to a narrow flight of stairs. "Your room is on the second floor. That kinda sucks because we have a pair of toilets on first. If they're busy you can use those in the community center. Quiet hours start at ten, and videos and music must be at low volume. Some of us are screamers during moments of passion, and that's the one quiet hour exception. Don't complain about the occasional late-night shriek, and you should be okay."

"I've had a long day and have a spiritual development session tonight. Think I'll join the ranks of the nappers. By the way, my name is Cliff."

"Too bad you didn't get Clint, like that cowboy guy. So, is it Clifton or Clifford?"

I hadn't thought about that one. "Cliff," I replied, "just plain Cliff."

I pulled off my boots and sank into my bed. The spiritual development seminar didn't amount to much. I heard most of it over thirty years ago in freshman-year World Religions class. The only new thing seemed to be something called dynamic meditation. Instead of sitting quietly, a seeker would search for enlightenment by expending large amounts of energy. I'd have been interested in hearing more about it, but the option was available only to *sadhus* and beaded seekers.

There were just seven of us grunts in the seminar—four young women and three even younger men. When class broke up, I stayed behind to chat with the other guys. Forget intelligent conversation. All they could talk about was their female classmates and how far they'd get during the tantric sessions. Older, wiser, and clued in by Professor Flanagan, I felt sorry for them: first, for their out-of-control hormones and then for the inevitable trips to the Shiva City Clinic to get their equipment checked.

I was about to climb into the sack when I remembered that a scorpion or man-eating centipede might be my nighttime companion. I sighed, stripped the sheets and blankets, turned the mattress, and inspected the pillows. All clear. I reassembled everything, unhappy that the examination would become a nightly routine. I wasn't worried about waking up in time for my first day on the job. There were speakers in my room and the portrait of Dev was equipped with a light attached to the frame.

My bed free of critters, and certain that I'd be awakened by the sound of chirping birds, I climbed into the sack and closed my eyes.

I awakened from deep sleep to the feel of a scorpion crawling across my chest. Without a second's hesitation, I pulled back the sheet and used a hard, horizontal swat to knock it off me. I raised my legs, then slammed them down preparatory to an attempt to clear the bed in a single leap. The effort was a failure. I caught my leg on something, heard a loud thump, and ended up on the floor. A hop upright and I was at the opposite wall.

An irritated voice came from the floor next to the bed. "Jesus, Buddha, Joseph. Some guys might have been disappointed, but no one's ever kicked me out of bed before."

"Sorry, I thought you were a scorpion."

"And the compliments just keep coming. You really know how to destroy a mood. I just wanted to rub your tummy a bit."

"You missed. You were a little high," I observed.

"It was dark. I think I better get back to my room. You might be cute, but you're more trouble than you're worth."

I recognized the voice. "Ma Prema?"

"None other."

I flicked on the overhead light. "Hope you're not hurt. By the way, thanks for getting me out of temporary housing. I appreciate it."

Prema unbundled herself, grabbed the bed to pull herself up, then stood. "You could have fooled me," she muttered and made for the door. "When I told Astra you were a little uptight, I had no idea your nerves were completely shot."

I didn't reply. There's no way a guy can talk himself out of a blunder like that. At least she didn't chew on me.

After closing the door, I turned out the light and walked over to the window to collect myself. The turn of a metal lever and a push allowed me to open it. Cool air rushed in. The crescent moon, even brighter than when I'd ridden the bus, lit the roofs of the neighboring *haciendas*. Two a.m., the courtyard was empty, and Shiva City quiet. No lighted windows, no streetlights, no pedestrians. I heard no radios or cars. No conversations drifted up from below. Coyotes whooped it up in the distance.

The desert is a lonely place.

Chapter 22

When I got to the Brickyard, I found Elvin leaning against the side of a pickup waiting for me. "Let's go," he said. "Today you're going to learn about making adobe."

The passenger seat was occupied, so I walked around to the back of the truck and climbed over the tailgate to join the guy and girl in the back. He was in my orientation group. I didn't recognize her. Maybe she was old enough to be out of high school. Neither had the Manoneeta look. I said hi, and they returned my greeting with noncommittal nods. Instead of taking us into the Brickyard, Elvin drove through the city, past the vegetable fields, into the scrub. We rode in silence until the truck stopped next to the face of an excavation in a small hill a few hundred yards from the Pecos.

Elvin opened his door and shouted, "Everybody out." My companions and I clambered to the ground and followed him past a pair of oversized skid loaders to a house-sized pile of dirt. After checking that we were paying attention, he pointed to the excavation.

"You can't make adobe from just any old dirt," he said. "You've got to have the right mix of sand and clay. We're lucky here at the ranch because this spot has some of the best adobe dirt you'll find anywhere. Every other Monday a crew comes out here to dig the dirt for the next two weeks. Most of you will never work here, but I thought you ought to see it."

Since I'd never work at the site, I tuned out while Elvin droned on about cubic feet, screening dirt, and re-rod mesh. He walked us from place to place, pointing out good dirt and bad, all the while regaling us with stories of ruined loads and bad bricks. After an hour of herding us around, he hustled us back into the truck and drove us to the Brickyard.

The tour proved to be the highlight of the day. I soon found myself shoveling dirt into a wheelbarrow and unloading it into one of those tanks that farmers use to water cows. Each of us turned out to be responsible for making a batch of adobe wet bricks—start to finish. Mixing up a tankful of muddy sludge was the first part of the task. When the glop reached the rim, I had to shovel it back out and haul it, wheelbarrow load by wheelbarrow load, to the forming lot where I shoveled it into wood-frame molds.

I found the stupidity of hoisting dirt in and out of an aboveground stock tank infuriating. Until Elvin took over, brickmakers worked in crews, a system he believed encouraged slackers to take advantage of the more productive staffers. According to my more experienced co-workers, his arrangement, now in its second day, was even less productive than the workflow he inherited. Though years of dancing had kept me in shape, after two hours of shoveling I wondered if I'd make it through the day. My muscles ached, mud caked my boots, and I was dizzy from the heat. Lunch wasn't that far away. I'd make it until then but doubted I would last the afternoon.

Dev, in one of his rare hands-on moments, came up with the system. Completely taken with his vision of an earth-friendly adobe city, he'd inserted himself into every aspect of the brick-making process. Though the guru considered machine technology good enough for collecting raw materials, he wanted the building blocks of his city to be the product of self-sacrifice and love. One thing for sure, his system got the self-sacrifice part of the equation right.

I was wondering whether my daughter's love was worth the misery when the sound of raised voices caught my attention. A glance over my shoulder revealed Elvin and a pair of brickmakers engaged in a vehement disagreement. Though I didn't understand what they were arguing about, he and the boys had gotten into a shoving match. When a particularly strong push detached Elvin's hat from his head, the other guy caught it, threw it on the ground, and stomped on it. The action appeared to take the wind out of everyone's sails. Elvin grabbed his hat and tramped off. The brickmakers went back to their work.

Elvin was nowhere to be seen when I joined the rest of the crew for lunch. The other workers looked as exhausted as I was. Save for a few remarks comparing Elvin to Adolf Hitler, nobody said much. My head had just begun to nod when I heard a woman asking for Amrit and Steven.

I looked up to see five pink-clad security guards, three women and two men, all packing side arms. Amrit and Steven stood up. The shortest woman spoke. "Guys, I hate to do this, but you know we have a policy against physical violence in Shiva City. Pushing and shoving another Manoneeta is assault. You need to come to Harmony House to explain your actions."

Everyone seemed cordial enough. Amrit and Steven joined the security detail with embarrassed smiles. One of the guards patted Steven on the back, and they left. I looked at my companions with a raised eyebrow. "What'll happen to them?" I asked.

I'd given up on getting an answer when Tanak, a beaded seeker, said, "We won't be seeing them again. Fighting is high on the no-no list. Someone will clean out their rooms this afternoon. They're gone."

Cherie, who'd ridden in the back of the pickup with me, asked, "Where will they go?"

Tanak shrugged. "No idea. If the folks at Harmony House think they can do anything with them, they'll be off to the Research and Re-education Center in South Dakota. One thing for sure, neither one will be seen in Shiva City again."

Cherie shook her head. "Seems harsh."

"Maybe, maybe not," Tanak replied. "We're trying to build a new world here. Not everyone is up to the task. What happens to those who can't make it is no concern of ours."

"Doesn't seem very caring," Cherie remarked.

Tanak shrugged. "You can't make an omelet without breaking an egg. We can't let the losers take us down."

His remark brought the conversation to a close.

———

Elvin returned to the Brickyard as our lunch break was about to end. "Okay, you yo-yos. Back to work. We'll be back to workin' in teams this afternoon. Newcomers, report to Work Area Five. Everybody else, go back to your assignments from last week."

I got up, ready to join the rest of the group, when I saw Elvin motioning to me. I joined him. His hat looked the worse for the wear, and its human-colon hatband was missing. "That worked out better than I expected," he said. "Two days of working alone instead of on a team and my biggest gold bricks crack and get hauled away. Baba Pappa says I'll have a couple of new workers tomorrow. The two of us are all buddy-buddy right now, but I've got the feeling I'm being set up."

Apparently, our evening conversation in the Kali Court dining tent put me in the position of Elvin's confidant. The guy must have been hard up for friends. "How's that?" I asked.

"I found out Dev wants an indoor meditation hall, one that'll accommodate four thousand, and he wants it made from adobe. As far as I know, it'd be the biggest adobe building in the country, and guess who just got told he'll get to oversee making the bricks? The way I figure, I'd need half the population of Shiva City."

"Is it even possible to build an adobe structure that big?" I asked. "They're going to need engineers and consultants up the ying."

Elvin shook his head. "If we don't have 'em here, they'll find them in the pods. I shoulda kept my mouth shut about problems in the Brickyard. This meditation hall project is impossible, and when everything goes to hell, Babba Pappa will see to it I take the blame. The Inner Circle gets mad enough, and I could end up at the Research and Re-education Center. I hear it's a bad place. If I don't like it there, where would I go? Don't have a family to speak of. That's the one bad thing about us People of Light: once you get used to bein' on the inside, leavin' is hard. Well, I better speed up and get to Station Five before the rest of you." He clapped me on the shoulder and strode ahead.

After a long, brutal morning, working as a team was a breeze. We turned out slop and fed the molds until late afternoon when we removed older, hardened bricks from their forms and turned them on their edges to promote uniform drying. I finished the day physically and mentally exhausted. Happy to have survived, I tucked my mud-caked work gloves into my belt and made for a dejected-looking Elvin sitting on the tailgate of a pickup.

"Say Elvin, you and I both know the Sattguru's workflow won't hold up to the new project. The way to manage this operation is to handle the mud with mixers and chutes like they do with cement."

"Figured that out a long time ago, but nobody wants to tell Dev his plan for making bricks stinks. He makes such a big thing about the sacrifice and love going into each handmade brick. I'm screwed."

No one would ever have called Elvin optimistic. His third day on the job and the guy was defeated. With an attitude like that, he would never have made a Cleatzy's salesman.

"So, give him something better," I said. "Back in college, I learned Buddhists like to paint prayers on slips of paper and put them on sticks outdoors They say each flutter in the wind sends the prayer to the gods. Tell Dev you'll put a tiny paper prayer in each brick, and his new center will be built of prayers. Or better yet, a little slip of paper with wise words from the world's great religious leaders. That way, the meditation center will hold the wisdom of the ages. He makes such a big deal about searching for the truth at the heart of all religions, he'll love it."

Elvin brightened up and slapped his knee. "Not a bad idea, but you'll never make a salesman, Cliff. The way to do it is to put one of Dev's sayings on each little paper."

I'd already thought of that, but it seemed too brownnose. Apparently, Elvin believed pandering was the way to go.

"Better yet," I chimed in. "Lose the sacrifice thing and build up the love and wisdom part."

Elvin stood, stretched, and headed back into the Brickyard. "Well, I better go check the hoses to see if we're ready for tomorrow."

He'd gone about twenty feet when he called over his shoulder. "You can go with me and do the talkin' when I take the idea to Babba Pappa. Somehow you got a way with words that softens people up."

It's called being a salesman, Elvin.

I left the Serenity Center and headed back to the *hacienda* no closer to finding Mike and still struggling with the finality of Dusty's death. My first encounter group had been a doozy. The last to arrive, I found my fellow grunts seated cross-legged on blue pillows and surrounded by space heaters. Our guide, a robe-clad *sadhu* named Sri Leela, waited until I sat and went into a song and dance about the defenses the unenlightened use to hide their true selves from others. Unwashed and misled souls that we were, the walls we'd built around ourselves kept us from seeing our internal beauty.

The first step in freeing ourselves from this self-inflicted incarceration turned out to be removing our clothing. I guessed Sri Leela was already free. She got to keep her robe. We rose and did as Leela instructed. Nobody seemed embarrassed about their lack of drapery. More worried about encounter-group protocol than the bodies of my colleagues, I fixed my gaze twelve inches above the other participants' heads and reseated myself without ogling the fairer members of our group. I might have slipped a little, but only because a brunette named Jan deserved admiration. After a brief struggle to refocus, I directed my attention to our guide as she continued her monologue.

"Tonight, I am going to ask each of you to tell us about your biggest loss. As you can imagine, the experiences we hear will be intense and may even arouse strong emotions in those of us listening. If that happens, don't bottle it up, share your feelings with the rest of the group. Remember, People of Light do not ask one another about their pre-Manoneeta past. The speaker will give as many details as he or she is comfortable with. We'll start with Thomas and go clockwise around the circle."

Thomas must have had an easy life. His biggest loss what that of his dog Buddy who got hit by a car when Thomas was thirteen. The guy barely made it through his story, bursting into tears at the end of it. The woman seated next to Thomas hugged him and soon was weeping too. Being enlightened, Sri Leela remained unaffected by the story. When the waterworks ceased, she got things moving again by calling on Clarissa.

I tuned out Clarissa's tale of woe. Sri Leela would call on me next, and I needed to come up with a tale of my own. The problem with continual lying is that sooner or later, cracks emerge in the fairytale castle you've built. They say the best way to avoid getting caught in an inconsistency is to keep your story as close to reality as possible. I came up with some real whoppers on my People of Light intake papers and had no idea if Sri Leela had seen them so decided to go with the worst thing that ever happened to me and tell the truth. It wouldn't be the whole truth. I'd go light on the details.

My turn came.

"I lost my wife to suicide. She took her life the day she discovered I'd been unfaithful to her."

You could have heard a pin drop. Stunned that I'd just blurted out the reality that haunted my every waking hour for the past eighteen years, I froze. When I opened my mouth to continue, no words came.

Sri Leela came to my rescue. "Thank you for sharing, Cliff. I know that was difficult."

Sharon, the woman across from me, stood. "Difficult?" she shouted. "What about your poor wife?" She stared down at me. "What you did killed her, and you come here and expect sympathy for your loss?"

My tongue came unglued. "I didn't. She was—"

"Dirtball!" a shaking Sharon screeched.

I looked down in shame, a mistake because it left me unprepared for what was coming.

Sharon threw herself across the space between us and landed on me, knocking me backward. "My sister killed herself because her husband cheated on her!" she screamed. "He married the dirty slut afterward like nothing ever happened."

Blows from Sharon's balled fists rained down on me. She flailed; I raised my arms to deflect the blows. We were naked. I didn't have it in me to fight back. Finally, hairy arms appeared from nowhere and pulled her off me. By the time I seated myself and cleared my head. Sharon was back on her pillow, crying. I felt for her. A loved one's suicide is something you don't get over.

"Sharon, thank you for sharing your anger with us," a seemingly unperturbed Sri Leela said from her pillow. "While we don't tolerate violence in Shiva City, group therapy can be intense, and exceptions are made. Cliff, if it's okay with you, we'll move on to the next participant."

Doing my best to look serene, I agreed. The rest of the session passed uneventfully. At least I think it did. I wasn't paying attention. Though Sharon had been so overwrought her blows were ineffective, her attack brought with it enough guilt to sink a cargo ship. If the People of Light viewed the all-nude circus I'd just experienced as therapy, their goal must have been to destroy people rather than help them.

I entered the *hacienda's* back door wondering if Astra's discussion group was still at it. She and my housemates met once every two weeks to watch videos of Dev's lectures and talk about them. Jokingly called Best of Dev nights, the events featured lemonade and all-you-could-eat popcorn. Attendance wasn't mandatory, but an unexplained absence was considered bad form.

Ma Prema proved to be the sole occupant of the TV room. Ensconced on the futon, she was watching a black and white film that I immediately recognized as Fred Astaire and Ginger Rogers's *Top Hat*. "Have a seat and some popcorn," she offered.

I could hardly say no after booting her from my bed the night before. I took a place on the opposite end of the futon. When she passed the popcorn bowl, I made sure to set it down between us. We chatted a bit but mostly watched. Though I'd seen the movie a dozen times, the "Waltz in Swing Time" number knocked my socks off. It's one of Astaire's best.

The movie over, Prema clicked the remote. "When I was little," she told me, "I watched this movie with my mom. For weeks afterward, I lived in a world where men danced and wore tuxedos. I took ballroom lessons when I graduated from high school, but then Mom got cancer, and I had to take care of her and the house. A few months after she died, Dad sprained his back and needed me at the garage. That's how I became a mechanic. Dirty fingernails and ratty hair didn't fit with my dreams of dancing, so I never went back to the studio. I know it's stupid, but I still dream of being swept across the dance floor by a man in a tuxedo."

She turned to me smiling and with a gleam in her eye. It weirded me out. Prema claimed to have second sight. I couldn't imagine what the twinkle in her eye might be about. Did she have a vision of me dancing in a tuxedo? A warning light flashed. The woman was dangerous.

I was sure of it.

Chapter 23

I found Elvin waiting for me at the entrance to the Brickyard.

"Get your butt down to the Mercantile Center and buy some blue clothes. As of this morning, you're a seeker."

"What? I just got here."

Elvin tipped his hat back, its human colon band returned to its place of glory. "Babba Pappa likes our idea and wants us to present it to the Inner Circle tonight. No grunt has ever been part of a proposal before the I. C., so he promoted you."

Elvin had gone to see Babba Pappa without me.

"Can he do that?" I asked.

"He sure can. Seeker status is no big deal. It's not like you're getting your beads or anything."

I hadn't been there long enough to earn any of Shiva City's funny money, and I didn't want to dig into my cash supply. "We just talked about this yesterday afternoon. Isn't this sort of sudden?"

Elvin stuck his hands in the pockets of his turquoise-blue jeans, looked down, and scuffed the dirt with his boot. He cleared his throat, looked back up, and said, "Look around you, Cliff. Five years ago, this was ranchland with two thousand Manoneetas living in tents. We didn't get where we are today by taking our sweet time with things, and we didn't get there by being stupid. We're People of Light, and we're building a new world. We'd be even farther along if it weren't for our biggest flaw—we're too nice. The I. C. shoulda pulled Babba Kam from the Brickyard and reassigned him a long time ago, but they didn't have the heart to do it."

This from the guy who yesterday said Babba Pappa was setting him up for failure. No getting around it, true believers are weird.

"Take the morning off, Cliff. Get your seeker stuff and think about what you're gonna tell the I. C. tonight and make it good. I won't be saying much. I get stage fright when I have to talk in front of a group of people."

After coaching me on how to act in front of the Inner Circle, Elvin got into his truck and drove off. The heck with planning for tonight. I turned right as I left the Brickyard and headed for Kali Court and its temporary housing. Finding time to look for Mike was difficult, and the morning off allowed me to nose around the place he likely called home.

When I got to the court, the place was nearly deserted. Most of the residents must have been out at their work assignments. I wandered through the dining tent and found a handful of stragglers finishing their breakfast. No luck. A trip to the kitchen area yielded a dozen staffers who kept asking if they could be of assistance. Though intent on helping a grunt, their earnest inquiries demonstrated how hard it was for an unfamiliar civilian to remain unnoticed.

I headed for the residential tents. The first was unoccupied. I walked down its center aisle—a passage lined with beds. A hodgepodge of shelves, trunks, and lockers placed between them gave the residents an illusion of privacy. As I prepared to leave the enclosure, I heard footsteps behind me.

"Excuse me," a voice said. "This is a seeker tent."

I turned to find a pink-clad security guard ten feet behind me. My civilian clothing had marked me as an outsider. His lack of a smile and holstered side arm were more than enough to ensure my cooperation. "Sorry," I said. "I'm new here and don't know my way around yet."

The guard looked at me with suspicion. "Residents of Kali Court have reported a problem with personal items gone missing. What are you doing here?"

"I'm looking for a guy I met yesterday. His name's Mike and he said he lives in temporary housing. He's a seeker but doesn't have his beads. Sound familiar?"

The guy appeared to relax. "Everyone in Shiva City works. Your friend will be at his work assignment. I need to see your ID."

I showed him the card Baldy gave me at check-in.

He examined it, then looked up, unfriendly again. "You've been here three days. You should have a job by now, and you should be working at it."

"My boss at the Brickyard gave me time off to go to the Mercantile Center and pick up a few things."

"This isn't the Mercantile Center. You should know by now that People of Light work hard and take their jobs seriously; you should do the same. I'm required to record this incident on my daily security report. You don't want your name to show up on it again. You can go now but do yourself a favor and stay out of trouble."

So much for finding Mike by hanging around Kali Court. I left the tent and made for the Mercantile Center. Outside the main door, I found a group clustered around a bulletin board. It didn't take long to realize it featured a notice the assembled Manoneetas considered especially noteworthy. I drew closer.

"I never thought I'd see the day," a bearded *sadhu* remarked. "Some of us waited years. Wait until this gets out. People are gonna be unhappy they're making it so easy."

A beaded seeker noticed me, gave a fake cough, and motioned with his thumb to indicate the presence of an outsider. Heads turned, and the crowd broke up as if by unanimous consent, leaving me feeling like I'd shown up at a nude beach with a camera. I walked up to the board to see what the hubbub was about. The source of the consternation must have been a blue notice titled Policy Change. It read:

The venerable Sattguru Devesha believes the current Dynamic Meditation Policy has become counterproductive. The exclusion of a large part of the seeker community from the profound joys of a form of meditation unique to the People of Light has led to the development of a caste system within our beloved city. Henceforth all seekers aspiring to the light shall be welcome at the weekly meditation at Devesha Meditation Grounds. Newcomers still must earn the privilege.

Whoopee-do. Another expectation to crowd into my schedule. It went without saying that participation was expected. There was one bright spot. If Mike was anywhere at the ranch, my chances of spotting him had increased substantially.

For a guy who has run a clothing store, the Mercantile Center's duds room felt small indeed. I'd noticed the space's Lilliputian size when I picked up my work gloves but missed the fact that there was no changing room. The People of Light didn't need to entice customers with elaborate displays. There just were three mannequins in the place: one dressed in scrubs, another in jeans, a work shirt, and a cowboy hat, and a third in a purple kaftan. A sign before each listed prices and instructed the customer to "tell us your size, and we'll take care of you." Off to the side, a female *sadhu* with shoulder-length hair and granny glasses sat behind a window. Next to it was an unillustrated list of prices for underwear. My takeaway: Male or female, if you shopped at the Mercantile Center, you wore boxer shorts.

"You don't have much of a selection," I observed. "Still, I see folks walking around in items you don't offer."

She gave me the Manoneeta smile. "You're not required to buy from us. Some people bring their clothes with them and dye them. Some do mail order. If you want to keep the clothes you have, we sell packets of bleach and dye, so you can color them yourself. It only works on natural fibers. You need to bleach your dark stuff before you dye it. Bleaching is hard on the item and reduces its life span, but it beats throwing it away. You can use the machines in your laundry room. Don't worry about the next person's clothes, almost everybody wears blue anyway."

I wasn't about to ruin the garments I bought at Barta's so picked up three sets of work clothes, a blue belt, and some scrubs. I'd learned that blue footwear was optional so didn't bother. I paid far more for fewer items than back in Cedar Rapids' Bohemie Town. The attendant disappeared for several minutes and came back with my order in a large cardboard box. I walked back to the *hacienda* thinking about those of us who'd disrobed the night before. Since we were grunts, we still wore civilian clothes. So, despite my curiosity, I left the Center with an unanswered question.

Did seekers wear blue underwear?

———————————

I donned my new scrubs and walked the mid-afternoon streets in the hope of catching a glimpse of Mike. Working the grid between Kali Court and the Mercantile Center for the second time, I spotted a lone figure heading in my direction. It didn't take long to recognize the rangy shape of Elvin.

"On my way to pick up a new shirt for our meeting with the I. C. tonight," Elvin said looking me up and down. "Wear clean clothes, and whatever you do, don't say a word until somebody asks you to. I'll introduce you and remind 'em how we make adobe bricks. After that, I'll call on you to tell them what we have in mind."

"No problem," I said.

"Now don't forget to say *shaanti* before you start and don't forget to say it when you're finished. Smile a lot and try to sound friendly. If they ask any questions, brown nose for all you're worth. Don't screw up. The last thing I want is to end up sewing clothes at the Research and Re-education Center."

I patted him on the shoulder. "We'll be fine, but now I'm curious. Re-education means learning to sew? Doesn't sound so bad."

Elvin raised his eyes to the heavens. "Your mother drop you on the head when you were a baby? Running a sewing machine twelve hours a day, seven days a week? They don't get no eight-hour shifts."

"Twelve hours a day?" I asked incredulously. "What on earth are they making?"

"Hospital scrubs. All the scrubs you see here are made in South Dakota. Not only that, we got a contract to supply scrubs to a bunch of hospitals. Last thing anybody wants is to get sent there."

I couldn't see the problem. "They try to send me there, and I'll just quit."

My boss shook his head. "Ain't that easy. There's nothing on the outside to compare with what we got here. Dev's a living god, the Manoneetas are saints, and Shiva City is paradise on earth. A man would be a fool to leave what we're building."

I'd pegged Elvin as a half-hearted Manoneeta. That wasn't the case at all. He'd swallowed the whole spiel: hook, line, and sinker.

"The bad part about re-education," he continued, "is you can't come back to Shiva City, no matter what. I know for a fact that if you don't do your time, there's not a Manoneeta in the world who will give you a job, let you visit a pod, or even talk to you. Cut yourself off from divine peace? Nobody's that crazy. It's never happened."

Elvin must have seen the doubt on my face. "It's true. Nobody ever left Shiva City of their own free will. They got booted out because they couldn't cut the mustard. Think about it. Even the folks who have part-time jobs in that hell hole they call the outside world can't wait to get back. And look at you, you've only been here a couple of days and work in a mud hole. You're barely one of us, and the last thing you want is to go back where you came from."

A week ago, I'd been Cletus Efferding, the operator of the best men's clothing store in Cedar Rapids. It seemed like another life, and despite my son's disappearance and Flanagan's warning, for some reason I wanted to help a bunch of New Mexico space cadets build the biggest adobe structure in the country.

The heat, the dust, the isolation, and scorpions aside, Shiva City was growing on me. Elvin wasn't so great, but most of the folks I met seemed nice enough—even if they were nutcases. It made sense to cut them some slack. The people on the outside weren't any better when it came to having a grip on reality.

I would have worried about my sanity except for one thing—I wasn't brainwashed.

Dressed in my new Manoneeta-blue cowboy outfit, I walked down Joyful Life Street as I made my way to our meeting with the Inner Circle. Elvin said he would wait for me outside the main gate of Blissful Haven, the *sadhu* neighborhood surrounding Dev's compound.

I found him leaning against the wall of a *hacienda* across the street from the entrance. We'd dressed alike except for footwear. Elvin wore his Krylon-sprayed dress boots. He peeled off from the wall as I approached.

"Ready?" he asked as I approached. "I've got our passes. Babba Pappa had a guy from security bring 'em to the Brickyard after lunch. Never needed 'em before today. The guy said somebody sent Dev a death threat."

"Loonies in Shiva City, imagine that," I replied.

Elvin said nothing; we crossed the street.

A pair of security guards blocked the entrance to the *sadhu* neighborhood. Carrying military-style assault rifles and packing pistols, they looked formidable. I'd passed the entrance several times during my stay. It had always been unattended. One of them led us to an oversized communal center in a four-cornered compound at least twice the size of ours. We entered a small waiting room lined by two benches. Our escort left, and I heard the click as he locked the door behind him. I assumed the Inner Circle awaited us on the other side of a pair of double doors.

We sat and waited. I was the first to break the silence. "Those guys would have been a lot scarier if I didn't know the guns weren't loaded."

Elvin looked at me as if I'd gone mad, an expression he seemed to favor when talking to me. "Cliff, you're as dumb as a trough of adobe mix. What makes you think the guns aren't loaded?"

"On the way in, my driver told me the guns are all for show. The idea is to scare the local cowboys so they don't bother us."

"Well, just wait until tomorrow morning. Security has target practice every Saturday and the range is a few hundred yards outside the Brickyard fence. It'll sound like World War III out there, and they ain't makin' noise for the hell of it."

We sat silently for a few minutes while I puzzled over the discrepancy between Elvin's report and Prema's explanation for the firearms. I'd yet to reach a conclusion when one of the double doors opened and a purple-clad *sadhu* motioned to come inside. He pointed to a short row of chairs that faced a raised dais where a dozen sadhus sat on pillows. I recognized Baldy and smiled. He ignored me.

Baldy was an exception in that most of the I. C. members looked to have been born on the Indian subcontinent. A guy in his middle fifties, wearing silver beads, rather than rosewood, cleared his throat preparatory to speaking. I assumed he was Dev's second-in-command, Babba Pappa.

After checking to see that his colleagues were paying attention, he began. "Tonight, we have a proposal to change the way we make adobe. As you know, Sattguru Devesha developed our brick-making workflow when we were a smaller organization with a modest view of what we might accomplish. The Sattguru is attached to the process because he appreciates the care and sacrifice that go into each of the bricks used to build our beautiful city. Our brickyard manager, Elvin, and a colleague are with us tonight to suggest ways in which we might increase our adobe production while remaining true to Devesha's vision. Elvin will kick off the discussion. Elvin?"

Elvin didn't say anything. I turned to see him frozen, unable to speak, his eyes marked by wild terror. He trembled; sweat poured down his cheeks. No chance he'd get control of himself. Great, the guy screws up, Babba Pappa gets embarrassed, and we're off to South Dakota before I find Mike.

I stood. "*Shaanti*. My name is Cliff Krabbenhoft. My colleague came down with a sore throat this morning, and after a day of the constant communication it takes to run the Brickyard, has lost his voice. With all due respect for Sattguru Devesha's ingenious and beautiful workflow, it will be hard to ramp up production in a way that will allow the timely completion of the new meditation center. Elvin, an experienced adobe artisan, has come up with some ideas he believes will increase the amount of adobe the Brickyard produces while honoring, even building upon, Sattguru Devesha's vision."

And with that, I went into full Cletus A. Efferding third-generation haberdasher sales mode. Customers like to choose, and an experienced salesman never puts the customer in a yes or no position but gives them options. I spoke about the variations we'd come up with for contents of the notes to be inserted in the bricks. After giving them the vision, I went straight to the practical considerations, everything from chutes and commercial mixers to having the mix brought in from outside in cement trucks. When I finished, there were no comments, so I *shaantied* them and sat back down.

If it's possible to fill a room with silence, I managed it. Several long minutes passed before someone spoke. It was Baldy.

"Mr. Krabbenhoft has given us much to think about. I suggest we wait until tomorrow to decide whether to approach Sattguru Devesha. Before we make any decision, I think it fair to mention that he has been here less than a week and has no experience in adobe construction. His line of expertise is the sale of men's clothing."

I turned to Elvin. He had doom written all over his face.

"There is something else you should know about Mr. Krabbenhoft, something that may have a great impact on your decision."

I'd been found out. The jig was up.

Baldy looked at his colleagues and paused for dramatic effect. "Cliff Krabbenhoft has been called. He told me of his meandering path to Shiva City. He had no intention of coming here, but a wave of peace overwhelmed him as his bus entered Santa Rosa. It was a call he could not ignore. It is his destiny, and tonight we have learned the reason he is here. Cliff may not understand it, but he has come here to move us in a new direction as we undertake the construction of our new meditation center."

As far as bigwigs go, Baldy didn't look like much, but he sure got their attention. The faces of his companions on the dais registered astonishment, and they began whispering to one another. The burbling went on until Babba Pappa cleared his throat.

"This is a most unusual development. Though I wish Babba Bahru brought the information to us sooner, it may be possible to bring this matter to Sattguru Dev's attention at my regular Sunday meeting with him. I suggest that we clear our minds through quiet meditation and then meet here tomorrow at noon. Elvin and Cliff, you may go."

Babba Pappa signaled that Elvin and I leave the room. No questions, no thank you, and no *shaanti*. Okay by me. I needed to get Elvin out of there before he went comatose. I stood, tapped him on the shoulder, and gently taking his elbow, led him back to the anteroom. By the time our escort led us back to the street, Elvin was back to normal and cussing me out for not telling him I was called to Shiva City.

"I couldn't tell you," I explained. "I don't even know what getting the call is about or why anybody thinks it's such a big deal. After all, when I got here, they assigned me to the Brickyard. I didn't ask for it."

"Every time I think you couldn't get any dumber, you manage to prove me wrong," Elvin groused. "You didn't choose the Brickyard; the Brickyard chose you. You were scheduled to work there because that's your fate. Just like it was your fate to get the call."

"Fate, shmate," I answered. "I showed up one day, and the powers that be put me in the yard because they had an opening."

"Bull!" snapped Elvin. "You didn't even know about the People of Light when you got on that bus in Oklahoma City. Why else would you be here?"

I bit my tongue.

Back at the *hacienda*, I found Prema, Swami Raj, and Astra in the TV room. Astra was the first to notice my arrival. For once, she didn't look spacey. She looked irritated.

"You've been holding out on us Cliff," she remarked. "You were invited to a meeting with the I. C. and didn't tell us."

"Bad form, Cliff," Prema chimed in.

I didn't want to get in Dutch with my housemates so pulled up a pillow and joined them on the floor. "I didn't think anyone would care that I talked to the I. C. about adobe bricks, and I haven't been here long enough to notice anything unusual."

As if naked encounter groups, second sight, astral projection, and worshipping living gods were everyday events.

Raj pointed a finger at me. "You didn't even tell us you got seeker status. None of us knew until you walked out of here tonight wearing blue. That's big news."

"None of us know what's going on," complained Astra. "Ordinary seekers going to dynamic meditation. Rumors about death threats against Dev, security people outside Blissful Haven. There's a new policy on part-time jobs that came out of nowhere. You show up, and in a couple of days, there's more strangeness in Shiva City than any of us can remember."

I barely knew these people, but it was easy to see they were upset with me. "Look," I said, "I didn't know anybody would be interested. I gave my boss a suggestion for a better way to make adobe, and the next day he tells me to buy blue clothes because I'm a seeker, and by the way, we're meeting with the Inner Circle to talk about the Brickyard. I didn't hear anything about a death threat until a couple of hours ago, and I don't even know what dynamic meditation is."

"Maybe Cliff is bad karma," Astra suggested. "Something about his aura doesn't seem right."

Raj, his hands laced across his belly, barely stirred from his almost prone position. "Give the guy a break," he mumbled. "Cliff doesn't have a clue."

Not as clueless as you lard butt.

"I sense that Cliff is getting angry," Prema announced.

Astra jumped in. "What do you know about the new policy on part-time work?"

Prema looked at me. "I sense Cliff is puzzled."

Damn the woman and her second sight.

Prema started in again. "I believe Cliff—"

"I can speak for myself," I interjected. "And what I want to say is you're the most paranoid people I've ever met. Ever since I got here people have been telling me what to do and where to go and saying I've been called and—"

"You've been called?" Astra interrupted, her eyes the size of fishbowls. "I've never met someone who's been called. That explains everything."

"What?"

Raj sat upright. "Those who are called are innocents. They come to us as agents of change but have no idea of what their contribution to the People might be. Your rapid promotion and appearance before the I.C. are understandable."

"Don't get a big head," Prema added. "Agents of change have influence, but they're still ordinary Manoneetas."

Astra pulled her shawl around her and leaned forward. "Yeah, a big deal, but not a big deal. You met with the Inner Circle today, but next week you'll be cleaning toilets with the rest of us."

The story of my life. Riding high one moment, wallowing in sludge the next.

Chapter 24

A cool morning greeted me as I stepped outside the *hacienda* wondering how to take advantage of my status as one who'd been called. I wanted to go to Dev's Sunday evening dynamic meditation event to look for Mike but discovered there were hoops to jump through. I wasn't trained in the technique, a requirement for attendance.

The morning's flutes and bird calls from Dev's portrait had been followed by an announcement that the I. C. planned to hold a dozen training sessions prior to tomorrow night's dynamic meditation event. They'd scheduled the classes in anticipation of unprecedented demand by Shiva City's unbeaded seekers. For many of them, it would be the first time they'd set eyes on Dev. Slots were limited. In-person registration was to take place at the security office and required a signed release from a work supervisor.

I made straight for the Brickyard, practicing the lines I'd use to persuade Elvin to give me time off for the training. I found him at the entrance, dressed in clean scrubs rather than work clothes, and leaning against a utility pole. He motioned me over.

"Been waitin' for you, Cliff. I need to find Babba Pappa to get my meditation training approved. I want you to supervise the adobe operation while I'm gone."

My opening. "I wanted to ask you to sign my—"

"Figured you would. I'll sign your release form when I get back. Then you can take time off to go down and register."

In other words, if I wanted training, I would need to supervise the works until he returned.

"The slots will fill up fast Elvin. I've been called. I don't understand why, but I get the feeling it's important for me to be at that event. It could even be one of the reasons I'm in Shiva City. If word got out the dynamic meditation session was a part of my call, and I wasn't there, Babba Pappa would be unhappy."

"If you're not there, it's because that's your fate," a stony-faced Elvin answered.

I came right back at him. "And an unhappy Baba Pappa would be yours."

Elvin grunted. "Seein' as how you're so special, I'll see if can get you registered without your bein' there."

And now to get out of the supervision. "I really don't know very much about adobe. It would be better if you put Tanak in charge."

Elvin detached himself from the utility pole, adjusted his surgeon's cap, and patted me on the shoulder. "You'll do fine, Cliffy boy."

"A lot could go wrong," I said. "Tanak knows adobe inside and out, and he's worked the yard a long time."

"You're a better choice," Elvin replied.

"I don't think so. Besides, I know the guy. He's not the type to appreciate you putting me over him. What am I supposed to say when he complains?"

I'd yet to see a bigger smile cross my boss's face.

"Tell him you've been called."

Tanak didn't seem to care that Elvin made me straw boss. Some of my other colleagues, eager to get their work releases for the training signed, didn't take it so well.

"I'd be happy to sign your work release forms," I said, "but Elvin didn't give me any of the paperwork." A lie. Even if I had the release forms, I wouldn't have dreamed of giving any of Elvin's workers time off. The guy would have my head.

That's when Tanak stepped in. "No problem, Cliff. The supervisor of the motor pool is a housemate and owes me a favor. I'll buzz over and get the paperwork from him." He turned to his fellow workers. "How many do we need?"

We had six aspirants and there was no point in having them start work since they'd want to take off as soon as I signed their forms. When Tanak left to fetch the releases, I asked them to wait while I sent the crews off to make mud. They did so without complaint. After all, their new straw boss was a good guy willing to sacrifice production to get his workers trained.

Tanak returned ten minutes later and passed out the paperwork rather than handing it to me. His co-workers responded with smiles and heartfelt expressions of gratitude. "I didn't know if Cliff had a pen," he announced, "so I signed his name for him at the motor pool."

When the last of the trainees departed, Tanak gave my hand a shake. It was one of those jobbies where you put one hand on the other guy's elbow to show how enthusiastic and sincere you are.

"You're a hell of a guy," he said. "Elvin never gives anyone time off. I really wouldn't want to be you when the boss gets back. You'll be shoveling mud nonstop for weeks." He paused. "Well, I better get to work. *Shaanti.*"

His mission accomplished, Tanak walked away. I'd misjudged the guy. Unhappy that Elvin put me in charge, he didn't bother with the uncooperative bully act. Instead, he stuck a shiv in my ribs and pulled it out slowly so he could watch me bleed to death. Nothing to do for it. I went over to the weakest of my newly formed crews to help them get the mud out, all the while picturing Tanak caught in quicksand, screaming for help. For some reason, my fantasy didn't involve coming to his aid.

And I thought I was bigger than that.

The security force took up target practice on the other side of the fence. While I couldn't say if the pink-clad Manoneetas were good shots, they went through a boatload of ammunition. I didn't hear the distinctive rat-a-tat of automatic weapon fire, but there was no doubt that most, if not all, of the force were firing semi-autos. The din proved to be as loud as Elvin predicted.

"I said, all the training sessions are canceled."

I looked up to see Sandee, a raw-boned giant of a woman, nearly in tears, holding out her release form. Apparently, she wanted me to take it. I did.

"What happened?" I asked.

She spoke, her voice nearly drowned out by the racket from the shooting range. "I don't know. A bunch of *sadhus* showed up at Harmony House, screaming at everyone to leave and get back to work. They practically pushed us out of line. It felt scary, almost like they were attacking us. Somebody started yelling to get security. Everybody got away as fast as they could."

I took Sandee's paperwork, and as she turned to leave, a siren wailed, and the small arms fire ceased. I heard shouting coming from the direction of the firing range. Doors slammed, engines roared, and gravel rattled against metal as vehicles left the area at high speed. I didn't know if Sandee connected the fracas at Harmony House to the abrupt departure from the shooting range, but I did. Shiva City's militia had just left to respond to a crisis.

Though the People of Light's definition of crisis might not square with that of the outside world, something big was going on. The idea of pickups racing through the streets, bristling with semi-automatic weapons in the hands of panicked security guards—amateurs all—scared the hell out of me. People could get hurt, and as boss for the morning, I felt responsible for the brickyard workers' safety.

I caught up with Sandee, now frozen by the sound of the siren. "Go to your crew and tell them to meet at the water tank. I'll gather up the rest."

I made the rounds in short order, then hurried to the water tank. The siren had my colleagues expecting something more than a how-we-make-mud meeting. Though they'd gathered quietly, looks of concern betrayed their uneasiness. I waited a moment for the stragglers and dove in.

"There was a disturbance at the big signup for meditation classes today. All the classes were canceled. The *sadhus* informing those already in line were visibly upset, and there is a report of pushing and shoving. Shortly afterward, the security force's target practice ended abruptly, and they sped off in their pickups. You've heard the siren. Given the circumstances, some of you might be more comfortable at home. You have my permission to leave if you wish but clear the mud from the tanks before you go."

Tanak greeted my announcement with a laugh. "Way to go, Cliff. You're on the job for a couple of hours and freak out over a siren test and glitch in class signups. We're busting our sweet Manoneeta butts to see people have housing this winter, and you—"

Attention! Attention! Shiva City is under lockdown. All residents are to put their work areas in order and go directly to their housing units. There are to be no exceptions. Finish up and go home.

A look toward the gate revealed the source of the sound to be a loudspeaker mounted atop a pickup. I glared at Tanak and mouthed a word rhyming with 'bass pole.'

A deserted TV room greeted me when I returned to the *hacienda*. My housemates had taken to their rooms, the only sounds being a chorus of birds and flutes coming from the illuminated portraits of Dev in their sleeping quarters. I went to my quarters where the dulcet tones continued. Curious to know what was going on, I opened the window and leaned on the sill. Nothing stirred in the courtyard below. Save for the rumbling of pickups, the streets were quiet.

I sat on the bed, kicked off my boots, and assumed the prone position. Finding Mike was more complex than I imagined, and though I arrived in Manoneeta heaven just five days ago, the reality of life on the outside had begun to fade. I couldn't say why, but the People of Light's outrageous plan to create a promised land in the New Mexico desert appealed to me. Stranger still, their wild-eyed plan to build a preposterously oversized adobe structure captured my imagination.

The Manoneetas had dreams; they hoped to make a better world. Slaving away to make Gib Sutherland even wealthier paled in comparison. Cleatzy's and Gib, artifacts of my love for Dusty, felt like leeches bleeding me dry, clinging to my skin because I couldn't cut the last of the ties connecting me to her. And as much as I hated to admit it, I liked it in Shiva City, the home to a cult that brainwashed Dusty and was now doing the same to my son. I'd spent the better part of a week with a bunch of wackos, working my butt off, bouncing from one inanity to the next, but compared to my life in Cedar Rapids, it felt like a vacation at a dude ranch.

Maybe the Manoneetas had it right. I had been called, and Shiva City was my fate. How else to describe the improbable circumstances that brought me here: falling in love with a former Manoneeta, a wedding disaster, a horrific murder, and the search for an estranged son in hope of earning the affection of a daughter I hardly knew.

I awoke to loud pounding.

"Cliff Krabbenhoft, please answer your door*."*

I opened up to the sight of three smiling, pistol-packing security people. My search for Mike in one of the Kali Court residential tents had come back to haunt me.

"Shaanti," the leader said. "We've been ordered to search your room. Please understand you haven't been singled out. We've been asked to go through the quarters of everyone who has been here less than a year."

Seeing no other options, I stepped aside to let them enter. "No guns, pornography, or stolen items," I joked.

Two female security officers entered the room. The third, a burly guy, stood blocking the door. He pointed to a spot next to him, "Stand here, this will only take a minute."

It took fifteen. The women checked everything. They opened and closed the window, dismantled the bed, and went through my dirty laundry. My underwear provided the younger of the two some entertainment.

"You should get blue underwear," she giggled. "It's not required, but your face might get red when you go to your tantric group and realize you're the only one in white."

I would have laughed it off, but her more mature partner had just removed the lower drawer from the wardrobe. I held my breath as the pink-clad snoop unpacked my neatly folded clothes, set them on the floor, and turned the drawer upside down. Without comment, she turned it back upright, then retrieved the still-folded scrubs, jeans, and shirts, placing them neatly back into the drawer. I'd wedged my Cletus Efferding driver's license into the underside of the groove holding the drawer's bottom. Though the woman couldn't have missed it, she didn't say anything.

I relaxed, a bit. The younger woman was going through my shaving kit when the guy at the door became positively loquacious. "Sorry about all this," he said. "You're our last search for this quadrant, so you'll be free to leave your room when we go. You and your neighbors can move around the compound as much as you wish, but no one is allowed outside the walls until further notice. You'll want to be on Dev Line at nine o'clock. There'll be an important announcement."

"Dev Line?" I asked.

"I should have realized you were new what with the white underwear and all," the big guy said. "Dev Line is a network of all the Dev portraits with the speakers behind them. The I. C. created the system so Dev could give us inspirational messages. He doesn't use it much, so it's become the community alarm clock."

Until then, I hadn't noticed that the sounds of the birds and flute music I'd fallen asleep to had gone silent.

"Hey Cliff," the younger woman called. "For a guy with a beard, you sure have a lot of razor blades."

"Yeah, I haven't decided whether or not to keep it."

She put the kit back on the nightstand, walked over to me, and gave my whiskers a playful tug. "Covering a face like that with hair, Sweetheart. It's a sin and offense to womanhood. If you ever want to lose that beard, I'll be happy to shave it off for you. Of course, I might not want to stop there, if you know what I mean."

I knew what she meant and wanted her to go away.

"Quit playing around," the guy at the door said. "Let's go if we're done. I'd like to get to bed tonight."

They left. I melted into a puddle that had nothing to do with the flirtatious, razor-happy guard. A close call doesn't come any closer than the one I'd just experienced, and I worried the woman who'd let me off the hook after seeing my Cletus Efferding ID might have a change of heart. It was time to find a better place to stash the card, so I went to the wardrobe to fetch it. I didn't have a location in mind but knew better than to hide it in my room again. Cletus Efferding's driver's license could reside in my pocket for now, but the sooner I got it securely tucked away, the better.

The near loss of my license gave me a new appreciation of its importance. I had no cash. If the situation in Shiva City continued to deteriorate, I might be forced to abandon the search for Mike and head home. I'd need money, and without an ID, a Western Union wire transfer was out of the question. No bank would touch me. Wondering how I could have been so casual about concealing it, I pulled out the wardrobe drawer and unpacked it. A quick survey of the underside took care of the problem, but I can't say its resolution brought me any relief.

My ID—it was gone.

After some discussion, my housemates and I opted to catch the nine o'clock Dev Line announcement in the TV room. Seventeen of us clustered around the oversized portrait of the Sattguru. Tubs of popcorn were in abundance. At nine sharp the recorded birds tweeted, and the flute fluted. A few minutes later the great Om sounded, repeating itself as it summoned us into a deep well of relaxation. At least that was the theory. Dev seldom communicated with Shiva City as a whole, and my companions were too keyed up to pay any attention. Static and throat-clearing followed the Om, and the program got underway.

Shaanti. This is Babba Pappa. A troublesome event took place in Shiva City today, one unparalleled in the history of the People of

Light. It is with heavy heart that I must report that someone has made an attempt on the life of Sattguru Devesha. Though the perpetrator has escaped, the Sattguru is, thankfully, uninjured.

Many of you are aware of the recent death threat made against the one who is our guide and inspiration. He has been the recipient of such threats in the past. The Inner Circle's response to the new development was to limit part-time work away from Shiva City. Other steps were examined and rejected as unnecessary.

As it turns out, the situation was worse than we could have imagined. We understood past threats against the Sattguru to be products of the disordered minds of blowhard ranchers opposed to our mission. This is not the case. The I. C. believes the perpetrator of today's assassination attempt is internal. Given the sophistication of the operation, it is not unreasonable to assume the culprit had accomplices.

Until the threat is neutralized, new security measures have been put in place. Going forward, no visitor or guest passes will be issued. Seekers associated with our P. O. L. pods will no longer come to our beautiful city to receive their beads but will do so at the local center. Shiva City will accept no new residents. Traffic leaving the city will be closely monitored, and only those associated with our work at the Sattguru Devesha Harmonic Convergence Center in Santa Rosa will receive exit passes. The Inner Circle regrets these measures are necessary but hopes they are adequate to ensure the safety of you, our citizens. Please report any unusual or suspicious persons or activities to the security office. We ask your patience in this time of great stress. We, the People of Light, will prevail. Shaanti.

The great Om returned, but no birds this time. Most of the room sat in stunned silence. A few chewed popcorn. Madhuk and Astra began to sob, and a guy named Cletus Efferding realized he'd just become a virtual prisoner in Shiva City, one unable to prove his identity to the world outside. Worse yet, someone had his ID, proof that he entered Shiva City under false pretenses—a deception a would-be assassin would surely resort to.

And Babba Pappa, what did he mean by neutralize?

Chapter 25

Sunday morning. Half-past eight with one down and seventeen to go. I finished brushing the porcelain and flushed the stool. Wanting to get the gut-wrenching part of the task out of the way, I started with the worst case, a blocked throne in the men's room.

Our *hacienda* had communal center cleanup duty this week, and as the newest arrival, my housemates put me on what they referred to as porcelain patrol. Concerned that I might take the job less than seriously, my compatriots let it be known that they and the compound council expected perfection. Manoneetas might be casual about social diseases, but they were over the top when it came to clean facilities. The fixtures got scrubbed every day.

Ma Shivani, our compound's mayor, inspected the communal center restrooms and showers each morning. Failure to meet her standards would put our *hacienda* on cleanup duty for an additional week. A statuesque, beaded seeker from Germany, Shivani was one step away from making *sadhu,* and a good report on her handling of the lockdown situation would likely put her over the top. Concerned that the citizens in her charge might chafe under the restrictions, she organized a compound-wide card party for the afternoon and scheduled an atypical morning cleanup in anticipation of the event.

I'd just poured the cleaner into the second bowl when I heard a woman clearing her throat behind me. I looked over my shoulder and recognized Shivani. She stood too close to the stall for me to step out. I rose as best I could in the limited space and turned to see what she wanted. Thank goodness my colleagues had mentioned she was one of those people whose dour expression belied a good disposition; otherwise, I'd have expected to be gutted with a butcher knife.

"I hear your name is Cliff. I've seen you in the dining room and stopped by to say hello."

I found it hard to believe she didn't come to check up on the job I was doing. "And you're Ma Shivani," I replied. "Pleased to meet you."

I put down my brush and took off a rubber glove to shake her hand. She didn't take it. Considering the location and my task, I could understand.

"Sri Mira was right when she said you'd look better without a beard."

"Sri Mira?"

"One of the security team that searched your room. She mentioned it when they stopped by the office to give their report."

I nodded. "What can I do for you?"

"You could take off your other glove and give the pair to me. I don't know where you found those, but they're worn out."

I handed her the gloves and she tossed them back over her shoulder. "We keep the new ones on the top shelf of the janitor's closet. You must not have seen them."

She took a step forward, crowding me back against the stool. I nearly fell.

"You have strong-looking fingers," she said as she slipped my hands up under the top of her scrubs.

Astra warned me Shivani was a maneater, and I absolutely didn't want her leaving tooth marks on me—anywhere. "Maybe this isn't such a good idea," I stammered. "Somebody could walk in on us."

I slid my hands out from under her top and leaned farther back. Too far—my knees folded, and I lost my balance. The lid was up; my backside got wet. To say Shivani looked stunned would have been an understatement. Her eyebrows rose to her hairline, and I could have slipped a basketball into her mouth.

"*Verdammter americanischer Clown!*" she raged and stormed off.

Mr. Smooth in the outside world, an unmitigated disaster in Shiva City. Tamara would never understand what I went through in my search for Mike. She just wanted her dad to find her brother, end of story.

And really, was that too much to ask?

Ma Prema, Swami Raj, Ma Astra, and I would have skipped Shivani's card party but for the promised treats—strawberry smoothies and all-you-could-eat almond cookies. On the way over, we discovered we were all euchre players so decided to sit together and play a few hands. We'd been at it maybe fifteen minutes when Shivani walked by and gave me the stink eye. Raj noticed.

"Whoa!" he exclaimed. "What did you do to get on Shivani's shitlist?"

I leveled with him. "She wanted to get physical, but I wasn't in the mood."

No way the details of my humiliation would pass my lips.

Raj raised his eyebrows and looked as if he was about to speak when Astra jumped in. "You shut down Ma Shivani? The mayor? And you kicked Prema out of bed. You sure have a funny way of making friends. Put that ace back in your hand. If you play it, I'll have to trump it."

Playing cards with Astra made for an otherworldly experience. She wasn't my partner and had just let me know what was in her hand. A few minutes earlier, Astra cautioned Raj not to bid because all her cards were of the trump persuasion.

"Astra, I don't understand," I said. "How do you expect to win when you keep telling the rest of us what's in your hand?"

"It's not nice to deceive others."

Astra didn't get the idea of friendly competition.

Raj waited until Astra and I finished speaking, then said, "You were selfish with yourself, Cliff. Ma Shivani may be the best mayor in

Shiva City. She does everything she can to see our compound has first-rate food and is as comfortable and clean. While no one would call her a warm, affectionate person, she has needs like everybody else. Being friendly would have cost you little more than a bruise or two, and Shivani deserves appreciation for what she does for us."

Raj's vision of a kindly civic-leader saint didn't square with my memory of a wanton she-devil who all but shoved me into a toilet and then cursed me out for it.

Prema took the game-winning trick. "Raj has some good insights. He's been a Manoneeta from almost the beginning and knows his way around. He survived the Babba Vivek years."

My deal. I shuffled and distributed the cards. "Who was Babba Vivek? What did he do that was so bad?"

Raj shook his head and sighed. "Babba Vivek was Sattguru Dev's right hand back in India. It's the role Babba Pappa plays right now. Dev is a spiritual leader. His mind is too perfect to be wasted on the day-to-day details of running an organization like the People of Light. *Sadhus* like Babba Pappa and Babba Vivek filter out the mundane world to allow him to function at his peak."

I passed on my chance to bid because I needed to function at my peak. It took all my control to avoid bursting into laughter at the thought that our adobe workflow was the product of a perfect mind. The attempt to restrain myself might have been impossible but for the sudden realization that Raj had been at the *ashram* at the same time as Dusty. The group was smaller back then. They likely knew each other.

"I get that part," I said. "Prema mentioned the Babba Vivek years as something to survive. What was it like back then?"

Raj put down his cards, puffed out his cheeks, and exhaled. "Hard times. Manoneetas getting kidnapped and hauled off to be brainwashed by people called deprogrammers. We never saw most of them again. There were problems with our school. A couple of teachers got involved with some twelve-year-old students. One got pregnant. Then grunts from Australia introduced some of the younger Manoneetas to laughing gas, and they started using it every day. There were rumors of violent encounter groups. Money was going out faster than it came in. To top it all off, the family of a neurotic American seeker contacted the Indian government and lied about us. They started investigating us, so we got into tax trouble.

Though Dusty shared the trauma of her kidnapping and deprogramming with me, she'd left out a lot. The Sutherlands were right to get her away from the *ashram* when they did. Steele and Consuela may have done it for themselves rather than their daughter, but the situation at the compound was dangerously unstable.

Raj continued. "Many of us believed Babba Vivek wasn't up to the job of running the *ashram*. Our community split into two factions: those who thought it Vivek's job to shield Dev from unpleasantness and those who saw Vivek as a control freak more concerned with consolidating his power than the good of the community. Strange things started happening to the folks who spoke out against Vivek. They'd get shifted to inferior housing or be barred from Dynamic meditation. Some just disappeared. We didn't know if they'd been kidnapped by deprogrammers or what."

Astra shivered. "Sounds terrible. I'm glad Babba Pappa is running things now. Shiva City is wonderful."

Raj rubbed his ample midsection. "Life is better here than it ever was in India, and the food's great. All because Babba Pappa found a way to get past the guards and into the Sattguru's house. Dev hadn't realized Vivek kept him so isolated he'd become a virtual prisoner."

Astra stopped shivering long enough to say, "I can't believe Dev didn't kick him out of the People of Light."

"If Babba Pappa had his way, Vivek would be long gone, but Dev believes in growth and forgiveness," Raj explained. "Things would have worked out if Babba Vivek didn't blame Pappa for the loss of Dev's trust. They may be People of Light, but Vivek and Pappa hate each other. Dev put the Re-education Center in South Dakota to keep them apart. Babba Vivek runs the place with an iron hand, and it makes money hand over fist. He believes he's proved himself, but Babba Pappa won't let him come to Shiva City, and Dev agrees. Vivek may be isolated and bitter, but he would never make an attempt on Dev's life. He wants his old position back—to be near Dev and have a role in the People's future. I doubt it will ever happen. The reason we have an Inner Circle is so one person will never again have as much power as Vivek."

"Looks like Babba Pappa has plenty of power to me," interjected Prema.

I wanted to hear more, but her remark brought the topic to a close and we picked up our cards again. I can't say I enjoyed Astra's loopy insistence on not deceiving her opponents. It reduced the play to pure luck. We might just as well have drawn for high cards. Though the smoothies and cookies were grand, between Raj's frequent returns to the buffet and Astra's helpful comments, our card game got too disjointed and weird for me. I yawned and threw in my cards.

"I feel a nap coming on," I fibbed. "Think I'll head back to the *hacienda*."

"Me too," Prema added.

Astra giggled. "Have fun, guys. Don't kick anybody out of bed."

"Hard to do if we're each in our own rooms," Prema replied.

We rose and walked back to the *hacienda*. Prema didn't have anything to say until we reached the door.

She tapped me on my shoulder to get my attention. "Listen up, Cliff. You're nothing but trouble. Don't mess things up for me."

I knew then Prema would never forgive my mistaking her for a scorpion. Stepping in front of me, she grabbed the door handle and marched in.

I followed and tried to continue the conversation. "But Prema—"

She held up a hand and scoped our surroundings. "Back off and stay away from me," she hissed. "I know you're not who you claim to be."

The woman didn't have second sight. Somehow, she'd seen my ID.

Chapter 26

I pulled out my bandanna and wiped my face. Dev Line's morning birds and great Om were followed by the voice of Babba Pappa thanking us for our patience and announcing the city-wide curfew had been lifted. He gave no update on the security situation but instructed us to report back to our jobs.

Consumed by worry, I found it hard to focus on my menial task—so much so that I dumped a shovel full of adobe mix alongside the wheelbarrow twice in a row. Prema had not only seen my driver's license, like as not she was the one who'd stolen it. Solid evidence of my false identity, its exposure would torpedo any attempt to find Mike.

Prema's actions were beyond understanding. I'd enjoyed our drive to Shiva City. She must have liked it too, or she wouldn't have crawled into my bed. Prema understood she ended up on the floor simply because she startled me. The next day, we enjoyed a pleasant evening watching TV, and I thought were becoming friends. Now she'd violated my privacy by searching my room, found my ID, and hated me. Not only hated me but had one up on me. If I lived to be one hundred, I'd never understand women. And as for Manoneeta women, it would be at least five centuries.

"Hey, Cliff. We did it!" Elvin's voice.

I stuck my shovel into the slop in the wheelbarrow and looked up to see Elvin heading my way, grinning from ear to ear. I sincerely hoped he wouldn't hug me. He didn't but stopped three feet away. Barely able to contain himself, he hopped from one foot to the other.

"Babba Pappa just sent a messenger. I'm supposed to meet him at two o'clock. I've gotta get back to Kali Court and get cleaned up. The guy who brought the news wasn't supposed to tell me, but he says they're going to have engineers work with me to design a new adobe process."

I stepped forward and shook his hand. "Congratulations, Elvin. You'll do a bang-up job, and the People will have a first-class meditation center."

Elvin removed his hat, held it in front of him, and nervously fingered the brim. "I'm not very good at this sorta thing, but I gotta say thank you. I wouldn'ta thought about puttin' those little papers into the bricks, and you took over when I got too scared to talk in front of the Inner Circle. I won't forget it, Cliff."

I was genuinely happy to see the man genuinely happy. "No problem. I want to see that new meditation center, too."

Elvin returned his colon-trimmed hat to his head. "You know, the other day when you bent over, I saw you're still wearin' white underwear. I'm gonna buy you a week's worth of Manoneeta blue. By the way, you're in charge for the rest of the day."

With that he turned and strode for the gate. I had to chuckle to myself. How could you not like a cantankerous crank who promised to give you underwear? My good mood lasted until an interruption at four o'clock. I was working with the crew, rotating adobe bricks when a security staffer in sunglasses ambled up.

"Cliff Krabbenhoft?" he asked.

My guts froze. "That's me."

"Babba Pappa wants to see you in the security office at six."

I tried for nonchalant. "Wonder what he wants. You happen to know?"

"He didn't say. The guy's time is important. Don't be late."

I gave him what I imagined was a friendly smile, hoping it didn't come off as a terrified grin. "Wouldn't think of it, and thanks."

A summons to see Babba Pappa at the security office. Panic set in. I wanted to run—get out of Shiva City as soon as possible. There could be just one explanation.

Ma Prema had squealed on me.

"Cliff Krabbenhoft?" the uniformed security guard asked. I didn't see a sidearm, but then again, why wear one when you're on desk duty. Fenced in, surrounded by desert, armed security at the exits, no vehicle, no money, and no time to plan, I didn't run. Instead, I walked to the security office going over the arguments I'd need to talk my way out of the false-identity situation.

"Babba Pappa is ready for you," the desk jockey said. "Just go on in."

I walked through a deserted secretary's office and found the purple-robed *sadhu* seated at his desk, scratching his ear, and staring into one of those personal computers that are all the rage. He didn't look up. The guy was so lost in whatever was happening on the screen. I coughed to get his attention.

He looked up, smiled, and rose, coming around the desk with his hand extended. Up close, he appeared older than he had at the I. C. meeting. I pegged him for my age.

"*Shaanti*, a pleasure to meet you, Cliff. That was an impressive presentation to the Inner Circle Friday night." He shook my hand. "Have a seat."

I sat, and Babba Pappa went back to his chair. Mindful that Pappa came out on the top side of a bitter rivalry by crushing someone whose rivals mysteriously disappeared, I wasn't prepared to let my guard down.

Dev's second-in-command adjusted his chair, then folded his hands on the desk in front of him. "You'll be happy to know that Sattguru Devesha is quite taken with the idea of building the world's largest indoor meditation center with adobe bricks containing the prayers of the great religions. The Sattguru understands humankind progresses by abandoning that which has served its purpose and embracing the new. To that end, he is determined that the attempt on his life will not delay our progress in building a new world, much less a meditation center."

So, the guy went for the each-brick-is-a-prayer option. I would never have guessed. My father's advice to give the customer a choice—even if it's a bad one—had once again proven true. Babba Pappa looked at me as if he expected a response, so I decided to go with the Cletus Efferding corollary. If in doubt, bury them in bull.

I nodded sagely. "A meditation center built on the world's prayers, a powerful image, one that should go far in getting Sattguru Dev's message across, one Manoneetas can be proud of."

"Well spoken," Babba Pappa replied. "I see by your intake form that you've worked in sales. Once you've been here a while and have a better understanding of what we're trying to accomplish, The I. C. may want to put you in a public relations role but for now, you've become a bit of a problem."

I should have seen it coming. He'd been softening me up. The other shoe was about to drop. Time to bury him in bull again.

"A harmonious environment is everything. I can't tell how deeply disappointing it is to learn I've struck a discordant note in the short time I've been here. I hope it doesn't complicate my quest for fulfillment."

Pappa held up his hand. "You misunderstand. You've been called. The role you are to play here is not yet clear to us. It may be to assist in getting the meditation center built, or it may be something entirely unrelated. Only time will tell. The situation is puzzling. You have no engineering or architectural experience, and your supervisor believes your talents are wasted in the Brickyard. I agree with him. In fact, I'd like to work you into a role in administration, but with the attack on Sattguru Devesha, things are in chaos, so I don't have any openings."

The guy could create a job for me with the snap of his fingers. When it came to BS, the man was no slouch.

"I appreciate your frankness, Babba Pappa. Let me assure you that I will wait patiently until the time my role within the organization becomes apparent. In the meanwhile, I will happily work anywhere you put me."

Babba Pappa nodded. "You have a marvelous attitude, one certain to make you a pleasure to work with. There is a position available, but I haven't mentioned it because your abilities exceed the demands the position would place on you. It's not much, but it will keep you close at hand if we need you."

As if shoveling mud wasn't the bottom of the barrel.

"I appreciate the consideration, Babba Pappa. Where do you want me?"

"Well, the office and security areas have been a disaster lately, and the janitorial staff isn't keeping up. Report to Swami Ravi in housekeeping tomorrow morning. He'll get you off on the right foot."

I nodded. "Thank you, Babba Pappa. I'll do my best."

"Glad to hear it." He leaned back in his chair. "There's one more thing. One so unusual that I can't think that it's happened before. When I told Sattguru Devesha about your presentation to the Inner Circle, he wanted to meet you. You've been a seeker for four days and have been here less than a week. Because of the security situation, I advised him to wait. He smiled and told me to check up on you."

La-dee-dah. Meeting Dev might be interesting but wouldn't do anything to help me find Mike.

"Don't worry, it's fine," I said. "Someone as precious as Sattguru Devesha can never be too protected."

Babba Pappa looked like I'd smacked him with a baseball bat. "Because you are new to our ways, you have no understanding of the unbelievable honor and absolute privilege you've been afforded. I've checked up on you as the Sattguru has requested. I'm concerned you lost your ID on the way to Shiva City. It hasn't turned up by any chance, has it?"

A trap. He'd fabricated the you're-so-valuable and invited-by-Dev tale to set me up. I answered truthfully but sidestepped.

"I don't have it."

"I feared as much." He put on reading glasses, pulled a paper from the stack on his desk, and scanned it "Still, your intake paperwork is in order, and I've questioned Elvin extensively. Is there anything you'd like to add?"

What the hell was the guy up to? Unsure of how to answer, I reverted to Efferding's bury-them-in-bull corollary.

"I can't think of anything. Some guys are bad at managing their finances but are good salesmen. Five will get you ten I can walk into almost any men's store in the country and come out with a job inside of twenty minutes. Being a first-rate salesman makes it easy to drift. I like the stability I'm finding here."

Pappa looked at me over the top of his glasses. "I don't know that your explanation for a somewhat checkered past helps very much, but then again, many who come to us have difficulties functioning in the hate-filled world outside. I'm going with my gut on this one. You will be meeting Sattguru Devesha at one o'clock tomorrow afternoon. Though you've been called, the decision has been a difficult one. The clincher was my interview with your compound's mayor."

It was my turn to look stunned. "Ma Shivani?"

"Yes. She said you were so timid you wouldn't hurt a fly."

Back on the prowl again, working the grid that comprises the forty square blocks that make up Shiva City. I hoped to catch a glimpse of Mike, but the city might as well have been on lockdown. The streets were almost deserted.

My meeting with Babba Pappa took a fair-sized chunk out of the part of the day when people were out doing errands on the way home from work. By now many of the city's residents would be nestled within the walls of their compounds eating, socializing, and going about their evening work assignments. I caught a few dozen people going to the Serenity Center. None looked even vaguely like Mike. I was ready to throw in the towel but decided to make one last pass by the Mercantile Center.

Though the center was closed, its courtyard benches attracted the occasional group interested in evening conversation. When I got there the seats were empty, but it was hard to miss the dozen or so Manoneetas clustered around a community bulletin board. Most were *sadhus*, but one of the seekers was the right height and had the same build as Mike. I wandered over and stood behind him to check him out. No dice, but the *sadhus* were all abuzz.

"Strange," a skinny guy said, "The Inner Circle permanently reduced to ten. It's been a dozen since Dev created it."

"Not so strange," a hawk-nosed woman *sadhu* replied. "Babba Kumar and Babba Vasant live in my compound. They're gone and their rooms are empty. We won't be seeing them again."

The skinny guy scratched his beard. "It doesn't make sense. The guys are senior *sadhus*. They've been with Dev for years. There's no way they'd get sent to Research and Re-education. And why is Dev shrinking the Inner Circle?"

"Use your enlightened noodle," the woman said. "Kumar and Vasant go back to the days when Babba Vivek was a big deal. Somebody tries to kill the Sattguru, and they're gone."

"No way they'd be mixed up in anything like that," a short-haired woman declared. "They're beautiful souls, kind and gentle. They love Devesha as much as anyone."

"Well, they're gone," the skinny guy said. "Gone the day after someone tried to kill Dev. It can't be a coincidence."

"What interests me is the situation with the I. C.," a pudgy little guy piped in. "Given everything that happened, why reduce to ten? Shiva City needs as many wise minds as possible right now."

"Why?" the hawk-nosed woman said. "Back in India, Kumar and Vasant were close to Babba Vivek. Babba Pappa is using the attempt on Dev's life to consolidate his power."

The skinny guy cocked his head, gesturing in my direction. "Uh, guys, maybe this conversation isn't appropriate right now."

Faces turned. The conversation wasn't seeker-level. The *sadhus* scattered, leaving me and the other seekers standing alone, wondering if we had body odor.

Frustrated by my inability to lay eyes on Mike, I decided to break Manoneeta protocol. "Any of you happen to know a guy named Mike from Iowa? I borrowed five bucks from him this morning and was supposed to meet him here to pay it back."

Almost-Mike glared at me and replied, his voice filled with contempt. "My, you're a nosy one, and your story is garbage. You're looking for someone and not to repay a debt. Most of us know better than to refer to another Manoneeta's past. If someone honored me with details of his life before Shiva City, I wouldn't have the bad manners to pass it on."

Almost-Mike wasn't my son so no point in sticking around. I made my goodbye shaanties and left.

I finished porcelain patrol at 10:30 p. m. I'd gotten a late start because my first tantric therapy session ran late. I didn't know what to expect but found myself pleasantly surprised when we kept our clothes on and gave each other neck rubs. Our group leader explained that the process of revealing ourselves to others would proceed slowly, and it might be several sessions before we shed our attire. Leave it to Manoneetas to do the unexpected. Nude encounter groups and clothed tantric sessions, in the upside-down world that was Shiva City, it almost made sense.

I returned to the *hacienda* and found the TV room empty. My housemates appeared to have gone to bed early. Knowing they'd gang up on me if not informed of tomorrow's appointment with Dev, I composed a note for the *hacienda* bulletin board—short and to the point.

> *Shaanti. I met with Babba Pappa and have an appointment to meet with Sattguru Devesha Thursday afternoon. The Sattguru requested the meeting. I imagine it has something to do with my suggested improvements to the adobe-making operation. Also, as of tomorrow, I have a new work assignment as janitor in the security offices. Cliff*

When I went back to pin it on the board, I discovered a penciled note on lined yellow paper. I'd missed it when I came in.

Big announcement on Dev Line tonight. Community-wide dynamic meditation originally scheduled for Sunday now on for Wednesday night. Training for those who need it starts a half-hour beforehand. Dev won't be there—security reasons. Rumor has it he's leaving for the serenity of the mountains in a few days to fast and do some uninterrupted meditation. Shaanti. Madhuk

I added my note to the rest of the clutter and returned to my room. Most of Shiva City would take part in tomorrow night's event, making it the best chance to spot Mike since my arrival. Optimistic about my chances and looking forward to a good night's sleep, I almost forgot to check my bed for scorpions. The realization hit me as my butt made contact with the mattress. Though tempted to throw caution to the winds and burrow in for the night, discretion won out over immediate comfort. I stood again and whisked the covers back. That's when I spotted it—dead center in the middle of the bed—my missing ID.

Chapter 27

I joined Swami Madhuk and Ma Astra for breakfast. I'd no sooner pulled up a chair when a drop-dead gorgeous brunette put down her tray and joined us. She was the first Manoneeta I'd seen who could have given Dusty a run for the money. I was trying to put my eyes back in my head when Astra spoke up.

"Cliff, this is Ma Nakti, she lives in our *hacienda* and just got back from Albuquerque. She earns her *hissa* dancing at the Silver Spur."

I nodded. "*Shaanti.* I've heard you dance there—a month on and a month off." Too bad the woman wasn't in my encounter group. I could think of 500 worse ways to pass the time than seeing Nakti naked.

"Well, it's all over with the Silver Spur now," Nakti reported. "The ban on outside work means I'll have to get a real job here in Shiva City. Can't say I'll miss dancing all that much."

"You might get a few days off," Madhuk noted. "Babba Pappa has to come up with jobs for 150 workers. Some folks may get assigned to the pods."

Nakti looked up from her tray. "Cream of Wheat, ugh. I knew something was up the minute we pulled up to the gate and saw four security people instead of two. I hope I don't get assigned to a pod. I've spent a lot of time in Albuquerque, but Shiva City is home. On the outside, I'd end up dancing full time to make *hissa* because of rent and groceries. Who needs it?"

Nakti's problems must have been too much for Astra; she gave her the Manoneeta smile and changed the subject. "Cliff is meeting with Sattguru Dev today. He's so new, he doesn't get how unusual it is to make a presentation to the I.C. and become a seeker in just four days. He's been here a week, and Dev wants to talk to him. Not only that, but Cliff is here because he was called."

Nakti looked at me appraisingly. "Don't let Astra's song of praise go to your head. You're still low dog on the totem pole where *hacienda* chores are concerned."

"There's nothing like shoveling mud and working porcelain patrol to keep a guy down to earth," I responded. Though my new janitorial position wouldn't involve a shovel, I expected it required a continuing acquaintance with the world of white ceramic.

Madhuk cut in. "Anybody brief you on how to act when you meet Dev?"

"Not yet," I replied.

"Whatever you do, don't speak unless spoken to. When I got my beads, I sat there for a full fifteen minutes, and he didn't say a thing. Finally, he got up and left. A *sadhu* handed me a box on my way out. Inside, I found a set of beads and a slip of paper with my new name on it."

Astra looked so excited I thought she might jump out of her chair. "When I got my beads, we talked for a half-hour and had tea. He seemed impressed I had the power of astral projection."

Madhuk looked pained. He sniffed and gave Astra the Manoneeta smile. "With Dev, it's not the quantity of time but the quality of the experience. Quietly sharing his perfection for a quarter-hour was the experience of a lifetime.

"The Sattguru and I talked about the beauty of making love," Nakti announced. "Our discussion topped the tawdry reality of the mere physical."

Now that they'd one-upped each other, my companions moved on to a rehash of the wisdom of the lockdown and off-the-wall theories about the reason for the attack on Dev. I'd heard it all before. Wanting to be on time for my first day on the job, I motored through my food and bid them farewell.

While the streets outside the compound weren't filled with Manoneetas, several dozen passed me on the way to work. None came close to looking like my son. I had become good at sizing up and eliminating potential Mikes and was as ready as humanly possible to identify him in a crowd. Failure to do so would mean formulating a plan to leave the ranch. As much as I liked the place, things were getting too weird for me to stay. The news of the additional security at the entrance gate worried me. Were they there to keep intruders out, or residents in? If I found Mike and convinced him to leave, our exit could get complicated.

───────────────

The security guy nodded, indicating that I was free to pass through the white gauze curtain and enter the room beyond. I parted the fabric and entered a sunlit space with walls, ceiling, and plush carpet done in soft white. With its gently filtered sunlight and snowy palette, the room had an airy, otherworldly feel about it. Thirty feet ahead of me on a raised platform sat the Sattguru. I'd been counseled to walk to a white throw pillow some ten feet from the dais and stand behind it. After pausing a moment, I was to bow my head, steeple my hands, and touch them to my forehead. After another brief pause, I could take my seat. I did as instructed.

I expected to see Dev in the lotus position, nestled on an oversized pillow, a bland smile on his face. Instead, I found him enthroned on a gold-trimmed, overstuffed white chair, sipping from a delicate cup, with a bland smile on his face. I bowed and sat. My position on the pillow put his slippered feet at eye level. Two armed bodyguards, dressed in white, rather than pink, stood in the corners of the room. Save for the need for security, the Sattguru business looked like a good gig. Everybody waited on you, and you didn't have to talk if you didn't feel like it.

The minutes ticked by. Dev sat with his eyes closed. His beard and shoulder-length hair had gone gray. I put him in his mid-sixties.

Either he was sleeping, or I was in line to get one of those silent sessions like Madhuk. I sat patiently, wondered why the guy wanted to see me if he didn't have anything to say. But then, finally, he did.

"*Shaanti*. I understand you've been called."

Dev spoke in a normal voice, soft but pleasant. Now that he'd broken the ice, I was free to talk, a good thing because his statement came from left field. The man had to know whether he called me or not. But then again, he could have been trying to trick me.

"Sattguru Devesha. Others have told me I have been called, but only you know if you've done so."

"Ah, but it doesn't work that way," he said in unaccented English. "The universe calls, and you have answered. Your mission here is unknown to me. It may be to help us build a new meditation center, or it could be more. Could be less. Time will tell."

I didn't respond but sat quietly as if I was soaking up the wisdom of the ages. Eventually, the silence got to me.

"Sattguru Devesha, if I may be so bold, why did you wish to see me? I appreciate the opportunity but can't think my actions make me worthy of your time."

His eyes twinkled. "I am a simple holy man who went to a demonstration on how to make adobe bricks when we began building our city. Two of the Inner Circle accompanied me. I chose my companions poorly. As a result, we returned to our community believing there was but one proper way to make adobe and used the setup we'd seen at the demonstration. Because I am the people's leader, those who saw the inefficiency of our operation hesitated to suggest improvements. I know not why as I am hardly an ogre. You came to us and saw the problem. Fate stepped in, and all the little cogs and levers needed to make the change fell into place. I have asked you here to reward you."

I knew better than to ask to get off janitorial duty and enough to do the humble groveling bit. "Thank you. It was nothing Sattguru Devesha."

"When you leave today, you will receive your beads, but first we must do something about your name."

I can kiss butt as well as anyone. "I don't know that I deserve the honor, but as you wish Sattguru Devesha."

"All seekers who have earned their beads receive a new name. For you, I have selected the name Cletus."

The room swam and a blue light flashed as the blood drained from my brain. Thank goodness my adrenalin kicked in just in time to keep me from falling over. Expecting to be hauled away, I looked first to one guard, then the other.

Fake it, Efferding.

"You are surprised by your new name? I couldn't possibly improve on the one you were born with. You will be Swami Cletus."

Shocked stupid, I couldn't think straight but continued to kiss butt. "Thank you, Sattguru Devesha. You are too kind."

"And now, Swami Cletus, you are thinking, 'How does Devesha know my name? Does he have psychic powers? Do spies report to him?'"

I was, kept silent.

"Let this be a lesson to you, seeker. A life of deception does not lead to happiness. Deceiving others becomes a dangerous habit. One deceit builds upon another until one day your soul can no longer find itself. Your quest is to free yourself from the lies entangling you. It will not be easy, but you will not experience peace until you do."

The guy had me nailed. Myra, my kids, marriage to Dusty, all screwed up because I didn't level with people. I would have lost my best friend Lumir if he weren't the most decent person I'd known.

"You may go now, Swami Cletus. From this day, wear the beads you receive on your way out to remind you of your quest. *Shaanti.*"

I shook so badly I could barely stand, but somehow made it to the door, all the while asking myself, "Should I stay in Shiva City?"

———

Back in my room, completely shaken. I'd reported back to the job, but my supervisor, Swami Ravi, took one look at me and shook his head.

"You'd better go home. You're a complete wreck, but don't worry. Meeting the Sattguru Devesha has that effect on many people."

The box of rosewood beads sat next to me on the bed. I opened the lid, took them out, and draped them around my neck. The neckwear didn't make me feel any different, but something had changed. A complete stranger had seen through me. Seen through me because I misrepresented myself when I came to the ranch.

Shoving the box onto the floor and flopping back onto the bed didn't make the situation any clearer. How did he know? Was there something to all this psychic mumbo jumbo, or did my once-missing ID have something to do with it?

My confusion was total. That much was sure. The cult and its members had a bad reputation. Sooner or later, those who joined the People of Light gave them all their money and for whatever reason, getting out wasn't easy. Members who crossed some ill-defined standards of behavior either disappeared or were sent for re-education. Putting all that aside, the people I met seemed incapable of harming anyone, and the Sattguru—

A knock at the door. I went to see who it was. Prema brushed past me, inserting herself into my room

"I need to talk to you, Cliff. I found your driver's license and ratted you out."

And I thought things couldn't get much worse. Anger rose. "Found or swiped?"

"I searched your room and found it on the underside of the drawer. I didn't know if I could use it for leverage, so I took it."

To say I didn't trust the woman was an understatement. She shouldn't have been in the *hacienda* at this time of day. "What are you doing here in the middle of the afternoon? You should be at the motor pool."

"I'm not at work because I get cramps at this time of the month."

She didn't look to be suffering. Not that I cared. "You snuck in and searched my room. That's low, really low."

"It's what I do, Cletus. I'm a private investigator—from Des Moines."

"Your snooping has me in hot water. When I met with Dev today, he knew who I was."

"Babba Pappa does too, you can be sure of it."

Then to add insult to injury, Prema sat on my bed. "Pull up a chair, Cletus. We have more in common than you know."

I wanted to smack her but put my hands on my hips instead. "No, you get off my bed, and you pull up a chair."

She rose and put her hands in the air. "Okay, okay. Sit wherever you want. I'll use the chair."

I retook the bed, angrier than ever. "Where do you get off breaking and entering and stealing my ID! You're a one-woman crime wave, a—"

"I'm working for Gib Sutherland."

"What?"

"He hired my firm to look into the murder of his niece. When I wired your information to the home office, they told me who you were. I nearly lost it. You can't begin to imagine how your being here doing the same thing I am complicates matters."

Prema's revelation took the wind out of my sails. Though she'd treated me badly, revealing the reason for her presence at the ranch was, in fact, an act of trust. It gave me as much on her as she had on me. Her position as a mechanic and shuttle driver could work to my advantage. I needed a link to the world outside.

"Things aren't what they appear to be," I said. "My presence here has nothing to do with Dusty. I'm trying to find my son. I don't know if he's at the ranch or in one of the pods."

"You must really like the kid to do so much to find him."

I'd already said too much. Prema might not know Mike was the reason my wedding didn't come off. If my son wasn't one of her suspects, I could inadvertently put him on her radar.

Worried, I fingered my new beads. "What did you get for turning me in?"

"More you'd ever believe. Not that it's going to help with my investigation."

"You took my driver's license and betrayed me. You owe me. Spill."

"I wouldn't have said anything, but I have a job to do and expected a big payoff. The information was big alright but no help to me. Turns out nobody tried to kill Dev. The whole thing was a hoax dreamed up by Babba Pappa so he'd have an excuse to get rid of Babba Kumar and Vasant. He's consolidating his power and is behind the Inner Circle's ban on outside jobs. He sees people who come and go anywhere but the Harmonic Conversion Center as a threat to his control. The pods are unhappy but accept the limitations on travel to the ranch because they believe it's for Dev's safety."

Prema's narrative didn't make sense. "I met with Dev today. The man may be a strange ranger, but there's no way he's so spaced out he isn't aware of a fabricated story about an attack on him."

"Don't underrate Babba Pappa. The guy's a genius. Dev believes Pappa saved his life by foiling the attack by Kumar and Vasant at the last minute. I can't say for sure, but I expect Babba Pappa laid the blame on a conspiracy cooked up by Babba Vivek and the South Dakota operation."

I rubbed my face with my hands. "I don't know what to make of all this. I'd like to help you out. I want to see Dusty's killers face justice as much as anyone, but I need to stay focused on finding Mike. Did you ever think you could be on the wrong track? The People of Light may have had nothing to do with Dusty's death. Her father Steele is a snake in the grass, a guy with lots of enemies. What better way for someone to get even with him than to kill his daughter?"

"You don't understand the detective business, Cliff. As long as my paycheck keeps coming, there's no incentive to solve the case."

Not only was the woman a snoop, but she had no problem with sponging off her employer. I decided to give her the benefit of the doubt. "You sound burned out. Maybe you should look for a new career."

"Been thinking about it. I want to open my own repair shop and need a stake. This is a good gig. I've been here for nearly two months and inflating my expenses. Add that to what I've already got saved and I'm almost there."

Prema didn't understand who she was dealing with.

"Be careful," I warned. "The Sutherlands don't live by the same rules as the rest of us. Gib's a skinflint. Even if you find Dusty's killers, you'll be lucky to see a penny of your fee."

Prema shrugged. "No skin off my nose. The agency worries about collections. I get my *per diem* and expenses anyway."

"If Steele Sutherland believes you defrauded his brother, he could come after you hard—maybe even pay somebody to break your bones."

"I can take care of myself."

At least he couldn't castrate her. She leaned closer, grabbed my forearm, and squeezed hard. "My gut is killing me. I've gotta go lie down. We'll need to talk—later. In the meantime, don't mess me up."

It would take time to process the new information but for now, I wanted to know who I was dealing with. "Before you go, there's one thing. You know my name, but I don't know yours."

She rolled her eyes, stood, and made for the doorway. When she got there, she turned, folded her arms, and gave me the death stare.

"My business is my business. Keep your mouth shut. You don't and I'll cut your throat."

Not about to let her intimidate me, I glared back. "Your name. Now."

"The handle's Mabel."

Chapter 28

Wearing my new beads, I stood at the intersection of Tranquility Street and Vishnu Avenue, across the street from the entrance to the Devesha Meditation Grounds. A half dozen armed security guards stood outside the gate. Their unexpected presence threw cold water on my plan to stand at the entryway and scan the faces of the entering Manoneetas. Though attendance was not mandatory, the big event would draw most of Shiva City's residents. Dynamic meditation time slots were sacred. No other activities could be scheduled. I skipped the evening meal to get my porcelain patrol duties out of the way and arrived early enough to catch the unbeaded seekers who needed training on their way in. I planned to attend the event as well.

Blue-clad seekers began arriving, chattering excitedly, most wearing scrubs and surgeons' caps. Though they approached the gate from three different directions, keeping tabs on them proved easy. Easy, until an agitated Elvin confronted me.

"How'd you get the beads?"

Focused on the new arrivals, I didn't think about Elvin's tender ego before responding. "Sattguru Dev gave them to me at our meeting this afternoon."

"Glory hound," Elvin snorted. "I spend the afternoon makin' mud while you're passin' time with the Sattguru. Without me, you wouldn't a had a chance at your beads."

I kept eyeballing the new arrivals. "Dev asked to see me. What was I supposed to do? Say no?"

"Look at me when you talk to me. It ain't right. I been here a couple of years and spent a year on the outside studyin' The People before that. You been here 'bout a week, and already met Dev."

Time to get the guy out of my hair. "The only reason Dev wanted to see me is that I was called. He says he knows as little about why I am here as I do myself."

Another little white lie. If I hadn't suggested a better method for making adobe, the Sattguru wouldn't have asked to see me. Since my meeting with Dev, I'd become more aware of how often I played with the truth.

Elvin shook his head. "That bein' called stuff is strange business. If Dev doesn't understand it, how are ordinary people supposed to? It was wrong for me to jump all over you. Babba Pappa will get me my beads all right, and tonight I get to do dynamic meditation without them."

The stream of seekers threatened to become a crowd. Elvin's interruption had already cost me the chance to ID a half dozen entrants. He clapped me on the shoulder.

"Sorry I lost my cool. Come on in with me, and we'll try to get a place at the front."

"Can't," I replied. "I promised some of the folks in my *hacienda* I'd meet them here." Another lie, but it beat telling him I was looking for my son. He nodded and left. I turned my attention back to the crowd. A half-hour passed, and the guards closed the gate. Those not already inside would miss the session. Not a worry for me, I had my beads and could get in later.

I noticed one of the guards staring at me and realized forty-five minutes of standing on the corner looking up and down the street might seem suspicious. I doubted any of them knew the attempt on Dev was a hoax. Babba Pappa wasn't about to let a phony crisis go to waste when he could use it to portray his forces as indispensable to the community's safety. Given that the Sattguru wouldn't be at the shindig, security was over the top.

Unwilling to call further attention to myself, I peeled my backside off the wall I'd leaned against, rounded the corner, and took up position outside the guards' line of sight. The new location would cost me the opportunity to do a comprehensive survey of the new arrivals, but I didn't want my unwarranted lounging reported to Babba Pappa. Showing up under a false name may have counted against me but hadn't put me on his blacklist. Since as many Shiva City residents were running from their past as were searching for enlightenment, a new arrival with a phony identity wasn't all that unusual. Despite all the fuss about simplicity and truth, honesty remained a challenge for many of Dev's followers. As a result, Shiva City's security would never be anything but haphazard.

As the time for the meditation session grew nearer, the trickle of beaded seekers and *sadhus* became a deluge. Twenty-seven hundred followers descended on security's narrow gantlet. A festive mood prevailed; no one seemed upset by the inefficiency. I scoped the crowd from several vantage points, then launched into the throng, eyeballing face after face. I got a look at something like two-thirds of the attendees before my overloaded brain refused to focus. None looked like Mike. Exhausted, I filed through the gate.

Inside I found most of Shiva City gathered on a large, well-trodden flat devoid of vegetation. Though I expected to see a large group milling around a raised platform, I found Manoneetas standing individually, spread out across the entire space. Most were stripping down to their boxer shorts, the women retaining their standard-issue bras. Small, neatly stacked piles of clothes soon dotted the field. I kept my scrubs on and breathed a sigh of relief at the lack of nudity.

Huge towers of speakers flanked each end of the dais. Dev's vacant throne stood in the middle, surrounded by huge baskets of flowers. Men and women, apparently musicians, sat behind a low row of microphones. I could make out cheesy-looking horns, tambourines, and drums—lots of drums. I knew the event was about to get going when I saw Babba Pappa walk onto the stage and take up a microphone. He *shaantied* us and began:

My friends, tonight marks the first of many nights when all seekers, whether beaded or not, will come together to participate in community-wide dynamic meditation. As you know, Sattguru Devesha has gone to the mountains to fast and meditate. His chair may be empty, but he is with us in spirit. If you have not yet felt his presence, you soon will do so. Remember the purpose of group meditation is to shut down our brains and open our hearts so that, together, we may find the beauty within. Let us now begin with our breathing exercises.

I lost interest in Babba Pappa when the gathered Manoneetas started in on their breathing exercises. The people in front of me looked as if they'd gone mad—bouncing up and down, taking such extreme breaths they looked like they were convulsing. Arms waved in the air, heads shook, hair flew. I realized they were altering their mental processes by hyperventilating. A 360-degree survey of the grounds revealed a sea of gyrating Manoneetas, all with their eyes closed. Unsure if they were peeking and not willing to draw attention to myself, I closed my eyes and put my heart and soul into it. My performance would have earned me an Oscar. I hyperventilated along with the rest of them, shook, and hopped. The thing went on for so long that I started to get lightheaded.

I quit when I heard Babba Pappa's voice say stop. I opened my eyes. The huge speaker setup came to life and the musicians started softly playing some kind of music from India. A few minutes later, Babba Pappa reappeared at the mic and said just one word:

Explode!

Someone must have flipped a switch, the musicians upped their tempo and the sound of their playing erupted from the speaker columns with ear-shattering force. People went crazy. They started dancing and shouting. Some screamed at the top of their lungs. One guy started doing somersaults and kept yelling for his mommy. The woman next to me spun around so fast that she got dizzy, fell, and threw up. Everyone kept their eyes open, and each looked hell-bent on outdoing the strangeness of the others. In retrospect, attending the training session would have been a good idea, but now I had to come up with something fast. Without giving it much thought, I started dancing around like I was walking on hot coals and shouting curses that would have embarrassed a longshoreman. If my actions hadn't been understated compared to those around me, I'd have felt like a complete idiot. After a minute or so, I flashed on the image of Steele Sutherland's fist coming at me and got really mad.

No need to fake anymore. I started punching the air, imagining myself knocking his teeth down his throat. I broke his nose, smashed both his eyes, and hit him below the belt. When I saw him go down, I screamed and kicked him again and again—in the head, in the groin, in his back. I repeated the sequence of the beating over and over until I heard Babba Pappa yell stop. I hate to say it but giving an imaginary Steele the beating of a lifetime felt good, very good. A little guilt would have been in order, but it's hard not to let it all out when everybody around you is doing the same thing. I decided if I ever had to do one of these dynamic sessions again, I'd replace Steele with Gib. As exhausted as if I had gone ten rounds with Mohammed Ali, I put my hands on my knees and found myself panting like I set the record for a three-minute mile. And then Babba Pappa gave the next instruction:

Howl!

All around me folks got down on their hands and knees and started making like lovesick coyotes howling at the moon. Three thousand people, I couldn't believe the noise. The guy beside me sounded like somebody was pulling his fingernails out. No wonder Dusty ended up in the funny farm. I made some half-hearted howls wondering how I'd make it through the foolishness when it occurred to me that the woman to the right of me had a good soprano voice. Since her howl was repetitive and my baritone isn't too shabby, I decided to harmonize. It didn't sound all that bad. I could tell she caught on to me when she dropped her tone a bit to bring us into better alignment. We kept improving and made some sweet music, coaxing one another to new heights. Stupid, but it passed the time. We bayed and brayed until Pappa's next command.

Dance!

My heart sank. All around me people gyrated the way they do in what passes for nightclubs these days. I've taught dance for over a quarter-century and know a hundred moves in a dozen different dances. Professional pride wouldn't let me sink to the level people refer to as boogying. I was ready to throw in the towel when I realized I could Lindy hop to the band's strange Indian rhythm. I broke into a few Lindy moves and came up with the coolest variation on the Shorty George I'd ever seen. Not wanting to forget it, repeated it, again and again, to burn it into my muscle memory. Engrossed in my project, the Pappa's next announcement brought me up short.

Freeze!

The music stopped, and everyone froze in their tracks, the gentle whisper of a desert breeze the only sound breaking the silence. After forty-five minutes of intense physical activity, the relaxation felt good. I closed my eyes to let the gently moving air wash over me and felt even better. I don't know how long I stayed that way, but the quiet ended when Babba Pappa shouted:

Celebrate!

Some of the people around me collapsed. Though there was no music, some went back to their so-called dancing. Others shouted at the top of their lungs. Some hugged; some cried. One guy lay on the ground shaking and foaming at the mouth. I stood still, at a complete loss, until a woman behind me put her hand on my hips.

"You dance," she said.

I turned my head. "Yup."

"*Conga* line!" she shouted.

I needed no encouragement and off we went, picking up other dancers along the way.

Bah-da-da-da-dah. Kick! *Bah-da-da-da-dah.* Kick!

We threaded our way past the bodies of collapsed seekers and groups of the more socially inclined. The musicians on stage noticed and came up with a makeshift Indian-style *conga* tune. We must have had 350 laughing, underwear-clad Manoneetas in our line before it finally broke up. On the way home I broke into my new and improved Shorty George move, strutting down Tranquility Street to the cheers of passersby.

I hadn't had so much fun in years.

I returned to a deserted *hacienda* where I found a poster board sign suspended from the TV room ceiling.

Swami Cletus, surprise! Your prabodhan party starts at 9:30 at the communal center.

My watch said ten. One thing about life as a Manoneeta. I never had a clue about what was going on. Nobody said a word to me about the shindig. Shaking my head at the strangeness of it all, I made an about-face and headed for the communal center. On entering, I found an elbow-to-elbow crowd sipping fruit smoothies and eating what looked to be ice cream from disposable bowls. Crepe paper streamers hung suspended from the ceiling as did a hand-lettered sign reading 'Congratulations, Swami Cletus.' Rock music blared from unseen speakers.

"Swami Cletus, you're here!" Astra tried to make her way through the mass of bodies but, petite woman that she was, failed. She waved at me to join her. I worked my way through the mob and when I finally reached her, was greeted with a big hug.

"Can you see Madhuk?" she shouted. "Over in the corner?"

"Yeah."

"We saved you a seat. Just push your way on over. I'll be right be-hind you."

I did, and she followed, putting her arms around my waist so as not to get sidelined. Madhuk sat with Ma Nakti, Mabel/Prema, and Raj. When we got to the table, I saw just one vacant seat.

"Looks like someone took your chair," Astra said. "Sit down before we lose that one too."

I did, and she sat on my lap before I had time to collect myself.

"What's this thing about?" I shouted.

Madhuk and Mabel shrugged. They couldn't hear me.

Astra whispered in my ear. "It's a party to celebrate the new swa-mi in our compound."

I used my normal voice. "Nobody told me. You're lucky I'm here."

Astra giggled. "We'd have celebrated without you. If you didn't make it, it would have been your fate."

"Too bad the room is so noisy. It's hard to talk."

Astra kissed my cheek. "Don't worry, they'll be gone soon. Nobody misses a *prabodhan* party*.* It's a big celebration—the only time we eat ice cream and cake. Servings are unlimited, and we're having straw-berry smoothies. That's why so many people are here. They'll start leav-ing when they've had their fill."

"Where's the food? I better get there. I don't want to miss out and have everyone tell me it's my fate."

Astra licked my earlobe. "Let go of your stress. Ma Shivani won't let that happen."

Images of Shivani backing me into the toilet bowl returned with a vengeance. I tried chasing them away, but they seemed determined to undermine what otherwise had been a nice evening. Astra started a loud conversation with Mabel that I couldn't hear anyway, so I sat qui-etly, content to wait for my dessert.

Eventually, the crowd began to thin, and the music stopped. I saw Ma Shivani headed my way banging two aluminum pans together, ap-parently a signal for silence. A pair of Stetson-wearing seekers, bearing an oversized bowl of vanilla ice cream and a large pitcher of strawberry smoothie followed in her wake. She quit whacking the pans as she approached our table and launched into an oration.

Tonight, we are celebrating Cliff's transition to Swami Cletus. It happened fast, but I hear he earned it by suggesting we build the meditation center with adobe bricks containing the prayers of all the world's religions. Our new temple to enlightenment will serve as a shining example of tolerance in a world still plagued with bigotry and war. Swami Cletus has been called to Shiva City. Many believe the universe put him at our disposal for the purpose of fulfilling Sattguru Devesha's dream of a center truly worthy of the People of Light.

That may or may not be, but of one thing I am certain. Swami Cletus was not called here to fill the lonely space in Ma Shivani's heart. So focused was he on his duties to our compound that he jumped into the toilet rather than allow himself to be distracted by my physical charms.

The entire room broke into howls of laughter as I felt the heat of embarrassment rise in my cheeks.

"Don't worry," said Astra. "We've already heard all about it. It's traditional to roast a new swami."

Shivani banged her pans and started in again.

So dedicated is Swami Cletus that he threw Ma Prema from his very own bed rather than lose the precious sleep that enables him to give his full attention to our cause. Sensitive soul that he is, he didn't want Prema to feel rejected, so he compared her touch to that of a scorpion crawling across his chest. Ma Astra likes to say that of all the Manoneetas in Shiva City, Swami Cletus is the most in need of our tantric classes, and so tonight, Swami Cletus, we present you with the swami's traditional ice cream meal. A parade has been organized in your honor.

Pans started banging in the far corner of the room, the crowd parted, and a half dozen seekers, dressed in their underwear and holding toilet brushes on their shoulders, marched up to the table. Shivani stepped to the side.

"Swami Cletus, we salute you," the leader of the group announced.

"Present brushes!" she ordered.

The ragtag group stood at attention, held their brushes out in front of them, and with more or less success, twirled them like batons.

"To the rear," the leader commanded.

The group turned, dropped their boxers, and mooned me. Giggling like hyenas, they tossed their brushes into the air and scattered. The crowd roared. I sat dumbfounded, Astra still on my lap, unsure of how to react.

"Say *dhanyavaad*," she whispered.

"Donnie avid," I said, waving at the assembled guests.

And with that, Astra got off my lap, and the servers presented me with my ice cream. The big entertainment for the night now over, many of the partygoers left. Most who remained lived in my *hacienda*. Mabel and Madhuk got up and cleared what appeared to be a small dance floor by pushing some tables aside while I sat with folded arms, trying to determine how insulted I should be. Moderate-volume popular music replaced the head-banging rock.

Mabel and Madhuk returned to the table. "I asked Madhuk to bring a few of his oldies cassettes along," Mabel said. "I thought some of us might want to dance."

I glared at her. "Nice job blabbing the scorpion business from one end of the ranch to the other."

Astra chimed in. "There are no secrets in Shiva City."

Raj chuckled. "What do you expect? This is a small town. Now everybody in the compound knows who you are, and a lot of them will become your friends. Lighten up, Swami." He grabbed Nakti's hand, and they went out to boogie. Astra floated onto the floor and danced alone. Her movements had nothing to do with the music.

"Raj is right," Madhuk observed. "One of the reasons we roast a new swami is to allow his colleagues to learn more about him. The other is to remind him not to get too full of himself."

Mabel patted my hand. "Lose your grouchy face and let's go out to dance."

I'd finished my ice cream but didn't want to. She rose and pulled on my arm.

"Okay," I said. "Just one, and I don't boogie."

We joined the others. Mabel's teenage lessons stood her in good stead. One dance turned into several; she was a natural. We'd just returned to the table when Frank Sinatra's *New York, New York* came up in the rotation.

I did a double take. "I thought this was an oldies tape."

Madhuk sniffed. "Get with the times, Clete. The song came out three years ago."

In my world, oldies came from the forties and fifties. Still, the song made for a hard-to-resist foxtrot. I led Mabel back on the floor.

The foxtrot is a traveling dance with big, sweeping moves. To do it properly, you've got to move around the floor. I wasn't in the mood to let the small space confine me and danced Mabel through the aisles between the tables and around the room. The lady could dance. As we glided through the room, I realized I had a problem. I'd been dancing at least four days a week for a quarter-century, too long to miss the warning signs. The languid mouth, the half-open eyes, a body gone beyond the music on the way to surrender. Emotional entanglement loomed. Wanting to put a stop to it, I danced her through the propped-open doors of the communal center and out into the garden. The music faded as we approached a small bench. I removed my arm from her back and led her to it. We sat.

"No," I said still holding her hand. "Not gonna happen."

Mabel blinked. "Why waste a good lead-in? Everyone thinks you've danced me away to take me back to the *hacienda* and ravish me."

I liked the woman. We were becoming friends, and I didn't want to hurt her. "Think a minute. The woman I loved was murdered two months ago. It's too soon. I can't."

Mabel tilted her head and looked up. "Life is for the living. It's too short to waste any of it."

She wanted to kiss. I took her shoulders, drew her in, and kissed her on the forehead, moved back. "I know life is short, but there's more to it."

"My friends call me Belle."

"I hope I'm in that category."

"You're hanging by a thread. Most girls aren't big on being rejected—especially twice. I never imagined someone would look at making love to me as a chore. You might not think it, but some guys even fantasize about me."

"It's not like that."

"Not like what?"

At a loss for words, I put my hand on top of hers. A coyote howled in the distance. It took me a while, but I finally came out with it.

"It's not about you. It's about what's missing."

"I hope you're not one of those guys who's looking for a wife."

She didn't get it.

"Actually, I'm looking for more, and that's what's missing—the magic."

Belle stood and crossed her arms. "I can't believe it," she muttered. "I finally meet a guy I'm attracted to, and he turns out to be a romantic."

She stalked off into the night. I stayed behind on the bench wondering why I ever thought we'd be friends. The woman didn't understand loss, and she certainly didn't understand me.

Chapter 29

A pile of lint, hair, and scrap paper collected along the front edge of my dry mop. Another twenty minutes and my second day at the security office would come to an end. I heard approaching footsteps and looked up to see Ravi, my boss, headed my way.

"Cletus," he said, "bad news. You know Swami Adnan?

I shook my head.

"He's the guy who comes in after you. Messed up big time and is on the way to South Dakota. He got caught stealing a tape deck from one of the communal centers, so you need to cover his shift. He does the I. C. suite and Babba Pappa's office.

"A problem, Ravi," I replied. "My *hacienda* has communal center cleanup this week, and I have porcelain patrol. I need to clean the heads after work, or the *hacienda* will be on again for another week."

"You'll just have to do it after your shift here. Let's go over what you need to do."

He handed me a checklist and gave me a tour of the areas I needed to clean. Since Babba Pappa stayed in his office until nine each night, Ravi told me to save the big guy's suite until the last part of my shift. Unhappy as hell that I'd get to bed at one and be awakened by flutes and chirping birds at 6:30, I nonetheless smiled pleasantly and got on with it. Sixteen hours of janitorial work might sound like a snap, but time crawled by. As instructed, I reported to the main security station at 9:00 p.m. Save for the gorilla of a guy sawing logs, his feet on the counter, the place was deserted. The dreamer was anything but beautiful and could have given Madhuk a run for the money as master of the yoga of sleeping. If noise counted for anything, the somnolent rumbling of his chest-deep *basso profundo* put Madhuk's nasal baritone to shame.

I gave his boots a sideways push. "I'm here to clean Pappa's suite and need the key."

Rip Van Winkle snorted and opened his lids. "Just a minute," he said. Raising his knees, he reached under his thighs and pulled out a drawer without displacing his feet. He extracted a ring with a single key on it. "This is a master. It works for all the doors in the area. Sign the date and your name on the clipboard. Return the key before you leave."

I took the pen dangling from a piece of string taped to the board and scrawled Swami Cletus. The only other name on the form was Adnan's. Since the commotion resulting from the bogus attempt on Dev's life hadn't resulted in a single request for the master key, more than one must have been in circulation. The People of Light had no understanding of security. They may have had firearms to burn, but a sleepy desk clerk gave me a key to the offices of the most powerful man in Shiva City without asking for identification. I returned the pen to its holder, grabbed my cleaning cart, and wheeled past the counter and through the anteroom used by Babba Pappa's secretary.

Pappa's office looked pretty much as I remembered it—semi-neat with a large desk, visitors' chairs, filing cabinets on opposing walls, and a conference table with a globe on it. His computer sat on the desk, its cursor blinking. Even if I wanted to see what was on it, I wouldn't have known how. I managed to suppress my laughter when Pappa mentioned he dreamed of the day when all the paperwork in his filing cabinets would be stored on a computer. Anyone with half a brain knew that the machines were only good for calculations and bookkeeping.

Two rooms away, Rip Van Winkle was back where he left off. The morphean noises rumbling from his prodigious nose were hard to miss. Not only was Rip fast asleep, but his position at the counter precluded a direct line of sight into Pappa's office. I doubted I'd get a chance to snoop like this again. Though I tidied up a little, for the most part, I nosed around.

Pappa kept his desk unlocked. I plopped into his swivel chair, and the ten minutes I spent going through it proved instructive. He used the file drawers to provide convenient access to the organization's most recent accounting and investment records. No orders or invoices, this was the big stuff. I'm not a financial whiz, but it was easy to see that worldwide, the People of Light were sitting on seventy-five million and probably more. Pappa might be the brains behind the organization, but how the man could be so careless with sensitive paperwork was beyond me. Professor Flanagan would have killed his firstborn to get his hands on this sort of information. I can't say the figures shocked me; they proved what everyone knew—the cult was loaded. Interesting information indeed, but useless to me and of no help in my search for Mike.

I looked at the two rows of Russ Bassett filing cabinets lining the longer walls of Pappa's office. Randomly going through them would be a fool's errand, but I exited Pappa's chair and made a pass around the room to give them the once-over. The labels on those to the right of Pappa's desk appeared to hold records from the People's time in India. Those on the left looked more current. A closer inspection of the cabinets' neatly labeled drawers revealed they ran the gamut of everything from donor information and construction projects to health care and personnel. A top drawer in one cabinet looked especially interesting. Its label identified its contents with a single word—Census.

Censuses list names of people and where they live, so I suspected the drawer represented my best shot at learning if Mike was affiliated with a pod or living in Shiva City. I gave the drawer a pull. It didn't budge. Pappa may have left his desk wide open, but his filing cabinets were locked, likely the work of a secretary with a better handle on security than the boss. I expected the key would be in the outer office and went to search for it.

I'd just entered the anteroom when Van Winkle snorted. Silence followed. Unsure of the situation, I walked out into reception and made for the restroom. I passed Sleeping Beauty without looking back and entered a small room I recently cleaned. After occupying myself with the tasks the room was designed for, I checked on Old Rip on my way back. Still propped in his chair, his head nodded. My best guess—Van Winkle was drifting in and out.

My shift was drawing to a close. I'd come too far and invested too much time in Shiva City to play it safe, so I returned to the secretary's office and made for the desk. No joy. It was locked. I looked around the room. Not much to see—a coat rack, a three-drawer file, an oversized bulletin board, some sets of open-faced shelving. With one ear open for sounds of activity on Rip's part, I checked the secretary's filing cabinet— locked. I was about to re-enter Babba Pappa's office when I spotted a small nail driven into the frame of the door to the big guy's lair. On it, hung two rings of keys.

I picked them off their holder and recognized the profile imme- diately—Russ Bassett keys. The company set the standard for high-qual- ity steel office cabinets. I'd ordered Russ Bassetts for Cleatzy's.

A tag attached to each ring identified it as the set to be used for the cabinets on the north or south wall, demonstrating once again the incompatibility of the Manoneeta lifestyle with sound security mea- sures. Labeled keys on display a few feet from locked cabinets. The only good thing you could say about the proximity was a self-respecting bur- glar would discount it as too obvious to investigate.

I took the ring for the north wall and picked up my dry mop on my way back to the Census drawer where I leaned it against a nearby cabinet in the hope of grabbing it and pretending to clean if someone came in. Though the odds the distraction would succeed were minus- cule, the illusion of having a plan gave me a sense of comfort.

There were eight keys on the ring. The correct one would unlock all four of a cabinet's drawers simultaneously. The fifth key I tried un- locked the cabinet with the Census drawer. Inside I found a series of files arranged by the names of states of the union followed by another series arranged by the names of countries. I pulled the folder for New Mexico and discovered an alphabetical list of names and addresses on the inside, each entry followed by a numeric code. The information on the sheets amounted to little more than a mailing list. I suspected the code represented a location where files containing more information on the person could be found. The People of Light claimed a worldwide membership of twenty-five thousand. There was no way detailed information on each of them could be stored in Pappa's office.

I started scanning the sheets and was surprised to discover not all New Mexico members lived in Shiva City. There were pods in Santa Fe and Albuquerque. More interesting was what I didn't find, a listing for Michael Hinkley. Maybe the information was dated. I went through the sheets again and this time discovered something I missed. A sheet at the back of the stack bearing the caption Addendum. On it were hand-written notices of new arrivals and departures. I found the entries marking my first full day in Shiva City and those for the reassignment of Swami Amrit and Babbas Kumar and Visant to Bison, South Dakota. Again, no Mike. My son must have been assigned to one of the pods.

Disgusted that I'd been wasting my time, I returned the folder to its location. About to close the drawer, I noticed an orange-colored file tab I'd overlooked. It sat at the back of the files arranged by the states of the union. The tab read Index, something I should have noticed the first time around. I pulled the folder and discovered it contained an al-phabetical list of names along with a notation for the state of residence. Again, no listing for a Mike Hinkley, but this time I was smart enough to look for an addendum and that's where I found him.

Hinkley, Michael, seeker, pod affiliate from Madison, Wisconsin to Bison, South Dakota.

I had yet to process the information when I saw a surly-looking Van Winkle standing in the doorway. "Whatcha doing in here?" he growled. "Nobody ever takes this long. Pack it up."

Dropping the folder on top of the others in the drawer, I stepped to the left, putting myself between the cabinet and the approaching guard. I was reaching for the broom and using my other arm to elbow the drawer shut as he came into full view.

"Just finishing up," I said as I headed for my cleaning cart.

Rip watched as I placed the mop in its clip. "I'll take the key," he announced, extending his hand.

I was ready to hand him the file keys when I realized I couldn't. They were still in the file cabinet's lock. How I found the presence of mind to reach into my pocket and hand him the master key, I'll never know.

"Don't forget to record the time on your way out," he said. "I'll lock the office."

"No problem," I said, and meant it. Compared to the blunder of leaving a ring of keys hanging from a file lock, scrawling the time on a sheet of paper was no problem at all.

Chapter 30

I kicked off the covers, plopped my feet on the floor, and stretched. Though I'd finished porcelain patrol at the communal center at 1:30 a.m., I felt well-rested. Maybe it had something to do with sitting quietly to the sound of the great Om and bird chatter, or maybe it was relief at finally knowing where to find Mike. I should have been concerned about the key ring I left in Babba Pappa's office, but the light shining through my window promised a beautiful morning, and I wasn't prepared to worry myself into feeling tired. After a quick shower and some oatmeal, I'd show up early for my shift. Maybe I could find a way back into Pappa's office to extract the telltale key ring from the filing cabinet.

I'd just exited the communal center shower and was on my way to breakfast when I spotted Belle lounging outside the dining room door. As I approached the entrance, she grabbed my arm. I felt the first crack in the cocoon of my morning bliss when she pulled me in the direction of the center's nearest exit.

"We've gotta talk," she insisted.

"But I'm hungry."

"Get over it."

Knowing it would be easier to hear her out than argue, I gave in and followed her out the door. An unwelcome feeling of *déjà vu* came over me when she led me to the bench where I'd rejected her advances.

Though unprepared for intimacy with anyone, I felt vaguely guilty. The good-natured residents of our *hacienda* slept with each other at the drop of a hat. By comparison, my rejection felt uptight and stingy. Though I wasn't ready to change my mind, remorse clobbered what little was left of my good mood.

"I found a letter from the agency in my Santa Rosa post office box," she announced. "I've been recalled, and my *per diem* ends in two days. I have shuttle duty the day after tomorrow. When I get to town, I'm going to pick up the rental car the agency has arranged for me and vamoose. I don't think you're going to find your son. You should come with me while you have the chance."

Time stopped. The world went silent. Either Gib Sutherland had given up on the investigation or law enforcement identified Dusty's murderers. Gib wasn't the type to give up.

When I found the presence of mind to respond, my voice sounded far away. "They've found Dusty's killers. Who were they?"

Belle winced. "I have no idea. The letter said my *per diem* was ending and gave me the skinny on the car, nothing else."

I realized I was holding my breath and exhaled, disappointment filling the space once occupied by air. "Mike was never here," I mumbled. "He's in South Dakota, but I'm not ready to leave yet."

Belle frowned, "You found out, and you're still here?"

"I didn't know until last night. The regular guy didn't show, so I got drafted into cleaning Pappa's office and started poking around in his files. Mike was with the Madison Wisconsin pod."

"You've got a better nose than I gave your credit for. Since there's nothing more you can do here, you can leave with me. The agency usually charges for rescues, but what they don't know won't hurt them. Wear the cowboy outfit with a blue hat and leave the scrubs and luggage behind. You'll ride out in style."

"I don't think I'm ready to go yet."

"Why in the hell don't you want to leave?"

"There are construction plans in the files. If I get assigned to clean Pappa's office again, maybe I can find the ones for the Research and Re-education Center. Besides, I could use a little more vacation."

Belle took my hands and positioned her face six inches from mine. I didn't want to kiss her and turned my head.

"Look at me, Cletus. Are you crazy? How are you going to get out of here? I can get you a pass into town and chauffeur you out through the front gate. What good is a diagram of the Manoneeta detention center? What are you going to do with it? Raise an army and invade the place so you can spring your son?"

Leaving before I formulated a plan to retrieve Mike felt wrong. "Maybe it'll help, and maybe it won't, but the more information I have, the better."

"Maybe it'll help, and maybe you've been here too long."

"I'll be okay."

She dropped my hands, grabbed my shoulders, and gave me a shake. "Listen up, Dumbo. No exit pass, armed guards at the gate, fifteen miles to town, search parties coming after you, and if they don't get you, the cowboys will. There are rumors of security hauling Manoneetas off the streets of Santa Rosa. The Inner Circle gets more paranoid by the day.

"I can take care of myself."

She pushed me backward, hard. "Shiva City place is starting to feel like an up-and-coming Jonestown. Think about it. A phony attempt on Dev's life, keeping new people out, making it next to impossible for Manoneetas to leave. Babba Pappa is consolidating his power. Things could blow sky high any day."

"Belle, get a grip. You should hear yourself. I won't be drinking any Kool-Aid. I'll be fine."

She sighed and let go of my shoulders. "You're going to stay?"

"I'm going to stay."

"You dumb sonofabitch," she said, then took my face in her hands and kissed me hard—too hard. If it had been Dusty, you'd have had to scrape what was left of my poor, dissipated body off the bench with a putty knife. The kiss was nice enough, but Belle wasn't Dusty. My lack of enthusiasm must have registered. Belle stood, and shaking her head, began walking away.

"Goodbye, Cletus," she said without looking back.

I didn't recognize the guard at the main security station but sauntered through the lobby checking to see if the door leading to Pappa's office was closed. It wasn't. A woman *sadhu*, cradling a cup of what I assumed was tea, sat at the desk in the outer room. Behind her, the door to Pappa's office stood open. I couldn't tell if Pappa was inside and certainly didn't have a plan for retrieving the key ring.

Having no good option, I went to the washroom, waited a minute or so, and exited, heading toward the big guy's office. I waved at the guard behind the counter, *shaantied* him, and strode into Pappa's anteroom as if I were expected. When the *sadhu* behind the desk looked up, I gave her my full-bore Cletus Efferding smile, before going into my song and dance.

"*Shaanti*, my name is Swami Cletus. Adnan, the evening housekeeper has been reassigned and couldn't make it last night, so Babba Pappa asked me to fill in for him. I expect I'll be asked to take the assignment again tonight. I'm new to housekeeping and want to get off on the right foot. Is everything ok? Is there anything I should be doing differently?"

A glance revealed both rings of file keys hanging on the doorframe.

My full-bore smile must have worked. The woman beamed at me. "*Shaanti*, Swami Cletus, nothing comes to mind. The wastebaskets are empty, I didn't see dust anywhere, and the offices are as tidy as can be expected. I appreciate your asking."

"Okay, glad to hear it. *Shaanti*."

I turned to go and was almost at the door when she called me back. I retraced my steps.

"There is something. This morning I found a ring of keys hanging in the lock in one of the filing cabinets in Babba Pappa's office."

Crap.

"The files are confidential," she said. "It's important they remain locked. Pappa has so much on his mind that he is sometimes forgetful. If you should see keys dangling from a desk lock or one of the files, please remove them and hang them on that little nail." She gestured to the doorframe.

"Be happy to," I replied. "*Shaanti.*"

Security, Manoneeta style. I spent the better part of the day expecting Ravi to approach me with the news that I'd be working Adnan's shift again. He never showed, but I would have been happy to. I wanted to know more about the workings and layout of the South Dakota center. Sensitive files, a sleepy desk attendant, easy access to keys, and the free run of Babba Pappa's office, coming up with the information would be a piece of cake. I cursed myself for not offering to take Adnan's place on a permanent basis.

Ravi finally showed up five minutes before my shift was over. I was about to wheel my cleaning cart into the closet off the main hallway when he rounded the corner. His voice preceded him. "The shift starts and ends at the janitor's closet down the hall. It's where we keep the timesheet."

I expected to see the new evening janitor following him. Three pink-uniformed security guards made their appearance instead. It took all of five-eighths of a second to realize I was toast. Nothing for it but to wait for them to arrest me. The guy in the lead didn't look happy, but then again, a cheerful countenance would have been hard for him. He had the eyes of a dead lizard.

Two of the guards brushed past me, stopped, and turned to face me. They'd taken the position to box me in between Lizard Face and themselves. Ravi started walking down the hall backward, putting distance between the operation and himself, but unable to look away. Lizard put his hand on the butt of his pistol and glared at me.

"What, no *shaanti*?" I asked.

He didn't look amused. "Swami Cletus, we have a policy against the abuse of a position of trust in Shiva City. You have taken advantage of your housekeeping responsibilities to rifle through sensitive files, compromising the security of the information found therein. This is a serious infraction. You need to come to Harmony House to explain your actions. Please come with us."

I couldn't help myself. "Found therein? You flunk out of law school?"

Not the smartest move. Lizard Face slapped me so hard my eyes bounced back and forth in their sockets. They say it's a double insult when a man slaps another man. The respectful thing to do is to haul off and belt him with your fist. Having been on the receiving end of a punch that fractured my eye socket, I'd take a slap any day.

Still, I couldn't let the insult pass by unremarked. "I hate to say this, but there is a policy against physical violence in Shiva City. Slapping another Manoneeta is assault. When I get to my hearing, I intend to inform them of your actions."

One second, I was having a spirited conversation with Lizard Face, the next I was on the floor, reeling from a second slap and getting kicked in the gut. I barfed.

"Get up!" somebody ordered.

I tried several times, finally made it. My predicament was far worse than Amrit and Steven's. They were taken into custody for shoving Elvin and stomping on his hat. Apparently, snooping through files was an offense of far greater magnitude.

Chapter 31

The room had no windows. A steel door set in a steel frame marked the exit. The only furnishing in the place was a galvanized slop bucket. I sat in a corner going over the events of the day. Pappa's secretary must have mentioned the misplaced keys to him. In my haste to close the cabinet drawer, I left the census folder lying on top of the others. What with being caught wandering through temporary housing and entering Shiva City under an assumed name, it wouldn't have taken much to realize I was searching for someone.

Though I didn't get a chance to go through the files for information on the Research and Re-education Center, things were working out. I'd soon be on my way to South Dakota to join Mike. The only way to screw it up would be to show up at my hearing and come off as a good guy. I wasn't going to let that happen. I'd just settled in for a nap and was on the border between wakefulness and sleep when the sound of an opening door brought me back to consciousness. I looked up to see a security guard whose tiny, rectangular-framed glasses would have been the center of my attention if not for his sporting the scraggliest beard in Shiva City. He held a tray covered with a cloth towel.

"*Shaanti*, I brought your dinner," he said with a shy, blissed-out smile.

If I had a mind to, I could have jumped him, shoved the tray in his face, and been out in the hallway in twenty seconds. Instead, I asked, "Do you know when my hearing is scheduled?"

He looked surprised. "You're getting a hearing? There haven't been any since the attempt on Sattguru Devesha's life."

News to me, not that I cared. They could just as well send me to the Center without one. "It was a fake, you know. The attempt on the Sattguru's life. Dev doesn't know it, but Pappa cooked the whole thing up, so he'd have an excuse to consolidate his power."

My food jockey smiled blandly and set the tray on the floor. "Interesting theory, but fate rules the universe. Babba Pappa will either be an influential leader, or he won't, but only enlightenment matters."

"I guess you're right. I expect fate has me going to the Re-education Center. Do you know when they'll come to pick me up?"

He gave me the Manoneeta smile. "I can't say as I do. Life is filled with uncertainty, and after all, time is relative."

The guy had to be the spaciest headcase in Shiva City. I wonder if Lizard Face assigned him to bring me my meal just to torment me.

"I suppose they'll take me there in one of the vans. I hope it's comfortable. South Dakota is a long way off. I expect they'll drive straight through and even then, it could take most of a day."

The deliveryman backed up a step and raised his eyebrows. "Not everyone goes to South Dakota because not everyone is amenable to rehabilitation. For some, fate has chosen a different destination.

"Where do they get sent?" I asked.

The guy smiled vaguely. "To meet their fate, of course."

———————————

The van chattered and rattled over the unpaved road. I lay in the cargo compartment, on my back, blindfolded, my arms duct-taped behind me, a ball gag stuffed in my mouth. There must have been a sale on the tape at the hardware store—they wrapped my legs from ankle to knee. Something looped around the tape on my arms prevented me from sitting up,

When I asked Lizard Face where they were taking me, I got the silent treatment and took a few swats to the head. My ears rang; one of them bled. A sincere thank-you drifted heavenward when I realized he wouldn't be part of the two-man crew taking me to my destination.

Save for Lizard Face, the guards hadn't been especially brutal. They weren't especially nice either. The last person who spoke to me was the guy who brought my dinner the night before, and what he said then hadn't been especially comforting. The bit about going to meet my fate unnerved me. Manoneetas talk about fate a lot, so I didn't know if he was spouting party-line blather or referring to something more dire. When I heard references to folks who were not seen again, I assumed they'd been sent to South Dakota or left the cult of their own volition. Now I wasn't so certain.

The rattling of the van indicated on a dirt road, but not going cross country—

the ride wasn't rough enough. That didn't mean the jostling didn't hurt. They'd trussed me up like a Thanksgiving turkey, and I had no means of cushioning myself against the jolts. Pinned under my back, my elbows banged the floor as we bounced. The unnatural position put so much pressure on my shoulders that I feared they'd be torn from my body. No matter how I cut it, things were going poorly. My well-being meant nothing to the cult leadership. Certain they intended to kill me, a bolt of anxiety shot through me, and I lost control of my bladder.

The ride smoothed out—pavement. I couldn't look out at the surroundings to determine the direction of travel because they'd blocked the windows of the cargo compartment so no one could see inside. Ten minutes after our turn onto the blacktop, I realized we'd entered a town, most likely Santa Rosa.

After a couple of turns, the van slowed and stopped. Between the road noise and blaring radio, I was unable to hear what the folks in front were talking about. The driver killed the engine. Too bad he didn't mute the radio. I could only catch a word or two, something to do with the rocker Bruce Springsteen and a hungry harp. The music suddenly went from loud to skull-splitting, and at the end of the harp song, just as abruptly ceased.

The van rocked and I heard a door open. "Springsteen's got a hungry heart. But he's got nothing on my stomach."

The other guy. "Don't I know it. Real food—finally. I'm ordering a pair of steaks and a baked potato."

"Yeah, loaded with sour cream. Lots of sour cream."

They must have stopped at a place to eat. The van rocked again; doors closed. No one bothered to check up on me. Steaks for lunch. They'd be gone at least forty-five minutes.

I had no intention of waiting patiently for their return. Attracting the attention of a passerby made for the best way out of my predicament, but my attempts to yell failed. I worked my jaws as hard as I could, but the gag didn't budge. My reward for the effort—profuse salivation. I swallowed, but the flow kept coming. Fearing strangulation on my own spit, I choked down the drool again and again, obsessively, unable to stop. A lifetime passed before I regained control of myself. I tried kicking my legs to make some noise and understood why they'd gone overboard taping them. I couldn't bend my knees. My arms had gone numb. My shoulders screamed with pain

July in New Mexico. The blistering mid-day sun beat down on the van. No air conditioning. Sweat flowed from every pore. It wouldn't take long for the cargo compartment to reach 130 degrees Fahrenheit. That's when I knew for sure. About my fate.

I'd been riding in an execution van. By the time the guards finished their steaks, Cletus Efferding would be dead of heatstroke. I didn't know how it would happen, if my organs would gradually shut down, or I'd strangle on my own vomit, but the result would be the same—lights out.

The execution process fit the Manoneeta conception of fate to a T. Those responsible would enjoy the comfort of believing they hadn't killed me because I met my fate in the back of an overheated van. No shooting, stabbing, or strangling, just nature taking its course on a hot day. Then just leave the body somewhere where it wouldn't be found, or where it would decompose enough to remove all traces of the cause of death.

I should have paid more attention to Professor Flanagan's discomfort with the group. I should have gone with Belle. But it was too late. I felt myself cooking from the inside out, my head felt like it had been smashed with a sledgehammer, my limbs shook uncontrollably. I screamed into the gag and started choking again. My brain flicked on and off like a light switch. Thoughts wouldn't come.

"Cletus! Come on, Cletus."

A shape floated above me. My cheek stung, then stung again. Someone was slapping me. A face came into focus—Belle.

Still in the cargo compartment, still shaking. No gag, no blindfold, pain, a hand holding a big knife.

"We've got to get out of here. Roll over. Help me out, damn it."

"Can't, too tight."

She grabbed my shoulder and lifted. My arm sockets shrieked in protest.

"It hurts. No!"

"Shut up, stupid, or I'll leave you here. Cooperate!"

An arm behind my back and rapid back-and-forth movements. Jostling that hurt like hell.

"Now, roll over."

My brain kicked in. "I don't think I can. Everything above my waist is numb."

I caught a glimpse of the hand and knife in my peripheral vision, felt something tugging at my legs—Belle sawing through the duct tape wrap.

"Now keep your mouth shut and listen," she hissed. "The guys in the restaurant won't be there forever, and we've gotta get you out of here. I'm going to put my arms around you and pull you into sitting position. Help me all you can."

It took a lot out of both of us, but somehow, we did it, and Belle went to work on the duct tape circling my wrists. My arms flopped when she finished. I had zero feeling in them.

"Let's go," she said and began pulling and tugging me toward the rear doors. I puked on her.

"Jesus," she said letting go of me and shaking her arms. "I never expected you'd be such a problem to rescue."

Losing the feeling in your upper body is no piece of cake. The absence of Belle's physical support nearly toppled me. Between her shoving and my feeble wiggling, we made it to the back door. How I was able to stay upright when she swung my legs out over the back end of the van was beyond my understanding.

"Okay," she said. "We'll sit here for a minute and a half. Work on moving your legs, and I'll start rubbing your arms. Maybe we can get some feeling in them. That's my car, ten feet away. The back door is open. You'll have one chance to get from here to there. No way I'm tangling with a couple of armed lunatics, so if you fall, I'm leaving you here. End of story, end of Cletus Efferding."

The lady meant it. I worked on moving my legs while she massaged my arms.

"By the way, no freebie. I've decided to bill you for the rescue, not that the agency will see a penny of it."

I noticed some barf on her frizzy red hair. It must have been mine. My thinking must not have returned to normal because I asked the world's stupidest question.

"How much?"

"You wanna negotiate?" Belle snapped. "You're not in the strongest of bargaining positions. Let's go."

I managed to stand, and as she turned to support me, I noticed the holstered automatic on her hip.

"I see you're ready for trouble."

"What?"

"The gun. I'm happy to see it."

"New Mexico's an open carry state, and you won't be happy to see it if you're not in the car by the time I count ten. I'll use it on you, Cletus. So help me God, I will."

I don't how we did it, but we got to the car where she managed to fold me at the waist and get my rear onto the seat. I lost my balance and flopped backward, my legs still outside the vehicle. She grabbed them, pushed, and slid me in another foot farther. I tried to help, but the struggle to get to the car did me in.

"Here's what we're gonna do," she said. "I'm going to hike your legs up, bend them, and close the door. Give me all the help you can, because if this doesn't work. I'm leaving you here, car and all."

"You'll lose your deposit."

She corrected me. "The agency will lose its deposit."

She pushed on my feet, my legs folded, and she shut the door. Though my boots rested on the window glass, I thought it best not to complain.

Randy Roeder

Chapter 32

I tossed the TV remote over to Belle. We were sprawled out on the twin beds in our room at the Blue Swallow Motel and unable to agree on a program. The local cable service wasn't much to brag about: a half-dozen stations if you counted the Weather Channel and CNN. I'd been switching between *The Powers of Matthew Star* and the *Dukes of Hazzard* in a futile attempt to keep us both entertained.

"I can't believe you pulled into a car wash and turned the hose on me," I groused. "The back of the car will get moldy before it dries out. It'll probably make us sick, and the rental car agency will go ballistic when they see the damage. They're going to charge you an arm and a leg."

"Complain, complain, complain. The nurse at the clinic said drenching you with cold water saved your life, Swami. You're lucky I had to fold your legs up to get you onto the back seat. I didn't know it, but legs-in-the-air is almost as important as a quick cool down. By the way, I'll take that thank you now."

"Thanks for showing up when you did."

"Let's hear the rest of it, Swami. You know, the thanks for the quick thinking and spraying you before your body shut down."

I turned my head to glare at her. She didn't notice.

"… and thanks for cooling me off at the carwash," I mumbled.

"No doubt about it. This is the luckiest day of your life. If I hadn't been in the motor pool and overheard those guys talking about taking you for a ride, you'd be trying to convince St. Peter to let you into that great ballroom in the sky. I knew something was wrong when they drove off with a cargo van. The transports to South Dakota have passenger seats."

"The luckiest day of my life all right. Two goons try to roast me alive, my shoulders might never work right again, my rescuer nearly drowns me, and I can't get any money because I have no ID."

"The luckiest day of your life because it was my second last day in Shiva City, and I had van duty. The luckiest day of your life because I stashed a wad of cash and a gun in the bottom of my toolbox and the foresight to grab an extra set of keys for the van you were in. The luckiest day of your life because your escorts broke the rules and went to lunch. I had no idea how to convince two armed guards to pull over and give you up."

The "luckiest day" song and dance was getting old. Pretending to be engrossed by the *Matthew Star* program, a tale about an alien prince with special powers trying to make it through everyday life in an American high school, I ignored the remark. Not that it did me any good. Belle was in the mood to converse.

"I knew you were in big trouble, but I didn't think they'd come down on you so hard and so fast. What on earth led you to believe you could stick it out in Shiva City?"

I sighed. She saved my life and was driving me back to Cedar Rapids, the least I could do was pretend I was interested in what she had to say. "I expected to get sent to the Research and Re-education Center, not cooked alive."

"It's a good thing you're not a detective, Cletus. You'd last two weeks—tops. I knew within a day and a half that the people in charge at Shiva City were dangerous. I don't see how you could miss it."

"Except for Babba Pappa, everybody I met seemed nice enough. Weird, but nice. Besides you're the one who told me the security guards' guns weren't loaded."

"I didn't know you from Adam and gave you the party line. It's never a good idea to go out of character when you're undercover. Getting into your bed that night, it was all part of the act. You know, sex-crazed cult member and all. You were cute, but I never really liked you until you kicked me out of bed."

No way I was going to buy that one. "Uh-huh," I said.

"No, really. I'd been at the ranch long enough that not sleeping with somebody was going to look weird. I thought you were cute and figured you'd be easy to handle."

Easy to handle, indeed. I didn't respond and stared at the TV. Matthew Starr was using his super abilities to make points with a girl enraptured by the high school's star quarterback. A guy who understands women doesn't need superpowers to attract them. Case in point, Belle climbed into my bed back in Santa Rosa with no encouragement from me.

"If you got out of hand, I knew you'd be the type to wilt if I came on strong. A lot of guys are like that, afraid they won't be able to satisfy a wanton, out-of-control woman. It's not that unusual and nothing to be ashamed of."

Me, wilting before a woman's passion? Belle didn't know what she was missing.

———

Wearing my new K-Mart clothes, I kept my thoughts to myself as Belle and I walked to a worn and dingy breakfast venue a few hundred yards from our motel. Though Belle's hosing had washed some of the urine and barf stains off my scrubs, I was too uncomfortable with their appearance to wear them in public. So Belle shopped for me, picking out what had to be the cheapest jeans and cheesiest shirt in the place. Afterward I'd washed my scrubs in the motel sink. The two outfits would have to do me until I got home.

My time in the Manoneeta death wagon brought with it the realization that some part of the People of Light organization wouldn't think twice about killing someone they believed had betrayed the cult. As loathe as I was to consider it, the group may indeed have been responsible for the hit on Dusty. They say that vengeance is a dish better served cold, but waiting five years for a payback? Seemed like a long time to hold a grudge.

Maybe it was my negative experience with the Sutherlands, but I had zero desire to exact retribution for the death of the woman who'd left me at the altar. My almost-wedding felt like an artifact from a distant life. Since arriving in Shiva City, I'd gone from a mud yard worker to a respected advisor to the Inner Circle. I was propositioned multiple times, threw a woman out of bed, took part in a nude encounter group, howled at the moon, and led a *Conga* line at dynamic meditation. I'd been beaded by a guru, feted by my compound, pulled off a burglary, jailed, and nearly murdered.

And every part of my body hurt. I dreaded the idea of a day in the car, but Belle insisted on reaching Kansas City before nightfall. In my condition, I didn't see how it would be possible. I had trouble keeping up with her as we walked to the restaurant. She waited for me at the door and picked up a day-old newspaper from a rack as we entered. Her head disappeared behind a wall of newsprint the moment we sat down. I picked at my food and stared at the walls.

We were on our post-dinner coffee when Belle peered at me over her paper. "So what now with Mike? You know where he is, but you can't get to him."

"I don't know. It's a tough one. "My daughter wants me to bring him back to her. I've already failed once at the fatherhood thing and don't want to do it again. Maybe there's a way to get law enforcement involved. The People of Light tried to kill me. Former members have disappeared. At some point, the government is going to step in."

Belle returned her mug to the table. "At some point. But right now, you've got no proof other than your own experience, and no one in Shiva City to back you up. Don't ask me to. I'm not about to get involved in providing corroborative evidence for crimes committed in New Mexico. Besides, Mike is in another jurisdiction entirely. It's going to take an interstate effort by someone like the FBI to bring the cult down. They'll want to dot the i's and cross the t's. Expect a two-year investigation. In the meanwhile, your son will be brainwashed and doing slave labor at the Research and Re-education Center."

"I don't need the FBI in my life, and now that I think about it, anything connected with law enforcement doesn't seem like a great idea. I'm still unhappy that the Linn County Sheriff's Department wanted to pin Dusty's murder on me. I don't understand why Gib Sutherland called off the investigation."

Belle twisted her fire-engine orange frizz into a ponytail and wrapped a doohickey around it. "I checked with the office yesterday. As far as they know there's been no arrest. The guy just called the agency and said to drop it."

The ponytail didn't look half bad. Belle was easier on the eyes without an unruly mop hiding her face.

I shook my head. "Nasty as he is, Gib loved his niece. She was the child he never had, the bright star in his life. It's not like him to drop something as important to him as finding her killer. It doesn't make sense, especially now that I know more about the People of Light. A few days ago, I would have laughed in your face if you'd told me they were killers."

"That's because most of them are good, if slightly confused, people. Babba Pappa and Babba Vivek, on the other hand, are power crazy and will do anything to keep control."

"They're not the only bad apples. Those guys who took me for a ride are nothing to write home about. I guess every tyrant has minions. There seem to be more than enough of them to go around. Must be a common personality defect."

"Minions or not, you need to spring your son before his mind is shot. Do you know about the research part of the South Dakota operation? They're developing improved sensory deprivation tanks and plan to sell them to rich clients."

I nodded at our waitress, who headed our way with a coffee pot. "Doesn't surprise me. The People of Light never miss a chance to make a buck."

"They have something like a dozen black-box tanks at the center they don't intend to sell."

"How do you know all this?" I interrupted.

"I know how to talk to people," Belle replied. "That's why I make a good detective."

"I know how to talk to people, too, and I never heard about the tanks."

Belle chuckled. "Well, it helps that I worked in the building that provides transportation between Shiva City and South Dakota."

"That, plus you're a born snoop," I added.

Belle leaned forward, "Seriously Cletus, sensory deprivation tanks can be abused. Rumor has it they developed the black-box tanks to keep workers compliant. Think solitary confinement on steroids. Pitch-black, in water up to your neck, light-proof, soundproof, no room to move around, no toilet—ten hours in one and you'd come out compliant as hell. Lower the thermostat from body temperature to sixty degrees and it wouldn't take that long. Drop it to near-hypothermia levels and it would take less time yet—assuming your victim doesn't die first."

I thought of Burl. "I know a guy, a former cop. His name's Burl, and he's gone private. Does body-guarding and the like. He wouldn't go to Shiva City because he's just getting his business started. He might be ready to travel before long and South Dakota is closer. I wonder if he could pull off a rescue?"

"No way one guy could do it unless he was on the inside. And even then, he might have to wait months for an opportunity to come up. Though it's harder than it once was, getting in and out of Shiva City is a piece of cake. The South Dakota site is the People's prison. Security will be tight. An infiltrator with no idea of how to act or what to say would be discovered long before he could mount a rescue."

Our waitress stopped by to top off our mugs. When she left, I got back to business. "What about the agency you work for? Could they pull something like this off?"

"Maybe, if all their people were as good as me. Unfortunately, I'm the best they've got. Getting your son out will be a nightmare. That sort of thing isn't my cup of tea. It's too dangerous, and if the law decides to get involved, they'd be just as likely to charge me for kidnapping as they would the Manoneetas. Tell you what, when we get you back to Cedar Rapids, I'll talk to this Burl guy. Maybe between the two of us, we can come up with something you can do."

Chapter 33

Belle and I arrived in Cedar Rapids just before noon on July 2nd. The pain in my shoulders had grown steadily worse. Our first order of business was a stop at the Mercy Hospital emergency room where Belle had to open the car door for me. After a two-hour wait, a nurse led me into an examination room where a doctor who looked to be all of sixteen years old clumsily manipulated my arms as I did my best not to scream at him.

"H-m-m-m," he said. "Looks like you have two dislocated shoulders. If you'd come in sooner, there'd be less swelling. Must hurt like the dickens. How did you ever manage to do it?"

"Chopping wood," I lied.

"I can't imagine how," he replied, "but if you're lucky, easy enough to fix. The swelling concerns me, but I'll try to manipulate the joints back in place. Sometimes that's all it takes, but if the injury is serious enough, we'll want to immobilize those arms."

I swallowed hard. "Immobilize?"

"Not as bad as it sounds. We put both your arms in slings."

Images of being unable to dress myself and gobbling my dinner from a bowl like a dog assaulted me. "How's that going to work? I live by myself." I explained.

The guy gave me the standard smile doctors use to calm an anxious patient. "It might not come to that, but if it does, we can make arrangements for a stay at a rehabilitation facility."

"Rehabilitation facility?"

"He picked up my chart and began writing on it. "Some of the area nursing homes have wings where patients can stay until they're ready to live independently. I'll have a nurse come in to give you a pair of injections. One will be a muscle relaxant, the other one will dull that pain while we get those shoulders popped back into place."

He left and was soon replaced by a smiling nurse. "Looks like we'll be working on those shoulders," she said as she prepped the syringes. "Two dislocated shoulders. Men your age need to be careful. You're past the weekend warrior stage."

My Florence Nightingale was handy with a needle. The injections took all of sixty seconds.

"Doctor Bonner doesn't believe in pain," she announced. "He ordered you the good stuff—morphine."

The nurse stepped outside for a moment and returned to gently fluff my pillow. She smiled down at me. "The doctor has been delayed by another patient. You can lie here and relax until he's ready to adjust those shoulders."

Settling into the softest pillow this side of paradise did wonders for my spirits, not to mention my powers of observation. I hadn't noticed my nurse was gorgeous—a woman possessed of beauty so radiant it bordered on angelic. Though she might have been near retirement age, the realization a man could spend a lifetime looking for a lovelier partner hit me like a Category 5 hurricane. Not wanting to miss the opportunity to become better acquainted, I asked her for a date.

"Marry me," I said.

She shook her head. "My third proposal this week. Get in line"

———————————

I talked the doctor out of putting my arms in slings by promising to stay home and rest. Three days of wall-to-wall TV convinced me I'd go buggy if I didn't get out of the apartment, so I got dressed and walked over to Cleatzy's, making sure I arrived after the place closed for the night. It would have been better if I stayed home. The struggle to open the door reminded me it would be some time before I'd be pain-free. I made my way to the office courtesy of the dim glow of the exit signs. A stack of invoices a foot high had accumulated in my absence. Unenthused about tackling them, I put my feet on the desk and picked up the coffee-stained copy of the *Gazette* Reg left on the desk.

I stifled a yawn. The front page didn't have much to say, but a short notice on the second more than made up for it.

Local Banker Takes His Life

The Board of Trustees of Merchants National Bank announced yesterday that President and Chairman of the Board James H. Sutherland died of a self-inflicted gunshot wound on the evening of Thursday, July 7th. Sutherland, 62, was the driving force behind the aggressive expansion of the business and is credited with turning a sleepy family-owned business into one of the state's premiere financial institutions. The son of MNB founder Walter J. Sutherland, the younger Sutherland joined the organization as a teller following his 1945 discharge from the United States Navy where he served as lead gunner aboard the USS Enterprise and was awarded the Navy Cross for heroism during the Battle of the Santa Cruz Islands.

Sutherland's work ethic and no-nonsense approach to the world of finance resulted in a rapid rise through the bank hierarchy and in 1956, he became MNB Executive Vice-President, a position he held until assuming the presidency in 1963. Known to all as 'Steele,' at one time or another, James Sutherland held positions on the State Board of Regents and the boards of Coe College, and the Cedar Rapids Country Club. He was instrumental in securing the Brucemore estate's affiliation with the National Trust for Historic Preservation and chaired the fundraising campaign that resulted in the restoration of the Paramount Theatre.

Roland Hillman, the bank's current Executive Vice-President, will lead the business through what he expects will be a smooth transition. According to Hillman, "One of Steele Sutherland's strengths was his insistence that decisions at the bank are too important to be left in the hands of a single individual. His foresight ensures that the MNB team has the breadth of experience necessary to guide us through the coming months. I speak for the entire Board when I say the death of Steele Sutherland represents a loss not only for Merchants National Bank but for the entire Cedar Rapids community.

An odd article sounding as if it was based on a Merchant's Bank press release. No statement from the family, nothing from law enforcement reports. Either the Sutherlands managed to keep a lid on the story, or the *Gazette* was caught with its pants down and ran with what was available. Since Steele and Consuela regularly played bridge with the *Gazette*'s publisher and his wife, I suspected the former. Odd, but my almost father-in-law's suicide humanized the guy for me.

A war hero, a man's man—good-looking, with money to burn, a popular and respected civic leader—Steele had it all, yet he'd been so distraught by the murder of his daughter that he killed himself. Who'd have thought the heart of a grieving father beat beneath his hard, manipulative exterior. Maybe it was time to let go of my bitterness over his obsessive control of Dusty's life and my busted eye socket. There's no percentage in hating a dead man—especially one traumatized by the loss of someone dear to the both of you.

Belle stayed on at the apartment for a couple of days, sleeping on the couch. She'd been fired from her job in Des Moines when her boss at the detective agency realized she played loosey-goosey with her expense account. I put her in touch with Burl, and she talked herself into a short-term project with Dietz Investigations. Job in hand, she drove to Des Moines, put her things in storage, and returned to Cedar Rapids in her personal ride, a well-used AMC Gremlin. After another night on my couch, Belle rented a sleeper in one of those big rooming houses on Fourth Avenue and Seventh. Not much comfort, but enough to tide her over while she looked for a long-term job.

We'd spent quite a bit of time talking about my options now that I knew where to find Mike. None of them were good. The best we came up with was a drive to South Dakota to ask the county sheriff to accompany me to the Manoneetas' Re-education Center. Once we got there, I'd ask to see my son. I wasn't too keen on the idea, so decided to get Burl's reaction to the scheme. I could pump him for details on Steele Sutherland's suicide while I was at it. With his law-enforcement connections, he'd be in the know.

I looked over at my in-basket and the pile of paperwork awaiting me and rose from my chair. It could wait until tomorrow.

———————

Burl ran his hand through what was left of his hair and planted his elbows on the blotter covering his desk. "Funny you should ask. Orrin got called to the house that night. The Sutherlands was playing bridge with his brother Gib and his wife. There was two other couples: Bunny Hamilton's folks along with the guy who owns the *Gazette* and his old lady. Anyway, it's getting on toward ten o'clock. Consuela Sutherland gets the bid and hubby ends up as the dummy. Since he's got no hand to play, he excuses himself. Everybody thinks he's going to the restroom. Instead, he goes upstairs, shoves a Smith & Wesson in his mouth, and splatters his brains against the wall.

Orrin shows up to secure the scene and finds out the dude who owns the *Gazette* freaked out and left before law enforcement could get there. The Hamiltons are goin' crackers and talkin' nonsense. Consuela Sutherland won't say a word without a lawyer. Brother Gib is the only one calm enough to talk about what happened. When Orrin's boss gets there, he orders him to go to the *Gazette* guy's house to get a statement. Had a hell of time, they was afraid to open the door for anyone—even a deputy. The whole thing was a zoo."

The Gazette's strange reporting of Steele's death now made sense. Its panicked owner bailed because he didn't want to become entangled in the investigation and the gossip that inevitably follows a high-profile suicide. From his viewpoint, the less coverage, the better. I couldn't help but think it strange that the Hamiltons and Sutherlands still socialized when their daughters had been the victims of a recent and grisly execution. The timing felt off. I wondered if the presence of Bunny's grieving parents at his home was the straw that drove Steele over the edge.

"Orrin is no slouch when it comes to giving you the hot poop," I said. "Consuela's wanting a lawyer seems strange. Any chance of foul play?"

Burl shook his head. "As far as suicide goes, a classic case. The gun wasn't wiped, and Sutherland's prints was the only ones on it. The powder burns and blood spatter looked right. The position of the body and gun made sense. Guy lost his daughter to a violent death a few months before. He offed himself, pure and simple."

"I figured as much. It's just there's been so much violence. First Dusty and Bunny and now Steele. When the Sutherland family's good fortune took a hike, it turned out to be a doozy."

Burl grunted in agreement. I took his stingy response as a sign he was done chatting and wanted the reason for my visit. I came right out with it.

"I'd like to hire you to go to South Dakota with me when I ask the Perkins County Sheriff to accompany me to People of Light center. You were a cop. You'll know how to talk him into it. Besides, you could spell me on the drive. I don't think my shoulders can tolerate two days behind the wheel."

Burl folded his hands, looked doubtful. "Belle said I might be seeing you. Orrin and I get along because we're brothers, but cops and sheriffs don't have much to say to each other. You'd have better luck if you got somebody from a sheriff's office to soften him up."

"Without somebody official there, it's unlikely they'll let me see Mike."

Burl leaned back in his chair, yawned, and stretched. He didn't want to go.

"What about Orrin?" I asked.

"Don't hold your breath. You screwed up when you got on your high horse at your apartment that day. That sort of thing honks him off. He ain't about to lift a finger for you."

I tried again. "I'll pay double your going rate."

Burl raised his eyebrows. A hesitation, I had him.

"Nope," he said after a moment's consideration. "Even with your girlfriend helpin' out, I got more work than I can handle. Too bad she's lookin' for automotive work. This Dietz Investigations business is gonna make me a pile."

"She's not my girlfriend."

"Whatever. Listen, my brother Orrin won't help, but Junior might. Never got over bein' rejected for the military police and is crazy about anything to do with law enforcement."

"What can Junior do for me?"

"Not a whole lot, but Junior is a Flying Farmer."

"A Flying Farmer?"

Burl looked at me like I possessed the mental capacity of a peanut. "It's what it sounds like, a club for farmers who fly airplanes. Junior lives in Wessington Springs, South Dakota. You can drive that far and fly the rest of the trip. Then you can make an aerial pass over that re-education place and see what it looks like before you go there. Take some pictures in case you have to come up with Plan B."

"I doubt I can talk the sheriff into going to the Center with me just so I can talk to my son."

Burl rolled his eyes, looked up at the ceiling, and then back to me.

"I thought you said you was a salesman."

His words brought me up short. After straightening my tie, I rose from my chair, plunked my hat on my head, and exited without another word.

Belle scoped out the scene at the Top of the Seasons Restaurant, impressed. Since Burl wouldn't go to South Dakota with me, I intended to ask her to accompany me to the People of Light's compound. I needed the moral support, and my shoulders weren't up for the hours behind the steering wheel. I hoped lunch in one of the city's top venues would soften her up.

She held her coffee cup with two hands and smiled at me over the top edge. "Is this a date, Cletus?"

I wasn't about to say yes and smart enough not to say no. "You saved my life, Belle. I want to say thank you for it. What with the stress of the drive back, the doctor visits, the pain pills, and digging out at Cleatzy's, I've been too preoccupied with my own problems to think of anyone else."

Belle put her cup down and rested her chin on her hands. "I'm happy things are settling down for you. I wish I could say the same. I've been checking the shops in town to see if anyone wants a good mechanic. So far, no takers. Thank heaven for Burl. If he didn't have the extra work, I'd have to dip into the money I've set aside for opening my own place. I'm damned tired of the detective business."

I reached out and touched her elbow. "They say if you give your dream a name, you'll have an easier time getting there. Belle's Automotive has a nice ring to it."

"Nope. I may go by Belle. But the sign out front is going to say Mabel's Auto Repair." Belle could be a last name, and I want everyone to know I'm a woman. Automotive could mean I sell things. I'm a mechanic and proud of it, so auto repair it is.

"Things will work out. They always do."

She shrugged. "Not always the way we want."

Belle had a point. I softened my face and gave her elbow the slightest squeeze. "Well, there is that. I didn't find Mike."

"But you know where he is."

My opening. "Burl agrees that the best way to get my son back is to have the Perkins County sheriff go to the Rehabilitation Center with me and stand by when I ask to see Mike. Right now, I can't drive that far. I'll pay you to drive me there and back."

Belle curled her lip and folded her arms. "So, this isn't a date."

"I'm in a pickle. It's stupid for me to go to South Dakota alone. Mike can't stand me. The big wheels in the People of Light hate me so much they tried to kill me. If anyone out there recognizes me, they might try to finish the job. I could use backup."

"Nobody said getting Mike to see the light of day would be easy but going out there is the best chance you've got. Shave your beard. You didn't know that many people at the ranch and Manoneetas aren't much for taking pictures. There are 900 miles between Shiva City and the Re-education Center, and the folks at the ranch are basically prisoners. I doubt anyone at the Re-education Center will recognize you. It's not like they'll be handing out wanted posters."

"Babba Pappa wants me dead."

"If you ever try the phony date routine on me again, you'll wish you were dead."

I held up my hands. "My arms won't take the drive."

Belle stood. "Quit hiding behind your injury and get off your butt. Do something about your son or write him off. If you try to bring him back, you might succeed. If you fail, your time and effort will be wasted. That's not the end of the world. Write him off and your daughter might write you off. That's not the end of the world either."

"But ..."

Belle held up her hand and shouldered her handbag. "You had a close call, but you're alive. Don't make me regret I saved your sorry ass. Make a decision and get on with your life."

I realized I still had my hands in the air and put them down.

"So, you're not going with me?"

Randy Roeder

Chapter 34

I popped the top on a second can of Budweiser, went back to the couch, and propped my feet on the coffee table. My arms ached. I'd driven the few blocks to take in a game at the minor league stadium but couldn't recall anything that happened before the seventh inning stretch. I had just finished singing "For it's one, two, three strikes, you're out" when it hit me. The hell with Cleatzy's, the hell with Burl, the hell with Belle, I would shave my beard and go to South Dakota by myself. Maybe I could convince Junior Dietz to fly me up to Bison. If he didn't, I'd rest my shoulders a day or two and drive the remainder of the way myself. If I struck out and came home empty-handed, at least I'd played the game.

The beer on top of the pain pills hit like a ton of bricks. I woke up at nine—maybe too late to call Lumir—but I did. He answered, and I asked if he'd be at his shop the next evening.

"I will be at Eddie's. He is grilling hamburgers. Tamara and Millie will be there too. Now that you have returned, Eddie will want you to come."

My daughter would be there. We hadn't spoken since she stormed out on me, and my news would not be good. She'd know I failed the minute she laid eyes on me

"I'll be there, wouldn't miss it," I said.

"Good," Lumir replied. "Did you speak with your son?"

"I didn't. He's not at the ranch. He's at their compound in South Dakota. It's their re-education center for cult members who don't measure up."

"It took two weeks to learn this?"

"There's a lot more to the story. Things have gone south in Shiva City, and it's become as close as you can get to a prison camp. The place in South Dakota is even worse. The South Dakota compound locks its discipline problems in soundproof tanks, in water up to their necks. There's no light, and the tanks are so small that the prisoners can barely move. The People of Light tank them until they're broken. They justify it by claiming they're helping those who are troubled by providing sensory deprivation therapy. It's a thousand times worse than the solitary confinement used in prisons."

"This news is not good, Clete. You must tell me everything. There will be ears who should not hear the whole story at Eddie's picnic, and I do not wish to wait."

I gave him the scoop—an hour and a half's worth. Lumir didn't have many questions, and when I finished, he made a request I didn't want to hear.

"I would like to meet this Belle woman who saved your life. I will tell Eddie you are bringing a guest."

Lumir bailed me out when I lost it after Dusty's murder. His phone call to my daughter brought her back into my life. Though Belle and I hadn't parted on the best of terms, honoring Lumir's request was the least I could do.

The next morning, I phoned Belle at the rooming house. Not sure of her schedule, I called at 7:30 to improve the chances she'd be in. One of the residents called her to what must have been a shared hall phone.

Belle sounded less than thrilled to hear from me. "This better be good. I was in the middle of a nice, warm shower, and now I'm standing in a cold hallway wrapped in a towel."

I gave her my best Efferding sales pitch and thought I'd struck out until I mentioned that Lumir and Tamara would be there.

"Let me get this right," she said. "Your daughter and the old guy who threatened one drug dealer and hanged another?"

"Lumir didn't threaten a drug dealer. He and his friends used their pickups to box the guy's car in; then they worked it over with baseball bats while he was still inside. The dirtbag was selling LSD to fourteen-year-olds. Lumir was ready to hang the other dealer because he murdered his granddaughter, not because he sold drugs."

"H-m-m-m," Belle intoned. "Didn't they both end up dead anyway? You talked so much in the car I kept zoning out."

If Belle didn't get the story the first time around, she'd have to wait. I sidestepped her question. "That was a long time ago. Lumir was only sixty-seven."

"I wish I paid more attention. You're more interesting than I gave you credit for. People you know have a way to turning up dead. Drug dealers, your wife, your fiancée, Steele Sutherland. There were some others, too."

I didn't want to go into a song-and-dance about a pair of dead hit men and their murder of my neurotic cousin. "Steele and my wife killed themselves."

"Dead is dead. Okay, I'll go. Meeting an aged vigilante and the daughter you abandoned should be a hoot."

"I didn't abandon my daughter."

"If you say so," Belle replied. "No need to pick me up. I'll drive myself."

I gave her directions to Eddie's—the long way around.

Eddie rented a small house in Bohemie Town a block and a half from St. Ludmila's Church. Though his home was small, his backyard wasn't. Lumir, Millie, Tamara, Belle, and I sat at a picnic table in the shade of a white oak the size of a three-story house. Eddie flipped burgers on a Weber kettle grill while we chatted. I noticed Tamara's frequent glances his way and doubted they had anything to do with the progress of the beef patties.

Though she tried to keep her sneak peeks subtle, any fool could see my daughter was head-over-heels infatuated. I found nothing positive in the development. Tamara led a sheltered life, not getting out much because she was taking care of the woman she called Mom. Eddie was a rough-and-tumble guy who'd been around the block more than a few times. Tamara was too innocent for them to have anything in common other than the purely physical. I wondered if we needed a father/daughter chat about birth control.

She'd hugged me when we saw each other. I didn't know if it was the unexpected affection or the shoulder pain from her enthusiastic grasp, but the action nearly brought me to tears. She looked good, and she looked happy. I worried she might spend the night with Eddie. Knowing Tamara would tear me limb from limb if I asked about her lodgings, I quashed my parental instincts and kept my mouth shut.

My daughter wasn't the only one taking an interest in the opposite sex. Lumir and Belle seemed to have hit it off. Belle's mother had emigrated from Eastern Europe and insisted her twelve-year-old daughter take polka lessons at a Polish social club. When Belle discovered Lumir was a polka dancer, she peppered him with questions about dance steps and button accordions. Lumir, basking in the warm glow of her attention, preened like a peacock. He was soon demonstrating steps for her.

Their mutual admiration session broke up when Eddie delivered a platter of hamburgers to our table. Our enthusiastic response emptied the platter before he seated himself, so he returned to his grill to make extras. Lumir, Belle, and I were responsible for the burger shortage—we'd taken more than our share. As we constructed our personal versions of the ideal sandwich, Tamara used the interruption to redirect the conversation from dancing to my search for Mike.

"Lumir says you went to New Mexico, got into some kind of trouble, and found out Mike is staying at a research center in South Dakota. Why didn't you go there to get him?"

I'd asked Lumir to keep his counsel. Apparently, he slipped up, and I didn't know how much he'd told her. "Well, getting Mike back to Iowa isn't that easy," I replied.

Tamara wasn't ready for excuses. "It would be if you tried."

As if I hadn't. My daughter and I should have discussed my stay with the Manoneetas before going to a cookout with friends.

"They tried to kill your dad," Belle cut in. "I got to him in the nick of time, or he'd have been a goner."

Tamara's eyes grew to the size of saucers.

"It's not as bad as it sounds," I said. "I stayed in a hot van too long and ended up with a bit of heat stroke."

Belle stuck out her chin and glared. "A bit of heat stroke? They tied you up, gagged you, and left you to roast in a van in the New Mexico sun. You were supposed to die in that tin can. Attempted murder, nothing less."

"Gramps?" Tamara looked as if she were about to cry.

"It wasn't so bad, Sweetie. I'm here, aren't I?"

Belle didn't know when to stop. "Gramps? I thought she was your daughter."

"Failed as a father," said Tamara. "And still failing because he doesn't believe in being straight with me."

I felt my face flush. When I arrived at Eddie's cookout, Tamara had given me an enthusiastic hug. Belle opens her mouth, and my daughter starts worrying about me. She opens it again a few seconds later, and Tamara calls me a failed father. I flashed angry. Time to absent myself before I said something I'd regret. I folded my napkin. "Thanks for butting in, Mabel."

"Your daughter is old enough for the truth," Belle hissed. "The People of Light are worse than any of us could have imagined. At the South Dakota center, they use isolation tanks to break the minds of people who don't fit in. Their idea of re-education means turning people into zombies who'll do whatever they want."

"Mike?" said Tamara.

"Who is this Mabel?" asked Lumir.

"Me," replied Belle.

I disentangled myself from the picnic table as what was supposed to be a pleasant *al fresco* event disintegrated in front of me. I'd already resolved to go to South Dakota to try to talk some sense into Mike. If I didn't make the effort, Tamara might try to do it herself, but physically and mentally, I wasn't up to the trip.

Belle wasn't done. "The People of Light might even be the ones who killed your father's fiancée. Some of them still blame her for being forced out of India."

"Excuse me," I said. "My shoulders are acting up and walking is the only thing that helps. I'll be back in a bit."

Not that any of my companions was dense enough to believe me. I willed my feet to move, and surprisingly, they did. I'd just turned my back to the table when I heard Tamara ask, "What's wrong with his shoulders?"

I made my exit, seething at my inability to present my daughter with an unsensational story of my search for Mike. Everyone at the cookout seemed to think they had a better read on Tamara than I did. What was the point of fatherhood if I couldn't control my relationship with my daughter? I walked up and down J and K Streets for a half hour before returning to something approaching a normal state of mind. Back at the picnic table, I found my companions sitting quietly, staring at their plates. Eddie broke the silence.

"We've talked among ourselves, and the others have asked me to speak. You've been through a lot, Clete—Dusty's murder, her family hijacking your business, someone trying to kill you, but we're your friends." He looked at Tamara, "... and family. Tamara is nineteen years old and has been taking care of her mother for four years. She's grown up in a less-than-ideal family situation. All that has made her stronger than you can ever imagine. You're doing her no favors by trying to protect her from the reality of the attempt on your life and the situation Mike is in. And lighten up on Belle. She was ready to shoot it out with two loonies to save your life. We're on your side. So, could you please just relax? And by the way, Tamara and I are dating."

What could I say? Outnumbered by my tablemates, I wasn't about to prolong my embarrassment by arguing. "Okay, I'll take a deep breath and ease up, but remember, if you hurt Tamara's feelings, there'll be hell to pay."

Tamara cut in, "No there won't. If there's any hell to pay, it'll be coming from me. I've told you before. Your role is to act like a father, not a parent. Remember?"

I sighed with resignation. "Got it."

My evident distress and abrupt departure seemed to take the shine off the evening. Tiptoeing around the obvious—the situation with Mike— Eddie and Tamara talked a bit about the rock concert they'd seen at the Five Seasons Center. Millie and Lumir reminisced about the good old days. I couldn't add much to either conversation.

About nine o'clock, Belle yawned. "I know it's early, but I need some downtime and a hot bath. The last few days have me completely worn out, and the mattress at the rooming house is so lumpy I'll have trouble sleeping.

Lumir didn't miss a beat. "A rooming house? Nonsense. I have a perfectly good spare bedroom and tomorrow I'll cook you up some bacon and eggs."

I didn't think it possible a no-nonsense eighty-two-year-old could become so easily smitten. That Belle was a half-century his junior seemed not to have occurred to him. I can't say I knew what my friend had in mind. It could have been anything from a late-night double solitaire marathon to a roll on the mattress. And to tell the truth, I preferred not to think about it.

Mrs. Hemsky looked as if she'd swallowed a pound of rancid butter. "Spending a night on a broken-down bed in an aged bachelor's excuse for a home? I wouldn't hear of it. I have a lovely guestroom with a new Sears mattress and a private bath. You'll be much more comfortable. We'll have waffles buried in strawberries and covered with whipped cream for breakfast. And Dearie, if you've ever tasted Lumir's coffee, you'll realize there are far worse things than drinking from a gas station toilet.

I assumed Millie had been oblivious to Lumir's fascination with Belle, but no doubt about it, Mrs. Hemsky intended to protect her turf. A quick survey of the table convinced me my companions didn't catch the motivation behind her offer. As much as I hated to see Lumir miss the opportunity to work his ineffable charm on Belle, Mrs. Hemsky's suggestion was the better option. Ninety-year-olds like Millie aren't made for jealousy and one of these days, Lumir's coffee would put somebody in the hospital.

The outcome: Mrs. Hemsky 1; Lumir 0.

Chapter 35

I pulled into an angled parking space in front of Ray and Jerry's Jack and Jill grocery in Wessington Springs, South Dakota. The pain pills had worn off; my shoulders ached. Unhappy with the turn things had taken at Eddie's cookout and unhappy with myself, I quit answering the phone, put Reg back in charge of Cleatzy's, and spent two days making the eight-hour drive to Wessington Springs, South Dakota. The burg was pretty much what I expected, a small plains town serving a declining population dependent on agriculture. Take away the local school and county courthouse, and the place would be in a world of hurt.

A glance in the rearview mirror brought me up short. It would take time to get used to the ridiculous handlebar mustache covering most of my mouth. Worried that a Manoneeta from New Mexico might recognize me with the beard and Mike might recognize me without, I opted for the middle course–one that left me looking like a Yosemite Sam's black-sheep brother half-crazed on locoweed.

Still miffed at Burl's slight on my sales abilities, I hadn't asked him for directions to Junior's farm. Rural areas being what they are, I reckoned the folks at Ray and Jerry's would know most everyone in the county. A surprisingly well-stocked operation greeted me as I entered the front door. A pair of farm-fresh high school girls staffed the check-out. As I approached the register, they greeted me with the sweetest smiles this side of heaven.

"Can I help you?" the taller of the two asked.

"I hope so," I said. "I'm looking for the Junior Dietz farm and need directions."

The girls looked blankly at each other. "We're from Alpena and work here after school, so we don't know everybody," the prettier of the two explained.

A man's voice from a nearby aisle piped in. "If you're looking for Junior, go on over to the Co-op. I was just there, and Junior's ordering feed."

The walls had ears. "Thanks, much obliged," I called back.

"Two blocks north and one to the east," the voice added.

I said goodbye, which must have been hilariously funny since the girls burst into fits of giggles. Setting out for the Co-op on foot, I arrived at a no-frills sheet metal building a few minutes later. The door proved stubborn, and my shoulder barked when I gave the extra tug needed to get inside. The aromas of oil, farm chemicals, and feed supplement assaulted me as I entered a display room stacked with bags and a collection of hardware that I took to be useful for work on farm equipment. A trio of life-size cardboard farmers promoting herbicides and fertilizer smiled at me as I passed them on the way to the service counter. The place felt downhome comfortable.

The guy behind the counter was chatting with a mountain of a woman wearing an oversized engineer's cap and pin-striped bibbed overalls. A mountain she may have been, but fat she wasn't. The lady was built like an ox. She and the clerk were involved in a discussion of the merits of something called Crossbow.

"You'll get a better kill with Crossbow than you will with Prowl," the clerk said. "Buckbrush is tough stuff and spreads like wildfire. You'll want to knock it down before it gets established."

Though I'd missed Junior, the folks at the counter could give me directions to his farm. Not wanting to interrupt, I took up a spot on the counter a polite distance away and waited for a break in the conversation. It didn't take long for the clerk to acknowledge me.

"What can I do you for?" he said, interrupting his chat with the Amazon.

"I need directions to the Junior Dietz place," I replied.

The clerk chuckled as the Amazon stepped toward me with an extended hand. "I'm Junior Dietz."

Though I'm sure my eyes betrayed me, I didn't miss a beat. I grabbed her massive paw and introduced myself. "My name is Cletus Efferding and your brother Burl told me to talk to you."

A grin and twinkling eyes told me she'd caught my surprise. They lit up a plain, sunburned face. Though her gender came as a bit of a shock, I liked the woman immediately.

"So, how's Burl doing?" she asked.

"His detective business is going great guns," I replied. "Between it and the security work, he has more jobs than he can manage."

"Glad to hear it, but why anyone would leave a police force job to go private is beyond me."

The guy behind the counter was hanging on every word.

"I have a business proposition for you," I said. "Is there a café around here where I can treat you to coffee and a piece of pie?"

"I'm almost finished with my order. Meet you at the Chuckwagon in ten minutes. You can walk there from here."

I followed her directions and came to a building with a mansard roof. It looked more like a small barn than a chuckwagon, but I had to give the owner credit. Folks tend to associate barns with manure, but a chuckwagon calls up images of bacon, pancakes, steak, and eggs.

And be that as it may, I still wanted pie.

Like everyone else in the Chuckwagon, Junior ate with her cap on. When she removed it to scratch the top of her head, a pair of ten-inch braids came tumbling out, giving all the explanation I needed for her overly large headgear.

"I'm named after my dad," she explained. "His name was Don and mine is Donna. Somewhere along the line, Burl started calling me Junior, and the name stuck. Now I don't answer to anything else. Have you ever thought of doing something about the Cletus handle? It's kind of uncommon."

Coming from anyone else, I would have been offended, but Junior's moniker made her a full-fledged member of the club of people with unusual names, so she got a pass.

"No, I like my name."

She nodded. "I married a guy named Oscar. He liked his name too, even though everybody called him Ockie. I never did—always used his full name. He passed away ten years ago, and I been farming on my own ever since."

Though a decade had passed, I could see the pain in her eyes. After losing Myra, it took eighteen years before I could love again. I hoped she'd fare better.

She tipped back the brim of her engineer's cap. "So, you talked to Burl and have a business proposition. What's up?"

"I want to hire you to fly me up to Bison, where I want to talk to the local sheriff. While we're up there, I'd like you to fly over a commune where a cult has a re-education center. I might want to take pictures of it."

Junior finished her coffee, flagged the waitress for a refill. "Okay, I'm interested. But you gotta admit, it's a strange request. Nobody goes to Bison, not even folks from South Dakota, and I never heard anything about a cult up there. You have a car and could drive. I don't want to get involved in anything fishy."

When the waitress refilled Junior's cup, I put my hand over mine. With my shoulders acting up, I'd have enough trouble sleeping without loading up on late-afternoon caffeine. Burl mentioned Junior had a lifelong fascination with law enforcement. The best way to enlist her help would be to lay all the cards on the table.

"I'm recovering from an injury caused by two members of the cult who tried to kill me by tying me up and leaving me in a closed van under the New Mexico sun. Another day behind the wheel isn't in the near future. The cult is called the People of Light. My son got involved with them, and I'm trying to get him out. He screwed up somehow, so they sent him to the Bison center for what they call re-education. Re-education means working him ten hours a day, seven days a week, and brainwashing him the rest of the time.

A grin crept over Junior's face. "Ten hours a day, seven days a week. I'd say they're training him to be a farmer except the hours are a little light."

I chuckled. "You have me there, but the scary part is the cult wants to break his mind, so he'll do anything they want him to do. He's already so indoctrinated that the idea of leaving would never occur to him, and even if he wanted to, he'd have to get past armed guards."

Junior let out a low whistle. "I can see why you need the sheriff. The boy's in a truckload of trouble going down a mountain pass without any brakes."

"That's only the half of it. I need the sheriff to get me into the place and stand by while I try to talk him into leaving of his own free will. That's a tall order because he's a true believer. Worse yet, he hates me."

"What happens if you can't convince him?"

I threw up my hands. "He's legal age, so he has to make his own decision. If he doesn't want to come. I'll have to leave without him. It gets even worse. If the People of Light deny he's there, I won't even get to see him. Weird as it sounds, the law is on their side."

My tablemate looked at me as if she wasn't buying it. "If it's as bad as you say, why bother?"

"Because I'm a father. Because he has a sister who loves him."

Silence. I'd just about thrown in the towel when Junior slapped the table. "I'm in, Cletus. Oscar and I tried to have kids. He wanted to be a father the worst way, but I was the one with medical problems. He never said a word about how much it bothered him, but I knew."

What a woman.

Junior nodded. "We'll go tomorrow."

My travel alarm went off at 5:30 a.m. Sleep had been elusive. The well-worn mattress in my room at Traveler's Motel had been home to one overweight pheasant hunter too many. Junior would be swinging by in a half hour to pick me up for our trip to the bustling metropolis known as Bison, South Dakota.

I still had my cowboy boots, but my jeans, Stetson, and western shirts were somewhere in New Mexico. I slipped the boots on and pulled the legs of my fawn-colored dress slacks over the uppers. Not wanting to look entirely out of place, I topped off with a white Fruit of the Loom t-shirt. Seeing no reason to wait in my room while a sunny July morning beckoned, I grabbed the backpack containing my new camera, sunblock, and the set of blue scrubs that survived my incarceration in the People of Light's death van. With my Cedar Rapids Reds minor league cap atop my head and a pair of Foster Grant shades on my nose, I walked down the short driveway to await my pilot.

Junior pulled up ten minutes later. I hopped into her International Harvester Scout, plunked my pack on the floor, and asked if we were going to the Chuckwagon for breakfast.

"No, I packed baloney sandwiches," she replied. "We'll eat on the plane."

I bid my dreams of a rasher of bacon, eggs sunny-side-up, and melt-in-your-mouth pancakes goodbye and settled in for the drive to her farm. Our route took us through hilly, rock-strewn grassland dotted with cattle. Plots of corn and alfalfa appeared in the flatter, less stony areas.

Junior brought up a country station on the radio and began humming *On the Road Again* to Willie Nelson's baritone. When the song finished, she turned to me and asked, "How far is this re-education center from Bison?" she asked.

I shrugged. "Don't know. I thought we'd fly around until we found it."

"You didn't do much research before showing up and asking me to fly you out there," she complained. "Hardly any towns in that part of the state. If someone says they're from Bison, they could live as far as thirty miles from the place—thirty miles in any direction."

"We'll be able to see pretty far from the plane," I replied.

"True enough. I keep a calculator in the glove compartment. "Do you know how to find the area of a sixty-mile circle?"

Taking Junior's well-used calculator, I started pushing buttons. "Always liked geometry class, one of my favorites. Never get to use it much."

My driver drummed her fingers on the steering wheel. "Okay, math whiz, what's the answer?"

"Two thousand eight hundred twenty-six," I announced proudly.

"That's square miles, Cletus."

"Oh," I said. "Guess we'll have to get directions in Bison and fly over it on the way back."

"Did you check on the airport?" Junior asked.

"Uh, no."

"I did, last night. I checked with a friend up there, and the municipal airport is temporarily closed. The Bison town council wants the land for a golf course and won't approve a budget. They're hoping the FAA will revoke the authorization. The nearest airport is an hour and a half away, and there's no car rental. It's a good thing I'm a Flying Farmer."

"How's that?"

"Number one, you'd be driving there alone if I didn't like to fly so much, and number two, I know every Flying Farmer in the state. Carl Gunderson has a place fifteen miles southeast of Bison. He's the friend I phoned last night. Carl will let us use his grass strip and lend us a pickup. He'd drive us around, but he's takin' a load of feeder calves to his brother's place."

"My planning wasn't so great," I replied, "but since you're a pilot you'll understand the method to my madness."

"There's a method?"

"I'm flying by the seat of my pants." A groaner to be sure, but I couldn't help myself.

Junior didn't laugh. "Flying by the seat of your pants is no joke. Every good pilot

learns how. Before I got instrument certification, I could only go out on uncloudy days. You'd think it would be a piece of cake, but it wasn't. I decided to fly to visit Burl one weekend. Studied the maps the night before and did really good until I was coming up on someplace called Fort Dodge and flew off the end of the map. I reached into my pouch for the second sheet and realized I left it at home. Landed in Iowa City instead of Cedar Rapids because I thought Highway 30 was four-lane and ended up following Interstate 80 instead. Didn't want to do that again so I studied up and got my instrument certification."

"Smart girl, eliminate the variables."

"It takes a while to get the hang of the instruments. I flew out to a Flying Farmer event in Wyoming through overcast so thick it scared me. I went down to get under it, and when I came out of the clouds, Devil's Tower was in my face. Learned to hard bank on that one. Guess I've made most of the mistakes a pilot can make, and I'm still here. Seat of the pants got me through every time."

I sat quietly, wishing Burl's sister had taken a more organized approach to flying.

"This is my land here," she announced. "Another half mile to the plane. When we get to the turnoff, hop out and open the gate. Be sure to close it after I go through."

When we got there, I did as directed. A few hundred yards later and we were parked alongside a small high-wing aircraft.

"It's a Cessna Skylane," Junior announced as she pulled the keys from the Scout's ignition. It's a four-seater and cruises at 167 miles per hour. If we're airborne by eight, we should land around nine."

"Not possible. I figured it for a 5-hour drive. We'd have to go something like 250 miles an hour to get there."

Junior chuckled. "You may be good at math but you're bad at geography. Bison is on Mountain Time."

We exited the Scout, and I watched as Junior freed the plane from its tie-downs and did her external pre-flight check. When she met my one attempt at conversation with a grunt, I understood she didn't want to be distracted.

"Okay," she said after several minutes of fiddling with the plane. "Get your gear."

I retrieved my backpack from the floor of the Scout. Junior went to the rear and reappeared with a thermos and a bread bag full of sandwiches.

We climbed into the plane, and I sat quietly while Junior finished her pre-flight routine. When she finished, she handed me a combination mic and headphone contraption.

"Put this on," she said. "It'll get noisy once we get moving, and we don't want to keep yelling at each other."

I put the rig on. She checked that we could hear each other, cranked the engine, and we started to taxi. The big noise didn't start until she gunned the engine to get us airborne. We bumped along a path in her alfalfa field until a hop got us off the ground. We were maybe eight feet in the air when a crosswind blew us over the barbed-wire fence that ran alongside her landing strip. I doubt if our wheels cleared more than a couple of feet.

"That was close," I said.

"Little crosswind," Junior replied, her voice barely louder than the static coming through the headphones. "Usually doesn't come from that direction."

As we climbed, she explained the relationship between air, ground, and wind speed. I smiled and nodded as though I understood. The concept was probably simple, but Junior's convoluted explanation was tough going.

She followed with a discussion of altitude. "I'm supposed to stay above 500 feet. The plane cruises nice at about a mile, but I like to see things, so we'll be flying at half that. If I see something interesting, I might go down for a quick look, and you'll get acquainted with the ground coming up at you at one hundred twenty miles an hour.

"It's ok with me if you want to take it slower," I yelled into my mic.

"Don't want to go too slow. Get much below sixty—the plane quits flying, and we're sort of out of control.

"Sort of?" I asked.

"I might be able to glide us in, which isn't as bad as it sounds. Except for a barn or a big boulder, all you can hit out here is a telephone wire or a cow."

I was processing the information when the plane made a sharp turn that resulted in us being at a forty-five-degree angle to the ground. My stomach felt like it was floating five feet above my head and ten feet behind me. I mentally reeled it back into place and started thinking about a barf bag.

"Sorry about the sharp turn," Junior said. "I got excited about showing you the farm and forgot you're not used to being in a small plane."

"I'm fine," I insisted.

"I heard you groan. Anyway, that's my main herd up over there—two-thirds of my 200 head. Top-of-the-line Angus. This isn't like Iowa. Out here, it takes ten acres of grassland and ten acres of cropland to support a cow. I own seven sections. Each one is a square mile. Took me and my husband nearly twenty years to put it together. Of course, I can't farm it all alone. I hire out what I can't do myself."

We flew around the farm for something like ten minutes before climbing to begin our trip in earnest. Junior's sharp turn was just the beginning of my discomfort. As time passed and the sun beat down on the plane, the claustrophobic cabin grew increasingly warm. The heat, combined with the persistent stench of aviation fuel, got me thinking of the barf bag again.

"Junior, could you turn on the air?" I asked. "It's getting warm in here."

"Ain't no air conditioning," Junior's voice crackled through the headphones. "We're flying full speed, so it's best not to open the window. Anyway, we'll be there in a little over an hour."

My mouth filled with petroleum-tainted saliva. No way I'd make it. I found the barf bag and filled it.

Despite the static, Junior's giggle came through loud and clear. "Fold the top of the bag over and crease it tight. I'll slow the plane down. When we get to speed, you push the window open and drop the bag. Don't throw it."

Junior slowed, banked the plane in my direction, and the bag went out the window.

I don't think it landed on anybody.

Chapter 36

Carl Gunderson had parked the pickup next to his landing strip and left the keys in the ignition for us. To say his ranch was desolate would be putting it mildly. Save for his buildings and a herd of cattle in the distance, an unbroken vista of browned-out grass spread from horizon to horizon in every direction.

"This place makes the land I saw in New Mexico look like a greenhouse," I remarked as I put my backpack in the box of Carl's pickup.

Junior adjusted the bill of her cap. "I heard it was bad dry up here. Never seen buffalo grass this brown in mid-July. No wonder Carl's truckin' calves to his brother's place. Wouldn't surprise me if they get some prairie fires up here before the season's out."

We piled into Gunderson's loaner and drove through twenty miles of nearly vacant, drought-stricken landscape. Bison, an anything-but-vibrant urban center one step above a wide spot in the road, looked like Paradise by the time we got there. The Perkins County Courthouse, a sleek, twentieth century building with a brick facade, stood in sharp contrast to the tired structures lining the town's block-long business district. With a population of 350 and the nation in the middle of an agricultural crisis, the burg was anything but humming.

Junior eased Carl's Dodge Ram pickup into a space at the rear of the courthouse. "You're sure now, that the People of Light center is at Bison and not Buffalo Gap or Buffalo," she teased.

The look on my face must have betrayed my utter exhaustion.

"It's okay, Cletus. I shouldn't have pulled your chain. When I got in last night, I phoned Burl. He told me you were running on empty. He didn't tell me you're running on fumes. Are you ready to do this?"

Running on fumes? The tank was dry, the vapor had evaporated, and there was no gas station in sight. Nothing to do for it but push on ahead. I put some conviction in my voice.

"Let's go kick some butt."

We entered a small, deserted lobby, looked at a series of arrows pointing to various county offices, followed one, and soon found ourselves at a door marked Sheriff's Department. I pulled on the handle, and we entered a sparsely furnished, surprisingly clean work area. A matronly woman wearing cat's-eye glasses with butterflies at the hinges stood behind the service counter. She glared at us as we approached.

"Hi," I said. "I'd like to speak to the sheriff about my son, he's being held captive at the People of Light Center."

A voice came from an office on the right. "Send him in, Marge."

"He's got somebody with him, Sheriff Hargrave," Marge shot back.

"Then send him and the somebody in."

"Sheriff Hargrave will see you now," Marge announced as she raised a section of the countertop to allow us to go through.

Since we'd already been invited in, her statement seemed unnecessary. The woman took her official sheriff's office gatekeeper role seriously. We passed through the opening and walked the eight feet to an open door. A retirement-aged guy with his hands locked behind his head and boot-clad feet sprawled on his desktop greeted us.

"Mornin'," he said and motioned toward a small conference table to his left. "Have a seat."

As we took our seats, he rose and called out through the door. "Marge, can you bring us some coffee?"

Women's lib may have made it to Cedar Rapids, Iowa, but had yet to reach Bison, South Dakota. Sheriff Hargrave joined us at the table. We introduced ourselves and made small talk about the weather and the trip from Wessington Springs until Marge returned with a tray and three steaming cups. After placing the cups, Coffee Mate, and artificial sweetener on the table, she turned to go. The woman might as well have taken a seat. I had no doubt she'd find a way to listen in to our conversation.

Hargrave got down to business as Marge's retreating butt cleared the doorway. "Your son is at the People of Light center?" he asked as he reached for his cup. Like me, he took his morning brew black.

"He's being held captive, I replied. "Their so-called Research and Re-education Center is nothing more than a slave labor camp where they send members who make waves."

Hargrave looked puzzled. "Don't know anything about a re-education center, but we haven't had any problem with the People of Light. They've set up a nice little business operation out on Bixby Road and mind their own business. They're polite. They don't drink. They pay their taxes and buy their supplies here in Bison. If Perkins County was home to more citizens like that, my job would be a hell of a lot easier. What makes you think your son is being held against his will?"

Convincing a man stubborn enough to wear muttonchop side-burns a decade after they became unpopular wasn't going to be easy.

"Most of the workers at the center have been brainwashed to the point that they have no free will. They force them to work at sewing machines ten hours a day, seven days a week. They're so broken they can no longer make their own decisions."

Hargrave nodded. "Long hours, but not that different from the kind of day the ranchers put in."

Junior giggled.

I gave her the evil eye. "Don't mind Junior. She's a farmer who doesn't know the difference between riding around in a pickup all day and being chained to a sewing machine."

Junior tucked her thumbs behind her overalls' bib. "Don't mind Cletus. He's a city boy who doesn't know the difference between makin' fence and makin' clothes."

Her light-hearted comment threatened to derail the conversation. I cut in as soon as she put the period on the end of her sentence. "I could give you details all day, but to make a long story short, I'm here to ask you to go to the People of Light center with me while I retrieve my son. I've been to their ranch in New Mexico and have an idea of how they operate. If I go there by myself, they won't let me in. Even if I do talk my way in, they'll make sure I don't see him."

The sheriff leaned forward. "Let's say that what you've told me is true. I can't go out there, ask them to produce the kid, and let you haul him away. Do you have proof of custodial parenthood? A court order?"

"My son isn't a minor. I just want to talk to him and convince him to come home. Maybe the shock of seeing me will shake something loose in his head. I've been to the cult's ranch in New Mexico. They have armed guards at the entrance who won't let anybody in. I'm sure it will be the same here. If you come with me, they might be more co-operative."

Hargrave sighed. "If your son is an adult, his associates are no business of mine. Unless, like you say, he's being held against his will. Do you have any proof? I just can't walk onto private property and demand they produce somebody the way they do on TV—not without a clerk magistrate's order. I know Jim Harrison, and he'll want more evidence than your say-so that your son is being held against his will. Do you have any letters from him? Statements from people who are on the inside?"

I rubbed my face. The guy didn't want to help. I counted to ten and used what my mom called my indoor voice. "I've lived with the People of Light. I know how the system works. Most members have been brainwashed to the point they can no longer think independently. My son is in worse shape than that. They're trying to break him. When he's not working, they keep him in isolation.

Sheriff Hargrave looked at a spot three feet over my head and stroked his chin. "Brainwashed, you say? They may have a weird religion and smile a lot, but all the People of Light I've met make sense when you talk to them. They may keep to themselves, but they believe in being good neighbors. Last fall they donated a new ambulance to the county emergency service. Out here that kind of money is hard to come by."

I looked over at Junior for support. She shook her head ever so slightly. I was on my own.

"They're trying to buy your goodwill with trinkets," I said.

Hargrave pointed his finger at me. "Trinkets? Our ambulance was fifteen years old. There's as many People of Light as live in Bison. The businesses in town are earning twice what they did five years ago. Everybody is smiling; everybody is happy. You're the first person to come into this office with wild stories about brainwashing and slaves. Tell you what, go find the clerk magistrate, get the paperwork, and I'll be happy to go out there with you."

Working with the man was like pulling teeth.

"I assume his office is in this building," I said.

"Other side of the lobby. But before you go, there's something you should know. Jim Harrison's wife teaches music at the high school. When the People of Light found out there was no budget for marching band uniforms, their leader had his workers sew up new ones. They did beautiful work and wouldn't take a penny for it."

I rose to go. "I'm sure the magistrate will be able to separate his personal and professional life."

The sheriff rubbed his chin and grinned. "One more thing, Jim's son runs the filling station on the east edge of town. The people you call brainwashers buy all their gas from him. He's doing so well he's added a diner to it. Everybody eats there because Jim's daughter runs the kitchen. She's the best cook in town. Her pies took the blue ribbon at the state fair two years in a row."

I stormed out of the office and through the workroom. It wasn't until I reached the Lobby, that I checked for Junior. When I did, she was right behind me, a crooked smile on her face.

"That went well," she observed.

Junior and I finished our baloney sandwiches and thermos of iced tea in the cab of Carl Gunderson's pickup. Junior devoured her Wonder Bread delights with the gusto of a starving panhandler at a wedding banquet. My portion of our larder came out to less than half. Not one to whine when things don't go my way, I made a brilliant suggestion.

"Junior, Hargrave mentioned the cook at the diner east of town makes the best pies in the state. We should check it out before we head back to the plane. Since we still don't know where to find the People of Light compound, we can ask about it while we're there."

"You might need to ask where the People of Light compound is, but I don't. Sheriff says it's on Bixby Road. There's an official State of South Dakota map in the glove box. Five will get you ten it shows a road that goes from here to someplace called Bixby."

Visions of my pie started floating away.

Junior crumpled the baloney-sandwich bag, leaned back in the seat, and stuck it in the side pocket of her bibs. I gave silent thanks that she wasn't one of those farmers who leave the side buttons of their overalls undone, exposing their drawers for all the world to see.

"We can look over the map at the diner," she said.

Happy we were on the same page, I gave a thumbs up. It took all of three minutes to reach our destination. I saw the vehicle as Junior turned into the parking lot.

Slapping the dash, I shouted, "Turn around! Back to the street—now!"

Junior swung back onto the roadway. "OK, what's wrong?"

"The van with New Mexico plates and flaming eye decal parked in the lot. It belongs to the People of Light. They're probably delivering prisoners to the Re-education Center.

"And?" Junior said, not taking her eyes off the road.

"I packed my Manoneeta scrubs just in case, and now they're going to come in handy. What's more logical than a true believer chatting up fellow cult members he runs into at a diner? Pull in behind that hair salon. I'll slip the hospital duds over my clothes. They're loose enough."

Junior sighed. "Fine, you can play detective, I'll have my pie at the counter."

We parked behind the beauty parlor, and I retrieved the scrubs from my backpack. The pants slid right over my trousers, but the top didn't cover my white T-shirt—a Manoneeta *faux pas*. I stripped off both and stuffed the tee into my pack. Still pulling on my scrubs top as I re-entered the cab, I heard Junior say, "For a city boy, you look pretty good without a shirt. You can help me make fence anytime."

I couldn't imagine helping Junior make fence. "I'd get sunburned," I replied. "Let's hit the diner."

Junior looked at me as if I was intellectually challenged and put the truck in gear. I slipped on my rosewood beads. They'd survived my detention. My surgeon's cap hadn't. I didn't know if the Manoneetas in the diner knew me by sight, but I'd worn a head covering in New Mexico and hoped my stubbly pate and extreme mustache made for an adequate disguise

The plan was to have me enter first and Junior come in a few minutes later. I'd pump the New Mexico folks for information while Junior enjoyed pie and coffee. Wishing our roles were reversed, I hopped out and made for the door. Though the place was new; the owner hadn't wasted any money on frills. The tables, lunch counter, and walls gave testimony to the wonder of Formica. Two beaded women dressed in pink sat at a booth by a picture window facing the gas pumps. Their regal bearing screamed *sadhu*. A solitary male seeker, also in pink, sat at a table halfway to the back of the room. Though all rode from New Mexico in the same van, his isolation from his colleagues was understandable. *Sadhus* didn't lunch with low-level seekers.

Knowing my place, I approached the guy at the table. "*Shaanti*. Mind if I have a seat?"

He looked up from the remains of an uninspired salad and pushed the chair across from him with his foot, a silent invitation to join him. Surprised by his lack of a return greeting, a violation of all Manoneeta expectations for politeness, I sat.

He raised an eyebrow. "What did you do to end up here?"

His defiantly rude opener brought me up short. Momentarily at a loss for words, I said, "Nothing."

"Nobody gets sent up here for nothing."

His response explained his attitude. He believed I'd failed the organization. As far as he was concerned, that made me *persona non grata*.

He gave me a once-over for the second time. "You look familiar."

I gave him my best full-on, space-case gaze of enlightenment. "I stayed at the ranch while waiting for my beads. Maybe you saw me then. I'm here in Bison because this is where my service is most needed. Before I took up my quest, I worked in the clothing trade. After Sattguru Devesha beaded me, I went back to my pod in Madison. Our *sadhu* believed my experience would help in marketing the People's hospital uniforms. She contacted the Inner Circle. They liked the idea and assigned me to work out of the shop."

He nodded. "*Shaanti.* My name is Phil. I worked at the Shiva City motor pool until they brought in a hotdog woman mechanic. Now, I'm the low dog in Shiva City security and drive the shuttle to the Re-education Center."

Bounced out when Belle came along. I wondered if he was bitter. "I'm Swami Aidan. Sorry to hear of your misfortune. Miss the mechanical work?"

"This is a lot better and way more important."

A gun can make you feel that way.

"Glad the new assignment is working out."

"I'm expecting to get called for my beads any day now. We just delivered a big-deal re-education case, and it went like clockwork. Doesn't always go that way. A few weeks ago, some guy escaped from a van. The driver and attendant were gone the next day. Screwed up so bad they didn't qualify for re-education."

Yeah, and got baked to death in the New Mexico sun.

Phil took a sip of what looked like iced tea. "I'll bet you're excited about the shindig you've got coming up in a few weeks. It'll be the biggest thing ever in your neck of the woods.

Time to bluff. I had no idea what the guy was talking about. "I've been on the road the past month, forty pods in thirty days—trying to get them involved in marketing our hospital wear. I'm so tired I don't know up from down. As soon as the shuttle gets here, I'm pitching my gear in the van and conking out."

"The pods must be as out of the loop as they say. They made the decision last week. You guys get the annual Guru Purnima this year. It'll be the first time Dev has been out of New Mexico since The People moved stateside. Imagine, five Bentleys and a half dozen Manoneeta vans rolling down the Interstate. That ought to get some attention."

No doubt it would. I hadn't heard of the Guru Purnima thing, but it was an annual event, so I came out with the only thing I could think of. "That time of the year again? Funny how you lose track of things when you're busy."

"Yup, can you believe it? Already the first full moon after the summer solstice and time to celebrate the wisdom of Dev. It'll be a blowout. Kind of makes me feel sorry for the folks who take up with the minor gurus. Your head guy, Babba Vivek, must be over the moon. I can't imagine a bigger honor."

Actually, most of the People of Light were over the moon.

A nice-looking waitress in her late twenties approached our table. I knew the town had a school, so there had to be younger residents, but she was the first I'd seen who looked to be under sixty. "What can I get for you?" she asked.

The hell with the Manoneeta diet, I ordered the peach pie with ice cream and coffee. On seeing Phil's raised eyebrow, I shrugged. "Unhealthy, I know. But you pick up some bad habits on the road."

"I was just wishing I could join you, but the *sadhus* I came up here with would give me grief all the way back to Shiva City."

"Manoneeta life's not easy," I said as my pie and coffee arrived.

"No need to rub it in."

"Couldn't help myself," I smiled.

My companion grinned, revealing a missing front tooth. He'd started to relax around me. I spooned down a chunk of the best peach pie to ever pass human lips. Doing my best not to moan, I went back to the business of fishing for information. "What with his history with Vivek, I can't imagine Babba Pappa is happy that Dev is coming to South Dakota for the big event." I gobbled more pie.

Phil scratched his beard. "What's that all about anyway? I feel like I'm the only person in Shiva City who doesn't know."

Finally, something I knew that he didn't. "Babba Vivek was Dev's right hand in India. He developed a problem with laughing gas, taxes didn't get paid, and people were getting hurt, so Dev put Babba Pappa in charge. When the People moved from India to New Mexico, Vivek was exiled to South Dakota to start the Research and Re-education Center. Vivek and Pappa have hated each other ever since."

Phil shook his head. "*Sadhus* quarreling over mundane trivia, everything we're trying to get away from."

I tsk-tsked. "Seems like building the new world gets harder each day. Nothing to do for it but hang in there. What's up with this big-deal re-education case you transported?"

Phil looked as if he wished I hadn't asked. "I'm not supposed to say anything, but this is so big, you'll hear about it the minute you get back to the Center."

"One of the Inner Circle?" I asked.

"Sort of, but bigger."

"Sort of?"

"We just transported Babba Pappa."

Out of my scrubs, back in the pickup, and waiting for Junior. Phil's revelation had knocked the pins out from under me. Worried that he would notice my consternation, I left the diner as quickly as I could without blowing my cover. Pappa's faked attempt on Dev's life had come back to haunt him.

It's not every day that the guy who wanted you roasted alive gets his comeuppance. I imagined Babba Vivek rubbing his hands with glee at the thought of breaking Pappa's very soul by condemning him to a chilly isolation tank. A better person might have taken some pity on the man for the mind-numbing misery he'd have to endure, but not me. The thought of Babba Pappa shivering for hours in a pitch-black void gave me a case of what my kindergarten teacher referred to as the warm fuzzies.

The only damper on my bliss was the realization my chat with Phil turned up nothing to help with the task of retrieving my son. I'd been so excited at the sight of the transport van in the diner parking lot I didn't realize my mission was doomed from the get-go. An inhabitant of the Re-education Center couldn't very well ask a visitor from New Mexico for details on the place where the inhabitant claimed to reside. Though I may have been shortsighted, I was out nothing but the price of pie and coffee and saw no reason to let a bit of failure rain on my parade. The vision of an emaciated, vacant-eyed Pappa, his mind too addled to form words, was an image for the ages, a treasure beyond price.

Chapter 37

The rocking of the pickup and thump of a closing door brought me back from the Land of Nod. I checked my watch.

"I've been out here for over an hour," I groused. "What took you so long?"

Junior took off her cap and shook out her braids. "I stopped to chat with those two ladies in pink sitting by the window." She put the key in the ignition, and the pickup rumbled to life.

"You did what?"

"Well, there were two sources of information in the restaurant you didn't bother with, so I thought I'd go over and check them out. They were a little weird, but they seemed okay."

"Okay? They drive people up here from New Mexico to get tortured."

"You should have talked to them."

"Wouldn't have done any good, I'm a lowly seeker. They're *sadhus* and wouldn't give me the time of day."

Junior grinned as we pulled out of the lot. "You really need to do something about your self-confidence."

"My self-confidence is fine. Their van's gone. I hope they didn't see me out here sleeping."

"They didn't. I walked out with them. The People of Light center is located next to a ghost town named Bixby. It's not on the map anymore, but the turnoff is six miles west of town. What did you learn from the guy at your table?"

"Only that they've just delivered the most important re-education case in People of Light history—the sattguru's right arm. The guy's name is Babba Pappa.

We rode in silence for a bit. Then Junior scratched the back of her neck. "How does that help us?"

"It doesn't," I admitted.

"Good job," she replied. "I hope you've got something better planned for when we get to the compound."

"I don't."

Junior groaned. Her reaction was unjustified. I'd been playing a long shot from the time I boarded the bus for New Mexico. Sheriff Hargrave was my last best chance for a payout. Lightening might yet strike, but only a fool could expect a positive outcome.

Not saying much, we rode through the desolate landscape. An endless row of wooden utility poles passed by on our right and a vacant blur of withered grass on our left. Now and again, a dusty lane appeared, and a wire or two split off the main line and followed a smaller row of poles to a barely visible ranch. I racked my brain, but despite all effort, came up with no better course of action than simply showing up at the gate and asking to see my son.

The pink, eight-foot-tall sign at the head of a well-maintained lane made no mention of the Research and Re-education Center. Instead, its navy-blue arrow and text directed us to something called Devesha Enterprises. A five-minute drive brought us to a gated opening in a tall chain-link fence identical to that in Shiva City. A guard house sided with those cheesy timber veneers used in the construction of fake log cabins stood just outside. With its cedar shake roof, the diminutive structure looked like it belonged at an entrance to Yellowstone Park rather than the gateway of a sweatshop hidden away in the far reaches of the Great Plains. The two pink-clad guys standing outside didn't do much to perpetuate the illusion. They looked more like escapees from a mental hospital than forest rangers.

I didn't want to negotiate through an open window so got out of the pickup as Junior rolled to a stop. Both men approached. The first, a bear of a man from the subcontinent, stood directly in front of me. The second, a pipsqueak, walked by me and assumed a position just behind my left shoulder.

"Can I help you?" said Bear-man. His name tag identified him as Swami Hari.

I gave him the friendliest smile I could manage. "I hope so. My son is staying here. There's been a death in the family, and I need to talk to him. He's just inherited his grandfather's farm."

I don't know where the line came from, but it wasn't half bad.

"I'm sorry for your family's loss," Hari said. "I hate to be the one to tell you this, but right now, we're having a little problem. Someone in the office let our liability insurance lapse. Until the matter is re-solved, we're only allowing order pickup and delivery."

Yeah, I believed that one. "Mike was close to his grandfather. We drove all night to give him the news. I'd hate for him to hear about it from someone else. Not just that, but the estate just got a top-dollar cash offer for the farm. It expires at noon on Friday. I'm the executor and need to know what he wants to do."

Hari looked to his left. Junior had exited the cab. She stood on her side of the pickup and stretched.

"Now Cletus, don't get your underdrawers in a bundle," she said. "We can wait out here for Mike. It's not like we don't have the rest of the day."

Hari nodded and his pint-sized companion rounded the pickup, taking up a position behind her. Good thing he had his gun. Junior could have broken the little twit in half, then yawned, and done some serious damage to Hari.

"My friend is right," I said. "We have time, so waiting's no prob-lem."

Hari shrugged, walked to the guard house, and returned with a pen and spiral-bound notebook. "I'll need to see your ID. Write your name, contact information, and message on this pad. I'll phone it in."

He didn't seem concerned with Junior, so I took the chance he wasn't going to ask for her ID. I put the pad on the fender of the pickup and wrote:

This message is for Michael Hinkley.

Mike. I know I'm not much of a father and we didn't part on the best of terms, but Tamara insisted that I come to speak with you in person. There's been a death in the family, you're mentioned in the will, and I'm the executor. I have paperwork for you to sign that will allow me to transfer your inheritance to you. Am waiting at the gate and have a notary public with me.

Cletus

I passed the pad to Junior. "That cover it?" I asked.

Junior didn't miss a beat. "Either of you guys willing to witness a document?" she asked the guards.

Apparently afraid of getting into trouble, the gatekeepers looked hopelessly at each other. Finally, the pipsqueak behind Junior said, "If it comes to that, I can do it. It's no big deal."

The matter settled, Hari took the note and checked my ID. He raised his bushy brows. "We've got a problem. Your name's Efferding and your son's is Hinkley. Doesn't add up."

"His grandparents on my wife's side raised him. That's one of the reasons our relationship is strained. He kept their name."

Hari snorted. "A life like that, the kid's lucky he found us."

Lucky to be held prisoner and brainwashed? I wanted to scream in the delusional douchebag's face. Hatred and rage surged through me. Summoning a reserve of willpower beyond the ken of mortal men, I kept my mouth shut.

Hari studied the note a bit longer, sighed, and returned my ID to me. He kept the note and returned to the guardhouse. Though I couldn't hear anything, I could see him through the shack's window, speaking into a microphone, nodding, and gesticulating. Though the Manoneetas must have used telephones to conduct their clothing operation, they weren't about give a mere security guard access to one. I stood silently, plotting my next move. Junior leaned against the driver-side fender.

Hari put down the mic and joined us. "Good thing you have all day. It'll take another hour." With that, he and his pal went back to the guard house. A half-hour later a golf cart drove up to the guard house. The gate opened, Hari handed the driver an envelope, and she returned in the direction from which she came.

Junior pulled a bandanna from her bibs and wiped her forehead. "It's too hot to sit in the cab, but I might as well turn the radio on. We can listen to it out here."

The sounds of the Oak Ridge Boys' "Elvira" drifted from the cab. I'd have preferred silence myself.

Junior hiked herself onto the edge of the pickup box. "Looks like you're gonna see him. Then what, Big Boy? Hope your plan is better than the last one."

I adjusted my Foster Grants. "The only thing Mike wanted from me the last time I talked to him was money for the cult. He hit me up for ten thousand. I'll offer him fifteen if he comes back to Cedar Rapids and talks to his sister."

"That's a good chunk of change."

"Not quite a farm, but worth every penny to prove myself to my daughter. I may not be anyone's idea of a good father, but I can do better than I have in the past."

We chatted a bit more while I kept an eye on the chain-link gate. Eventually, I made out a vehicle heading in our direction. As it drew closer, I identified it as a golf cart. The driver wore pink, a figure in blue, Mike, sat at his side. The cart was a six-seater. The back four seats held security guards, each cradling an assault rifle.

My son looked like he'd aged fifteen years. The gate slid to the side, and that's when I realized I'd been had. The guy in blue wasn't

Mike at all. He was a decade older, with the same coloring. He climbed out of the cart and walked toward me smiling all the way.

There are times when you can take the Manoneeta smile at face value. This wasn't one. The phony-baloney grin honked me off. I folded my arms and scowled.

The smile disappeared from the guy's face. He stopped five feet from me.

"Your son, Michael Hinkley, refuses to see you. He asked his supervisor to send me in his place. I am Swami Kalap. My law degree is from the University of Minnesota, and I represent our center on all things legal and financial. You may give me the papers. I'll take them to your son and see they are properly signed, witnessed, and notarized."

As if I had any papers to give him.

I stood my ground. "Surely you can see my problem. Being the executor of a large estate is a major responsibility. Having Michael Hinkley sign in my presence is the only way I have of knowing that he actually gave his consent."

Kalap frowned. "Your request goes far beyond the requirements of the law. The signature of your son in the presence of a notary and witness who can testify to his identity is sufficient and demonstrates you have done the job expected of you.

I stepped forward and jabbed my finger into his chest. "I see Michael Hinkley, or I leave with the documents. I need to ensure he's not signing under duress."

Kalap backed away. Four stone-faced security guards hopped off the golf cart and assumed positions facing me, their rifles at a forty-five-degree angle. Hari and his companion, hands on their holsters, joined them. I looked back to see Junior still sitting on the box of the pickup, her expression blank.

The cult's lawyer looked less than happy. "Your son's state of mind at the time of signing is an issue for the courts, not the executor." His face reddened with anger. "You've just assaulted me in the presence of eight witnesses. I intend to file a petition to ask the court to remove you as executor of the estate. Your behavior indicates you are unfit for the job. Notices of pending estates are public record and no problem for me to locate. You'll make it easier on yourself and Mike if you hand over the documents."

I spat into the dirt. "Not gonna happen."

"Have it your way. The lane leading out to the road is private property, and you are trespassing."

I wanted to give him more grief, but when I looked back to check on Junior, she turned her head in the direction of the road, indicating it was time to go. Game over. Cletus Efferding had lost. Head and shoulders slumping, I trudged back to the truck. Junior hopped off the edge of the box, opened the door, and took up position behind the wheel. After one last look at the gate, I climbed in. Blinking hard to keep the tears in my eyes from flowing down my cheeks, I looked at the floorboard as Junior turned the truck around and drove us back in the direction we'd come.

When I raised my head again, we were off the lane and back on the main road. I stared glumly through the windshield. "Well, that's it. The jig is up. The law's against me, my daughter won't forgive my failure, and my son is doomed to live out his life as a brainwashed slave. It's not like I can take an army to invade the place. There's nothing to do for it but go home. Why I ever thought flying over the compound to take photos would be useful is beyond me. We don't need to waste the time."

Junior flexed and unflexed her fingers as she made minor adjustments to the steering wheel. "I don't know about you, but I had fun today—almost like being an undercover cop. You tried a bluff, and it didn't work. So what?"

"Some fun. I blew it and have "loser" tattooed all over my face."

"Burl never told me you were a quitter. I think it would be damn useful to take those pictures. How else will I find my way around when I get inside?"

My head began to throb. I closed my eyes and rubbed my temples. "Let it go, Junior. It's over."

"Maybe for you, but not for me."

I didn't want Junior playing cop on my account. The woman was a gem, but it was time to cut and run. I looked across the cab. Both hands were still on the wheel, but an envelope protruded from the first two fingers of her right hand. "Take it and read," she said.

I reached over and retrieved the tan envelope. Nice stationery, with nothing written on the outside surfaces and the flap unsealed. Reaching inside, I retrieved a matching sheet neatly folded into thirds. Opening it revealed an embossed flaming-eye letterhead followed by a professionally engraved text.

> *The People of Light cordially invite* Donna Dietz *and guest to the Guru Purnima festival celebrating the wisdom and benevolent guidance of the light of the world, the Most Divine Sattguru Devesha of Kanpur. The observance will take place July 24th, 1983, at the Sattguru Devesha Learning and Research Center at Bison, South Dakota, between the hours of noon and midnight. Though gratitude is traditionally expressed with tributes of candles, flowers, sweets, fruit, and prayer, financial contributions are greatly encouraged.*
>
> *Sattguru Devesha will speak at 8:30 p.m. and lead the dynamic meditation session which is to follow. Invited guests who wish to participate in the meditation session are asked to attend a 7:00 p.m. orientation to prepare for the experience. Visitors will be required to show this invitation and identification prior to admittance.*

Junior's name appeared in ballpoint to an underlined space left blank for the name of the invitee, and it appeared that the name of the Re-Education center had been modified to make it sound more presentable. I sat dumbfounded.

Junior cleared her throat. "And this is where you say, 'Congratulations, Junior, how in the hell did you manage that?'"

We'd been aloft for maybe five minutes when I just had to go through it one more time. "So, you told them you were a big rancher, and they just gave you the invitation?"

Junior turned toward me and displayed the same smug grin she'd been wearing ever since she let me see the invitation to the guru celebration. "It didn't hurt that I was really interested in their beliefs. Just imagine, giving up everything you know to follow a religious leader. Kind of like the first Christians when you think about it."

"I don't think the early Christians locked people in cages and roasted them alive. At least not for the first few hundred years or so."

"You've got a point, but you get more out of people if you're genuinely interested in them. I let those ladies talk about themselves before I told 'em good help is hard to find, and I was getting tired of the cattle business. Said there must be more to life than workin' from dawn till after dark runnin' the biggest spread in Jerauld County. Told 'em I'd sell out but wouldn't know what to do with myself afterward. After that, they were on me like burs on wool socks."

"I get that part, but a special invitation?"

"I played it farmer dumb."

I wasn't sure I heard correctly through the headphones. "Farmer dumb?"

"That's what we call it around here when you run circles around city folks by acting like you got kicked by a steer once too often. Said it sounded like joining the People of Light might be what I was lookin' for, being I was so lonely and all. Strung 'em along like wire on fence posts."

"I can't believe you were so obvious. Folks can get spacey when they meditate too much, but *sadhus* should be way over that."

"Never underestimate the power of farmer dumb. Only two hundred invitations goin' out, and that includes People of Light. I got one. Sometimes I kick myself for not going into law enforcement. Woulda been good at undercover. Better get your camera ready. Looks like their compound up ahead."

A cluster of buildings appeared in the distance. All we'd seen from the gate was the fence, a water tower, and the guard house. The reason became clear as we drew closer. A small rise stood between the gate and the center. It wasn't much but served to screen the center's buildings from approaching vehicles. Our altitude made it hard to see much more. I asked Junior to drop down a bit.

"They won't shoot at us, will they?" she asked.

"I don't think so," I replied. "But what the hell, you only live once."

Junior banked the plane for another pass. "If they do, you'll be going down with me."

We dropped down a bit. Since Junior's Skylane was designed with an overhead wing, I enjoyed an unobstructed view. Still, it was hard to get a good angle on the Center. I shot a half dozen frames as we passed over the compound but doubted they'd show much.

"Is there any way you can tip the plane to my side?" I asked. "And maybe go a bit lower? I'm not getting very much."

"Sure," said Junior.

I waited for her to alter our course, but she kept flying in the same direction—away from the Center.

"Change your mind?" I asked.

"Well, you're not so sure we won't get shot at, and we just flew over the place twice. Doesn't make sense to give them any more time to get a welcome posse organized. We'll do some sightseeing and come back later. What did you think of the layout?"

"I was so busy with the camera I didn't have time to see very much. I'm pretty sure they don't have a swimming pool."

Junior turned to look at me. "I didn't have all that distraction. Compared to that ranch you were talking about, this setup is small potatoes. I don't know how much land they've got, but if I know my distances, they only fenced in a square mile. And then there's that fence within a fence. There's just one building in it, so I guess it's the prison part of the operation."

I put my camera down, settled into my seat, and took in the scenery. Not that there was much to see. Our altitude added little charm to the featureless plains we'd already driven through. The desolate view had a stimulating effect on Junior. Where I saw nothing, she saw cattle trails, the foundations of abandoned buildings, and abandoned corn pickers poking up through weeds and scrub. I discovered Junior could identify crops from the air, could determine the size of the farms and ranches spreading out below us, point out dry and almost dry riverbeds, and estimate the capacity of the grain elevators we passed over. After what seemed like two hours to me and maybe fifteen minutes for Junior, we made a turn and headed back to the Rehabilitation Center.

"I'll make a long, banking curve to our right as we fly over," she announced. That way you'll see more ground through the window. I'm allowed to go as low as five hundred feet, but that would make us an easy target if some crackpot decides to use us for target practice. I'll drop down to something like a thousand feet and hope they won't feel threatened enough to shoot. You'll have to work fast because I don't intend to slow down."

Getting good pictures through glass wouldn't be easy but opening the window and taking pictures through the windy, narrow gap didn't seem feasible given the speed at which the ground would be passing by. When Junior began her descent, I was ready. She brought the plane in for the low sweep. Hoping the light meter in my camera was up to the task, I began the point, click, and film advance sequence. My timing was pretty good. I managed to get off sixteen of my remaining eighteen frames before we passed out of range.

Junior's laugh crackled through the headphones. "No bullet holes in the airplane, and photo mission accomplished." The woman must have sensed I was pleased with my work. She turned and gave me a big grin and a thumbs-up. Some quick camera work on my part immortalized the moment, and I knew without a doubt I'd just taken one of the best photos of my life.

"I don't suppose that town of yours has a place with a 24-hour turnaround on photo developing," I said.

"I think the drugstore sends them to Mitchell. It'll probably take a week."

"Too bad, I can't wait to see how they turned out. Guess I won't know until I get back to Cedar Rapids."

"You could stay out here and help me make fence without your shirt on while you wait for the pictures."

Junior was a great gal and all, but I nipped the suggestion in the bud. "I've got to get back to Cleatzy's. I've been away a lot, and the place needs attention."

"I reckon then, you're not interested."

"Not in making fence. Shoveling mud down in New Mexico was more than enough physical labor for a while."

I knew Junior was serious about making fence, but Myra's suicide and Dusty's murder destroyed any illusions I once had about intimate relationships. Though I expected Junior's social life was something less than she wanted, I refused to feel sorry for her. She was the type of woman men love to talk to but seldom dream of. Too bad for them. There was a hell of a lot going on behind that plain, sunburned face, and I had no doubt she would land a keeper one day.

"I'll order two sets of eight by ten prints and mail the second to you as soon as I pick them up. You can study them on your end, and I'll do the same on mine. I'll come up a few days before the Guru Purnima, and we can make plans to go in and find Mike."

"You're missing a few things, Cletus. Say we find Mike. How are you going to get him out?"

"We'll improvise," I replied. "There's no way we can plan for what might happen once we get there."

"That might sound good to you, but there ain't much that happened today that speaks for the quality of your improvisin'. Besides, what makes you think I'm gonna fly up there and take you to the wingding as my guest?"

Junior's reply took the wind out of my sails. I hoped she wasn't honked off because of my lack of enthusiasm for fence-building.

"I know you have a farm to run," I said, "and don't expect you to drop everything to do me a favor. I'll pay whatever you think is fair."

"Money's got nothing to do with it, family has. You want to fetch your son, and I want to keep my brother happy. Burl made me promise I wouldn't go back up there again if we left without Mike."

"What's he got to do with this?" I asked.

"Everything. He called a few days ago to say I might be seeing you and could pick up a few bucks flying you up there. I did that. You want to do any more about your son, talk to him. I'm not about to involve myself in his detective business without his say-so. We get along so good because we know where the fences are and respect them."

"But I haven't hired Burl," I countered. "We don't have a business relationship, so you're free to do what you want."

"That may be true, but what I want is for you to find your son, and the best way to do that is to hire Burl."

Chapter 38

My second full day back in town. I checked in at Photo Pro, paid for and picked up two sets of eight by ten glossies. I dropped one pack in a manila envelope addressed to Junior and dropped it off at Federal Express. My next stop, an appointment with Burl at his office. The radio blared back to life as I turned the Cordoba's ignition switch. An announcer was in the middle of a KCRG news update.

... as FBI investigators carried box upon box of files from the side doors of Merchants' National Bank and into a pair of plain, unmarked vans. Officials have refused to comment on the nature of the seizure though rumors of corruption and financial mismanagement have grown from a whisper into a roar.

In a moment, Denny Frary with the weather ...

The station's news updates invariably ended with the weather, so I clicked over to a music station. A federal raid on Steele Sutherland's bank less than two weeks after he killed himself. There had to be a connection. I gave him the benefit of the doubt when I assumed his self-destruction was the result of grief over his daughter's murder. Now I wasn't so sure. Yeah, the guy wanted grandchildren, but I saw little evidence that he respected or loved his daughter. Dusty was simply a means to the end.

I didn't want to believe it at the time, but my friend Lumir was right when he insisted the rich were a breed apart, a god-like subset of humanity with concerns unfathomable to mere mortals. Dusty may have been an exception to the rule, but the hearts of her calculating family had long ago shriveled into avian gizzards hellbent on grinding up the little people who got in the way.

Preoccupied with such cheerful thoughts, I made my way to Burl's spartan storefront office. I parked in front, put a paper clip on the photos I kept for myself, and took the packet in with me. If anything, the place looked even drearier than the last time I visited. "Jeez, Burl," I said by way of greeting, "you really need to do something with that fifty-cents-a-sheet paneling. It's contact paper over composition board for Christ's sake. What are your clients going to think?"

"They won't think nothin'. Half of 'em seen so many movies they think a private investigator's office is supposed to look like a dump. The other half are happy they're not funding my extravagant lifestyle. You oughta lose that mustache, it makes you look like a walrus."

I chose to ignore his comment. "I've got a bone to pick with you. I suppose Junior's called already."

"She did and said it didn't go so good. You didn't get to see him. She couldn't tell if he didn't want to lay eyes on you or if the guys at the gate was lyin' through their teeth. At any rate, you struck out."

Burl had a way with words.

"Not struck out," I said, "Let's say the game's been delayed pending a guru festival. Junior won't help me out unless you okay it."

Burl fingered the stainless-steel chain he wore on his wrist. "That's what she said, huh? Well, you don't know the whole of it. She called me when she got home that night. Junior wants to see you get your son back but doesn't want to go up there with you because she thinks you'll mess up again. Belle and I think she's right."

Just then the bell on the street door tinkled. Burl looked at the watch on his chainless wrist. "Right on time," he said.

I turned to see Tamara, a huge bag over her shoulder and a small leash in her hand. The leash terminated in a dachshund that might have weighed ten pounds on a good day. "Hi, Gramps," she said. "Weird mustache. My dog's name is Loomie. I named him after Lumir."

"Cute little guy," I replied. "You still in Cedar Rapids? Find a job yet?"

Tamara's face darkened. "For a father who's come home empty-handed, you're starting out on the wrong foot. You could have tried a hug and *it's good to see you.*"

Messed up again. "I'm sorry, Tamara, but I worry about you."

Tamara put down her bag and took a seat. "Burl told me about the Guru Purnima festival yesterday. I called Eddie, Lumir, Mrs. Hemsky, and Belle. We invited Burl to a meeting last night and decided I'm going to the big guru celebration with Junior. After all, I'm the one Mike will want to see. It'll be easier for me to convince him to come back home than it would be for you."

I raised my voice. "I won't allow it! The People of Light are dangerous, and there's no way I'm going to let you go up there. If—"

A sharp bark, followed by a growl, interrupted my outburst. The yelp and throaty rumble brought on the realization I'd overplayed my hand. I didn't have the courage to look back at Tamara and face her disapproval.

Burl folded his arms on his desk. "Damn it, Clete. They're not going to haul your daughter off in the middle of a big festival, and now you got the dog all excited. He pees in here and I'm sending you the cleaning bill. You've got no standing in this one. Your friends put down a retainer; they're my clients now."

I hopped out of my chair. "Clients! I let my business go to hell, chase off to New Mexico, where I almost get murdered. Then I *schlep* myself off to Buffalo Butt, South Dakota, where I get abused by a tinpot hippie lawyer and a county sheriff straight out of the 1960s. And now I'm not wanted? And if you think I'm going to pay for getting a decade's worth of dirt out of your cheap-crap carpets, you better guess again."

"Cool your jets, Gramps!" Tamara's voice brought back memories of the fourth-grade teacher who caught me kissing Janice Tebbe's hand.

What I thought of as kissing Mrs. Galusha referred to as 'slobbering all over the poor girl's arm.' Old classroom habits die hard, so I sat down, properly chastised.

Burl shook his head. "You gotta get a grip. Nobody said they was cuttin' you out. You're gonna be part of the B team."

"Whoopdee-do," I complained, "the junior varsity. Okay, so what's the B team do?"

"There'll be four of us: me, Eddie, Belle, and you. We'll be armed, and if things go haywire—say the People of Light won't let Mike go or he doesn't want to leave with us—we're in charge of the extraction."

Cruising down First Avenue the next day, I forgot the stoplight at Nineteenth Street and almost rear-ended a pickup truck. I detest spacey drivers but gave myself a pass. The KCRG morning news had blown my concentration to hell and back. One of the station's reporters found a leak in the wall of silence surrounding the federal investigation into Merchants National Bank. The FBI suspected an executive at MNB was laundering money for Anthony 'The Mortician' Abato, a higher-up in the Chicago syndicate.

While the news report did not identify Steele Sutherland as a target of the investigation, it mentioned his suicide and the murder of his daughter as misfortunes that had befallen the closely held business. The implication was clear. Dusty's murder and Steele's suicide were a byproduct of his involvement with the mob.

I was certain of more than that. Tony the Mortician had Dusty killed. Maybe Steele fudged the numbers or wanted out of their arrangement. A crooked banker is an asset. As unhappy as a mob big shot might be, it didn't make financial sense to bump him off in a fit of pique. Far better to send a message he couldn't ignore. The bigger, the better. Dusty's gruesome death fit the bill.

Shaking my head, I pulled into a parking space in front of Ole's Ham & Egger, and except for the near-miss at Nineteenth Street, had no memory of how I made the drive. Steele just wasn't blowing smoke when he threatened to hire somebody to castrate me and break every bone in my body. With his connections, he'd have had little trouble finding the muscle to do it. Though my wedding to his daughter hadn't come off, he'd done nothing to carry out his threat. Still, the guy might have stewed over the situation and acted on it one day. Call me vindictive, but I was just as happy the man was dead.

I grabbed my envelope of aerial surveillance photos, inserted pictures of Mike that Tamara gave me, and made for the door. Ole's diner seemed a strange choice for our meeting. The owner had crowded in as many booths and tables into his hole-in-the-wall diner as possible. Conversations could be easily overheard, and our neighbors would risk neck injury as they stretched in their seats to take a gander at the photos we'd be passing around. Belle discovered the place on her third day in town and offered to buy our breakfast if we met there. A generous offer to be sure, but a poor location for a B team meeting.

Though my friends put down a retainer to secure Burl's services, I was on the hook for the rest. My part of the bill dwarfed theirs, coming in at fifteen thousand dollars—the average worker's annual income. It seemed a substantial sum to secure the services of what Burl referred to as his 'agency.' The term seemed a little grandiose since as far as I knew, Belle was his sole employee. I could have walked away, but doubted Tamara, Eddie, Lumir, and Millie would miss an opportunity to say they were disappointed in me. Worse yet, I'd have been disappointed in myself.

I ordered a coffee and took another look through the aerial photos while waiting for the team to arrive. The water tower Junior and I spotted stood next to the largest structure on the property. Flat-roofed, with a loading dock on one end, I pegged the building as the production facility and warehouse for the cult's hospital uniforms and isolation tanks. Across the road lay a set of four quadrangles, each surrounded by a dozen rectangular structures with a larger building in the center. The similarity to the residential layouts in Shiva City led me to identify them as housing units with communal buildings as their hubs. Junior flew low enough on our last pass for the photos to show quite a bit of detail. Most of the Center's buildings featured gabled roofs that looked to be shingled. Knowing what I did about Manoneeta aesthetics, I'd have wagered a bundle of cash that the cheesy guard shack set the pattern for the appearance of the structures on the other side of the gate.

The fenced-off square building Junior noticed on our first flyover sat isolated, a little way from the rest of the compound. I remained convinced it was the People of Light's prison. The other buildings were harder to identify.

A vacant area to the side of the quads looked as if it might be an outdoor meditation ground. A single road ran through the middle of the compound and terminated in a turnaround at the back fence. Except for the segment near the buildings, it looked little used.

I looked up to see Burl and Belle enter the restaurant. I waved. Eddie followed on their heels. "Not the best location for a meeting," I observed as they sat. "There's no privacy or room to spread out our photos."

Belle took the chair opposite me. She'd tied her bushy red mane in pigtails. Two-thirds hair and one-third face dominated by oversized green eyeglasses, I found it hard to believe there was a person in there somewhere. "The place will be deserted in a half hour," she replied. "Trust me, I'm already a regular."

Choosing among the breakfast options proved no problem. Having a thing for ham and given the name of the establishment, the decision was an easy one. After flagging a waitress and determining that Ole's Belly Buster—a slab of processed pork the size of a dinner plate— was large enough to meet my requirements, I placed an order. "And three over-easy eggs on top," I added before she left.

"I don't know how you do it," said Belle. "The way you shovel it in, you should weigh 300 pounds."

"I have discipline," I replied as I returned my photos to their envelope. "I put on twenty pounds to help disguise myself before I went to New Mexico. It's taken nearly three weeks, but I'm almost back to normal. Another four pounds and I'll be there."

Belle raised her eyebrows. "I doubt discipline had anything to do with it. You must have the Midwest's fastest metabolism."

I was about to point out that Belle's attitude could result in me calling her Mabel again but held my tongue as the others exchanged gossip. The dig would have served no purpose, and the prompt arrival of my ham and egg plate soon took precedence. The dish proved so tasty I complimented Belle on her choice of breakfast venue instead. Burl and Eddie did the same, and by the time the four of us were on our third coffees, morning rush was over.

Burl surprised me when he reached down, produced a briefcase, and extracted one of those maps inscribed with lines that show the elevation of hills and landforms. "This is one of those topographic maps," he announced. "Between your photos and this map, we should get an understanding of the layout of this place. But before we get to that, we need to spend some time on the basics."

"It's important to recognize there's a good chance of failure," he continued. "Including Junior and Tamara, we got six people to look through a crowd of something like four or five hundred. Junior and Tamara are gonna cover the group at the big meditation wingding. The four of us will search the rest of the compound. It's a lot of territory. We won't get through all of it, and any guards who see us are gonna be suspicious. Say we locate Mike; our problems are just beginning. We still gotta get him out. If he comes willingly, and they let him go, we're home free. That's a big 'if.' If not, the best case is we sneak him out; the worst is we kidnap him."

Burl paused and looked over at Belle. "We kidnap him, we gotta a sticky problem. Belle's been thinkin' it through."

Belle frowned and shook her head. "Thinking it through and up against a brick wall. All those stories about chloroform or knockout gas are fairy tales. You're as likely to kill someone as render them unconscious. If Mike doesn't leave under his own power, we'll have to gag him and take him out through a hole in the fence. All I can come up with is strapping him to a stretcher and lugging him back to a pickup truck. We might have to carry him a half mile or more inside the fence and then another quarter mile or so out to the truck. Of course, it would be a lot less work if we put a gun to his head and convinced him we're crazy enough to use it if he doesn't cooperate."

I thumped the table. "A gun to his head? Absolutely not! He's messed up enough already without believing his father is crazy enough to have somebody kill him. You're nuts."

Belle's face fell. "Sorry, that last part didn't quite come out right. I was trying for a joke to lighten the mood."

Burl cut in. "The upshot is we'll have to carry Mike out through a hole in the fence if he don't cooperate. He'll have to be gagged and restrained. Junior and Tamara will leave the way they came in—through the gate. That leaves the four of us to get him to the truck. Two transporting and two covering our butts. We'll alternate."

"We could use a *travois*," I said.

My companions looked as if I'd taken leave of my senses.

"A what? asked Eddie.

"Didn't you guys watch any old westerns? A *travois*."

A glance at Burl and Belle indicated that they had no idea of what I was talking about. I tried again. "A drag, a set of poles that's hitched to a horse or dog. You tie your load to it, and the animal pulls it. They're sort of triangle-shaped and work pretty well over ground where a set of wheels would just be in the way. It'd be almost as lightweight as a stretcher. Lumir could make one designed to be pulled by two people."

"Oh, one of them travises," Burl grunted. "Might be better than a stretcher. It'll have to be light. Even if we don't need it, we have to carry it into the compound. Talk to Lumir."

"Did you hear back from Junior?" Belle asked.

Burl, his mouth full of scrambled egg, nodded. "She called during the Johnny Carson show last night." A bit of egg yolk fell onto his lime-green polyester shirt. The shirt was bad, but paired with his checked cranberry pants, the effect was horrific. I kept it to myself, but the egg was the best thing on the guy.

When Burl wiped his face with his napkin, the egg rolled down his front and disappeared behind the edge of the table. "Junior looked at the surveillance photos you sent. She found what looks like a dry wash that leads from an abandoned road to a spot near the outside fence. She took her Cessna up there to check it out firsthand and then ate supper somewhere in North Dakota. On the way back, she flew over the compound again, in the dark. Most of the perimeter fence is unlit. The lights are concentrated on the entrance side of the property and that bunch of buildings next to it."

Looks like we have another thing going for us," I interjected. "Guru Purnima is celebrated during the full moon. The night will be bright enough to help us pick our way through rocks and brush."

"Or make us better targets for the security guards," Belle added.

I was thinking about a response when Eddie cleared his throat. "I haven't seen the aerial photos, and I still don't know what Mike looks like."

Burl and I took Eddie's hint and unfolded the map and brought out the photos. Immersed in speculation and planning, we lost track of time until an irritated counterman barked at us. "Either place another order or leave. It's almost lunch, I got tables to clean and a floor to mop."

Belle turned in her seat. "Sorry, Ole."

As we got ready to leave, Burl gave us our assignments. Each of us would be responsible for procuring our own firearm. Since I had the least shooting experience, he wanted me to use a scattergun. I remembered Lumir's shotgun, illegal since it had been shortened. "A friend of mine has a cut-down 12-gauge, pump action. It's on the short side of the law. Bad idea?"

Belle looked to Burl. Burl shrugged and looked back to Belle—her decision.

She nodded. "I think Cletus is going to need all the help he can get."

Burl sighed. "Get it if you can.

We decided that Eddie, with his knowledge of electronics and band equipment, would be best at finding small, hand-held walkie-talkies. Belle was charged with acquiring blue hospital scrubs.

Burl rubbed his unshaven jaw. "We'll ask Millie Hemsky to sew pockets for hiding the handhelds inside our scrub tops."

"Does Millie sew?" I asked.

Eddie rolled his eyes. "Millie is ninety years old. Every woman that age knows how to sew. Maybe she could add loops for holding flashlights.

"I like the loops," Belle said. "Manoneetas wouldn't think walking around with the flashlight hanging from your scrubs was weird; they'd think it was cool."

"Good idea," said Burl. "We're lucky they wear hospital uniforms. Scrub tops are loose enough to hide shoulder holsters.

"What about me?" I asked. "Am I supposed to walk around with a shotgun inside my pants leg?"

Belle drained her cup. "How about a little creativity, Cletus? Roll it up in a yoga mat. Do it right. and you might be able to get off a shot without unrolling it."

Ole, now holding a rag and bucket, yelled across the room, "I ain't got all day. Move it."

We did.

Chapter 39

Lumir and I sat in his cluttered workshop. "You can use my sawed-off shotgun," he said as he handed me a mug of near-toxic coffee.

The gun held bad memories for me. I once borrowed it without his knowledge to scare off a vicious drug dealer who'd been threatening him and his family. The pump-action gun worked only too well. The guy took one look at it, panicked, and ran into the path of a speeding car. It wasn't one of his better days. After the incident, I surreptitiously returned the gun to Lumir's house, and to this day he didn't know the gun he inherited from his father caused a premature death. Not that he would mind. As wise and kind-hearted as he is, my friend has a streak of vigilantism in him. His experiences in the First World War left him with a clear understanding of the difference between good and evil. He has little tolerance for degenerates.

I shifted in my chair. "I thought about your gun and appreciate the offer, but the People of Light security force is well-armed. I've decided to go with a semi-automatic. I don't expect to use it, but if things go bad with their security crazies, the extra firepower will be a godsend."

"Suit yourself," he said. "Now what is this travis thing you want me to build?"

I explained the concept.

Lumir shook his head. "It will be sad if you must gag your son and tie him up. You are doing it for his own good, but he may never forgive you."

"If he doesn't want to come with us, it's either that or leave him there. Besides, I don't think he can hate me much more than he does already."

"There are no limits to hate," he said. "It is sad, but it is true. And in the face of hate, goodness can go only so far. You are trying to do the best by your son, but in the end, you may lose him to his hostility. You must be ready for that. I am glad I am not in your situation."

"I'd like to think you're wrong, but the longer I live, the more I realize positive outcomes are hard to come by. I tried to find Mike for the sake of my daughter, but now there's more to it. Saving my son from the People of Light is a chance to prove to his mother that I was worth spending some of the limited time she had on this earth with me. He's in a cult because I failed her and after that, failed him."

Lumir straightened in his chair and rubbed his back. "There are times for thinking about mistakes and times for action. Let us get back to this travis you're talking about. When I was on graves detail, I hauled over a hundred bodies out of ditches and rivers and carried something like another hundred over open ground. There is no single device that will meet your needs."

"I understand that Lumir, but we have to be prepared for Mike's resistance."

"I will make a travis frame you can disassemble to create a stretcher. I wish I could make this trip with you, but your friend Burl called to tell me I am not welcome."

It was hard hearing the hurt in Lumir's voice. Worse yet, I was responsible. Knowing my aged friend expected to accompany us to South Dakota, guns and all, I'd asked Burl to find a way to keep him from participating. I never imagined he'd brush him off over the phone. Thank goodness for the *travois* construction project.

"I wish you were coming, but Burl insisted on complete control of the operation or his agency wouldn't get involved. For what it's worth, you're the only one I trust to come up with the solution to our transport problem."

"Yet this man has no problem involving your nineteen-year-old daughter in his scheme. I hope you knew what you were doing when you hired him."

Time for a diversion.

"Lumir, I need to know more about picking out a shotgun and ammunition. I'm not sure about the bore size and the best shells for it."

Seemingly distracted from his personal disappointment, Lumir put his hands on his knees and leaned forward. "You must choose a twelve-gauge. A ten-gauge would throw more lead, but they are not useful at close range. Using slugs sounds good, but in a pinch, you will not have time for a careful aim. People swear by double-aught buckshot, but my father used nothing but the number one size for deer hunting. That way, he got more projectiles per shell. Still, you might want something a little larger, say single-aught buck. If you choose three-inch magnum shells, you'll get an extra ball or two, but be sure your gun is chambered for them. If you put a three-inch shell in a gun with a two and three-quarter-inch chamber, it may blow up."

I knew all this but wanted Lumir to feel involved in our project. "I'll pick up some single ought buckshot. When I get my new semi-automatic, will you saw off the barrel and stock for me?"

"Of course, I will. When do you need it?"

"In three days."

My answer met with a string of Czech profanity followed by "... and make this travis device, too? I will have to work day and night to get so much finished in time."

"I'll buy the shotgun and bring it over tomorrow," I offered meekly.

Following another string of Czech profanity, my friend slowed down enough for us to go over the details of the proposed travis. By the time I left, Lumir was going through his stacks of lumber looking for suitable stock for the poles. Yup, he'd have to shorten the gun and build the carrier in just three days. No time for fretting or feeling left out, just a concentrated effort to make the deadline.

In a better mood, I whistled as I ambled back to the Cordoba and headed off to Fin and Feather sporting goods to pick up a shotgun. Finding a semi-automatic twelve gauge that took three-inch magnum shells was no problem. Ammunition was another matter.

"It's a special order. We don't stock it because Iowa doesn't allow buckshot for deer hunting anymore. Now, I know a guy who reloads empty casings ..."

A half-hour before I left the apartment for Cleatzy's. I put my empty cup on the kitchen counter, alongside the box of reloads I bought from Blaze Krouse the night before. It was a shady transaction all around. Blaze lived in a rundown one-story house in Paris—an unincorporated burg on the Wapsipinicon River a half hour's drive from Cedar Rapids. Paris didn't amount to much. After passing a sign informing me I was on the Left Bank, I encountered a cluster of decaying houses and mobile homes. A leaning mailbox disfigured by a barely legible scrawl identified the Krouse residence.

I pulled into the yard of a structure in no better condition than its neighbors, exited the Cordoba, and made my way to the front entrance. An unshaven guy in a threadbare t-shirt and camouflage pants answered my knock. His grease-stained cap may once have matched the trousers tucked into his half-laced combat boots, but the grime obscuring its fabric made it hard to determine. He said something I didn't quite hear because the hound chained to a doghouse forty feet away was raising such a racket.

"Bomber!" he screamed. "Shut up!"

When Bomber kept baying, the man stormed past me, marched to the doghouse, and kicked him. A whimper followed, then silence.

"Ya gotta let 'em know who's boss," he said, hitching up his pants as he came back my way."

"You Blaze?" I asked. "Tom Jelinek said I should talk to you. I need some three-inch twelve-gauge ammo. Single-aught buck."

Blaze took up a position in front of his screen door and looked me over. "Tom Jelinek, huh?" He paused. "Now, I don't know much about the reloadin' business, but sayin' I was to find you some ammo. It wouldn't come cheap."

A thin woman smoking a cigarette appeared at the door. I'd have sworn her pale, blue-veined skin had never seen a ray of sunlight. Topped off with stringy hair that looked as if it had last seen shampoo when Gerald Ford was president, the lady made for quite a sight. She opened the door a few inches and shielded her eyes.

"Blaze, who's that?"

"Nothin' to worry about, just a guy lookin' for ammo. Get back inside."

She disappeared. I felt nothing but relief that Blaze wasn't about to invite me into the house. Technically, he wasn't licensed to sell me his reloads and his talk of "finding some ammo" constituted a less-than-clever attempt at a cover for his reloading operation. I wanted to get my business done and leave.

"How much?" I asked

He named a ridiculous price, and I agreed to meet it. "I think I can find somebody who'll do it. Come back tonight at seven. There'll be a ten-dollar handling charge for my trouble. No checks."

Blaze had not only gouged me on the price of the ammo, he gouged me on the gouge.

I glared at the shells on the countertop once more, grabbed the Mr. Coffee, and poured another cup. I turned on the TV as I passed it and headed for the couch to catch a piece of the *Today Show*. Flopping down on the most comfortable piece of furniture I have ever owned, I caught the tail end of a news segment on transportation.

Apparently, a bunch of spaced-out cultists can't caravan a half dozen Bentleys down the Interstate without attracting attention—especially if they're trailing a fleet of vans decorated with flaming eyes. Jane Pauley and Brian Gumbel were milking the story for all it was worth. The visuals included helicopter shots of what Gumbel referred to as the "parade," stills of the sattguru, and footage of Manoneetas dancing in their underwear. I don't know how much of the piece I missed, but references to a "sex cult" and the use of the words like "secretive," "mysterious," and "orgies" told me the show's producers were as interested in ratings as being informative.

I thought about how Jim Jones and his followers reacted when the press and politicians started poking around his compound in Guyana. An outsider gets shot, they believe their way of life is threatened and that afternoon, they're drinking cyanide-flavored Kool-Aid. The sooner we got Mike away from the People of Light, the better.

Chapter 40

I bounced six inches into the air and dropped down hard onto the metal bed of Eddie's pickup. The nearly abandoned South Dakota road my companions and I traveled was home to some spectacular ruts and crevasses. Sure that a backward glance into a mirror tomorrow would reveal a bruised butt, I grabbed the yoga mat and stuffed it under my backside. Belle, seated in the box beside me, didn't seem bothered by the rough ride. I wondered if the posterior padding Mother Nature gifted the female of the species made for a better experience.

Adding insult to injury, a fine layer of grit settled on me. It wouldn't have been so bad, but the dust stirred up by the pickup and blown back on us by the incessant Great Plains wind found its way into my lungs, eyes, nose, and ears. Belle and I soon found ourselves plagued by intermittent fits of coughing, and if my eyes were anywhere as bloodshot as hers, it would be days before they looked normal again.

Up front, Eddie was driving, and Burl riding shotgun—literally. He'd appropriated my sawed-off without asking. I put up with it because I had to. We agreed he would have complete control once the operation got underway. Though it seemed like a good idea at the time, I now wished Belle were in charge. The lady would never ask for my gun and mentally, she had twice as much going for her as her boss.

The B team spent the night in a budget motel in Sioux Falls—Burl and Eddie in one room, and a platonic Clete and Belle in another. After later-than-usual burgers and shakes, Belle and I returned to our room in time for the KPLO ten o'clock news. We learned the media frenzy around People of Light had yet to abate. I watched as a reporter for one of the South Dakota stations buttonholed a female *sadhu* outside a gas station restroom and asked about the big festival. He got more than he bargained for. The woman grabbed his microphone and began a discourse on the Harmonic Convergence, the Gateway of the Moon, and dynamic meditation—all unintelligibly delivered and accompanied by a vapid Manoneeta smile. The reporter let her go on long enough to convince his viewers that the People of Light had truly lost their minds. He had to wrest the mic away from her.

Our pickup caromed into yet another rut, bringing me back to the present by delivering a painful jolt to my tailbone. I turned to Belle hoping conversation would distract me from my aches and pains. "What do you make of all the publicity the Guru festival is getting?" I yelled. "Will it help us or hurt us?"

"Help, I think. I'm hoping a horde of reporters shows up right outside the main gate. If we're lucky, they'll use helicopters to get fly-over footage. The more distractions, the less likely we'll be noticed."

"I doubt they'll fly over at night. Not enough light for the cameras."

Belle shrugged.

I was getting strange vibes from Belle. Yesterday she'd been all smiles and chatty and didn't mind sharing a room with me. I'd been on my best gentlemanly behavior, but today she treated me like I spent the night trying to get into her pants. One of my friends, a now-deceased car dealer, had the habit of saying virtue is a waste of time because it is seldom rewarded. The older I get, the more I realize he was on to something.

We rode on in silence until the pickup lurched to a stop and Eddie opened his door to call back to us. "We're at the dry wash."

Low banks rose on either side of the pickup. The wash was three feet lower than the surrounding grassland. As a hiding place for the pickup, the spot was less than ideal. In the bright moonlight, a casual observer might notice the top of a vehicle parked in a low spot. The same risk of exposure would hold for trespassers walking up the wash on their way to breach a fence. We'd have to be careful.

Belle hopped out of the box and lowered the tailgate. Gimped up by the rough ride, I crawled to the rear of the pickup, sat, and lowered my feet to the earth as Eddie and Burl came round the truck to join us. Burl returned my shotgun, and after we checked to see our walkie-talkies were in good order, he went over our communications protocol, closing with a few words of caution. "Remember, these things squawk and can draw unwanted attention. That's why Junior and Tamara are sharing one—less noise in a crowd. Remember, no use of handhelds except for emergencies or announcing you've got Mike. Remember our code and keep all communications as short as possible."

After double-checking that we understood, he grabbed a pair of bolt cutters from our equipment bundle and started up the dry wash with Eddie, hitching his pants as he walked. Neither of them looked as if they felt comfortable in their scrubs. Too bad, they'd be walking farther than Belle and me. Their assignment was to breach the perimeter fence near the turnaround for the single road that ran the length of the compound. Belle and I were to create a second opening where the wash came closest to the fence. Given the risks inherent in our mission, two exit options seemed the minimum. More would have been ideal, but after some discussion, we opted to be conservative. Each additional opening would increase the chances of discovery.

Since Burl and Eddie had the farther walk, Belle and I were responsible for transporting Lumir's *travois*. He'd done a grand job. Not only could the thing be converted into a stretcher, but its leather harness could be adjusted to allow for either one or two people to drag it. We unloaded it from the pickup and strapped a bag containing my yoga mat, two pairs of handcuffs, a roll of duct tape, and a bolt cutter to it.

I couldn't see the reason for the extra set of cuffs. "What's the second set for?" We'll only need one for Mike."

"You," Belle quipped. "If you're a pain in the ass, I'll use them on you." She adjusted her shoulder holster. "I'll carry your shotgun. You can pull the travis."

The woman was as bad as Burl. "That means I'll be unarmed," I protested. "No way."

"When you're strapped into the travis, you won't have the freedom of movement you'll need to bring your gun around."

I looked down at the rig. "Believe me. If things go to hell, I'll find a way."

Our eyes locked, each of us ready to go to the mat over the issue. I stood, my arms folded over my chest, doing my best to look as stubborn as the male of the species can be. After a few moments of silence, Belle capitulated.

"I believe you will," she finally said. "Harness up. No way I'm pulling that thing. This is your son's rescue."

"But I'm not getting paid for it," I complained as I stepped into the harness.

"Burl's only giving me fifteen percent."

"That's highway robbery," I replied, strapping myself into Lumir's contraption.

"Tell me about it, but if Burl paid me what it's worth, you wouldn't have the money, and your son would stay here."

I'd been taking Belle for granted. I accidentally tossed her from my bed and in my grief over the loss of Dusty, spurned her romantic overtures. Despite my treatment of her, she'd rescued me when Babba Pappa's crew tried to turn me into a pot roast, and now she sincerely wanted to help me rescue my son. Too bad the woman was bossy, lacked social polish, and wasn't better looking. We'd never make it as a couple. And then there was Eddie. Talk about misjudging the guy. The only skin he had in this game was his love for my daughter. I must have been out of my mind when I worried that he wasn't good enough for her.

Feeling small, I leaned into the harness and began dragging Lumir's *travois* up the draw. Though I soon learned to avoid the occasional oversized stone and scattered clumps of prairie sage, the device worked well. The going was easy enough that I was soon lost in thought. The world might be full of flakes, but I was lucky enough to have people like Lumir, Eddie, Tamara, and Belle in my life. As for my son, I doubted he and I would ever agree on the extent of my responsibility for his unfortunate adolescence. Still, I owed him, and the least I could do was give him the chance to function in the world outside the cult.

"That should do it," I said as I snipped the last bit of wire from the chain link fence. A yank, a pull, and a perfect three-foot square of woven wire separated itself from the Re-education Center's enclosure. The lack of a trail on the far side of the barrier fence indicated the Manoneetas were not in the habit of patrolling their perimeter. Once again, I found myself mystified by their odd notions of security. The absence of a regular patrol reminded me of the keys hanging on a wall near the locked files in Babba Pappa's Shiva City office.

Judging by the music and noise coming from the occupied part of the compound, the organizers of the Manoneetas' dynamic meditation session were doing their best to set a record for the wildest party in South Dakota history. While not the norm, rumor had it that mass fornication sometimes followed a particularly robust celebration. I wondered if tonight would become one of those occasions. If it was, the news people would get their money's worth. I turned to see Belle staring intently at something in the palm of her hand.

"What are you looking at?' I asked.

"A compass. I'm taking a bearing on the light post up ahead. How else are we going to find our way back here?"

"Hadn't thought of that. Glad you did."

No answer. Being the perfect gentleman when someone wants you to maul them can lead to ill feelings.

"So far, a piece of cake," I said. "No problem with the fence, the *travois* works great, and not a security guard in sight. If the rest of the operation goes this well, we'll have Mike out in a few—."

A blast of light turned night to daylight. I dived for the dirt as the blinding glare exposed us for all the world to see. The ground shook as an ear-splitting blast washed over me. I rolled on my back and readied the sawed-off.

"Don't shoot me. It's an aerial bomb," cried Belle. "They're setting off fireworks."

A smaller blast followed, silhouetting her against a fountain of red and green stars. I stood and brushed myself off.

"And you can leave off with this "trav-wuh" business and call it a travis like the rest of us," Belle huffed.

This time, I didn't answer, but crawled through the opening of the fence and motioned for her to push the travis through. After she did, I informed Belle it was her turn to pull. "I need ready access to my shotgun. In a pinch, it will be better than your pistol."

"You're not winning any popularity contests, Cletus. Swing that gun around like you did when that aerial bomb went off, and somebody's gonna get hurt."

At least we were still speaking to each other. Belle checked her compass from time to time as we headed for the light post. The constant popping of the glittering fireworks worked to our advantage. Anyone passing the time outdoors would have their eyes on the sky, and the extra noise would provide cover if the use of firearms proved necessary.

We walked a quarter mile and paused at a rusted-out metal drum lying on its side. The moonlight and overhead light show were coming through for us. The fenced-in building we identified at the Center's lockup was visible a few hundred yards ahead. Belle unharnessed herself from the travis. "We'll leave the rig here and come back for it if we need it."

I watched as she took another bearing, nodded, and removed her handcuffs and duct tape, my yoga mat, and a bolt cutter from our equipment bag. I wrapped the sawed-off in the yoga mat. By placing my hand inside the roll, I'd be able to get off a quick shot, but one with a big disadvantage. There was a chance that the shell wouldn't clear the ejection port, causing the bolt to jam. I re-wrapped the bundle for a looser fit but remained uncertain the spent casing would clear. It wasn't worth the risk. The mat would have to come off, delaying a second shot by precious seconds. Too late now, I should have practiced the move in advance.

"Okay," Belle said. "This is where we start acting like a couple more concerned with a romantic stroll than the big festivities."

"Let's hope it works," I replied. "It's hard to imagine a Manoneeta more interested in an evening walk than partying with the sattguru."

"Maybe, but we'll be a lot less obvious than if people see us sneaking around. Your yoga mat might make them think we're intent on some outdoor fun. What's better than whoopee under the fireworks?"

"There is that," I conceded.

"Yeah, especially if the guy doesn't have a dead battery."

"Common sense and basic human decency don't necessarily imply a dead battery." I took up a position at Belle's side, and we started off.

"If you say so, but the human decency part sounds more like an excuse than an indication of character."

I bit my tongue.

Chapter 41

Not a soul in evidence as we approached the fenced-in building we'd identified as the lockup. Having no better plan, we circled the structure, walking a dozen feet outside the tall, razor-wire-topped fence enclosing it. Three times as long as it was wide, the building's imitation log walls were broken by just two openings—a window and a door on the side facing the developed part of the Research Center. The place screamed prison, and the lack of an emergency exit indicated the folks who built it weren't concerned with the safety of the occupants.

Light shone from the single window and spilled into the yard from the open door. I couldn't be sure, but it looked as if the gated opening in the fence was secured by a single padlock. The place gave me the creeps. Looking almost abandoned and staffed by an indifferent security force, the dismal structure reeked of hopelessness and despair. I prayed to God that Mike had never crossed its threshold.

Belle and I returned to the back side of the building.

"Any ideas?" I asked. "I can't think of anything but cutting a hole in the fence and going in with guns drawn."

"That's what I like about you Clete, you're subtle. So subtle that somebody's gonna get killed. You're right about one thing though, we're going to have to cut through the fence."

"And then?"

"We go round to the front and improvise."

My companion's idea didn't do much for me. "We don't know how many guards there are or how they're armed. We don't know if they have a telephone. We could get cut down at the doorway."

Belle positioned her face six inches from mine. "The last thing we'll do is throw caution to the winds and rush the door. I don't know what we'll run into either, but you're making me nervous. We'll cut through the fence and then check things out. Sure, there's risk, but let me ask you something. How'd your first marriage go?"

I didn't answer.

"And your second marriage?"

"You know it didn't come off."

"And your son, he likes you right?"

"He hates my guts."

"And your daughter, she worships you, right?

"Hardly."

"And you're happy about the way your almost-in-laws stole your business?"

I shook my head.

"Then what do you have to lose?"

"My life."

"Doesn't sound like that much to me."

Mad as hell and cussing under my breath, I grabbed the bolt cutters from her and went to work on the fence. My savage snips made short work of the chain link. I threw the bolt cutters on the ground, grabbed the sawed-off bundle, and crawled through the opening. Belle followed.

"Okay now, don't go off half-cocked," she said as she stood. "Hey, is that blood on your cheek?"

I rubbed my hand against the side of my face. Nothing.

"Not there, here." She leaned forward and kissed me just below the ear.

"What the hell are you doing?" I asked, my irritation obvious.

"Now if you die, you won't go to that great beyond unkissed. So, let's go upfront. You cover me while I peek through the window."

We walked to the lockup's front corner where I clicked the shotgun's safety button to the off position. Belle, her nine-millimeter in hand, sidled up to the window. I shook the yoga mat off my gun and stepped a few feet away from the wall, ready to blast the hell out of anyone coming out the door.

No one did.

Belle drew away from the window and motioned me back to the corner. "You won't believe it. The front door's wide open and two security guys are just sitting there playing cards."

"Manoneeta security," I said. "I wonder if there are any more?"

"Don't know, but it looks like the Guru Purnima gig has thrown a monkey wrench into the Center's routines. Everyone and his brother will want to see Dev. I want to take advantage of that. Here's the deal. First, you reengage the safety on the shotgun."

"What!"

"I heard you click it off. Put it back on. That's a scattergun, and I want you to think twice before you shoot. There's a chance I'll be in the line of fire."

I didn't understand how she could hear anything with all the noise from the fireworks but flipped the safety button back on.

"Good. I'm planning to trick them into coming outside. If they both come out, you make for the doorway as fast as you can. The idea is to keep them from re-entering the building. If only one comes out, stay where you are."

"If they both come out, and I get to the door, what happens next?"

Belle shrugged. "I don't know."

"If only one comes out. What are we going to do?"

"I don't know."

"You call this a plan?"

Belle put her hands on her hips. "It's like this, Cletus. Planning gets you only so far. At some point in any operation, you have to rely on yourself and the judgment of the people you're with. That means you make it up as you go along. For the life of me, I don't know why I'd trust you in a pinch, but despite all evidence to the contrary, I do."

"Thanks for the vote of confidence."

"Stay here, and don't disappoint me," she said and strode toward the fence, keeping out of view of the jailers inside. When she reached her destination, she turned and headed for the lockup's open door.

"Hey guys," she called as she continued up the path. "Looks like you left the front gate unlocked."

A guard with a bushy beard and ponytail appeared in the doorway. He turned his head back toward the room. "Jeez, Paco. Just for once could you pay more attention to what you're doing? We're Manoneetas. That means we're supposed stay in the moment."

A muffled voice came from inside and the bearded ponytail started down the path with Belle. Just before they reached the gate, Belle stepped back, swung her arm, and the guy went down with a grunt. She motioned me over.

I made my approach with one eye on the doorway. By the time I got there, she had her gun to his head. She jabbed the barrel into his skull. "One peep and your brains are wet dog food. Got it?"

The guy didn't say anything, so he must have got it. He didn't make a sound when I slapped Belle's cuffs on him, and he didn't complain when I removed his shoes and stuffed a dirty sock in his mouth. Belle taped his legs together, took his sidearm from its holster, and removed the magazine. After checking that the chamber was empty, she tossed the gun into a patch of weeds and the clip in the opposite direction.

"You blackjacked him?" I asked.

Belle nodded. "Thank God for the fireworks. I doubt the guy inside heard anything. I want to get him out here before he has time to think anything's wrong. Get back to the corner and stay out of sight."

I made tracks and watched as Belle pocketed her sap and ran up to the open doorway. "Something's wrong!" she cried. "Your friend bent down to check the lock and fell over. I think he passed out or something. There's blood coming out his mouth."

Paco appeared in the doorway, and as he brushed past her, Belle laid him out with her leather wonder. He screamed, I think, but with the noise of the celebration, it was hard to know. Paco got the same treatment as his companion—right down to the dirty sock in his mouth. His silence assured, we dragged him into the shadows alongside the building. Given the flashes of light from the fireworks, it wasn't much of a hiding place, but we weren't about to take him any farther.

We went back to retrieve his friend. "You're pretty good with a blackjack," I said. "Why didn't you just knock them out?"

"Because I don't like killing people. A blow to the head or neck is a good way to off somebody. The idea is to cause incapacitating pain. That's why I went for their shoulder blades."

I shivered at the thought of what the man was going through. "For a mechanic, you know a lot about this stuff."

"When I got my first PI job, they partnered me with a guy who was a special forces trainer. Five months later, they sent me out on assignments by myself. It was sink or swim, but I was ready."

The first security guard was sobbing into his sock when we got to him. We grabbed him by the arms and dragged him back to the shadows. I suspect the tugging made his shoulder hurt like hell. If the People of Light security forces hadn't tried to kill me, I might have felt sorry for him.

We took our prisoners' keys and approached the lockup's open door. Though we didn't expect additional guards, we advanced with caution. Once there, Belle—handgun drawn and pointed at the entrance—made a lateral leap to the side of the door opposite me. My sawed-off leveled, I went in first.

The room was empty—not just of people, but devoid of anything but a table covered with playing cards, two chairs, and a pair of lunch pails. Centered on the reinforced back wall was another door, this one closed. Built of sturdy oak and crisscrossed with wrought iron bands, the door was designed to open with an inward push rather than a pull. No doubt about it, the thing opened into a detention area. Belle and I caucused.

"I imagine it's locked," I said.

"And with more security on the other side," added Belle. Her hand held one of the sets of keys we'd taken from the guards. "One of these should open the door. I'll unlock it, open it a crack, and stand aside. We'll wait a minute and if nothing happens, you give it a hard shove. I'd recommend stepping aside afterward. You know—the hail of bullets thing."

"Why me?" I asked. "You have the special training."

"You have the sawed-off. Besides, no one in their right mind stands in front of the guy with the scattergun. That's why you went first last time."

"Oh."

Chapter 42

We stood next to a pair of cafeteria tables in the center of a deserted common room. A dozen or so molded plastic chairs sat stacked in a corner. Though I should have been happy about the lack of excitement, our well-planned entry had proven a letdown. The place was some sort of a prison alright. Oak doors similar to the one we'd just unlocked lined the side walls of the room. Each stood ajar, and each opened into a cell containing a blanket-covered army cot and the sorriest excuse for a toilet I'd ever seen. To the rear of the common room stood yet another iron-reinforced door—closed and apparently locked.

"This setup is giving me the creeps," I whispered. "There were people here, and not that long ago. The bedding still stinks."

Belle stepped closer. "The sooner we get out of here, the better. The building isn't that big, so I'm guessing there's just one more room. Same fire drill as before. I unlock, we wait, then you go in first.

The keys she'd lifted worked. I pushed the door partway. No reaction. The room before us was unlit. I removed the flashlight hanging from the loop Mrs. Hemsky had sewn on my scrubs. Holding it under the shotgun's forearm, I went in and stepped aside. Belle followed. No gunshots. The room felt empty. Empty, except for a shadowy collection of coffins resting on the concrete floor.

I felt the wall behind me, found the switch, and flicked on the lights. Two rows of vault-like boxes appeared. Twelve in all. Nine with lids up, three closed.

"These must be the isolation tanks," I said. "They're so ugly I can't imagine somebody buying one."

"They sure as hell aren't commercial models," Belle replied. "We're looking at full-blown People of Light brainwashing boxes. And if I'm not mistaken, some of them are occupied."

The tanks weren't the only thing in the room. A maze of overhead pipes connected to what looked to be a large water heater in a back corner. Nearby, a wall-mounted service panel sprouted conduits that carried electricity to clusters of pumps and meters interspersed with the tanks. To our left stood a cage containing a crude toilet like those we'd seen in the cells.

Belle started for the first tank. "Let's get moving. This building has one exit. If anyone shows up, we're trapped."

I put down my gun and went to the second of the closed tanks. The lid wasn't locked. I raised it. Empty.

"This one is sealed," Belle muttered. "There's got to be a way to open these things."

She must have been looking for a lock that would accept one of her keys. The lid on the tank behind the one I'd just checked was closed. I gave it the once-over as I approached. A handle partially concealed by a recess seemed the obvious candidate to gain entry. I twisted it and raised the lid. The pallid face of an adolescent girl, her eyes closed and her head resting on a piece of molded plastic, greeted me. The light must have bothered her. She screwed up her face and began whimpering.

I turned my head. "Belle, you better come over here. I'm out of my league on this one."

"Got a live one and can't handle it?" she asked.

"Over here, now! This is no joke. It's a girl. Looks like she'd be in junior high." And then I froze, unable to process the horror confronting me.

Belle shoved me out of the way. "I'll take care of this. Go over and check the other box. We haven't got all day."

Happy to leave the girl in Belle's capable hands, I went to the last box, turned the release, and opened the lid. Thank God it wasn't a child. An unshaven face struggled to adjust to the unexpected light. I stared as its mouth opened and its sunken features began to rearrange themselves. It took a few seconds, but then I knew without a doubt. Babba Pappa.

Images of my near-death in a tin can van came back with a vengeance. White-hot fury surged through every cell in my body. I lifted Pappa's head off its rest and pushed it down into the water. He was so weak he offered little resistance. I practically giggled. And then, damn it, a wave of pity for one of the vilest men alive overwhelmed my lust for revenge. Feeling cheated by some strange moral code drilled into me as a kid, I pulled his head back up, put it back on its rest, closed the lid, and relatched it.

Belle had the girl out of the tank and on the floor. The kid, shaking like a leaf in a shabby wet swimsuit, didn't have the strength to sit or stand. She still hadn't opened her eyes, and she was still whimpering.

Belle stood, faced me, and put her hand on her hips. "Okay Cletus, this is where we part company. I've been hired to help rescue your son, but there's no way I'm leaving this girl behind. I can't do it."

"I wouldn't want you to. We'll get her squared away somehow and after that, I'm off to find him on my own."

"She's too weak to walk. The only way she's leaving is on the travis."

I did some quick mental gymnastics. Mike was somewhere in the compound and most likely able to walk. Burl and Eddie were already searching for him. If I found him, they'd be available to help with the extraction. The girl was in more danger. I lifted her and turned to Belle. "Let's get the kid outside this trap."

Belle retrieved my shotgun and took the lead. As we passed through the cell-lined room, she took a detour to fetch a blanket. I put the still-shivering girl on the floor, wrapped her in it, and scooped her back up. "You're going to be ok, Sweetie," I whispered. "Everything is alright. You're safe now."

As we reached the outer room, my eyes began to water. If I didn't know better, I'd have thought the guys who'd been guarding the place had a serious tobacco problem. The air reeked of smoke. My walkie-talkie squawked in its pocket.

Abort! Abort! Front gate.

Belle retrieved her handheld, put it to her mouth. Her response rose from the speaker of my device.

No way, José.

Her reply informed our partners that contrary to statement, we understood the mission had ended and we'd meet them at the main entrance.

Distracted by the acrid haze in the air, I coughed as I processed the information. Something was wrong. The smoke was too foul and dense to be a result of the detonation of black-powder fireworks. The Manoneeta's decision to mount a pyrotechnic display in the middle of a drought was a mistake. They'd started a prairie fire, and their shingled, faux-log buildings would be all it would take to transform a grass fire into an inferno.

Belle motioned for me to stay back. "You wait with her while I fetch the travis." She ran to the door and disappeared, taking the sawed-off with her. Her absence left me without a firearm. I put the girl down, told her in my kindest voice to stay put, and went to the door. I peered out. Panicked Manoneetas ran through the haze. I ducked back inside when I saw a trio of security guards carrying assault rifles materialize in the smoke. I didn't think they were coming our way but was taking no chances.

Belle's absence galled me. For all her training, she ran out the door leaving me with an incapacitated girl and no gun. I went back to check on the girl. The child was either passed out or asleep, but at least she was breathing. I looked at my watch. If Belle didn't return within the next few minutes, the girl and I were leaving. I went back to the door and the reality of our situation became clearer. The wind-blown bits of ash floating through the air glowed red at the edges. The fire was close. So close that I could feel the heat on my face. Gun or no gun, the kid and I couldn't stay. If we didn't leave, Belle and the travis would be of no use to us.

I turned to gather up my charge. As I kneeled to take up my burden, I heard a voice behind me shout.

"Freeze or die."

I froze.

"Now, hands in the air. Stand."

I raised my hands, stood, and turned. The guards must have left an open padlock dangling from the hasp on the gate. A security punk, rifle at ready, stood silhouetted in the doorway.

"I need help," I said. "We've got to get this girl out of here before the building goes up in smoke. She can't walk."

"If the two of you are in here, it's because you're a danger to the People."

I recognized the voice. My son, a true believer to the core, and worse yet, a security guard. Maybe they'd tanked him into submission. Maybe not. The how and why didn't matter. He'd turned into a monster.

"Mike, a junior-high girl isn't a danger to the People of Light, and she doesn't deserve being burned alive."

Until that moment, I don't think he realized who I was.

"Kali, the goddess of death, will decide if the girl lives or dies. That's not the case with you. She has delivered the world's worst father to me. I decide if you live or die. Kali is the goddess of vengeance, old man. It's not looking good for you right now."

The Manoneetas in South Dakota must have taken to the Hindu gods business in a big way. I figured my odds of survival at less than ten percent, but I wasn't going down without a fight.

"Let's say you kill me. Then what? You'll still be unhappy, and the damage you'd do to Tamara would last the rest of her life. She's broken-hearted because she hasn't heard from you. Do you know we're at the Purnima Festival tonight just so she has a chance to talk to you?"

I took a step closer. Mike shouldered his rifle and took aim.

"Let me kill him! The bastard raped my daughter."

I turned my head. Belle stood in the doorway, shotgun leveled. I hope it was a bluff. If she pulled the trigger I'd go down too.

Mike didn't turn. "Bullshit, he's going down."

The girl in the blanket screamed. She may have been a waif, but she had the lungs of a harpy. Mike turned the gun in her direction.

"No, Mike!" I shouted. "I'm the one you want."

The distraction gave Belle the opportunity she was looking for. She tossed her shotgun aside and launched herself forward, blackjack in hand. She didn't need it. Her weight knocked Mike to the floor. As he fell, his rifle discharged. I rushed to the girl to see if she was hit. She wasn't, but to say she was terror-stricken didn't begin to cover it. I turned to see Belle cuffing Mike.

"A third set of cuffs?" I asked.

"No, I wasn't going to let those guards I sapped burn up. I let them go."

"You let 'em go! What if they come back after us?"

"Right now, I think the only one in the place who's worrying about who's a prisoner and who's not is Mike. Everybody is doing their best to get out before the whole place goes up in flames. We should, too."

The building was beyond hot. It was high time to vamoose, but I was still mad at her. "Your training had a hole in it. I can't believe you waltzed out of here without leaving me a gun."

"I left you without a gun on purpose. I figured if you had one, you'd try to use it and both you and the girl would get killed. This way, if you got shot, they'd be more likely to leave her alone. Face it, Cletus, she has a lot more life ahead of her than you."

I stood there with my mouth open. Belle was right that the child's life came first but wrong about my ability to come up with a solution that didn't endanger her.

Belle grinned at me. "Ready to go? You carry the little miss, and I'll sweet talk Mike into coming along with us."

"Where's the travis?"

"No time. Probably ashes by now."

I went over to the girl. She'd broken the silence with her scream but appeared to have gone back to a catatonic state. I rewrapped her in the blanket and picked her back up.

Belle prodded Mike with her toe. "Ready to go, Sport? You've got two choices: come along or burn up."

I guess Mike didn't want to be burned alive. He stood, and we left the building, taking the path to the front gate. The incessant Great Plains winds had brought the flames to the compound's buildings. The heat was unbelievable. Roofs blazed; the fire roared.

I looked back. Flames danced on the lockup's cedar-shake roof. The sides of the structure were already beginning to burn. A building ahead of us belched flames. Thick, choking smoke made it hard to breathe and obscured the scene before us. I don't know where I got the strength, but I managed to keep the girl on my shoulder despite being bumped by fleeing Manoneetas and dodging a vehicle barely under the control of its terrified driver. Five minutes into a brisk trot, a coughing fit seized me, and my muscles gave out. I was losing my grip on the girl.

"I don't think I can go any farther," I gasped.

Belle didn't miss a beat. She tripped Mike so that he fell to the ground. "I can fix this. Put the girl down."

I did, and she handed me her sidearm. "Watch your boy for me. If he gets up, shoot him in the crotch. I'll have a ride for us in no time. And by the way, Mikey, your father has spent the whole summer looking for you—even after Babba Pappa and his friends tried to kill him."

Belle checked the chamber on the sawed-off, walked maybe 150 feet, and took up a position alongside the street.

Mike sneered. "Like I believe you did any of that."

I gave him my best death stare. "If we get through this without me shooting you, ask Tamara about my summer."

I had no doubt that Belle would try to hijack a vehicle. Without support, the odds of her success were small. I turned to my son.

"Okay Mike, for once in your life, do the right thing. Stay with the girl while I help Belle get us a ride out of here. If we're not back in a few minutes, try to get some help. You can leave her here to die and try to outrun the flames with your hands cuffed behind your back. Without the kid, I doubt anyone will stop to give you an assist."

Woozy and coughing, I assumed a position across from Belle. As one of the Manoneeta vans approached, she stepped into the center of the road, fired a warning shot into the air, and brought the gun done again, pointing directly at the windshield. As the van slowed, I walked into the roadway and pointed the nine-millimeter at the driver's window. The sadhu behind the wheel stopped and rolled it down.

"Out," I ordered.

"What are you going to do, shoot me?" he asked.

I didn't answer but pointed the gun to a spot four inches in front of his nose and squeezed the trigger. Much to his dismay and that of his passenger, the front window on the other side of the cab disintegrated. The guy almost knocked me down trying to get out of the vehicle. Belle approached the car, her scattergun now in one hand. She jerked on the passenger door and removed the dazed and almost certainly deaf passenger.

She leveled the gun at him. "Get moving before you burn up."

I don't know if he heard her, but the guy scrambled off in the direction taken by the driver. Our ride secure, Belle got behind the wheel.

I walked back to Mike and the girl. He still sat next to her. I don't know how much he saw through the smoke-filled air, but it must have been enough to realize I'd fired into a car with people in it. My son looked at me as if he might be next. Belle pulled the van up to us, and I put the girl in the middle seat. My son, still cuffed and shaking like a leaf, got in of his own accord and took the seat at the rear.

I reached into my pocket for the handheld and heard Belle's unit squawk as I spoke into it.

Bird in hand. Bird in hand. Meet at rendezvous.

A moment of silence followed and then ...

No way, José.

"What kind of animals would do that to a child?" Belle asked as she parked our hi-jacked van next to my Cordoba. It was the first she'd spoken since we made it out of the madhouse surrounding the compound.

I raised my finger to my lips. The kid, belted into the seat behind me, still looked out of it, but there was no way to know if what we said made its way to her brain or not. Belle nodded. She got it.

"You worried about Mike?" she asked.

"Sandwiched between Tamara and Junior in Gunderson's pickup, he's pretty much stuck. They won't stop until they get to the plane. Where's he gonna run? It's out in the middle of nowhere. Same thing once they get to Junior's farm."

"I mean about his future. What's going to happen now?"

"No idea. A wise woman once told me that planning gets you only so far and at some point, you have to rely on yourself and the people that you're with. Mike, Tamara, and I have a lot to work out."

"Your daughter was happy to see him. She didn't seem too thrilled with the handcuffs."

"We should have ditched the bracelets before she saw him. I'm glad you were the one who unlocked him. It made you look responsible for the situation."

"I was. I'm the one who cuffed him, remember?"

"The way Mike was crying when his sister hugged him, and the look on her face—it made the whole thing worthwhile. Whether he hates me the rest of his life or not, I'll know we did the right thing."

"Changing the subject, are you sure we should drive all the way to Mobridge? It's a two-hour drive."

I didn't answer, but opened the windowless door and exited, brushing a few stray bits of glass from the seat of my pants. I walked to the front of the van, and leaned against it, gesturing for Belle to join me.

"The girl's gonna need first-rate care," I said as she took up position alongside me. "There's nothing in Bison. Even if there was, I don't trust Sheriff Hargrave. He's so enthused about the People of Light, who knows what he'll do? He might try to charge us with grand theft auto and kidnapping. I fired into the van to get those *sadhus* out. If they file a complaint, he could make a case for attempted murder."

Belle shrugged. "I wouldn't get too paranoid. What with all the commotion, Hargrave will be so overworked, it'll be weeks before he can see straight again. Besides, we'll be over the county line in less than an hour."

"It's not just the county line. There could be state charges. As soon as the girl is settled in, we can hightail it to North Dakota. It's the long way home, but why take chances?"

Belle laughed. "If you're that worried, let me give you something else to chew on—a federal charge for interstate flight to avoid prosecution."

"Thanks a lot, Sunshine."

"Actually, I'm more worried about Eddie's pickup than anything. It's a long walk back to Iowa. You think it burned?"

"No idea, but we'd better get going."

Belle launched into a coughing fit. She sounded like a lovesick basset hound with galloping pneumonia.

"You in any shape to drive?"

She glared and held out her hand. "Keys."

I handed her the keys to the Cordoba. She took them and made for the driver's door. I walked back to fetch the girl, thinking about the effect of trauma on kids, wondering if she'd ever be normal again. As I picked her out of the van, the horrors of the evening caught up with me. My eyes started to water.

Not yet, Efferding. Get a grip. You can let it all out when you get home.

Though I repressed the sobs, a tear ran down my cheek and landed next to the girl's nose.

Her lids fluttered and opened a crack. Her mouth trembled and her lips parted.

"Thank you," she said.

Chapter 43

I stood next to the podium in one of the banquet rooms at the Longbranch Restaurant waiting for my bride to arrive. I thought the location odd, but when I insisted male guests wear formal morning dress, my wedding planner, Tamara, removed me from all decision-making and sent invitations informing guests and members of the wedding party to "wear clothes you feel good in." Since Mike's rescue, our relationship had blossomed. I acquiesced because I wanted to keep it that way. Convinced that wearing a tuxedo before six p.m. had something to do with the disaster that occurred the last time I tried to marry, she'd allowed me my choice of dress. I must say I looked grand in a swallowtail coat, striped pants, and white vest.

Burl stood behind the podium. He had sent away for one of those "marrying Sam" certificates and would be officiating. He'd done his best to dress for his role—green plaid trousers, a burnt-orange shirt, a red plaid necktie, and maroon blazer. I didn't know if they were the clothes that he felt good in or not, but it finally dawned on me that Burl was colorblind. He had to be. The guy custom-ordered lime green upholstery for the lavender Cadillac de Ville he bought with his cut from the fee for Mike's rescue.

The shebang was a modest one, but I could have spent more on it. The girl Belle and I rescued from the People of Light turned out to be the runaway daughter of Ethan Garraway, a prominent Wall Street broker. He invited Belle and me to spend a week with his family at their Connecticut home and paid our airfare. The guy was so sincere we took him up on the offer and enjoyed a great visit. He and his wife were as unlike the Sutherlands as you can get. Their daughter Addie, happy but still shaken by her captivity, treated us like heroes. When Belle and I returned home, we were stunned to find generous checks from the Garraways waiting in our mailboxes.

I leveraged the gift to free Cleatzy's from the clutches of Gib Sutherland. Gib was facing a five-to-ten stretch in federal prison for his role in his brother's money-laundering scheme. He was lucky. The body of mobster Tony 'the Mortician' Abato washed ashore on Chicago's South Shore Beach after rumors surfaced that the FBI had taped him discussing Dusty's murder.

Addie Garraway made out better than her tank-farm companion Babba Pappa. Found in his isolation box, Pappa was one of eleven Manoneetas who didn't make it out of the conflagration. The press had a field day pointing fingers at everyone from the state governments of New Mexico and South Dakota to the FBI. They in turn blamed the Immigration and Naturalization Service who passed the buck onto the local fire department and law enforcement. Sheriff Hargrave lost his next election, and Dev disappeared, eventually turning up in Switzerland.

On her return to Cedar Rapids, Belle added the Garraways' gift to her savings and started the auto repair shop she always dreamed of. Located in a new building on Blairs Ferry Road, her business was hitting it out of the ballpark, expanding from two service bays to five. Much to the dismay of a dedicated following among the residents of the northeast quadrant, she put her foot down on the idea of further expansion.

The opening bars of Mendelson's Wedding March sounded. Eddie, perched on a stool in the back corner of the room, was thumping out the tune on his electric bass. I hadn't realized it, but the guy was a genius on an instrument usually relegated to the background. My daughter stood next to him, dressed in a black leather jacket and skintight pants, sheet music in hand. Who'd have thought there were words to the Wedding March? They were in German of course, but she'd spent several evenings with Herb Wiese, a professor at Coe College, getting her pronunciation up to snuff.

Tamara and Eddie lived in sin over in Bohemie Town. I wished they'd tied the knot but doubted it was to be. Tamara was responsible for the biggest change at Cleatzy's. She joined the operation as a junior partner, wanting to buy in with the trust fund I set up for her, but I wouldn't hear of it. The girl may have brought no capital to the business, but she had the ideas. Tamara operated a boutique within the store, selling non-traditional fashions to the younger set. She was good at it and took on so much of Cleatzy's paperwork that I found time to reopen the dance studio.

I doubted Mike would unexpectedly mess up this wedding. He'd reviewed his college German and stood next to Tamara. When she started singing, he joined in, his soaring tenor blending harmoniously with her alto. My son wore a flowered yellow dress for the occasion—something I doubted he did in South Dakota. He was so traumatized by his experiences with the cult that he spent a half year in a residential care facility. At the end of his stay, he accompanied Tamara and me on a mini-vacation to Junior's farm. He liked it so much he asked to stay. The life agreed with him. Junior watched over him like a mother hen and put him to work at hard physical labor. He'd never been so happy.

Our relationship had experienced its ups and downs. He found it hard to accept the fact that I left him with an abusive grandfather, and I found it difficult to forget he'd been a split second from killing me. We'd talked about it and were dealing with it. Forgiveness is a journey, not a destination. My son and I were on the way.

The door at the back of the room opened. Arm-in-arm, Lumir and Junior, our best man and matron-of-honor, solemnly entered. Lumir looked great in the white linen suit I sold him over a decade earlier. Junior, having taken Tamara's dictum to wear clothes she felt good in, wore new pin-striped bib overalls and her well-washed engineer's cap. I couldn't tell for sure from my vantage point but had no doubt the top quarter of a red bandanna protruded from her back pocket.

The flower girl came next. There'd never been any discussion of an alternative candidate. Blushing sweetly and scattering rose petals as she went, Millie Hemsky wore a pastel pink frock and enough costume jewelry to sink a battleship. A sweetheart through and through, she continued to ignore Lumir's standing marriage proposal. She'd recently confided in me that she did it to keep him on his toes.

My bride appeared, dressed in white, a radiant smile on her face, looking lovely. Ours was one of those courtships where you don't realize you're growing on each other until it hits you over the head. She walked alone. When asked if she wanted someone to give her away, she refused quietly, but firmly, with something along the lines of "no way in hell."

I stood patiently, savoring the moment, filing the memory away for the future. When she got to me, I took her hands and smiled like a seventh grader touching a girl for the first time. I'll never forget the look I got in return—a full-blown, unadulterated auto mechanic's grin. Throwing tradition to the winds, we kissed before the ceremony began. The smooch over, she stepped back to look at me, and I did the same. The sight of my beloved was one to treasure—right down to the red Mabel's Auto Repair embroidered on her white coveralls.

I hadn't known that family is as much about a feeling as it is genetics. A man couldn't do any better than the people gathered for my wedding. No doubt about it, Cletus Efferding was a lucky man.

Acknowledgments

I am indebted to Eileen Thomas for her understanding of the landscape of northwest South Dakota and her recollection of life in 1980s Wessington Springs, and I'd be guilty of neglect if I didn't mention Crista Carter, a transplanted New Mexican who taught me more about scorpions, centipedes, and single-ply toilet paper than I wanted to know. I doubt that either one knows how much our casual conversations did to bring this story to life.

I want to thank my editor, Shannon Ryan, for wrangling my prose. His suggestions are always sound and did much to improve the quality of the text. This book wouldn't exist without the support of Dylan Moonfire, the proprietor of Typewriter Press. His faith in my writing and willingness to go to bat for me did much to get this volume across the finish line. And once again, thanks to Jenn Roeder who came through with a cover that does everything it's supposed to do.

And then there are the readers of the many drafts of *Sins of Deception*. Bill Hart deserves a prize for the number of times he's gone through the story. A stickler for detail and consistency, Bill did much to uncover some of the quirks that creep into a much-revised tale. Nancy Kraft, an avid reader of suspense, detective, and thriller fiction, put the icing on the cake when she gave the final draft a thumbs up, her official "good read" seal of approval.

Others who've helped refine my ideas along the way include Ciuin Ferrin, Jeff Morrow, Nick Tharalson, Prateek Viswanathan, Aime Wichtendahl, and Laura Prendergast. You've taught me so much.

To learn more about the author and his books visit the website: randyroeder.com